Inspirational Romance Reader

A Collection of Four Complete, Unabridged
Inspirational Romances
in One Volume

• Contemporary Collection No. 4 •

A Whole New World
Yvonne Lehman

The Fruit of Her Hands
Jane Orcutt

A Matter of Faith
Nina Coombs Pykare

Eagles for Anna
Catherine Runyon

BARBOUR
PUBLISHING, INC.
Uhrichsville, Ohio

A Whole New World

Yvonne Lehman

YVONNE LEHMAN, an award-winning novelist, lives in the heart of North Carolina's Smoky Mountains with her husband. They are the parents of four grown children. In addition to being an inspirational romance writer, she is also the founder of the Blue Ridge Christian Writers' Conference.

Dedication

**To Cindy and David
Two beautiful people—inside and out.**

Chapter One

Amber Jennings, what are you doing here?

Amber groaned inwardly as she stepped inside the plushly carpeted reception room of the Pasetti Modeling Agency, San Diego's finest. It didn't help to settle her nerves that the receptionist was a stunning blond, her flaxen hair pulled back in a sophisticated chignon, looking as if she herself had stepped off the pages of some fashion magazine.

"What can we do for you?" the young woman asked when Amber approached the desk. At closer range, she could see that the woman's eyes—an unusual tawny gold, flecked with green—were dancing. Empathy. . .or amusement? Amber couldn't be sure.

The smile was sincere enough, though. "Do you have an appointment?"

"I believe the employment office called. I'm Amber Jennings. . .here about the secretarial job you advertised in the classifieds."

The receptionist, whose nameplate read Lynn, ran a tapered, polished nail down a list, then looked up. "Mr. Pasetti will see you shortly. Just have a seat."

Amber settled herself on a cream-colored leather couch, trying to ignore the whole flight of butterflies that took off in her stomach. She couldn't help staring at the blond, now taking a telephone call. She was wearing a bone-colored dress, set off by gold earrings and choker. Glancing around her, Amber could see that everything in the room—low-slung sofas arranged around glass-topped tables—was some tone of gold or ivory. Except for the greens, of course. Potted palms, ficus trees, and hanging baskets of lush greenery brought in a touch of the outdoors. Amber looked down at her good navy suit—the best thing she owned—and cringed. This place was like nothing she had ever seen back home in North Carolina. In these elegant surroundings, she stuck out like a sore thumb.

Catching herself drumming her fingers nervously on her purse, she laid it aside, picked up a magazine from a table, and began to leaf through. This issue featured some of the high-fashion Pasetti models, and feeling a fresh wave of anxiety, Amber threw down the magazine and picked up her purse again, fiddling with the clasp. This was just not going to work.

She ought to cancel her appointment and leave right now, before she had to face the embarrassment of hearing, "Don't call us. We'll call you!"

At that moment, an attractive brunette entered the office and spoke to the receptionist loudly enough for Amber to hear. So she wasn't the only person applying for this job! The petite young woman sank into a seat near Amber and offered a forced smile. Apparently too excited to sit still, she jumped to her feet and proceeded to pace the room. In her high heels and flame red dress, the other applicant made Amber feel even more plain vanilla than she had before.

Still, in business school, she had been taught that first impressions were important, and choosing one's interview outfit could make or break your chances of landing a job. Navy, she had learned, signified stability, diligence, and perseverance. That's why she'd decided on this conservative suit and simple white blouse. Still, maybe the instructor hadn't had in mind a fancy job with a modeling agency!

Now the brunette was studying the photographs on the walls, and Lynn rose to explain. For the first time, Amber noticed that the gorgeous receptionist was very, very pregnant. Could it be her job someone would be filling?

Overhearing her explanation of the photos, Amber recalled her own year with an advertising agency back home. She knew something about such layouts, which often focused on a single physical feature—a hand displaying a ring, a foot modeling a shoe, even a perfectly formed ear studded with a diamond or other precious stone. Although she recognized the concept, she also realized that these photos were much more sophisticated than others she had seen. The Pasetti Agency obviously catered to the elite publications.

There's a place for both, Amber told herself resolutely, resisting again the impulse to bolt from the room and forget the whole thing.

A closed door near Lynn's desk bore the name Anton Pasetti in gold letters. The door opened, and another tall blond exited. After a brief assessment of Amber and the brunette, she stopped by the desk. "He asked me to wa—a—ait." She closed her eyes dreamily and sighed.

Lynn gave a knowing smile. "He's probably checking your references. Good luck."

Still in a daze, the blond nodded and drifted to a chair across the room. *Well, so much for that,* Amber decided. The woman had probably already landed the job. In fact, she could be a model herself, with that great bone structure set off by arched brows and silver-blond hair. She'd fit right in. Even her color scheme was right.

Self-consciously, Amber put her hand to her own hair. She had pulled it back, pinned it into a simple twist, and fastened it with a barrette. The color, a dark brown, was far from spectacular. In fact, her only decent feature was her eyes, and even they were just a little more than *run-of-the-mill*, she decided, lapsing into one of the quaint expressions she often heard in her part of the Tarheel State. Some folks had said she was pretty, but she'd never believed them. All she could remember were those miserable preteen years when her eyes and mouth had been too big for her face.

As a Christian, though, she'd never relied too much on her looks. As her grandmother had always said, "Pretty is as pretty does," which was Aunt Sophie's rough translation of 1 Samuel 16:7: "Man looks at the outward appearance, but the LORD looks at the heart." Still, to be surrounded by all this feminine perfection was a little daunting. "Mr. Pasetti is so good-looking," the tall blond gushed, giving Amber just another sharp reminder that some people didn't share her views.

"And single, too," Lynn said in a loud whisper from behind her hand. "Oh, excuse me." She responded to the low beep on her intercom, pressed a button, and listened. "Yes, sir. I'll tell her." She leaned forward. "Jan, Mr. Pasetti thinks you have beautiful hands," the blond gasped and appeared ready to faint, Amber thought, "but not for typing." Lynn hastened to add, "If you're interested, he'd like to use your hands for a layout."

"My hands?" She held them up in front of her as if they were not attached, then blinked. "Well. . .sure! I mean. . .of course! I've always wanted to be a model!"

Lynn nodded. No doubt she'd heard that line before, Amber concluded. The brunette closed her eyes. Amber couldn't help thinking she was probably praying that she'd get lucky, too. *If she does, then maybe I'd have a chance at the secretarial job, after all.* Lynn had to call her name twice before the message sank in. "Amber Jennings, you may go in now."

Amber took a deep breath and rose, dropping her purse, then bumping into a table in her effort to retrieve it. Feeling like a klutz, she made her way to the door with the gold lettering, turned the brass knob, and stepped inside.

There was time for only a glimpse of the room and the man behind the desk when suddenly she was blinded by a beam of southern California sunshine streaming through the undraped window at his back. She could barely make out his tall silhouette, with very broad shoulders, standing to greet her. She squinted and turned her face from the light.

"Sorry," he apologized in a deep baritone voice, "I didn't expect that sudden burst of splendor. The sky has been overcast all day." He turned and released the raised miniblinds, then adjusted them to keep the golden rays at bay. "I confess I'd rather be outdoors than in, and far from the city, I might add. San Diego is like a concrete jungle, and the eighth floor of this building is not much better than a cage in the zoo. Much too confining."

As he spoke, head turned, she took in his striking appearance— muscular build, dark hair curling at the collar, strong profile. Everyone had said he was handsome. But she hadn't been prepared for this!

He turned to find her staring openly, and to cover her confusion, she plunged in before he could initiate the interview. "Confining?" She gave a wry laugh. "My entire cottage would fit into this one room!"

"That's quite a southern drawl you have there."

Was he mocking her? "Well, I'm not surprised. I've lived in the South all my life, actually in only one small town in the South."

He picked up some papers from his desk and flipped through them. "Swanna—how do you pronounce the name of the place?"

"Swan–na–no–a," Amber sounded it out for him. "It's a small town in western North Carolina."

"Never heard of it." He looked up from the file folder in his hands. "What does it mean?"

Despite the fact that Swannanoa had been home for all of her twenty-two years, she really didn't know. But she wasn't about to admit it. "I've. . . heard two different stories," she said uneasily. "Some say it means 'pleasant valley,' while others say it means 'pig path.' "

"Pig. . . ?" She could see him struggling to suppress a smile before coughing into his hand.

"Actually," she went on miserably, just wanting to get this over with, "I think it's probably named for an Indian chief."

"Then you have some Indian blood?"

The only person who had ever mentioned such a thing was Aunt Sophie.

"I think my father's father had a smidgen of Cherokee in him."

He nodded, studying her intently, as if she were a painting in a museum ...or a bug under glass. "That...er...'smidgen,' " this time the smile crept through, "no doubt accounts for the cheekbones and the vivid coloring—especially those eyes."

While she was trying to figure out if he was pleased or displeased with the possibility, he read from the application form: "Amber Elizabeth Jennings?"

"That's right," she answered politely.

"And I'm Anton Pasetti." The lilt of that deep resonant voice gave the sound of music to his name. "Have a seat, please." He gestured toward the chair beside his desk.

While he glanced over the application form, Amber twisted the clasp on her purse. He looked her way when she clicked it shut. Feeling foolish, she slid the small handbag out of sight, then folded her hands together on her lap, making sure that her skirt fell demurely just above her knees. *And remember not to cross your legs,* she could hear her instructor say. Instead, she slanted them properly—in the parallel position.

She knew it had been only a very few minutes since she'd entered the room, but it was beginning to feel like forever. She tried to concentrate on the room. Here, too, the decor was in neutral tones, with photos on the walls. Unlike the reception room, this one was dominated by Mr. Pasetti's desk of polished cherry. Triple the size of a normal executive desk, this one could easily accommodate large portfolios and photo spreads.

She had been told that there were two job openings and that Anton Pasetti would be interviewing those applying for the position of his personal secretary/receptionist. Amber had felt qualified for either. Now, she wasn't so sure this was the job for her. For some reason she couldn't fathom, this man made her feel distinctly uncomfortable.

"You worked with an advertising agency in North Carolina," he said, glancing briefly at her.

She nodded. Just as she was beginning to relax a little, something on the form caught his attention, and he lifted his eyebrows. "You had two promotions within a year?" He leaned back, swiveling his chair to peer at her quizzically.

Feeling warm, Amber put her hand to the high neck of her blouse, then abruptly dropped it to her lap. *Don't let them see you sweat!* came to mind.

She was aware that she didn't sparkle like the brunette outside, nor was she the cool and collected type, like the blond. Close scrutiny would tell him she was just a small-town girl. But she was a good secretary, and the advertising agency in Asheville, although small, was quite successful.

All the information was right there in front of him, on her resumé. But she suspected he wanted to hear her version of the facts. Still, it was probably best not to mention that the owner of the ad agency was also the uncle of her former fiancé. "I graduated from a reputable business school, Mr. Pasetti," she said, plunging in. "After that, I worked for the agency for a year."

He swiveled the chair back to the desk and covered the papers with a large hand. "You worked there a year," he echoed, "took a three-month leave of absence, then returned to the agency for three months?" Leaning forward, he propped his forearms on the desk. "Weren't you happy with your work, Miss Jennings?"

"My leave of absence had nothing to do with the work," she said quickly. *Careful, Amber, don't sound so defensive.* She shook her head slightly and stared at the window, where the stubborn sun trickled through the blinds, spearing her in the angle of its beam, but casting Anton Pasetti into the shadows. She wished she could disappear as easily. But the spotlight was on her, his penetrating gaze probing memories, emotions she had no desire to explore.

She had come here, to this fascinating land of sea and sun, to escape what had happened. But right now this disturbing man was making that impossible. Shifting her gaze to him again, Amber looked across the wide expanse of desk at the man frowning down at her application. She noticed the determined thrust of his jawline, softened by a slight indentation in his chin. Funny. She'd never thought much about chins before. But his was different. Was it that the dimple made him appear less intimidating, more vulnerable? Boyish, even? She focused on the dimple. Anything to get this interview behind her.

After a moment of awkward silence, she realized that he was focusing on her hands, clenched in her lap.

"You're engaged to be married?" he asked brusquely, his eyes locked on the diamond ring on her third finger, left hand.

Heart racing, she looked down. She'd forgotten to take it off! How could she have been so careless? She'd meant to remove the ring as soon as she arrived in California, but had never found the proper moment, nor the proper place to keep something so significant. In the meantime, it had felt perfectly natural on her finger. Now it was too late. And any explanation she might try to make would sound lame.

"You're engaged?" he asked for the second time.

"Yes." She felt the hot color flood her face at the lie. "That is. . .I mean . . .no." She shook her head helplessly. "It's. . .really hard to explain, Mr. Pasetti."

Anton Pasetti turned in the swivel chair to face her directly, apparently annoyed. "I'm not trying to be personal, Miss Jennings. It's just that I'd prefer not to hire someone who might soon marry and leave us."

"Oh, I have no intention of marrying," she blurted out, and, seeing the sudden question in his eyes, amended, "that is. . .not now. I'm only interested in my career."

A comprehending sneer curled the corners of his mouth. "Ah, your career. A secretarial career, I take it."

Amber's chin went up, and she met his gaze head-on. "That's the job I'm applying for, Mr. Pasetti."

"Yes." He hunched his shoulders. "But I also know—from experience—that most applicants have their sights set on modeling."

Amber momentarily forgot her uneasiness. "Well, I have no such illusions, I can assure you. We both know I could never be a model."

His eyebrows shot up and the cynicism settled about his lips again. "And why not, Miss Jennings?" he asked, looking at her nose. Was there a smudge on it?

Distracted, she shifted in her chair. "I'm not tall enough."

At that remark, he threw back his head and laughed heartily. But his laughter didn't bother her nearly as much as the boldly assessing gaze that swept her from head to toe. She didn't know what this man wanted, but apparently it wasn't a secretary; it was a target for all that bitterness and frustration that crackled in the atmosphere around him!

He cleared his throat and drew his brows together in a frown. But the arrogant grin belied his fierce look. "Height isn't everything in the modeling business. Certain products don't require that a model be tall. . . ." He paused, a twinkle in his eyes that she now realized were not black, but a smoky gray, and nodded meaningfully toward her hand. "Engagement rings, for instance."

Amber gasped at the implication. He must be thinking she'd worn the ring to call attention to her hands! She determined to hold her tongue and get out of there as soon as possible.

Anton Pasetti glanced at her nose again, then turned calmly to study the papers in front of him. His tone was entirely professional as he continued. "There are plenty of executives who would give their eyeteeth for a woman whose ambition is to be a secretary these days."

Fortunately, before she could say she had all the eyeteeth she needed, he pushed a button on his desk phone and asked Lynn to get the North Carolina advertising agency on the phone. He gave the name and address Amber had written on the form, then glanced at her, his gaze again lingering on her nose.

Just as she put her hand to her face, he warned, "Don't do that. You'll make it peel." He chuckled. "You really should be more careful in the sun. A pink nose detracts from your best feature—your eyes."

Flustered, she didn't know whether to thank him for the compliment or punch him in his own perfect nose! But his next words dispelled any notion that he had intended to flatter her.

"Aren't you rather warm?" He scanned her long-sleeved suit and the white blouse buttoned all the way to the collar.

By now her flaming cheeks must surely match her nose. "I. . .I haven't had an opportunity to buy any new clothes yet. It's still wintertime in North Carolina in March. And, as you mentioned, it was cool and overcast here this morning."

"Mmm. Well, at least the suit's in good taste—for a secretary."

Not your secretary! she considered flinging back at him. *No way would I want to work for you!* In a few short moments, he had managed to insult her hometown, humiliate her, and render her speechless. He obviously was the kind of man who dominated those around him.

After everything that had happened, she needed new experiences, new friends, a fresh start. Until now, she had felt the Lord had led her to California, to heal. But now she was beginning to wonder if she had heard Him correctly. She certainly didn't fit into the fast-paced, flashy California lifestyle, much less the office of the impossible Anton Pasetti!

Chapter Two

"Mr. Jackson," Anton Pasetti's voice broke into Amber's silent monologue.

While he chatted with her former employer over the phone, she took stock of her situation. She really had to find a job soon, before her carefully hoarded funds ran out. Maybe she ought to reconsider—that is, if there was a chance in the world she'd be offered a position here. She eyed Mr. Pasetti's strong profile, trying to gauge his mood. What was Mr. Jackson telling him? She'd been assured that Ken's uncle would put in a good word for her. He'd even been the one who had suggested she contact the Pasetti Agency as soon after arriving in San Diego as possible. Mr. Jackson, "Uncle Jack," as he'd insisted she call him after her engagement to his nephew, had hired her on at his small ad agency and had praised her efficiency and creativity.

She darted another glance at Mr. Pasetti. He was frowning again.

He swiveled slowly in the brown leather chair, turning his back on her. Uncle Jack must be telling him about the accident. Well, she had come over two thousand miles to escape that very thing. She had to get out of here.

Amber jumped to her feet and was moving toward the door when a rumbling baritone halted her in her tracks. "Miss Jennings," he called in an irritated tone, "would you mind very much if we finished this interview?"

Reluctantly, Amber returned to her chair and perched on the edge, not daring to look him in the eye. If he mentioned Ken, she'd scream.

"Well, that's that," Mr. Pasetti said. Good. It would soon be over. "Mr. Jackson gave you an excellent recommendation. Superior, in fact." He hesitated before going on. "Normally, our applicants come here with their well-written resumés, their beautiful faces, and their lips literally dripping honey. It's refreshing to have a genuine secretary apply. You did say you had no aspirations at all to be a model?"

She knew by his tone of voice that he didn't believe her. Giving him a level look, she spoke as positively as she knew how. "As I've already told you, I haven't the slightest interest in modeling."

He drummed his fingers on the desktop. "Then are you really that unaware of your own potential?"

It sounded like a trick question. Well, she was tired of his games. She squared her shoulders and stood once again, keeping her mouth shut before she said something they'd both regret.

In one fluid movement, he was on his feet, hand extended. Puzzled, she allowed his brief, firm handshake.

"Welcome to the agency, Miss Jennings."

"Welcome?" Her eyes widened and she blinked in surprise. Then she narrowed her gaze. Was that sympathy she detected in his expression? She felt a stab of resentment and something like guilt. Anton Pasetti was the last man on earth she would have chosen to know about her past. But there was little doubt that Uncle Jack had told him. If so, Pasetti was probably giving her the job because he felt sorry for her. Maybe he figured her heart was broken.

On the other hand, Anton Pasetti hadn't really seemed very interested in her one way or the other, but only in hiring a capable secretary. Just for an instant she felt a twinge of envy. Unlike the blond and the brunette in the reception room, she was far from model material. But what difference did that make? She had the job for which she was most qualified. As for Mr. Pasetti, she'd do her job, but she'd do her best to steer clear of him as much as possible. Like oil and water, their personalities just didn't mix.

"Tell the other applicants they may leave, Lynn," he was saying into the intercom. "And take Miss Jennings to Charis."

❧

Lynn had a cocky grin on her face when Amber returned and they were alone in the reception room. "I had a feeling you'd be the one to get the job."

"Really? What gave you that idea?"

"You didn't swoon over the photos, the magazines," she glanced toward her boss's door and dropped her voice, "nor, apparently, over Mr. Pasetti."

"Oh. And I thought I was hired because of my qualifications."

"That, too," Lynn admitted, hoisting herself out of her chair to shake Amber's hand. "Congratulations."

"Oh, and congratulations to you," she said, dropping her gaze to the expandable front of the receptionist's smart maternity dress.

Lynn gave her bulging tummy a fond pat. "Thanks. I've decided to stay home for a while with my children. My three-year-old has grown so fast that I don't want to miss any more of these early, formative years."

Amber nodded. "So yours is one of the positions open?" For the first time, it dawned on her that she hadn't been told which of the two positions she had been hired to fill.

"Yes. The other is at the opposite end of this floor. I'm to take you down there right now. Come on."

Lynn guided her down a long corridor and past several closed doors. Amber learned that the entire fifteen-story building was owned by Pasetti Enterprises, with several floors leased to other businesses. Anton Pasetti's penthouse apartment occupied the top floor.

The end of the hallway opened into a huge room, divided into cubicles. From there, another receptionist directed Lynn and Amber to an inner office.

Seated behind the desk was the most strikingly beautiful older woman Amber had ever seen. Silvery hair was swept back from her face in a dramatic short cut. Even when the corners of her eyes crinkled slightly with the welcoming smile that seemed to emanate from deep within, her beauty was only further enhanced. And when she stood to shake hands, Amber could see that the woman's figure was trim and toned. Her dark gray suit with a printed silk scarf at the neck was the perfect foil for vivid blue eyes that sparkled with warmth.

"Amber Jennings, this is Charis Lamarr, vice president in charge of employee relations," Lynn introduced them.

"Call me Charis," she began as Lynn waved and left to return to her office. "With Lynn's second child arriving soon and one of my secretaries on permanent disability, we're in dire need of help around here."

"Oh, so I'll be working for you!" Amber felt a wave of relief wash over her. "I'm looking forward to it," she said with utter sincerity.

A look of mild surprise altered the woman's classic features. "Most women would jump at the chance to work for Anton," she flicked her gaze to Amber's left hand, "but I see you're engaged."

Amber felt her spirits take a dive. Why had she done this to herself— invite speculation? She took a deep breath. "My fiancé was killed several months ago."

"Oh, I am sorry." The blue eyes sparked with sympathy. "It must be very difficult for one so young to have experienced such a loss."

Amber was tempted to shrug the subject aside. But she supposed she should be honest and up-front with her new employer. "I wear the ring out of a sense of loyalty to Ken," she explained, "not because I can't accept the fact that he's dead."

The genuine concern in the older woman's expression prompted more of a confession than Amber had intended. "At first I tried to make some sense of the accident. But it seemed such a waste. I even blamed God for disrupting my plans. I know now it was He who finally gave me the courage to accept Ken's death." Her pulse quickened as it always did when she shared her faith with a stranger.

Charis walked over to the window, her back to Amber for a moment. The sun had apparently disappeared behind the clouds again, lending a dismal quality to the room. Charis's voice was equally subdued when she spoke. "I know what you mean, Amber." Her shoulders heaved beneath the fine fabric of her suit.

"Then you're a Christian, too?" Amber asked hopefully.

The older woman turned then with a rueful smile. "A relatively new one," she admitted. "I'm still learning to trust the Lord. I had a dear friend whose example I'm trying to follow. She, like your fiancé, died young, and the closer she came to death, the more confident she was that God was with her." Her voice had taken on a tone of wonder. Then, with a wave of her hand, she dismissed the subject. "Perhaps we'll talk at another time. Right now," she went on, sitting erect and looking every inch the vice president of a prestigious modeling agency, "let me explain how we get things done."

Amber listened intently as Charis explained the procedures. The company briefed all incoming staff on good grooming, makeup, poise, and etiquette.

"In short, a mini modeling course," Charis summarized.

Amber's momentary confusion gave way to dawning awareness. Of course. The tools of the trade. This agency's business was to obtain advertising contracts for its models, so all employees were expected to be well-informed. There was even a modeling school on the ninth and tenth floors, she was told.

Grooming, poise, etiquette. . . While Charis talked on, Amber's thoughts strayed. She could sure use some tips in at least one of those areas. If she could just learn how to keep her cool, such as during that recent encounter with Mr. Pasetti. . .

She snapped her attention back to the present just in time to hear the last of the briefing before Charis stood to signal the end of the interview. "So, Amber, on Monday morning you'll begin your training period."

Amber felt her cheeks heat. Had she missed something while her thoughts wandered to the opposite end of the building? "Did you mention how long the training sessions will take?"

"It depends upon the person," Charis replied with a thoughtful look on her face. "We don't put our office staff through the same extensive training our models receive. But we do expect our employees to give customers an impression of the Pasetti look."

The Pasetti look. Flawless features, sleek figure, well-coiffed hair. In other words, physical perfection. What ordinary woman could possibly measure up? It was all so superficial.

Yet the women she'd met so far, Lynn and Charis, were much more than pretty faces. They were warm, caring people. And Charis, at least, was a Christian. Maybe glamour was not altogether incompatible with Christianity, so long as one's motives were right. Besides, it was a job in a field she knew well, although this time the advertisers would be selling something less tangible than tools or toothpaste. This time they would be selling a look: "the Pasetti look."

For a moment, recalling her earlier encounter with Anton Pasetti, Amber felt a stab of anxiety. But it passed quickly. At least she wouldn't be working directly with Mr. Pasetti himself. She looked down at her engagement ring and was freshly reminded of her loss, and of Mr. Pasetti's curious scrutiny.

She'd told her immediate superior the truth, so she didn't owe him a full explanation. But lest he suspect she was too frivolous, or worse, too irresponsible for a job with the agency, she'd continue wearing the ring for a while. She'd just have to postpone, for a little longer, making a complete break with the past. It certainly couldn't do any harm. Could it?

❧

Amber steered her blue Escort out of San Diego, "the concrete jungle," as Anton Pasetti had called it, and was soon speeding along the palm-lined freeway. Because it was not rush hour, the traffic moved quickly, matching her exhilaration at having landed a job, one that far exceeded any expectations she'd entertained that morning. Without having worked a single day, she had the distinct feeling that she would gain much more from the Pasetti Agency than she could ever give it.

Twenty minutes later she turned onto a smaller road, which led to the shopping center near her new home. She splurged on several items—a basket of ivy to hang in the kitchen window, a fern, and a couple of bright toss pillows for the living room to add a personal touch to the cookie-cutter motor-court unit she had rented. She wouldn't buy any new clothes yet, at least not until she consulted with Charis Lamarr as to the image she needed to project.

After parking beside the scraggly palm at the back of the cottage, she entered the small efficiency kitchen. The cottage was nothing special—only a living room, bedroom, and bath beside the eat-in kitchen—but she had been glad to get it. A distant cousin of Uncle Jack's, who operated a service station, had recommended this motor court when she had asked about rentals.

"You might get a house or apartment now, but you'd only have to move in a couple of months," he'd warned. "Once the vacation season begins, landlords raise the rents. But a motor court won't be too expensive, even after the first of June."

He must have taken a look at her grungy jeans, tennis shoes, and three-year-old car, and concluded she couldn't afford the fantastic California prices.

He was right.

The small, white stucco house with the flat red roof was so typically Californian, a far cry from the familiar brick, stone, or log homes in North Carolina. But she had an idea she was going to enjoy her privacy. And she was within walking distance of the beach just across the highway.

Uncle Jack's cousin had given her his address and phone number in case she needed him. She was grateful. It made her feel a little more secure, knowing someone to call in an emergency, although she'd probably never have to use it. In fact, that was one reason she'd left dear Aunt Sophie. Although her dad's sister had always made Amber feel welcome, she often wondered if Sophie would have married or had a career if she hadn't taken on an orphaned child.

Looking around her now, Amber had to smile. This modest cottage didn't begin to compare with her aunt's two-story Georgian, where Amber had had an entire floor all to herself. But she was satisfied. It felt good to leave the nest and spread her wings. And today, she decided, she'd made a good start.

After tossing a green salad, Amber took the bowl and a glass of iced tea and settled on the couch, only half watching the television set in the corner. She twisted the diamond ring on her finger and felt again an overwhelming sense of guilt. Not only were her own feelings "abnormal," but she'd given the wrong impression to Anton Pasetti.

Still, she was glad she had come. Here, in her own little retreat, she could face the truth about her situation with Ken. Back home, well-meaning friends had smothered her with kindness, assuming she was brokenhearted. Of course, she'd always been fond of Ken. They had attended the same church all their lives. Two years older, he had first sought her out at a singles' Christmas party when she was in her last year of business school and he was a junior at N.C. State. She'd been flattered by the attentions of an "older man."

After that, he'd come home almost every weekend and they'd continued to see each other. The next summer Ken had asked her to marry him.

The proposal had come as a surprise, though in retrospect, she couldn't believe she hadn't seen it coming. They'd been together almost constantly, and their friendship had deepened. But she hadn't been sure how to answer him. Oh, it wasn't that she didn't care for him. He was her best friend.

Initially, it hadn't been his looks that had appealed to her, though he'd been nice-looking enough. Light brown hair. Hazel eyes. Medium build. It was his warm personality, his love for people that had drawn her like a magnet. The compassion that had led him to believe he was being called into the ministry.

Ken was a great guy, all right. The kind of man Amber respected and had always thought she would want to marry. A girl would have been crazy to turn him down. So she hadn't. She'd accepted his ring.

In no time at all, the news was out. Aunt Sophie, who had taken Amber in after her parents died, was ecstatic. All her friends were green with envy. So the wedding plans were in motion almost before Amber knew what had happened.

Simultaneously, Ken's uncle, Jack Jackson, had offered her a job with his advertising agency. Ken had wanted to marry right away, but some nagging doubt caused Amber to stall for time. Just because he was that kind of person, he went along with her suggestion that she take the job with his uncle while Ken finished at State. And during his senior year,

Amber was promoted to his uncle's personal secretary, then advertising assistant.

In the fall, after graduation, Ken began seminary, and they set the wedding date for the week before Christmas. But as the date neared, Amber grew more apprehensive. Bewildered by her lack of emotion, she prayed often.

She remembered what her pastor had once said about being sure one's plans were in harmony with God's plans. "First of all," he'd said, "don't try to justify something the Bible says is wrong." Well, there was certainly nothing wrong with marrying Ken. "Beyond that, keep your communication lines with God open. Pray, and listen. Listen to the circumstances God puts in your path. Listen to your feelings."

But that was just the problem. Where Ken was concerned, she had no feelings. At least, not the kind of feelings she would expect to have for the man she was going to be living with for the rest of her life.

So Amber had listened. She listened to her girlfriends who sometimes dreamed aloud of their wedding night, when they would experience sex with the man they loved. Instead of looking forward to that night, Amber dreaded it. The thought of being intimate with Ken was embarrassing. Oh, she enjoyed his kisses, the warm security she felt in his arms. But anything more than that. . . Even now, it was difficult to imagine. What was wrong with her? Was she some kind of freak? Or worse? Had her parents' deaths left her unable to respond normally to love?

When her singles' group prayed to be able to resist the natural physical urges of their bodies, she only mouthed the words. She knew Ken was having difficulty waiting, but for Amber there was no temptation. Maybe that was a blessing. Maybe she'd feel differently after they got married. Now she'd never know.

"I can't go through with it," she'd finally confided to Aunt Sophie just a month before the wedding.

Aunt Sophie had patted her on the arm. "Nonsense! It's just wedding jitters, honey. Everyone has them. They'll pass."

But it wasn't just an attack of nerves. And it hadn't passed.

Amber made up her mind to return Ken's ring. But during the November rains, his car had skidded and crashed on the rain-slick highway on his way home from seminary for Thanksgiving. He had died instantly of a broken neck, so the police report stated. *Better that than a broken heart?*

Amber could only wonder since she'd never had the chance to break their engagement. Now it was her chief consolation. At least he had died believing she loved him as much as he loved her.

Uncle Jack had kindly offered her time off until the first of the year, the weeks designated for her wedding and honeymoon. When she returned in January, she'd asked Uncle Jack what she ought to do with Ken's ring.

Through watery eyes, he had looked down at Amber. "He'd want you to keep it to remember him by." Aunt Sophie had said pretty much the same thing. "True love never ends, honey. Just because he's dead doesn't mean he isn't still alive in your heart." Of course, Aunt Sophie didn't understand. She'd never married. Instead, she'd dedicated her life to her nursing job and caring for Amber.

Rather than feeling grateful for such generosity, Amber had felt the noose tightening around her emotions. She'd never escape reminders of Ken, never be able to forget her own ambivalence. But removing Ken's ring would seem heartless to these dear people. Not only that, but she had become a kind of martyr in her hometown, where daily she heard, "I don't know how you manage to bear up so well, dear. You're truly an inspiration!" or, "We do so admire your courage, Amber."

"I have to get away," Amber had finally told her aunt. She'd bought the secondhand Escort with the insurance money her parents had left her, and because she and Ken had talked about a honeymoon in Florida, she'd decided to travel as far away as possible—in the opposite direction.

It had been Uncle Jack who had given her the idea of coming here to San Diego where he had lived as a boy. "And when you come home," he'd said, "there will be a place for you in the agency."

She smiled at the memory of the kindly man and his earnest offer. But she'd seen the last of North Carolina winters. She'd found a seaside paradise of rocks and cliffs, salt-sea air and swaying palms, and red poinsettias growing wild along the roadside. She had already made one new Christian friend. And she had the faith to believe that there would be other friends and challenges and a new life. Maybe even a new love, someone who could thaw her frozen heart.

Sorry, Uncle Jack, she thought, *you won't be seeing me anytime soon. This is home now.*

Chapter Three

If they could see me now! Amber frequently mused in the days after her arrival in San Diego. *Small-town girl makes it in the big city!*

The eighth floor of the Pasetti building, with its many offices and shops, was itself much like a small town. On the very first day of the training program, she was given a tour, along with Kate Harvey, who had been hired the same day as Amber. Kate was just out of business school and let Amber know right away that she admired her experience in the working world.

"My dad's in the military and was transferred here three years ago," Kate said in her exuberant way, wrinkling her perky little nose. "I know what it's like to move around a lot and have to make new friends. So from now on, I'm it!"

Amber grinned. "Well, that's an offer I can't refuse." Who could resist Kate? With her big eyes and gamine features, she resembled an eager puppy. And there wasn't a bashful bone in her body. Amber found herself wishing she, too, could be more open, less self-conscious. Yes, Kate Harvey would be good for her.

During the complete beauty makeover, Kate never left Amber's side. She was there to applaud the results of the tips on eye makeup and to mourn with Amber when her long dark hair was trimmed to shoulder length and parted in the middle.

"Shake your head from side to side." Following the stylist's instructions, Amber found that the soft waves that framed her face fell right back into place.

When the makeup artist commented that her skin was like magnolia petals, she blushed. "Ah," he added approvingly, "that's the color we want." He applied the cheek rouge lightly, trying to duplicate what nature had just accomplished.

"Scarlett O'Hara had nothing on you. Hourglass perfect," the wardrobe expert commented on her figure. "With your dark hair and fair skin, you'd be a knockout in vivid colors. Let's try something."

Although she'd never worn the bold color before, when a length of fuschia fabric was held up to her face, the reflection in the mirror didn't lie. She had to agree that the color was flattering.

Later, she couldn't help but laugh, wondering if all this were just a part of the Pasetti plan to build her confidence. "I feel like a model instead of a secretary," she told Kate.

"Isn't it fun? Goes to show that, in my case at least, you can make 'a silk purse out of a sow's ear'!" Kate struck a playful pose. "How's this for a makeover?"

A touch of green eye shadow gave depth to the dove gray eyes, and the short cap of light brown curls suited Kate's outgoing personality. "I don't mind being a secretary here," she told Amber. "Even that position is glamorous."

There was thorough training in general office procedures, as well. Both Lynn and one of Charis's most experienced assistants briefed Amber and Kate, giving them on-the-job assignments: handling phone calls, greeting clients, and learning the company computer system. The time flew. Over the weekend, Amber and Kate found another mutual interest: shopping. On Sunday, they attended a little church near Amber's cottage and went out for lunch together afterward. In the afternoon, Amber called Aunt Sophie, who was thrilled with Amber's new job and the fact that she had made friends, especially "that fine Christian woman at work," her aunt said. "My prayers are being answered, honey!"

When Amber mentioned Uncle Jack, she was surprised to hear that Aunt Sophie was cooking supper for him and that he'd be arriving "anytime now."

"Oh, I'm so glad you're having company in, Aunt Sophie. Jack Jackson is such a nice man."

There was a prickle of curiosity along with the little stab of guilt. Her aunt had never complained about missing out on a personal social life because of her care of Amber. But if anyone deserved a "nice man"—someone to take care of her for a change—it was Sophie. "Have fun, you two!" Amber said, and smiled as she replaced the receiver.

❧

Three weeks slipped by, and at the end of the day on Friday, Charis called Amber into her office. Her smile was as warm and charming as ever. "We've had a little. . . change of plans."

Wondering about the "we," Amber looked at her expectantly.

"Mr. Pasetti has decided he wants you as his personal secretary."

Amber froze in her seat.

"Do you have some problem with that arrangement?"

"Oh, don't think I'm ungrateful," Amber roused herself enough to say. "I just thought. . .that is, I'd hoped to work for you."

"What a nice compliment. And I can't say I'm not disappointed that we won't be working together more closely," Charis said kindly. "But we must take ability and experience into consideration as well as personality type. Kate is a dear, but I'm afraid her effervescence might annoy some of our clients. Also, you must know she finds Anton absolutely fascinating." She laughed softly. "It was a blow to his ego to learn that you don't."

"Why would he think a thing like that?" Amber was almost amused. As far as she was concerned, everyone in this new world of high fashion was fascinating.

Charis gave her an appraising glance. "I feel I can trust you, Amber, though I wouldn't confide in just anyone. The day he hired you, Anton felt you didn't particularly like him. And I must admit, I have noticed. . . a certain reserve when you're around him.

"Oh, not that you're anything but unfailingly courteous and respectful, just a little distant. None of that hero worship he's come to expect in a new employee."

Amber stared down at her manicured nails and wondered how to respond. It was true that she respected Anton Pasetti for his business acumen, but she certainly didn't idolize him just because he happened to run a worldwide empire. Her aunt, maybe, for taking her in and being a mother to her. Or someone like Ken, who had planned to spend his life in the ministry, telling others about Jesus. But this cocky, self-important man? No. It wasn't hero worship she felt.

"Of course I understand," Charis continued, following Amber's gaze to the engagement ring on her finger. "Right now, you probably feel as if you could never be interested in any man again. But that could change. . .after you've had a little more time to heal. There are some fine young men in San Diego." Amber couldn't bear to look into the woman's face, so she said nothing and kept her head bowed. "I want you to know that my prayer group is remembering you."

Amber dropped her head even lower, hoping her hair would conceal any expression of dismay. "Thank you," she mumbled, feeling like a moth caught in a spiderweb. Was there no way out of this? She must clear up the misunderstanding about the ring. But now didn't seem to be the time. When she glanced up, she didn't miss the look of sympathy in Charis's eyes. "I. . .hope Mr. Pasetti didn't think I was being rude."

"No problem, dear. Anton is completely convinced you'll be the efficient, detached secretary he needs. And—I hope you don't mind—I also told him that you're a Christian." Surprised, Amber lifted a brow. "Oh, don't worry. He was very pleased to hear it. Said dedicated Christians make the best employees."

"What about Mr. Pasetti's beliefs?" Amber couldn't help asking. "Is he a Christian?"

"Not that I know of," Charis replied somewhat wistfully. "Quite a few of my friends in the business are in the same boat. It's almost impossible to persuade people they need the Lord when they have so much of this world's goods." The corner of her mouth quirked in a wry smile. "I know. I've been there."

Amber nodded. Her association with the rich and famous was limited, but she had already discovered that in these new surroundings, her faith was not always understood. At least Kate was willing to discuss it. But most of the others seemed to feel that choice of lifestyle, including what one believed about God, was a personal matter. Which, to Amber, translated: "None of your business!" A couple of people had even laughed it off "Oh, you're from the South, aren't you? What's it called. . .the Bible Belt?"

How could she make them understand that her faith was not something to be endured, but was the most important part of her life?

Judging from what Charis said, Anton Pasetti, too, probably considered her faith quaint but harmless. She forced a smile. "I'll do my best for Mr. Pasetti."

"Good girl. I knew I could count on you. Anton and I both feel you can handle the additional responsibilities rather than being just another secretary in the pool." Her blue eyes danced. "Not to mention that the salary is better."

Charis extended her hand, and Amber noticed, as she had on the first day they met, that the older woman was wearing several large rings on her fingers, including a wedding band. "Just give it a try, and after a few weeks, if you don't feel it's the right spot for you, we'll see what we can do."

Amber was touched. The woman was a walking example of the Pasetti ideal, always charming and tactful, always putting the other person at ease. It was the kind of assurance Amber needed on the last day of training; on Monday, she would begin working directly with Anton Pasetti.

Although she had seen him only from a distance during the past few weeks, she had not failed to notice him when he dropped by to observe some aspect of the training sessions. Always, she had had the feeling he had been watching her, evaluating her, and weighing her assets. There was some satisfaction in knowing she had met some kind of criteria.

But at the back of her mind, there was the niggling sense that there would be times in the weeks and months ahead when she would wish she had never met the man!

Chapter Four

On Monday morning, a tall, crystal vase of deep red roses was waiting on the desk when Amber walked into the reception room of the Pasetti Modeling Agency.

"Somebody's birthday?" she asked Lynn as she parked her purse in the desk drawer.

"They're for you."

"For me?" Amber eyed her skeptically, then slipped the small card from the envelope attached and read it out loud. "Welcome, Amber! Anton Pasetti."

Contrary to her weeks of training in poise and self-control, she brought her hand to her mouth in an involuntary gesture of surprise. "Is this. . . standard operating procedure?"

Lynn shrugged. "I wouldn't know. Anton's mother hired me five years ago." At Amber's puzzled expression, she laughed. "Don't try to analyze it. Just enjoy."

Amber was bending over to inhale the fragrance of one perfect bud when she heard movement behind her.

"Good morning, Anton," Lynn greeted him, then busied herself at the file cabinet.

Lynn called him by his first name? Amber knew an employee could take such liberties only if the employer had invited it, or if there were no clients around to overhear. But what was she expected to do? She'd better play it safe.

Turning to glance over her shoulder, she was temporarily distracted by the fact that he was so much taller than she remembered. "Good morning, Anton," she blurted before she corrected herself in a professional, three-week-trained tone, "Uh. . .I mean, good morning, Mr. Pasetti. And thank you for the roses. They're very beautiful."

He returned the greeting, adding softly, "And so are you, Amber."

Her intake of breath was audible as she lost her composure for the second time in as many minutes.

His manner changed abruptly. "Oh, don't take it personally. Beauty is our business here, remember? Our models, secretaries, even the waitresses in the cafeteria are expected to be beautiful."

He was still talking as he walked over to the coffee urn and poured himself a cup of coffee. "My mother, who founded this agency on the philosophy that every woman is innately beautiful, believed that with the right clothes, the proper hairstyle, and careful makeup, even the most homely can be attractive."

Why did he have to add a disclaimer to what had seemed like a simple compliment? Flustered, Amber tried to cover her self-consciousness. "Well, she must have been right, because I certainly haven't seen anyone around here who is unattractive."

He peered at her over the rim of his cup, one dark brow lifted.

Realizing how he must be interpreting her casual comment, she wondered if she had already committed the unpardonable sin by Pasetti standards. One of two things might be grounds for dismissal: developing ambitions to be a model or developing designs on the boss!

Almost immediately she felt a stiffening of resolve. She didn't care the first thing about being a model. Besides, she had always believed that true beauty was far more than mere outward appearance. Pasetti training addressed part of it, emphasizing courtesy and consideration for others. But there was another kind of inner beauty, Amber knew, and that was a humility and selflessness that came only from a heart transformed by God.

As for Anton Pasetti, she had to admit that his "outward appearance" was enough to make any woman do a double take. For example, this morning he was dressed casually in dark pants and a creamy white silk shirt, open at the neck, that emphasized his tan. But he was her boss and at least ten years older than she. More than that, they were from two different worlds and—*What am I thinking?* she groaned inwardly.

Muttering something about getting a cup of coffee, she moved past him and toward the urn. She began to relax only when she heard his office door open and close behind him. *Well, Amber, you've managed to get off to a fine start!* she berated herself. *That man and I just don't speak the same language!* But she suspected that their dismal inability to communicate had little to do with her southern accent.

Lynn closed the file drawer with a snap, breaking Amber's reverie. "Come on. I'll show you around. We'll start with the storage closet since you'll be needing some supplies before long." She led the way to a door on the opposite side of the room, opened it, and motioned Amber inside.

Amber took note of the well-stocked shelves. From floor to ceiling, all kinds of office supplies were arranged in neat stacks—from boxes of computer disks and fax paper to paper clips. While they were safely out of earshot, she ventured a question. "What's it like to work for Mr. Pasetti?" she began, keeping her tone light. "I mean, what kind of person is he?"

"He's really a fine man," Lynn replied after a thoughtful pause. "And incidentally, he wasn't flirting with you just now. No offense, but why should he? He has the most beautiful women in the world literally falling at his feet."

Amber felt justifiably reprimanded. According to Charis, Anton Pasetti needed a sensible secretary, not one who would distract him from his work. Well, Amber was nothing if not sensible. And she hadn't the slightest intention of becoming another name on his list of ardent admirers.

They left the storage room and Lynn closed the door, moving to a pile of mail on the desk. She thumbed through as she continued, "He's pretty demanding, and sometimes you'll wonder if you can possibly get everything done. But that's the kind of business we're in. Sometimes things can't wait until morning, so there's some overtime that goes with the territory. Oh, don't worry," she assured, spotting Amber's look of distress, "Anton is all business at times like that.

"And he's fair. He won't expect you to pull off the impossible all by yourself." Lynn gestured toward a smaller desk. "That's for the days when you're swamped and need to call in a backup. All you have to do is check with Charis, and she'll send someone over. It's all going to work out."

❧

During the week, Lynn briefed Amber on her duties, watching over her shoulder as she got the hang of it. By the middle of the week, Amber was on her own, fielding questions on the phone, drafting contracts for models, and sorting Mr. Pasetti's personal mail. And by the end of the week, she had even learned to tell when he was too busy or preoccupied to pour his own coffee, and began to take it to him on a tray, along with the mail and business section of the *Wall Street Journal*.

On those mornings he never looked up from his desk, but barely acknowledged her presence with a nod or a wave of his hand. Even when he called her in to use her laptop to take down a a business letter, he dictated with a brisk authority that did not invite response. On Thursday evening, one contract required two hours of overtime, but he made no apology. "We'll stay until this is finished," he said. And when the final draft was delivered to his desk for his signature, there was not a word of thanks.

At the end of the day on Friday, just after Lynn had packed up her things and left for the last time, and Amber was getting ready to lock up, a gorgeous redhead burst into the office, demanding to see "Anton." *She practically purred his name,* Amber thought with a trace of annoyance.

Amber had seen Gina around the building a few times and knew she was the model being considered for a shampoo commercial for television, which accounted for one of the reasons they had been so busy all week. Well, they couldn't miss with Gina, Amber had to admit, eyeing the young woman's luxuriant mane of fiery red hair.

Amber pressed the buzzer, but Mr. Pasetti was already on his way out of his office door. Spotting Gina standing near Amber's desk, he beamed, white teeth flashing in his tanned face. And with little more than a perfunctory, "Good night," they left without a backward glance. Was this some unscheduled business appointment? Amber shrugged. Since she hadn't been invited along to take notes, she supposed it must be more personal than professional. But it was no business of hers.

She glanced at the roses. They looked about as wilted as she felt. At the first of the week, she had put an aspirin in the water to keep the buds from opening too soon. But now she could see that the flowers couldn't possibly last until Monday. Might as well get rid of them. With a sigh, she tossed them into the trash can.

Suddenly, she wished she could be working instead of facing what promised to be a lonely weekend. Kate was going away with her parents. The singles at church usually had their own weekend projects lined up. She supposed she could clean the cottage, but with only one occupant— a neatnik at that—it wasn't really dirty. Maybe she could go shopping for accessories to go with some of her new outfits. But why bother? She certainly didn't have any dates lined up. She'd met a few guys, but after noticing the diamond on her finger, they'd kept their distance.

On a whim, she tugged at the ring, but it wouldn't come off. Shrugging aside a twinge of guilt, she locked up and left the office.

❧

Accustomed to business hours during the workweek, Amber awoke early the next morning. She stretched, feeling the pull of little-used muscles. There had been no time for physical fitness with a new job and settling into her new living quarters. Better do something about that.

In the kitchen, she spread a bagel with low-fat cream cheese, then nibbled while she spooned coffee into the pot. After her light breakfast, she threw on a pair of shorts and a tank top and sprinted across the highway to the beach. By the time she reached the shore, she was wide awake.

The sun, rising behind her, slanted its rays across the turquoise water, more calm than she had ever seen it. No swells. No waves. Nothing to disturb the glassy surface; it was much like a lake. She felt the bittersweet tug of nostalgic memories of family vacations beside a lake in North Carolina. She had always loved going there—until her parents had been drowned in a boating accident and she had moved in with Aunt Sophie. Neither Amber nor her aunt had returned to the lake since. Still, the ocean was different.

A breeze blew up, riffling the water and sending gentle waves washing up on the beach. Amber began to run. She jogged steadily until she came to a rocky section of shoreline. When she felt the pebbles underfoot, she slowed to catch her breath, panting in the fresh sea air. With the blood singing in her veins, she felt a sense of exhilaration like nothing she had felt since she and Ken had played tennis together.

Looking back down the beach, she saw that her footprints, chased by the sea, had already disappeared. There was nothing to indicate from which direction she had come, or where she was going. She had run halfway across the country, it seemed, not toward anything in particular, but away from something. Now she must allow the past, like her footprints in the sand, to be washed from her mind.

At that moment, Ken's diamond glinted in the sunlight. Amber glanced at her hand, then out over the ocean. Burying her toes in the warm sand, she squared her shoulders. It was time. Today she would take off the ring and put it away. Today it would be over.

She watched the sun skidding into a hazy blue sky and, with a little ache in her heart, she breathed, "Good-bye, Ken."

Chapter Five

It was Gina who first noticed the missing diamond. "No ring?" she asked Amber when she breezed in unexpectedly on Tuesday. Her tone was more condescending than concerned. "Well, I'm sure there's another nice young man out there somewhere. Anton's in, I suppose?"

Amber lifted her hand to press the intercom button. "I'll let him know you're here."

Gina shot her an exasperated look. "Oh, that's not necessary. He'll see me."

"I'm only following Mr. Pasetti's orders. I'm to announce anyone—"

"But I'm not just anyone, honey." Gina tossed her glorious hair and swept past Amber and into Anton's office.

Amber felt her face flame with hot anger. But later, when her boss said nothing about his unexpected visitor, Amber could only assume that Gina was right: She was not just "anyone." After that, the redhead spared few words for Amber, but barged into the executive office whenever she pleased.

࿐

In the following month, the agency buzzed with activity. Mr. Pasetti was either preparing for or conducting one business meeting after another. There were endless luncheons and dinners and board meetings. For the most part, Amber handled the job without difficulty, though she often called Lynn for advice and Charis for extra help.

One situation Amber hadn't counted on was the stream of models coming in to see Anton. Some came at his request, to discuss the details of an upcoming contract. These he treated with cool courtesy. Others came in, weepy and red-eyed, disappointed over some job they'd failed to snag. These he referred to Charis.

"I've had enough trouble with women hounding me," he told Amber one morning in a rare moment of openness, "without letting them cry on my shoulder when a deal goes sour."

They are broad, she was thinking, inadvertently glancing at his very masculine, very impressive set of shoulders. Well, he could be assured she wouldn't be blubbering all over those manly shoulders! However, with him peering at her over the rim of his coffee cup, a trace of blue glinting in his dark eyes, she felt an uncomfortable warmth creeping through her body, all the way to her hairline.

"What a becoming shade of pink," he observed conversationally. "Too bad our makeup department can't bottle that glow."

Pleading a pile of work on her desk, Amber fled just before the flood of color returned. Just the week before, she had given his roses an aspirin to retard their opening. Right now she considered popping one in her own mouth, then scolded herself under her breath, "Stop it right now, Amber! That's unprofessional behavior. So what if this is the first time the boss has noticed that you're not a machine!"

ða

By the end of May, the pace at the office had slowed long enough for the executives to catch their breath. Amber was using her laptop in Mr. Pasetti's office when she caught him staring at her left hand. Was this the first time he had noticed the missing ring?

He broke his stare, stood, and turned toward the windows, flexing his shoulders to work out the kinks. Amber had the feeling he'd rather be elsewhere, probably somewhere with Gina. He had finished his dictation, so she rose to leave.

He must have heard her movement, for he turned and faced her. "Say, Amber, how are the RSVPs coming along for the picnic?"

Supervising the publicity and recording the reservations for the company's annual get-together had occupied a great deal of Amber's time lately, but it wasn't high on her list of personal priorities. Even though everyone from Charis Lamarr to the custodian had been invited, she wasn't even sure she wanted to go. It had been a long time, a very long time, since she'd attended a party. That last time had been with Ken. "We've heard from most of them."

"I assume you're planning to be there." The inflection of his voice left no room for speculation.

"I. . .haven't decided yet."

He appeared shocked. "No one ever refuses an invitation to a Pasetti picnic," was he only pretending to be stern? "unless it's a dire emergency. We've even had employees come with broken legs."

At the absurd idea, Amber had to laugh along with him, then looked away from his disconcerting gaze. This relaxed, more congenial Anton

Pasetti only confused her.

"You have other plans?" he pursued. "A world cruise, perhaps?"

"Oh, nothing so glamorous." She was trying desperately to keep the conversation light. "I'm afraid my boss wouldn't give me that much time off."

"Right you are!" Anton was emphatic. "Good secretaries are hard to find. And your boss is too smart to let her get away." Abruptly the tone of his voice shifted slightly. "You still don't like me, though, do you, Amber?"

She eyed him quizzically, but he had turned again to look out the window. "I realize that in the workplace it's best to keep things on an impersonal basis. And to be honest, it's something of a relief to know that you'll not be pestering me for a modeling contract. I think every one of Charis's secretaries has cornered me at one time or another—in the elevator, in the coffee shop, and even in the parking lot."

Amber allowed a fleeting smile. It was a well-known fact and the topic of a lot of office gossip.

His voice mellowed as he faced her again. "So I appreciate your sensible approach to our working relationship. However, let me make myself clear. Your. . .aloofness doesn't have to extend past closing time."

His eyes met hers briefly, but she couldn't make out the expression in them. In fact, she wondered what he was getting at, although she wasn't about to ask.

After an awkward pause, his voice once again took on a more businesslike tone. "I thought you understood that your services might be required after hours."

"Of course. Lynn told me. And during our training, Charis. . .Mrs. Lamarr instructed all of us about office hours." She would not let his arrogance ruffle her. "I don't mind working overtime once in a while. But I don't understand what that has to do—"

"Don't you know by now, Miss Jennings," his exaggerated patience making her feel like a school dropout, "that a great deal of business is conducted during social events?"

"You mean. . .the picnic?"

Looking smug, he silenced her with an uplifted hand. "Exactly. I had hoped you might be available. Your presence would be. . .helpful. But if you have more important things to do, by all means, do them." She could only stare. "I'll just get someone else to help with the cleanup afterward, as Lynn did last year."

He moved his chair nearer the desk and began to sort through some papers. She felt dismissed.

Thinking it over, she supposed this request wasn't so different from his orders to "Bring the Burman file, Amber. We have to see him over lunch," or "Get a replacement for your desk. I'll need you to take notes at a called board meeting this afternoon." Looking at it that way, the picnic was just part of her job. "If you need me, Mr. Pasetti, of course I'll be there."

With only a nod to acknowledge that he'd heard her, Amber returned to her desk, her mind in high gear. She'd have to take something other than casual clothes, in case of another called meeting of the board or something equally significant. At least she'd learned that a Pasetti employee must be prepared for anything. Lynn might have some tips, too.

At home, Amber picked up the phone and called her. "What kind of cleanup does Mr. Pasetti expect after the picnic? I would have thought the caterers would arrange for that. But he seemed to want me to help. Said you'd done it last year."

"He didn't ask me, Amber. I volunteered. But I must have done some terrific job for him to remember." Lynn went on to explain that Anton had plenty of hired help for his elaborate bashes. "But there are usually a few stray items the others miss. You know what a perfectionist Anton is. Or. . ." there was a long pause, "maybe he just wants to enjoy your company after everyone else has left."

"Ha! I doubt that!" Amber snorted. "What he wants is a cleaning lady!"

But Lynn's parting words lingered long after they had hung up. Enjoy her company? Ridiculous! Anton Pasetti was surrounded by the most beautiful women in the world. Lynn herself had reminded Amber of that earlier. Why would he want to spend time with her? Maybe he was just trying to prove a point. The man's ego probably couldn't tolerate the thought that at least one woman wasn't wild about him! Well, she had no desire to fall for a guy who no doubt discarded women like other men cast off an old pair of shoes.

As the date of the picnic neared, Amber asked Kate to ride to the affair with her. Her friend even agreed to help with the cleanup, so they could leave together afterward. With Kate around, there would be no chance of an awkward confrontation with Anton Pasetti. Just what she wanted, right?

❧

The noon sun, dead overhead, blazed mercilessly in a hot sky, striking sparks, it seemed, from the frothing ocean. Kate and Amber, in the Escort, followed a teal green Suburban packed with Charis's employees. The road curved along the coastline, climbing gently but persistently into the hills.

At last the caravan turned onto a brick driveway flanked by tall, carefully trimmed hedges. Farther up the incline could be seen the tops of swaying palms. And perched atop the cliff, a gleaming white structure that reminded Amber of something from a tourist brochure.

"There's even a bell tower!" Kate exclaimed, bouncing out of the car.

Even with her sunglasses, Amber had to shade her eyes against the bright sunlight to see an enormous tower suspended from the top of the two-tiered structure.

"The architecture of the house is patterned after the old Spanish missions," explained Donna, one of the secretaries, as she got out of Charis's van. "But just wait till you see the back!"

Amber gestured for the others to lead the way. Their sandals flapped against the terra cotta tiles as they walked across the front of the house, under an arcade supported by tall, slender columns. Between each pair of columns was an arch, and beneath each arch, a massive container of tropical flowers.

They turned a corner to another arcade that extended all the way to the back of the house, stopping at a pair of black wrought-iron gates. Donna unfastened them, swung the grillwork open, and, with a sweep of her hand, announced, "Welcome to paradise!"

Mouth agape, Amber stepped through the gates and into another world. At the center of the tiled patio was a fountain, guarded by two carved stone lions. Sparkling water spewed high into the air, then fell back to the base again in graceful arcs. A low wall encircled the patio. Several of the guests who had arrived earlier had already found seats there and were chatting in congenial groups.

Beyond the patio Amber could see the formal gardens: sculptured shrubbery, an occasional tree for shade, and a riot of flowers.

"You two going swimming?" Donna spoke up, pointing to the pool and cabana beyond the gardens.

"Count me in!" Kate waved a tote bag packed with her swimming gear.

"You go ahead," Amber told her. "I'd like to walk around for a while first."

Kate and Donna hurried off, and Amber made her way over to the fountain to catch some of the cooling spray. The sun was beating down, and she welcomed the breeze drifting through the courtyard, stirring the wisps at the back of her neck. Good thing she had taken time to pull her hair into a ponytail.

Looking around, she was relieved to see that most of the other women were dressed as casually as she, in shorts and scoop-necked shirts. Apparently the Pasetti look could bend if the occasion called for it. Only a couple of models had chosen sundresses, but they were lounging in the coolest part of the patio, under the arcade.

"Drink, miss?"

Amber turned to find a middle-aged woman in a crisp white uniform, holding a tray of iced beverages.

"Oh, thank you." Amber selected a tall glass of clear liquid, garnished with a sprig of mint.

Other uniformed employees—the men in white jackets with gold buttons and black pants—circulated among the guests, serving hors d'oeuvres—plump pink shrimp nested on lush beds of lettuce, dainty finger sandwiches, hot canapés.

So this was the famous Pasetti picnic! It was like no other Amber had ever attended. No mounds of golden fried chicken. No ants. No juicy watermelon eaten down to the rind, with a seed-spitting contest afterward.

Amber tentatively brought the liquid to her lips. The drink was wonderfully refreshing—some kind of iced concoction of whipped fruit—and, to her surprise, no alcohol. *Anton Pasetti must share at least some of my convictions,* she thought. Or maybe he was only protecting his models' health and welfare.

"Hi, Amber." A familiar male voice called from behind her, and she turned to see Ron Jordan, a male model from the agency, with his friend Jim Meyers, who worked in advertising.

"Ready for a swim?" Ron flashed a million-watt smile. He often did shoots featuring those perfect white teeth—toothpaste ads, tanning salons, that kind of thing.

"I don't think Mr. Pasetti would approve," she teased, glancing at the fountain.

Ron chuckled. "Not here! Jim tells me there's a pool. Come on down."

Keeping up with the long strides of the two men, Amber had little time to appreciate the gardens and promised herself she'd revisit them before the day ended.

Since she hadn't come prepared to swim, she waited at a table shaded by a wide umbrella while they changed in the cabana. At one end of the Olympic-sized pool were several diving boards, set at varying heights. Following the gaze of the bystanders, she turned to see a figure poised on the high dive.

Anton Pasetti did not look anything like a businessman today. His bronzed body gleamed in the sun, and something silver glinted at his neck. Typical of his style, his dive was executed with perfect skill and grace.

When he broke the water and pulled himself from the pool in a single fluid motion, she gasped. She had known his shoulders were broad, but had not guessed at his lean, muscular physique. *He must work out in a gym or health club,* Amber suspected. *That body takes work.*

She looked on as he waved to a youngster—an employee's child probably —splashing nearby. Midway down the side of the pool, a lifeguard sat erect, watching.

Kate called to Amber from the shallow end, and she called back. When Anton spotted her, he stood and made his way over to her table, his dripping form towering above her. Her eyes swept upward, and a flash of sunlight caught the silver chain that rested above the patch of dark hair, wet and curled, on his chest. She dropped her gaze in embarrassment.

"Hadn't you planned to swim, Amber?"

"Oh, I'd rather watch," she said quickly, grateful for the children's antics in the pool that gave her an excuse to look away. "Everything here is so. . . beautiful," she finished feebly.

She risked a glance. He was wiping away a drop of water that was sliding down his nose from the lock of hair plastered over his forehead. It was the first time she had ever seen a single hair out of place; it gave him a young, boyish look, despite the silver at his temples.

"You do swim?"

She nodded, playing with the stem of her glass. "Believe it or not, I used to be pretty athletic. Spent many a summer at a lake in my younger days. . .Mr. Pasetti." She still didn't feel comfortable calling him by his first name, not even at the company picnic.

He laughed, his teeth white against the darkening tan of his face. "Well, you're not quite ready for a retirement home, so far as I can tell,

Miss Jennings." His bold gaze swept her from head to toe. "Just what do you enjoy doing for recreation, now that you're an old lady?"

Now he was making fun of her. She thrust out her chin. "Tennis is my sport."

"Oh?" He lifted a water-slick brow. "You'll have to schedule a game with Charis's husband. He's practically a pro."

She shook her head. "Then I'd be no match for him. I'm just an amateur." Hoping to change the subject, she scanned the surroundings—the tiled poolside, fringed with waving palms, the manicured lawn sloping down to the terrace. "You have a lovely place here, Mr. Pasetti."

There was a twinkle of amusement in his eyes. "Then remind me to give you a guided tour of the house later." With a little salute, he strolled away, speaking to other guests on his way back to the diving board.

The perfect gentleman, Amber thought, *that's all it is. He's charming and polite to everyone.*

She took the last sip from the glass, set it on the table, and started in the direction of the house.

"Amber." Hearing her name, she saw Charis Lamarr, impeccable in an ice blue linen pants suit, standing in the arcade behind the patio. A tall, lean man, who appeared to be in his sixties, was at her side. His deep tan contrasted with a shock of white hair. "Come meet my Leonard," Charis called gaily.

"Ah, another beautiful model." Leonard Lamarr took her hand and kissed it in the continental manner.

Amber smiled at the twinkle in his eyes. "Afraid not. I'm just a secretary."

"She could easily be a model, though," Charis agreed, walking over to find a seat in the shade. Leonard brought another chair for Amber. "But Anton has hired her as his assistant. I told you about her, Len."

"Not quite everything, my dear."

With a musical laugh, Charis laid her hand over her husband's sun-browned one. Amber felt a bit uneasy under Leonard Lamarr's close scrutiny. Why was he studying her like that?

Seeing Amber's puzzled look, Charis explained. "Len has a line of cosmetics, specializing in eye makeup. Since he often uses our models in his advertisements, it's only natural that he views every woman he meets as a possibility."

"Oh, I'm not the one for your line, Mr. Lamarr, though I'm flattered."

"I realize I'm an old codger, Amber, but I'd consider it a favor if you'd just call me Len."

"All right. . .Len." Amber settled back against the cushions, feeling more at ease with this friendly couple than she had felt all day. Despite their good looks and prestigious positions, they might be the grandparents she'd never known.

They chatted companionably. Amber learned that it was Anton's mother who had improved the property, styling the house after the Spanish missions so prevalent in southern California, adding wings, and planning the exquisite gardens.

"It's truly magnificent," Amber breathed, still stunned by the beauty around her.

"Anton's mother was lovely, inside and out," Charis said with a trace of sadness. "We all miss her so much, particularly Anton, of course."

"Speaking of the devil," Len gestured toward the garden.

"Len!" Charis reprimanded with a helpless shake of her head. "We love that boy as if he were our own," she confided to Amber.

Her gaze following Len's gesture, Amber spotted her handsome boss. From out of nowhere, as if she had been awaiting the moment to make her entrance, Gina appeared at his side. She was wearing a copper-colored bikini that emphasized her lush curves and echoed her glorious hair, which was partially covered by a floppy, wide-brimmed hat. Her pale skin—a translucent ivory—looked as if it had never been touched by the sun and, if it were, it would freckle.

Anton was still in his wet swim trunks, but the rest of him was dry, including his tousled hair, which now curled over his forehead. Once again, Amber was reminded of a naughty little boy, whose eager zest for life, like the unruly curls, could not be contained.

Gina, like some tawny predator, moved in to stake her claim, touching the silver chain at his throat and laughing up into his face. Chuckling at something she had said, Anton looked fondly down at her, his hands grasping the ends of a towel slung around his neck. *They're a stunning couple*, Amber thought with just a touch of envy. *I wonder if anyone will ever look at me like that.*

She turned her head to find Len's gaze fixed on her. She squirmed, embarrassed to be caught like a kid outside a candy store. Well, she wouldn't be so transparent again. She was about to strike up a conversation with Charis when Anton came striding toward them, his business with Gina apparently at an end.

"You may have yourself a challenge here, Len," Anton said as he joined them. "Amber tells me that tennis is her game."

"Oh, I'm no match for a star," she corrected.

"Any starring role for me was over many moons ago, my dear," Len said, then chuckled. "Still, I'd like to take you up on that challenge one of these days. But at the moment, Anton, it's her eyes I'm interested in. I'm sure you've noticed."

Amber felt herself on the hot seat again as all three heads swiveled in her direction. "My eyes? They're just an ordinary mouse brown. You're teasing me, Len."

"Len?" Anton seemed surprised. "Now how do you rate a relationship with my secretary on a first-name basis? I'd venture to say you two have never met before today."

Leonard winked. "Always did have a way with beautiful women."

Anton flicked his towel lightly at the older man in a gesture of affection, Amber suspected. Lulled by their easy camaraderie and the warmth of the day, she relaxed even more. But when the Lamarrs and Anton fell into conversation about the upkeep of the grounds, as if it were home to all of them, she began to feel like an intruder.

"There's Kate," she said, seizing an opportunity to leave. "We promised to spend some time together, since we're the newest additions to the agency."

"The family would be a more apt description," Len corrected. "And most welcome additions, I'm sure."

Amber turned a grateful smile on this man who had set her so at ease from the beginning, and she wondered at the kindred spirit between them. He must be a Christian, like Charis. She'd noticed that with most people who shared the same faith in God, there seemed to be an instantaneous bond, just as there was an invisible wall separating her from those who did not—like Anton Pasetti.

The older couple rose to leave. "See you later, you two," Charis called with a waggle of her fingers.

Amber jumped to her feet. No way did she want to be alone with her enigmatic boss. Besides, he was probably just as ready to be rid of her. She managed to excuse herself and walk away without tripping over the loose tile at the edge of the patio.

On her way to catch up with Kate, Amber thought of Len's remark about family. That concept seemed to be Anton Pasetti's goal for the agency. If it really was a family, then Anton was the head. Everyone did look up to him. But why shouldn't they? Of course they admired him; he was a successful businessman, the man who signed their paychecks. Still, today she had seen a different side to Anton Pasetti, a more human side, a genuine caring for others. It reminded her of the day he'd asked her to find out what Lynn might need for her new baby and had then, on his own, arranged for a baby nurse for the first two weeks.

It would be nice to be part of a family again, she mused. As a child, she had assumed her parents would always be around loving her, protecting her. Later, she had believed Ken was her safe harbor. But of course, it was out of the question to lean on Anton Pasetti. She had decided long ago never to allow herself to care deeply about a man who was not a Christian.

Now, remembering his masculine appeal, his charm and consideration, she tried to shut out an errant thought that a man who cared about older people and babies must not be all bad!

Chapter Six

Brushing away a loose strand of hair straggling from her ponytail, Amber walked over to the fountain where Kate was standing with Jim and Ron. The three had changed back into their casual clothes, their hair still wet from their shower. "Have a good swim?"

"Just enough to work up a huge appetite!" Ron replied with a dazzling smile.

Jim glanced at his watch. "You'll have to hang on for twenty more minutes, pal. When Anton Pasetti says dinner will be served at six o'clock, that's exactly what he means."

"No problem," Kate said with a shrug. "We can walk around the gardens until then."

&

When they returned, servants had opened the French doors and were inviting the guests to come in.

"This is not exactly the way I'd pictured the picnic," Amber whispered to Kate. "I expected to eat off a tablecloth spread on the ground."

Kate wrinkled her turned-up nose. "I can't imagine an ant daring to crash this party!" she said with a giggle.

From the foyer, the guests entered a spacious room with dark tile and paneling. Long tables were set along the walls; behind them stood waiters in tall white hats, serving elegant food onto china plates. It was a veritable feast, with every imaginable delicacy—thin slices of roast beef and pork, fajitas, tacos, and quesadillas to offer the flavor of the Southwest, several rich casseroles, and a cornucopia of fruit, topped with a plumed pineapple and cascading from the center of the table. Another smaller table contained trays filled with pastries and a Mexican flan.

With their plates filled to overflowing, the guests found their way back outside through another pair of French doors and seated themselves at one of several tables or on the low wall encircling the courtyard. The entertainment began when most of the guests had put their plates aside and sat sipping their beverages. Strolling guitarists in Mexican costumes, complete with sombreros, paraded around the patio, serenading them.

At the close of one sprightly number, the musicians took seats on the edge of the fountain and began strumming a love song. A man with jet-black hair and a white shirt tucked into his black breeches and a woman in a long, ruffled red dress, made a dramatic appearance from opposite sides of the courtyard. While the man stood rigid, arms folded over his chest, the woman began to dance to the song, sung alternately in Spanish and English.

Amber was intrigued. The woman tossed her flowing raven hair, tapping her feet with staccato steps to the music, slowly at first, then with increasing speed. The tall lover stood aloof while she whirled around him, inviting him to join her with a look. Finally, he could remain indifferent to her wiles no longer and entered into the dance, expressing in every movement his love for the beautiful señorita.

The dance stirred Amber deeply, at some level she dared not acknowledge. When it was finished, she applauded along with the others, then let out a long sigh. *It was only a dance*, she reminded herself. The couple were not in love; they were performers, paid by Pasetti money.

And, as many of the guests began to drift away, Amber recalled why she was here in the first place. Anton Pasetti had summoned her to clean up after the picnic. She'd better get busy.

"I'm going to get my change of clothes and makeup kit from the car," Amber told Kate, feeling a strange letdown. "I may have to take notes for a meeting. If you'll stick around, we'll clean up when I get back."

"Amber?" Kate could not conceal her excitement. "Would you mind terribly if Jim took me home?" Her eyes were pleading.

Amber could never refuse her friend. "Of course not. That's great. You two go ahead, and I'll see you Monday."

"But you asked me to help pick up, and I'm feeling really guilty about this."

"There won't be that much to do," Amber assured her. "Unless Mr. Pasetti does have a meeting scheduled, I'll be out of here in no time. Now, scoot!"

"Well, I think Ron is going to ask to take you home," Kate added with a sly grin.

That was no surprise. Amber had already figured it was coming. But she had work to do first. She hurried to the car, retrieved her things, and went back to the house to find a guest room. Not quite sure what the evening would bring, she had packed a full skirt and multicolored blouse appropriate to the surroundings. She slipped on a pair of strappy sandals and gold dangling loops in her ears, then repaired her makeup and brushed out her ponytail until her hair hung softly around her shoulders. Mr. Pasetti should have given her a little more information on the kind of meeting he would be holding. But this would have to do.

Jim and Kate were leaving when she took her case back to the car, and Ron gave a low whistle. "Wow! I'm surprised Pasetti hasn't signed you as one of his top models."

She waved aside his compliment. "I thought you two guys came together," she said, gesturing toward Jim, who was helping Kate into his car.

Ron's grin was contagious. "Nope, I drove—just in case I came across some gorgeous woman who needed a ride home. How about it, Amber?"

"Thanks, Ron, but I have my own car."

Apparently he wasn't going to give up easily. "One of us could follow the other, and we could go somewhere for coffee or a nightcap. Or even dancing?"

Amber had to laugh at the ridiculous pose he made, arms poised above his head like the flamenco dancer. "Maybe some other time, Ron. I have to do some work for Mr. Pasetti before I leave."

Ron looked disappointed, but added quickly, "Have time for a turn in the gardens?"

"Sure. He hasn't called for me yet, and I should be able to hear him when he does."

With the approaching dusk, lights had been turned on—thousands, it seemed—miniature stars twinkling from the trees and lamps positioned throughout the grounds.

To add to the aura of fantasy, the lamps shimmered with halos created by a mist drifting in from the ocean.

"How long have you been with Pasetti, Ron?"

"About six months." He slowed his stride to match hers. His shirt, a pale blue, brought out the color of his eyes. "I'd never had any intention of becoming a model. But a scout noticed me when I escorted the homecoming queen during football season my last year in college." He grinned. "It's not too bad. A pretty lucrative business, considering the other jobs out there. And there are perks, like meeting other models of the feminine persuasion." He slanted her a mischievous look. "Are you sure you're not one of us?"

"Very sure. I'm just a secretary—which reminds me, I'd better see if Mr. Pasetti needs me now."

The crowd had thinned, and as Ron began to move away reluctantly, she returned to the patio. Just as Lynn had told her, the hired caterers had missed a few stray cups and glasses, and she picked them up to stow in a huge trash bag.

Gina was the last to leave. The redhead stood very close to Anton as she told him good night, her green eyes almost begging for an invitation to stay. But he laughed down at her good-naturedly and, drawing her hand through his arm, moved toward the arcade and the parking area.

On their way past Amber, Gina hissed, "Better get home and get your beauty sleep, honey. Anton expects his little secretaries to be fresh and dewy-eyed."

Amber bristled and bit back a sharp retort. The woman was impossible! *A gentle answer turns away wrath! A gentle answer turns away wrath!* she quoted Proverbs 15:1 furiously to herself, then managed a halfway genuine smile. "Good night, Gina."

"I could have helped you, Anton," the redhead pouted.

"And dirty those beautiful hands? Not if I can help it. I need you for that important hand lotion campaign, remember?"

Gina's answering smile was radiant.

Amber had to hand it to her boss. He knew how to let a girl down easy. Still, Gina lost no time. Catching up with Ron, she slipped her arm through his. "Ronnie, darling," she purred, "would you walk me to my car?"

"Sure thing." He waved to the others and he and Gina took off.

As soon as they were out of sight, Anton turned to Amber, his manner suddenly stiff and formal. "There's really no need for you to stay. If you'd rather leave with Ron, you're free to do so."

"But what about your. . .business? I thought there might be a meeting."

For a moment Anton looked puzzled. "Business?" Dawning awareness crossed his features, and he replied with amusement. "We have just conducted our business, Amber. Meeting adjourned."

Amber stared at him. He seemed to be enjoying himself immensely. Then it struck her. "You mean. . . ?" she gasped, spreading her hands helplessly. "You mean you used me. . .to make Gina jealous?"

His grin broadened, and he threw back his head and laughed heartily.

Amber clenched her fists. Lips taut, she struggled to control the cold, creeping rage that threatened to engulf her. "Mr. Pasetti," she said icily, surprised at the steadiness of her voice, "pardon me if I fail to see the humor in this. Your personal life is your own business. But when you begin to use other people for your little games. . ."

He took a step toward her, holding out his hands in a conciliatory gesture. "Forgive me if I've offended you. But all's fair in love and war."

Afraid he might touch her, she quickly turned away. Her skirt swirled about her legs as she went to the fountain and sat on the edge of the wall surrounding it.

"If those lions were not made of marble, I do believe they'd flee for their lives," he said, walking over to stand in front of her.

Jumping to her feet, Amber was about to brush past him to leave. But he anticipated the move and his hand shot out, grasping her arm in a firm grip. "Why does it matter so much, Amber?"

The truth doused her anger like a blast of water on a fire. She felt suddenly drained and void of emotion, except for her trembling legs and a pounding pulse.

Did it matter? Perhaps not. Hadn't she sensed that he was the kind of man who thought of women as trophies to be added to his collection? It was wishful thinking to believe otherwise.

"Before I leave, Mr. Pasetti, I want you to understand what I think of your. . .juvenile games. I may be younger than you, but I feel it only fair to warn you that I refuse to work—"

"Miss Jennings!" he exploded, taking hold of both her arms and preventing her escape.

His captive, at least for the moment, Amber stood in front of him, chest heaving. She had hoped to quit her job before he fired her. But now—

"You've said quite enough," he warned. "We're not at the office now. We're just a man and woman trying to have a conversation. And this thing about your being young won't wash. You're all grown-up now and, from my observations, wise beyond your years."

"Let me go."

Ignoring her request, he continued, his voice carefully controlled. "It would seem, Miss Jennings, that we are two of a kind."

She could only gasp. How dare he think they were anything at all alike!

"Ah," he smirked, "you think I can't see through you? Whom do you think you're kidding, little Miss Innocent? If you're going to accuse me of playing games with Gina, then perhaps I should remind you that your own actions have been highly questionable."

Amber blinked as he went on. "You came to my agency, sporting an engagement ring from a fiancé who—we later learn—is deceased. When I was finally told the true circumstances, you seemed not at all concerned about your loss, only about the job. I decided right then, Miss Jennings, that you had never really been in love."

How could he possibly know that? She had barely admitted it to herself! She lowered her eyes, feeling the quick sting of moisture behind them.

He wasn't through with her. "Then you worked on the sympathy of the entire agency, allowing them to believe you were grieving over your fiancé. Yet today you spent an entire afternoon and evening with Ron Jordan, a man you scarcely know."

Searching her mind for a way to redeem herself, Amber was speechless.

"And what about the remark Leonard Lamarr made about your eyes? You know he's in the makeup business. Is that why you cozied up to him, calling him by his first name? And right in front of his wife, too! Have you been using your job—and me, for that matter—in order to break into modeling?"

"That's not true! I have never—" she choked out, her words barely audible.

"Never?" he asked curiously.

Her gaze lifted to his, drawn into the dark depths against her will. She felt as if her heart would stop. *Please, Lord, don't let him try to kiss me!* She closed her eyes, feeling a wave of dizziness sweep over her. When she went limp in his arms, he tightened his grasp, then released her. "I'm sorry. I didn't mean to hurt you."

Feeling her legs about to give way, she sank down again onto the wall of the fountain.

"It seems we've arrived at a stalemate, Amber," he said, his voice husky. "You've made accusations against me, and I against you. You say I'm wrong. Maybe so. Maybe I've misjudged you. But that could go both ways, you know. It's possible that you've misjudged me, too."

She felt his assessing look, but could not bring herself to look up at him. His next comment was almost amiable. "Could be you'll discover I'm not such a bad guy, after all."

Hadn't she reached that conclusion herself not very long ago? But that was before—

He dropped down beside her and took her hand. She was too stunned to resist. His words, his fingers caressing her knuckles were hypnotic. She hadn't the faintest idea what to believe anymore. Did he truly think she was devious, a woman with ulterior motives? If so, why was he still trying to make another conquest? Or was it just that he was the ultimate con artist?

He released her hand, then stood, pulling her to her feet. His smile was beguiling, his eyes filled with sincerity. "Let's start over, Amber, without the distrust, the suspicions. You let go of your preconceived notions about me, and I'll ask you to forgive me for accusing you unjustly."

Amber hugged her arms to herself, feeling chilled in the cool night air. How could she make such a deal with him? Everything he'd said about her was not untrue. And she couldn't help but be suspicious of him still because he had asked her to stay under obviously false pretenses.

And yet, she wasn't up to another verbal battle. Before she had an inkling of how to respond, he asked softly, "Couldn't we be friends?"

Friends? After tonight, she wasn't sure. But she could answer honestly, "We haven't had any problems at the office."

"True," he replied. "But I'm speaking of after-office hours, when you're not an employee but a beautiful young woman, whose eyes seem to reach inside the soul, whose sweet lips are made for kissing, and whose soft, southern drawl melts the heart."

She caught her breath. He was playing games again. That line was straight out of some movie. She turned away. He was wrong about one thing—she was not wise beyond her years, not wise at all. "I'm afraid our lifestyles are too different for there to be anything for us outside the office," she said, then added, moving toward her car, "Good night, Mr. Pasetti."

His next words stopped her in her tracks. "Different. . .because you're a Christian?" She didn't move. "I'd like to talk to you about that. It's one reason I asked you to stay tonight."

How clever of him. If he knew anything at all about Christianity, he would know there was no way she could refuse such a request. She turned her head slowly.

She had never been so frightened in her life. She was afraid of his clever tricks, his quick wit. Afraid of her own vulnerability. She breathed a quick, silent prayer.

Then Anton was beside her, holding out his hand. "We'll talk," he said gently. "But first, like the pompous, arrogant materialist I am, I'd like to show you my home."

Chapter Seven

Anton steered Amber through the house, describing each room in detail. She tried to forget the incident at the fountain, tried instead to concentrate on the gleaming tiled floors and rich carpets. Light from ornate chandeliers glowed softly, illuminating the many paintings lining the wide hallways.

"An El Greco!" she burst out, forgetting everything else in her delight.

He slanted her a sidelong glance, then back at the painting. "My mother's favorite," he explained. " 'Adoration of the Shepherds.' But you know the painting as well as the artist, of course."

"Of course." So she had caught him off guard, for a change. "I know his style. He's famous for painting elongated figures."

"Some critics say he was mad," Anton put in, testing her.

"Others say he had bad eyesight," Amber returned, then cut her eyes around at him. He seemed amused—and pleased. But she was no connoisseur of the arts, hadn't traveled widely or trained extensively. He would know that anyway; her resumé spelled out her business school education and her family background. A small town would not be likely to provide the rich opportunities that were a natural part of his heritage.

"Two semesters of Art History at the University of Asheville." She ducked her head, then looked up at him with a contrite expression.

Now that he was smiling at her, blue glints sparking his smoky eyes, she dared to take it a step further. "Another reason I remember El Greco is because he spent most of his life in Toledo. At first," she admitted sheepishly, "I thought the biographer was talking about Toledo, Ohio—not Spain!"

"Art History was not my best subject, either, Amber. Seems I thought it was. . .an irreverent expression!" He seemed to reconsider telling her just what he meant by that.

They smiled at each other, and she felt no qualms at all this time in accepting his offer to continue the tour.

By the grand stairway, Anton stopped before a pair of portraits. "My mother and father."

The dark-haired woman reminded Amber of the beautiful Spanish dancer she had seen earlier that evening. The eyes in the portrait, however, were not those of a flirt, but of a warmhearted, gracious lady. Next to her portrait hung that of a ruggedly handsome man, his chiseled features softened by light brown hair that fell in soft waves from a center part.

Anton's golden bronze complexion and dark coloring were obviously from his mother's side of the family, while his stature was probably from his father's side. She risked a glance at him and caught him staring at his mother's picture. A man who loved his mother—and wasn't ashamed to show it.

As if suddenly aware of the tense silence, Anton started up his tour guide monologue. "This wing," he gestured toward the front of the house, "living room, salon, formal dining room, ballroom, is used primarily for entertaining. You've seen most of that. Since it would take much too long to explore the entire house, I'll take you through the living quarters."

Anton had implied that his personal quarters were small and informal compared to the more public areas, but Amber was stunned by their size and elegance. In the dining room, the walnut table and chairs hardly seemed informal to her, nor the lavish ornamentation and lovely rich colors of the Oriental rugs used in the rooms. The living room furniture—covered in suedes, velvets, and leather—repeated the deep reds, golds, blues, and emerald greens of the carpet.

"Many of the furnishings are contemporary," Anton explained, "but Mother was partial to the Mediterranean influence."

"It's breathtaking."

They returned to the hallway, and Anton led her up the stairs that spiraled up to yet another floor. As they walked along the landing, she could look down on the first floor, where the crystal chandelier cast diamond-shaped patterns of light onto the tiles below.

"The doors to the right lead to suites," Anton pointed out, "but this is my favorite." Stepping forward, he opened a door on their left.

Amber walked into a very masculine study with leather couches and overstuffed chairs, dark paneled walls, floor-to-ceiling bookcases, and a walk-in fireplace. He pulled a cord at the side of the deep red velvet draperies under Moorish arches, and the draperies parted, exposing glass doors, and on the other side, a balcony protected by a black wrought-iron railing.

Anton slid open the glass doors, and they walked out onto the balcony, breathing in the cool night air. At one side was a garden table and chairs. As if on cue, an elevator door opened onto the balcony and a uniformed servant trundled a wheeled cart over to the table. Anton pulled out a chair for Amber.

The servant poured coffee and set a tray of delicate pastries on the table, then lit two candles in heavy, silver candlesticks. "Thank you, Mitchell. That will be all." Anton dismissed him with a nod.

Amber took a sip of the hot coffee, then picked up a pastry. Avoiding Anton's gaze, she looked down at the formal gardens below. She was very near tears. It had been a long day, and her emotions had taken a roller-coaster ride. Now the very peace and tranquillity of this place was almost too much.

Anton was waiting. She really ought to say something. A Pasetti employee was always cool and collected, always knew the right thing to say. "Well, Amber?"

It might not be the Pasetti way, but she could only be honest. "I feel. . ." she hesitated and allowed herself to lock onto his gaze. Funny. The candlelight was reflected in his eyes, making them glisten with a silvery sheen. Then a breeze stirred, and the candle guttered and almost died, shadowing the strong planes of his face. "I feel as if. . .as if I've been introduced to your mother."

In the silence that followed, she wondered if she had offended him by bringing up a painful subject.

At last he spoke up. "I've had many compliments on this house and grounds. . .but no one has ever said a thing like that before." He regarded her thoughtfully, and she felt another prickle of apprehension. "You are a very perceptive young woman. All of this," he said, with an encompassing sweep of his hand, "is a product of my mother's good taste and perseverance. My father would have lost everything through his gambling and drinking if Mother hadn't taken over and kept the business going. I watched her struggle. After my father died, she continued to carry on, without much help from me, I'm afraid." He gave a bitter laugh and picked up a heavily carved silver spoon, twirling it as he went on. "I've often regretted the time I spent abroad instead of staying here to help her," he sighed, "but I was young and impulsive—and stubborn."

Amber forgot that he was her employer, as he told of the cancer that had destroyed by inches what had once been a vital and beautiful woman. There were tears in his eyes when he looked up. "But the illness brought her closer to her God. That's when she designed the house, using the architecture of a Spanish mission and installed the bell tower, where the carillon plays at dusk each day. Her idea was that in those few moments, at least, the faithful should remember their Creator. I'll show it to you sometime. On a clear day, you can see our private beach from there." He choked. "Mother used to shoo me away from her bedside to go there when the suffering became too great, saying she could signal me with the bell if she needed me. She lived four long years like that."

It was all Amber could do to restrain herself from putting out a hand to comfort him. But he had not finished.

"It was during my mother's years of illness that I began to grow up, assume more responsibility for the business. I promised to keep the business going. But she laid the groundwork for our success. I simply inherited the results of her hard work."

Stunned by this revelation, Amber could only sit, allowing him to absorb the peace of the evening. Finally, she ventured a comment. "You work very hard, too," she said softly. "I'm sure your mother would be very proud of you."

He let out a long sigh. "Yes, I can feel a sense of accomplishment in that, at least. But it was my mother who set the pace. This house reflects her tastes, her spirit. . .though I suppose someday my wife will make some changes, add her own touches to the place."

His wife. Amber wondered if Gina would be the next Mrs. Pasetti.

Anton's voice was quiet in the stillness, a stillness strangely enhanced by the distant lapping of waves against the shoreline. "It was my mother who taught me that possessions are cold and impersonal, totally without meaning—unless there is someone to share them. She was right."

"Your mother. . .was wise as well as beautiful."

"She'll always be a part of me." He lifted his head and narrowed his gaze speculatively. "It's good to remember those we have loved, but there comes a time when we must face the fact that life goes on and we have other duties and obligations to the world—and to ourselves."

Amber shivered slightly in the evening breeze. Was he going to ask her about Ken?

"My mother had a way of accepting whatever came as God's will,"

Anton went on. "When she was too weak to hold her Bible, I sat beside her bed and read to her for hours." His tone was laced with pain as he lifted the silver chain at his throat.

For the first time, Amber noticed a small cross attached. She had to know. "Are you a Christian then, Mr. Pasetti?"

He shook his head. "No, I wear this cross in her memory. Oh, I tried it. When the pain seemed unbearable, I asked that unseen God of hers to give her peace. . .to take her pain away. . .or release her in death." Anton regarded Amber with such intensity that she knew he was speaking the truth. "When neither prayer was answered. . ." He shrugged, then spat bitterly, "How could I trust in a God who would allow such suffering?"

Amber squirmed under his penetrating gaze. She understood his confusion, his frustration. "Sometimes I've wondered, too, where is God?" she admitted. "Why does He allow such terrible things to happen? Why did He let a boating accident take my parents from me when I was only seven? On the other hand, if God stepped in to prevent all evil, then we'd be nothing more than puppets. What father wants his children to love and obey him because they have no other choice?"

Anton was still studying her, watching, waiting, as if nothing she had said so far had registered with him. She rushed to her conclusion. "At least, with God's help, we can get through painful times. We can know that someday, either here on earth or in heaven, everything will be all right."

Anton snapped out of his reverie. "Oh, so God is a crutch," he said, his voice tinged with skepticism.

Amber hesitated only a moment. "If you had a broken leg, you'd use a crutch, wouldn't you?"

He nodded, somewhat reluctantly, she thought. "And we are broken, twisted, weak inside. All of us," she added pointedly.

Her words apparently did not faze him. Instead, he shifted the subject. "Amber, you lost the man you were going to marry. You might say God took him. Why?"

Amber averted her eyes. "I. . .really don't know. But I do know that God has a plan for me. . .either with or without a husband. I'll just wait until He leads me to the right man."

"And of course that man will have to be a Christian to be a real man in your eyes." There was no mistaking the sarcasm edging his remark.

Amber picked up her spoon and stirred the half cup of coffee that didn't need stirring. The ensuing silence was loaded. Whatever she said now could make or break their tenuous relationship. But she wasn't about to lie!

Still, she wasn't expecting his next comment, delivered as nonchalantly as if he were speculating on the weather. "I wonder what God would do for me, if I became a Christian."

"Maybe nothing you think you want. But you can be sure it would be best." She couldn't believe she had spoken so boldly—to Anton Pasetti, of all people!

"Your honesty is. . .quite refreshing. It's one of the things I've come to admire about you."

"I guess I am blunt sometimes," she admitted. "And I also have a temper."

"So I've noticed." His serious demeanor gave way to a slow grin. "Some women are even more beautiful when they're angry."

Her wariness surfaced again. He was probably thinking of Gina. But he really shouldn't be talking this way. Still, he might just be testing her. Or maybe this whole conversation had been a ploy to add her to his collection.

She had to admit she was beginning to feel as human as the million and one other women who found Anton Pasetti attractive. She was determined, however, that he would be the last to find out. "I really should go," she said, keeping her voice—if not the rest of her—coolly detached.

He was on his feet instantly. Probably he had just been waiting for her to leave so he could call Gina. It was still early.

"Let's take the elevator." He led the way to the corner of the balcony where he pressed a button beside a pair of recessed doors.

When they slid open, he motioned her inside. At the bottom, they stepped into an alcove off the kitchen. Mitchell was sitting at a table drinking coffee, while a couple of uniformed women were putting dishes away.

"Mitchell, would you follow us in Amber's car, then drive me back?" Anton asked.

"Oh, I wouldn't want to put Mr. Mitchell to any trouble," Amber protested.

"You know your way around these freeways?"

"Not too well," she had to admit. "Maybe if you just gave me some directions. . ."

The women had stopped their work and were staring openly. Mitchell looked embarrassed, or sympathetic; she couldn't tell which. She saw the glance he gave Anton, whose smug look resembled that of the cat who swallowed the canary.

"Your keys, please," Anton said.

Amber fished them from her purse and handed them over. "Come along." Anton slipped her keys to Mitchell, then guided her, with a light touch at the small of her back, out to his car in the garage.

Without a word, she followed the deft movements of his hands as he steered the big Mercedes out of the garage, whipped it around, and turned toward town.

From the passenger's side, Amber looked out the window. The seascape spreading across her line of vision was black velvet studded with diamonds, mirroring the night sky. Here and there a froth of whitelike lace rode in on the waves as they rolled to the shore. For several moments, neither one of them said a word as they drove through the night.

"You and Ron Jordan seemed to hit it off rather well," Anton said when he finally broke the silence.

Amber hadn't given Ron another thought, but now she recalled that he and Gina had left together. Was Anton jealous? How ironic if his plan had backfired.

When she didn't comment, he continued. "The night is young. If you'd left with Ron and the others, you'd probably be out there, too." He gestured toward the beach, where several cars had pulled off to park.

Amber still didn't speak, but she kept her head turned toward the ocean. He was right. But for some reason she did not regret the evening spent at Anton Pasetti's house.

With a flick of his wrist, Anton wheeled the car off the road and parked on the sand near the other cars. Over her shoulder, Amber could see Mitchell pulling up in her little blue car, a short distance behind them.

"Shall we walk on the beach?" Anton asked, apparently amused at her wide-eyed expression.

Amber cleared her throat nervously. "I can't walk very far in these heels. But I did bring along another pair."

She retrieved them from her bag and put them on, not sure what her boss planned to do next.

He stood quietly, studying the moon-washed shore. "It's been a long time since I've seen the beach at night. . .in the company of a young woman."

Now that was a surprise!

The sea breeze felt good on her flushed face as he reached out to tug her along, steadying her in the shifting sand. From here, they could see several couples playing in the water. Others walked along the beach, hand in hand, while some sat on blankets, locked in romantic embraces.

They hadn't walked very far when Anton stopped and turned to face her. She felt as if the surf were pounding in her ears as he tilted her chin upward with his thumb and forefinger. "Is this what Ron would have done?"

"Oh, he'd probably have thrown me in the ocean!" she quipped, hoping to dispel the sudden tension between them.

Anton's mood did not alter. "Then he would have rescued the lovely damsel in distress. . .and kissed her?"

"Oh, I doubt that!" She laughed uneasily and twisted out of his grasp, not daring to look into those eyes, luring her into their dark depths. She chafed her arms where goose bumps were blossoming. "It's chilly out here. We'd better leave."

Anton shrugged and led her back to the car. She was relieved when he started up the engine immediately, then switched on the radio. There was no need for conversation, other than the necessary instructions to her cottage.

When they arrived at the motor court, she motioned to Mitchell to park under the palm tree, then waited while Anton pulled the Mercedes in behind her Escort.

Without waiting for Anton, Amber hopped out of the car and hurried over to the butler. "Thank you, Mr. Mitchell. I hope this hasn't inconvenienced you too much."

He bowed formally, but his smile was warm. "Not at all, miss."

Anton took the key from her and unlocked the back door. She switched on the kitchen light, and they stepped inside. At least she hadn't left dirty dishes in the sink!

"Check to see if everything is all right."

He's always bossing people around, she thought, but she kept her thoughts to herself. Still feeling awkward, she attempted a joke. "There's nothing here anyone would want."

When he didn't budge, she made a quick inspection, then reported back to the kitchen. "All's well." She held out her hand for him to shake. "Thank you for a beautiful day."

But it was not a handshake he gave her. He lifted her hand to his lips and planted a light kiss before releasing it. She felt a tingle of pleasure, then reminded herself that it didn't mean anything. Even Len Lamarr had kissed her hand. Must be another Pasetti thing.

"Glad you enjoyed the picnic. . .at least some of it, anyway. Good night."

He melted into the darkness before she could catch her breath. "Good night," she called after him.

She locked the door, then leaned against it, listening to his footsteps retreating down the gravel driveway, then the soft hum of the Mercedes as Mitchell backed and drove away.

She stared down at her hand where he had branded it with his lips. Like a silly schoolgirl, she considered never washing it again. His cologne lingered in the air—subtle, yet stirringly masculine.

Tonight she'd seen another side of Anton Pasetti. . .and had felt an unexpected side of herself. She wasn't at all sure what to do about either one.

Chapter Eight

On Sunday morning the shrill of the phone blasted away the last remnant of Amber's dreams. She sat up, every sense instantly alert. Anton?

But it was Ron. "How does a trip to Tijuana sound to you?" *How can any human being sound so cheerful so early in the morning?* she grumbled to herself. "With Kate and Jim?" he went on.

"I'm. . .barely awake," she said, stifling a yawn—and her disappointment. "I didn't set my alarm."

"Have your coffee and we'll pick you up in about an hour."

"Wait a minute! Let me think." She swung her legs over the side of the bed and grabbed for her robe. "Why don't you three join me for church and we could go afterward?"

There was a brief pause. "If those are your terms. . .sure. You have yourself a deal. I'll tell the others."

"The church is on the beachfront, strictly casual for tourists," she said. "So we can dress for Mexico and leave from there."

Amber took her time getting ready. She washed her hair in the shower, then wrapped it in a towel, turban-style, while she sat at her tiny kitchen window, looking out on her own "formal" gardens—one lonely palm—and sipping a cup of coffee. Had last night been a dream? Had she really spent time alone with the most eligible bachelor in San Diego?

Amber forced her thoughts from then to now. Maybe she shouldn't have cut a deal about going to church. But whatever worked.

So far, only Kate had ever gone with her to the beachfront church, and not every Sunday at that. Why was it she seemed doomed to failure when it came to sharing her faith? Like last night, when Anton Pasetti had confessed that he'd tried to bargain with God. Thinking back to her answer, she flinched. She'd come off sounding like a Pollyanna. He probably thought she was hopelessly unsophisticated and had turned her off without hearing a word she'd tried to say.

But then his beloved mother had tried, too, and although he apparently loved and respected her greatly, she hadn't succeeded in leading him to Christ, either.

Glancing at the kitchen clock, Amber took her cup to the sink, then padded back to the bedroom. She chose a yellow pants outfit, then tied her nearly dry hair back with a yellow ribbon. The natural curl would spring into shape without much coaxing. At least, she had that much for which to be thankful.

Since she'd be in the sun most of the day, she applied a light makeup base with sunscreen, a little lip gloss, and a touch of mascara. There. That should take care of the outside. She wrinkled her nose at her reflection.

When she heard Ron's car in the driveway, she hurried out to meet him.

He gave a low whistle when he saw her. "You look like sunshine on a summer morning. And take a look at this weather. Not a cloud in the sky. It's going to be a great day!"

Amber slid into the front seat of Ron's Mustang and turned to speak to Kate and Jim in the backseat. Even though Kate had been attractive when they'd first met, she was positively glowing these days. *That's not entirely due to Pasetti magic,* Amber knew. *I think Jim has a lot to do with it.*

Still, she was concerned that her new friends didn't glow with the joy of the Lord. Even Anton knew that, with all his beautiful possessions—including his women—life could be empty. During the church service, he and her friends were on her mind like a ceaseless prayer.

❧

Right after the service, they headed for the border, ready for a day of fun. As they strolled through the Mexican tourist town, the four of them laughed and joked, and weren't too particular about what they ate.

"Junk food once in a while won't kill us, I hope." Kate made a face and popped a burrito into her mouth.

For a while, they could forget they were products of the Pasetti Agency. But it all came back when Ron bought two wide-brimmed sombreros and plopped one on Amber's head.

"Souvenir," he explained, covering his own blond hair with the other. Amber suspected he was conscious of the bright sun on his fair skin.

Jim did the same. "Wouldn't want Pasetti women to burn their pretty little noses," he said, adjusting Kate's hat, then tweaking her pretty little nose.

Getting into the festive mood of the day, Amber splurged and bought a Mexican skirt and blouse from a street vendor. Ron presented her with some heavy, outrageously colorful Mexican jewelry.

"I dare you to wear that getup to work tomorrow," Kate said, mischief sparking her big, round eyes.

"I'll do it!" Amber couldn't believe she'd said that. But as the day wore on, her natural reserve just seemed to melt away. Once, when she was alone with Kate for a minute, she even opened up enough to tell her friend her deepest secret—that she hadn't loved Ken as much as she thought she ought to love the man she was going to marry.

"You shouldn't feel guilty about that," Kate chided. "Look how many people think they're in love, then their marriages break up. But," she dropped her voice to an excited whisper, "I think Jim might be the one for me. Would you believe we knew each other in junior high school— back when our dads were in Annapolis? Except I was a scrawny thirteen-year-old girl and he wasn't the hunk he is today!"

Amber felt much better after her confession and Kate's announcement. In fact, she even allowed Ron to kiss her good night when they returned late that evening, regretting it almost immediately. She'd have to make it very clear to him that she wasn't ready to consider anything more than friendship.

❧

By Monday morning she was also regretting having accepted Kate's dare. "How do I get myself into these things?" she grumbled. "Still, a promise is a promise."

But not until she arrived at work did she realize she might have made a huge mistake. She was at the coffee urn, just starting to pour a cup, when Anton walked in and stopped abruptly.

Amber cringed as his gaze raked her from head to toe. She could only imagine what he must be thinking as he observed the sight she made: hair pulled back on one side to expose the dangling earring that matched her flamboyant necklace; off-the-shoulder peasant blouse; full black skirt, hand-painted with brilliant peacocks; black high-heeled sandals. Even her complexion, kissed by the weekend sun, had darkened a shade. She must look like a gypsy!

Anton strode toward her, and she backed away until there was nowhere else to go.

"Tijuana special?" he asked, trapping her between himself and the wall. He touched the bauble at her ear. "Cute."

Granted, she was not dressed properly for the office. But in spite of her trembling lips, she managed to defend herself. "The jewelry was a gift. It's only courteous to show one's appreciation, isn't it? Even Pasetti philosophy teaches us to consider the feelings of others."

"So this is all compliments of the generous Mr. Jordan?" His eyes swept over her again.

"Just the jewelry," she put in hastily. "I bought the rest myself. But I wore it. . .on a dare. I'll go change." Not meeting his eyes, she tried to duck around him, when his tone halted her in her tracks.

"Miss Jennings! You're. . .not. . .going. . .anywhere."

Surprised, she looked up to see a smile tugging at one corner of his mouth. "You're fine just as you are. It's only that, after seeing you, I'm wondering whether I'll get any work out of my male employees today." He broke into a grin and then a chuckle.

"What's going on here?" Charis wanted to know when she heard the laughter and stepped into the room. One glimpse of Amber brought a gasp. "Amber Jennings, is that you?"

Anton answered for her. "Yes, indeed, would you believe that beneath all that cool competence beats the fiery heart of a Spanish señorita?" With one last appraising look, he turned and walked into his office.

Amber stared at the door that closed firmly behind him. Cool? Ha! Hadn't he guessed how often he'd left her uncomfortably warm? To the boiling point, to be exact!

She sighed. "I really goofed, didn't I, Charis?"

The older woman looked sympathetic. "Well, I wouldn't make a practice of wearing costumes to the office. But since you did, I'm glad you chose this particular outfit. Nothing Mexican or Spanish would offend Anton." Her lovely face broke into a smile. "You know, Amber, sometimes it's good for a woman, no matter how beautiful, to break out of her mold. Makes a man sit up and take notice."

"Oh, but I wasn't trying—"

"Oh, of course not." With a speculative glance out of the corner of her eye, Charis breezed out of the office, her final comment trailing over her shoulder. "But you accomplished it just the same."

❧

It didn't take long for others in the building to notice Amber's new look. The men were openly admiring, while the other women were either complimentary, catty, or critical. As Charis put it later, "Without the Lord in their hearts, they can't understand the concept of rejoicing in other people's successes."

When Amber ran into Ron in the cafeteria, his mouth dropped open. "Wow! Is this the same woman who went south of the border with me last weekend?" But she had to turn him down when he asked her out for the following weekend. Better not encourage him, lest she drift into the same dead-end pattern that had made her so miserable with Ken.

Anton Pasetti, on the other hand, was all business for the remainder of the day. Even when he summoned her to discuss the minutes of the last board meeting, he acted as if their intimate talk at his home and their morning encounter had never taken place.

In fact, he paid her no attention at all until he walked out of his office at closing time. Pausing, with his hand on the knob of the outer door, he winked. "Good night, señorita."

≈

The following day, Anton informed Amber that he and Gina would be leaving for New York for a week or so, in connection with the shampoo contract. And during the next few days, he was completely preoccupied with details of the upcoming trip.

"The reservations are made?" he asked on one occasion.

Amber nodded. "Yes, sir. Everything's ready." She had all the information at her fingertips: airline tickets, adjoining room reservations for him and Gina at the hotel in New York, and a schedule of appointments.

On Wednesday, the day of departure, Anton paused at Amber's desk. "I need to see you. . .in the coffee shop." His brusque, businesslike tone matched his dark suit.

Automatically, she dialed Charis's number and requested a secretary from the pool to cover her desk. Then she pulled up the file her boss would undoubtedly want to review and printed out a copy.

They stepped into the elevator and the door closed.

For some reason, even though there were only two of them inside, the small enclosure seemed more cramped than usual. She was relieved when they reached their floor.

With a light touch under her elbow, he guided her to a booth. Her skin tingled beneath the honey-colored fabric of her sleeve. But his gesture was, of course, entirely proper. He was, after all, the boss and she, his employee.

Settling herself in the booth, she glanced at Anton, wondering if she would ever get used to his proprietary manner. He had hired her; he didn't own her! Still, he probably subjected all his employees to the kind of scrutiny he was giving her now. Probably wanted to make sure she was measuring up to agency expectations. But it was more than a little disconcerting.

Anton ordered coffee for them and Amber opened the file.

"What's that?" he asked.

"The file on your trip, Mr. Pasetti. I have a copy of everything and a schedule complete with times, places, and contact people."

"The woman never lets me down," he mumbled to himself. "Now close that file. Just make sure you put it in my briefcase before I leave."

She eyed him questioningly. His smile was relaxed, not at all professional. . .but friendly. Gone was the preoccupied expression of the past few days. Amber could handle his office manner, but this? She was grateful when the waitress brought their coffee and set it in front of them. She concentrated on the swirl of steam rising from the cup while Anton stirred cream into his.

"I don't mind hard work," she said, lifting the cup to her lips and taking a careful sip.

"You've proven your point. But the workload shouldn't be as heavy while I'm away."

What did he expect her to say? "Of course," Amber replied lightly, and glanced around the near-empty room. "You know that old saying: 'When the cat's away, the mice will play.' "

Anton laughed. "Not you, Amber. But promise me you will take some time off."

Amber hesitated. Was this another test? "I prefer work to boredom."

"Boredom?" He cocked a brow. "What about all your young friends?"

She could have bitten her tongue! Why had she brought up the subject? But there was no way she was going to explain that she was trying to hold Ron at bay, and that Kate and Jim were so absorbed in each other, Amber barely saw her best friend these days.

"Feel free to use my house. . .the gardens. . .my private beach. Mitchell or one of the maids could show you around. As you know, it's quite secluded if you want to be alone. Or, if you prefer, you might entertain your. . .friends. I suppose you're still seeing Ron Jordan?"

"Not often."

"Getting too serious, was he?" Anton didn't wait for an answer. "You keep a tight rein on your emotions, don't you, Amber?"

She didn't look at him. "I'm all right." Her boss was probably only concerned about an employee who wasn't leading what he considered a "normal" life. And to a man like Anton Pasetti, that included intimacy with the opposite sex.

Yet it was not Ron's kiss she sometimes dreamed about, but the burning light pressure of Anton's lips on the back of her hand.

"I do hope you are. . .all right, Amber." Anton's voice was soft, gentle. "I value you very highly, you know."

Feeling his gaze on her in the uncomfortable silence, Amber could not trust herself to look at him. Unconsciously she lifted her arm and glanced at her watch, then quickly lowered it.

"There's no rush, Amber." Anton chuckled. "I'm the boss, remember?"

That's one thing I try never to forget, she was thinking and made a feeble attempt to laugh. A man and his secretary should be able to have a cup of coffee together without stress.

"Do you like New York, Mr. Pasetti?" she asked, trying for a casual tone.

"Very much. The pace is even more hectic than in California, believe it or not. But I thrive on activity. One has the sense of accomplishment, of getting things done." There was a small, secretive smile. "Still, there are evenings, after a busy day, when there is time to gaze out of a window far above the city and watch the traffic below. Up there, it's a whole new world."

Caught up in his mood, she sighed. "Sounds romantic."

"Only if one isn't alone."

Well, he certainly wouldn't be alone. Gina would be with him. Amber dabbed at her lips with the napkin. "I'm sure you'll enjoy your trip."

"Much like you," he was saying, "I find pleasure in work. But I've learned the art of relaxation, as well. I wonder if you have."

"You have enough to do without worrying about me," she retorted, took a sip of the coffee, and grimaced. It was cold.

"I do worry about you, Amber," he said suddenly, leaning forward. "I sense that something is closed off in that interesting mind of yours. Now, while I'm away, you take it easy. That's an order."

Amber responded to his playful tone with a little salute. "Yes, sir!"

"Good. Ready to go?"

She nodded and picked up the file. They walked out of the coffee shop and back toward the elevator. Inside the cubicle, Amber watched the lighted buttons registering the floors as they passed—3. . .4. . .5. . .6. . .7 . . .8. Instead of stopping on the eighth floor, however, she was amazed to see the buttons blinking on all the way to the fifteenth.

As the doors opened, Anton motioned her forward with a nod of his head. She stepped out into a carpeted hallway. "My apartments," he said. "For the sake of convenience, I often stay here after a late night with a client. Sometimes I conduct business here."

I'll just bet you do, Amber thought.

He led her through a huge living room, up several steps, and through another doorway that opened onto a rooftop garden.

She couldn't restrain a gasp of pleasure and walked over to look over the edge of a wall. "Oh. . .I didn't realize it would be so far down."

"Heights bother you?" he asked, coming up behind her to steady her with a hand at her waist.

"N—not really. It's just that back home, there wasn't anything this tall—except for the mountains, of course. It's strange, looking straight down like this. The cars look like toys."

"Can't even hear the traffic from here, can we?" He narrowed his gaze. "You have flown, of course."

"No," she admitted, embarrassed. She gave a helpless shrug. "No wings."

He laughed at her little joke. "You'll have to try it someday. It's the only way to travel."

She looked down again at the traffic far below. "The air must be thinner up here."

"Think so?"

She glanced at him in time to catch the quirk of one eyebrow and the slight smile of amusement playing around his lips. "Well," she said determinedly, "I know it's a little harder to breathe."

"I see," he said. "And you're sure it's height that causes that sensation?"

The next moment he had spun her around to face him. She inhaled sharply. Kept her eyes on his tie. Felt the gentle pressure of his hands on her arms. Yes, it was definitely height that caused her breathlessness—but not the height of the building.

"Tell me good-bye, Amber," he said softly. "And, please. . .call me Anton."

Before the whispered name was off her lips, his own were pressing against hers. His fingers tightened momentarily and then he released her. Slowly he stepped back and walked over to the door, holding it open for her.

In the elevator again, she floated down to the eighth floor. Time seemed suspended. Had the last few minutes really happened? The door opened and she turned toward the office, with Anton right behind her.

Hold your head up. Walk confidently, she quoted the Pasetti rulebook. *It was only a casual brush of the lips. It's done all the time.*

A shiver tingled down her spine. Who was she kidding? This was Anton Pasetti, king of a dynasty. No woman in her right mind would refuse him a simple farewell kiss. And that's all it was, wasn't it?

❧

For the next hour, Amber worked feverishly, checking and double-checking the file that Anton would take with him. When he was ready to leave, she watched him slide the file into his briefcase. He seemed distracted again, as if the kiss had never occurred.

When Gina came in, he greeted her with a devastating smile. Amber couldn't help thinking how like a cat the redhead appeared. She was positively purring!

Amber watched with a twinge that was very like jealousy as they moved toward the door of her office. Then Anton swiveled on his heel and pointed a finger at Amber. "Remember."

Remember to relax while he was away? Or remember the tender scene in his private garden?

This time his dazzling smile was for Amber. But it was Gina who walked away on his arm.

Chapter Nine

On Saturday evening, Amber sat on the Lamarrs' terrace, surrounded by exotic shrubs in lavish bloom. The three were sipping minted tea and enjoying the warmth of the evening after a superb dinner.

Amber had felt perfectly at ease in accepting Charis's invitation to their home, a large contemporary as elegant and graceful as the owners. Anton had implied that once one is an adult, there are no longer age distinctions. She felt that the same principle applied to Christians. In her relationship with Charis and Len, there was a bond that transcended any so-called "generation gap."

Even in such congenial company, though, there was a nagging apprehension. Tonight Anton and Gina would meet with the owner of the shampoo firm. Gina would probably land the contract, and then she and Anton would celebrate. How they would celebrate, Amber wasn't quite sure. All she knew was that, in matters of the heart, she and Anton Pasetti were poles apart.

Charis's soft voice broke Amber's reverie. "Excuse the interruption, but your mind is undoubtedly miles away, dear."

About two thousand or so, Amber figured. "Oh, I'm sorry!" But she hadn't been daydreaming about North Carolina. Actually, in her mind, she was in New York City, standing above the traffic in a skyscraper among the clouds. The setting was romantic. The man was tall, dark, remarkably attractive. The woman had a riot of red hair and luminous green eyes.

"Well, wherever you are, hold that thought, Amber, my dear," Len put in. "That's exactly the look I'd like to capture for an ad I have in mind. Mysterious. . .haunting. . ."

Amber was startled, then amused. During dinner Len had mentioned something about using her as a model, but she couldn't believe he'd been serious.

She took another sip of her tea and concentrated on what Charis was saying. "I was wondering if you'd like to see an old movie, Amber. It might interest you. Our daughter, Layla, had a part in it."

A daughter? Neither Len nor Charis had ever mentioned children.

Amber was curious. "I'd love to."

Len led them into a small room with soft leather couches surrounding three sides. He pulled down a screen on the blank wall, then went to the projection equipment, which apparently was always set up for a showing.

"There she is. That's our Layla." Charis's tone was wistful as a striking young woman came into view. A close-up revealed the same light blue eyes as her mother, and platinum blond hair that curled about an oval face framing small, delicate features.

"What a beautiful young woman." Taking a sidelong glance at Charis in the subdued lighting, Amber thought she detected the glimmer of a tear. What was that all about?

Then, concentrating on the feature-length movie, she lost herself in the story. Even with a bit part, Layla was an impressive actress, and Amber wondered where the young woman was now.

When the lights came on, Len rose to reset the projector.

"She was our only child," Charis explained in answer to Amber's unspoken question. "She died seven years ago, when she was about your age."

In the next few moments a bittersweet story unfolded, more touching than the movie. The young woman who had had everything: beauty, talent, opportunity, "and Anton," Charis finished.

Amber stared. Was that why he had never married?

After all these years, was he still in love with Layla?

"They often spoke of marriage," Charis went on. "But Layla was driven to succeed in her career." She paused. "We adored her so. I'm afraid we spoiled her completely."

Len looked up from the projector and leveled a searching look at his wife. "It's pointless, darling, to condemn ourselves."

"I know; you keep reminding me that hindsight is a waste of time. But I can't help it, Len. God has forgiven the mistakes we made with our daughter, but there are still lessons to be learned."

Amber suddenly felt that she was eavesdropping on the most intimate conversation between a husband and wife. Their wound was still raw. . .as raw and tender as her own unfortunate engagement to Ken. And now, she was beginning to wonder if she was stumbling into another relationship that would prove just as fatal.

"We gave her everything but the most important thing of all," Charis's eyes were filled with tears, "faith in Jesus Christ. We didn't know Him ourselves. . .then. Now we'd give anything in the world if we could have her back just long enough to. . ."

Amber had to look away from the pain in the woman's eyes.

Len went to Charis, cradling her in his arms, comforting her. "We're not sentimentalists living in the past, Amber," he explained over his wife's head. "We just wanted you to know that we understand the cruel blows life can deal. But we've also discovered that God's grace makes it possible. . .to bear such a loss."

How well she knew. "I don't know how people handle those times without faith in God," she added softly, wondering how Anton had survived two tragedies without Him.

At last Charis lifted her head. "It was losing Layla that sent Len and me to our knees. We probably would have put it off indefinitely, even with Anton's mother trying to talk sense into us for years. After all, it's not that we didn't believe that there was a God; we simply didn't trust Him enough to run our lives or our business."

A watery trail of mascara trickled down the older woman's cheek, and she blotted the tears with a tissue. "Maybe the Lord is giving us another chance. . .sending you to us. We've come to care for you very much, Amber. We sense that you're a very private person. . .that you don't open up easily. But if you ever want to talk. . .please know that Len and I are here for you."

Amber didn't know what to say. She was touched, of course. But Charis and Len thought she was still grieving a beloved fiancé. What would they think if they knew the truth?

"Thank you. . .for sharing." It just didn't seem the time, after such a dramatic testimony, to admit that while she regretted losing a dear friend, she was definitely not suffering from a broken heart. "Maybe I should be going home now," she finished quietly.

"What's this about leaving?" Len protested. "I was looking forward to a game of tennis. You did say you were pretty good, didn't you? I expected you to prove it."

Amber laughed, and the awkward moment passed. "You're on!"

❧

Later, at home, Amber reflected on the evening. Her winning game with Len. Their relaxed conversation, the easy camaraderie. The amazing revelation about Layla, the poor, lost daughter. . .though there was much more to that story. Amber was sure of it.

Another part of the conversation came back to her now. She hadn't planned to replay that little scenario, but the thoughts came anyway. If Anton had loved Layla, how could she have asked for anything more?

And what about Anton? Did he still think of Layla, still miss her? He had told Amber that his mother had taught him that, no matter what, life goes on. Did he really believe that? Or, without his mother and Layla, was he merely. . .existing?

Chapter Ten

On Tuesday Anton called to report that Gina had signed a contract with the shampoo firm. She would be posing for a magazine layout and four television commercials. Therefore, she'd remain in New York for the shoot, while he returned to the office the following week.

Amber wondered what Anton would say when he learned what his secretary had done in his absence. Len had cajoled her into posing for glamour shots, wearing his eye makeup. "Your eyes are perfect for my line," he'd insisted.

"Come on, dear. Humor him," Charis had added with a pleading note in her voice.

The pair had proved an irresistable combination. So she'd given in.

❧

"Do you have plans for the weekend?" Charis asked Amber on Friday afternoon.

"Nothing pressing." She certainly wouldn't turn down an invitation for another evening with her new friends. Besides, she was on a roll in tennis. She'd won her last game with Len six–love.

"Good. I'm having a small dinner party at my house. Anton will be back, you know. And he vows he prefers my home cooking to any of those marvelous restaurants in New York." Charis laughed. "I think it's the atmosphere he likes. He knows he can relax with us."

Amber stifled a groan. *Well, I can't. . .not if Anton is there!* But it was too late to back out. She had already admitted that she had no plans.

"Come early so we can play some tennis. Anton enjoys the sport as much as Len."

Friday evening and all morning on Saturday, Amber was a basket case. How many other guests were the Lamarrs expecting? Who would be Anton's date? Gina, of course, was not available. The shoot would take at least a couple of weeks. But Amber was pretty sure her boss would not be lonely long.

She bought a new white tennis outfit to complement her deepening tan, grateful that her skin hadn't burned in the dazzling rays. Then she was furious at herself for caring how she looked!

On Saturday afternoon, Amber parked her blue Escort beside Anton's big Mercedes in the Lamarr driveway and jumped out. By now she had learned that she could usually find Len and Charis on the terrace, so she walked around to the back of the house. All three, the Lamarrs and Anton, were sitting at an umbrella-shaded table, sipping tall drinks. There was no sign of anyone else. Had Anton come alone? Maybe his dinner guest would join them later.

"Here's my favorite tennis partner now!" Len called, springing to his feet. Charis gestured her toward a lounge chair near Anton.

"Hello, Amber." Anton's dark eyes swept her casual outfit—slacks, shirt, sandals. "That looks like a real California tan. You must have followed the boss's orders."

Ignoring his remark, she dropped into the seat Charis had pointed out. "I trust your trip was successful."

"Very, thanks to my efficient secretary. I followed your schedule, Amber, and everything went off like clockwork. And I see you've taken my advice and spent some time off in the sun."

When she still didn't answer, Charis spoke up. "No, Anton. She didn't."

He drew his brows together in a mock scowl. "Insubordination will not be tolerated at Pasetti Enterprises, young lady."

In the wake of the laughter that followed, Amber protested mildly, "I didn't need a day off. I relaxed on the weekend." Her mouth was strangely dry, and she was grateful for the iced lemonade Len set before her.

"You mean Charis isn't the slave driver I am?" Anton teased.

"Your secretary is full of insults today, Anton," Len interrupted, pretending to be hurt. "She calls beating me in tennis relaxation. Believe me, it was anything but."

"Perhaps we can turn the tables on her," Anton said. He finished his drink, set the glass down, and stood. "Are you game?"

She glanced at the two men. They were enjoying this far too much. "No fair for the two of you to gang up on me!"

Charis laughed. "I think I could make it even. Let's chance it. I hope you brought a change."

"Of course, just like you taught me; but what about dinner? Is there anything I can do?"

"Not a thing. Tillie has everything under control in the kitchen. Now, run get your things and you can use one of our guest rooms."

Amber retrieved the small case she had packed and followed Charis into the house. On the way down the hall, she couldn't resist asking, "When will the others be arriving?"

"Others?" Charis turned a quizzical look on her. "Oh, there will be no other guests. Just the four of us."

Amber had begun to suspect as much. What must Anton think? That she had asked the Lamarrs to set this up?

On the court, Amber's hands felt clammy, her knees shaky. "I don't think this is going to be my day," she confided to Charis.

"Don't worry about it. It's only a game."

Only a game, she thought. *The way some people play games. . .*

The speeding ball, the quick strokes, the pauses before serves—all passed by in a blur to Amber. She bit her lower lip for better concentration. She could see that Anton was enjoying himself immensely as he moved back and forth across the court in smooth, muscular strides.

It was an easy win for the men.

"Don't think that lets you off the hook, Amber," Len said on the way back to the house. "I'm still determined to beat you in singles. Today's win I have to attribute to Anton."

"I might have had something to do with our losing, too," Charis noted lightly. "But there's always another day. Right, Amber?"

Now that the set was over, Amber felt herself relaxing. "The two of us will have to practice so we can beat them in doubles next time." She shrugged aside the worrisome thought that it was no fun living as a single in a doubles world, then excused herself to freshen up.

After a quick shower, Amber slipped into the mint green dinner dress she had brought, smoothing the full skirt. Studying her reflection in the bathroom mirror, she touched the bodice that dipped to a V in front. Long sleeves of the soft material buttoned at the wrist. Matching green sandals completed the outfit.

After applying fresh makeup, she brushed her hair, grateful for the cut and natural wave as the shining strands fell softly below her shoulders. The sun had brought out golden highlights, she observed approvingly.

When she looked into the mirror for a final inspection, she realized that she barely resembled the same young woman who had fled to California over four months ago. She was almost. . .beautiful. Inside, too, she seemed to be changing. But she wasn't sure it was for the better. The guilt was almost gone. But she was still unsure of herself. Was she hoping that Anton would echo what the mirror was telling her?

Don't be silly, Amber, she chided herself. *You're too sensible. . .too cool and competent for that kind of nonsense.*

Leaving her apprehension behind, she went into the kitchen where Charis had promised to show her a few gourmet cooking tips.

"Mmmm. What is that aroma?" Anton asked, sticking his head around the door.

"Out!" Charis ordered, aiming her spatula at him. "Amber and I can handle this."

"Not until you tell me what it is."

"Poulet Ö l'estragon."

"Ah, chicken," he translated, to Amber's great relief. "Okay, okay, I'm going," he promised, holding up both hands to ward off Charis's mock blows as he backed out of the kitchen.

"Chicken?" Amber had to laugh in spite of herself. "I'm afraid my French isn't very good."

"Casserole—roasted with tarragon," Charis explained. "First, it's trussed, then browned in butter and oil and roasted in a covered casserole with herbs and seasonings."

"You've never eaten anything so tender," Tillie put in.

The three put the finishing touches to the broiled tomatoes, green peas, stuffed mushrooms, and *pommes dauphines.*

"French potato puffs," Charis translated at Amber's raised eyebrows. "Now, since Tillie doesn't like too many hands in her kitchen," she said, untying her apron and laying it aside, "let's go find the men so she can serve dinner."

In the informal dining room, Charis and Amber filled Anton in on office news and learned some of the details about the shampoo deal. Even though it was more painful than Amber wanted to admit to imagine her boss and Gina in that romantic setting, it did feel good to be included in the inner loop of agency talk.

After dessert, coffee was served in the sitting room.

Anton leaned back in a lounge chair and stretched out his long legs. "It's good to be back. Coming here is like coming home, Charis."

"It's home anytime you want it to be, Anton. You know that. You're like the son we never had."

If Layla had lived, Anton might have become their son-in-law, Amber thought with a jolt, and wondered if she had read their thoughts. Her cup rattled against the saucer as she placed it on the table beside her chair.

Just then, Len rose to his feet. "There's something I want you to see. Be right back."

Rather than subject herself to Anton's disturbing gaze, Amber walked over to an open window, allowing the night air to cool her face. She remained there until Len returned. He switched on fluorescent lighting set into the ceiling, and the room was flooded with brilliance.

After placing a leather-bound portfolio on the coffee table, he flipped it open. "Come take a look, Amber," he said, patting the cushion beside him. She obeyed.

"You, too, Anton." Charis motioned to the spot on the other side of her husband. "You'll want to see these."

Amber recognized the photographs instantly. She had posed for those pictures, albeit reluctantly. Now she wondered how Anton would view them.

He took his time, studying each one intently. "This would be one of our models, of course. But there's something else, about the expression. . ." He leaned forward to inspect the pictures more closely as his voice trailed off. Looking up, he quirked a brow, glancing past Len to Amber. "But this model has. . .brown eyes."

Len turned the page to a full-face photo of Amber. She held her breath, waiting for his reaction.

When it came, it wasn't the explosion she had expected. It was worse. "I. . .see," was all he would say.

"It was just a joke," she put in uncertainly, suddenly feeling like the victim of some conspiracy.

"Oh, it's no joke," Len told her seriously. "You're a natural for the 'haunting' look we're trying to project for our new campaign."

" 'Haunting'?" she croaked, and cleared her throat. "As in 'ghostly'?" Her attempt to lighten the atmosphere failed miserably.

" 'Wistful,' then. There's a certain sadness in your eyes, Amber." She could see that Len was dead serious now as he turned to Anton. "Can't you see it? It's dynamite! There's a whole story behind that look. And it'll sell, or I have no business trying to pitch beauty products!"

Aware that Len was about to stumble onto her secret, Amber changed the subject. "Have you always worked in the cosmetic industry?"

"No," he replied slowly, "not always."

"I know. I'll bet you were a tennis pro."

"No, my dear." Len closed the portfolio. "I was a psychiatrist. It was my wife who was in the beauty business." He glanced over at Charis, his voice strained. "Oh, I dabbled in a few projects, but I joined her only when it became clear that. . .well, let's just say I was much like the shoemaker whose family went barefoot."

A somber silence settled over the group. No doubt he was referring to Layla, the beloved daughter. Amber found herself wondering again what had caused her death. An accident, like Ken's?

Amber stood and walked over to the window. From here, she could barely make out the shoreline, where a choppy sea sent waves crashing against the beach. Even in the near darkness, she could see the foam spewing into the air. Ugly dark clouds scudded angrily across the sky. When had the weather changed? Well, whenever, it mirrored the storm brewing in her soul.

Feeling a masculine touch, she jumped. But it was only Len's arm around her shoulders. "Now I'm in the beauty business full-time, and dabble in tennis with lovely young women on the side," he said, his old self again. "And one of these days, I'm going to beat you in singles!"

"Promises, promises!" She gave him an affectionate pat. "But it'll have to wait for another day." Out of the corner of her eye, she saw that Anton had drifted off into a world of his own. "Thanks for a lovely evening."

Anton got to his feet when he saw that she was about to leave. "I'll walk you to the car."

Outside, jagged streaks of lightning split the sky. But there was no rain. And there was no conversation on the way to the car, either. Instead, a sullen silence fell between them.

When they reached the car, Anton barred her way by leaning against her door. Amber had no choice but to halt in front of him. The expression in his eyes was veiled, even in the half-light, but his face looked grim and stormy.

Of course! The photographs! But surely he wasn't taking them seriously. She had only agreed to pose to end Len's pleading.

"I hope you understand that those photos weren't my idea," she said with a trace of embarrassment.

"Len is a client," Anton stated flatly. "He apparently wants you to advertise his product. Unless you refuse or he changes his mind, that's how it will be."

"But if you. . .disapprove—" she began, and stuttered to a stop at the look of contempt on his face.

"That's my business, remember?"

"But I'm a secretary, not a model."

"Try telling that to Len."

"He also thinks I'm a tennis pro."

He shrugged. "As long as you're posing for photographs and winning matches, then I suppose you qualify," he snapped.

Funny. She had noticed a softening toward him in the few days before he left for New York. Now, just as she had begun to care for him, she felt she didn't know him at all. It shouldn't matter what Anton Pasetti thought, but for some reason she wanted him to believe that she was not serious about modeling.

"I'm your secretary first. Any other. . .project. . .would be temporary." She watched, but his stern expression didn't change. "Tonight. . .in there. . .you seemed—"

"Surprised?" he finished for her. "Believe me, I wasn't surprised to find out you'd agreed to pose for Len." The muscle in his jaw clenched. "It was just that the expression in the eyes reminded me of someone else." Silhouetted against the threatening sky, he towered over her like the stormy hero in some gothic novel. "The critics said she had the most photogenic eyes they had ever seen."

Layla! The truth dawned on Amber just as a crash of thunder sounded overhead. That was it! That was why Len and Charis had taken her in and treated her like their own daughter. Why even Anton had appeared drawn to her.

"I have to go," she said, feeling any explanation she might give would fall on deaf ears.

He reached for the door handle and opened the door. She slid behind the wheel, while he bent down to speak through the open window. "Just think of the publicity." His tone was laced with sarcasm. "I can see the headlines now: 'From Memos to Model Overnight!' Only you and I know it wasn't 'overnight,' don't we. . .Miss Jennings?" he flung at her. "You didn't waste any time, did you? You took advantage of my first business trip!"

The verbal assault felt like a physical blow. He believed she had deliberately set out to do this, had insinuated it all along. Amber clenched the steering wheel. She must not let him intimidate her. "I do not want to be a model!" she insisted. "I refuse to be."

"Oh? You're full of surprises, aren't you?"

"Anton Pasetti, sometimes I despise you! So go ahead and fire me now!" She plunged the key into the ignition and started the engine. It sprang to life.

"Fire you?" He spat out the words. "That would only make it easier for you to pursue another career—probably with a competitor! And don't tell me you wouldn't! Or that anyone taking one look at you wouldn't hire you on the spot!"

The wash of joy that flooded her ebbed at his next words. "What you didn't have in the beginning. . .Pasetti Agency gave you!"

She was quite aware that she had begun to desire his compliments, to need them as much as a thirsty flower needs rain. Now all she wanted was to hurt him as he had hurt her. "You can't bear to think you might be wrong about a person, can you? That every female who comes into your office is only interested in becoming a model. . .or," she forced the words past her aching throat, "or in you!"

He seemed momentarily taken aback, then shrugged. "Regardless of what you think of me, the Lamarr deal would be profitable all the way around. I'd suggest you consider it, Miss Jennings. Besides, since the agency has taught you to make the most of your beauty, surely you realize the obligation on your part."

"No!" she retorted, hating his placid manner, hating most of all his distrust of her. "I earn my paycheck. I don't owe you anything more. Why can't you just let me do my job. . .and leave me alone?" She gunned the engine, ready to spin off.

But something in his expression held her. "Secretaries can be replaced," he called over the roar of another crash of thunder, "but how many beautiful women could give Len Lamarr the pleasure of launching the career his own daughter missed? Since you've gone this far, Amber, could you refuse him now?"

She couldn't take any more of this. She pulled away, her tears blinding her just as heavy drops of rain splatted against the windshield. Switching on the wipers, she dashed away the tears with one hand. In the rearview mirror she could see Anton standing where she had left him in the sudden downpour.

On the way home, she calmed down enough to think more clearly. It was easy to see why he didn't trust her, she had to admit. It did look pretty suspicious, as if she'd wangled her way into Len's life to gain his approval. And she had consented to the photo session, though she hadn't expected anything to come of it.

Now it was too late. Anton obviously felt she was obligated to follow through, but he would never again trust her, never believe that she was different from other women.

The few times she'd tried to share her testimony with Anton were now worthless. Somehow, she had to prove to Anton that she was telling the truth about her motives, her goals, her faith in God. But she couldn't help but wonder if even God Himself could undo the mess she'd made of things.

Chapter Eleven

In the next few days, the office was a zoo. Anton had to be briefed on what had taken place during his absence, and follow-ups had to be made on his business contacts in New York.

For Amber, the worst part of her job all week was to type in her own name on the contract for Lamarr Cosmetics.

Her gaze kept turning to Gina's photograph on the wall of the office. Gina had modeled for the line last year, and Amber felt those green eyes flashing her a warning not to sign. Actually, she had no intention of signing the contract. Still, she was expected to draw it up, along with others, for Anton's Thursday night dinner date with Len.

After lunch in the cafeteria on Wednesday, Amber was back at her desk when Anton stopped by. He was holding a leather tote bag in one hand. "Have someone cover for you," he ordered in his most Pasetti-professional tone. "I want you to go with me."

She called Charis for a replacement, then got her purse and emergency makeup kit from the bottom desk drawer and followed him out the door.

Without another word, he took her arm and steered her toward the elevator. All the way to the first floor, he didn't break the silence. Amber figured there was an important meeting with some client. Must be a difficult one, too, judging from that stony expression. On the other hand, he wasn't carrying his briefcase.

In the parking lot, he opened the car door for her. "Hold onto this," he said, tossing the bag into her lap.

He walked around to the driver's side, slid behind the wheel, and started the car.

On the freeway, he sent several curious glances in her direction. "Aren't you going to ask where we're going?"

Amber shrugged. "I assumed you'd tell me eventually," she replied coldly, keeping her eyes straight ahead.

Just as suddenly as the sun breaking through dark clouds after the rain, his manner changed. "It's a lovely day. Much too nice to be cooped up in an office, don't you agree?"

Now her suspicions were aroused, and she just couldn't resist asking,

"Where are we going?"

"Does it matter?"

"I like to be prepared."

"You will be." He laughed, nodding toward the tote bag in her lap. "Take a look."

Amber opened the bag and pulled out a brown-and-white-checked, two-piece swimsuit. It looked like something Gina would wear. But Gina was still in New York. Feeling around in the bottom of the bag, she found a white terry beach wrap, trimmed in brown. "We're going to a photographic session at the beach." No doubt they would be meeting the model at their destination.

"Partly right." He smiled a secretive smile.

"We're going to a photographic session. . .but not at the beach."

"Try it the other way around." He turned off the freeway onto a familiar exit.

Silently, she returned the swimwear to the bag. No need to ask any more questions. She knew where they were going. Instead, she looked out the window while Anton made the expected turns, moving relentlessly toward his beachside estate.

When they arrived, she made no effort to get out of the car but waited for him to walk around and open the door. He stood, waiting while she stepped out, dragging her feet.

"Come now, Amber," he said in a smooth voice, "must you look so stricken?" A quick gleam lighted his eyes and his lips tilted slightly upward.

She refused to give him the satisfaction of thinking she could be charmed by his congenial manner, as if they were off simply to enjoy an afternoon together. There was some devious motive lurking behind his actions, and she would be on guard every single minute!

He sighed. "Come along. There's something we need to discuss in the library."

She trudged silently beside him, begrudging every step, hearing the echo of their feet against the tiles. He opened the wrought-iron gate, and she walked onto the back patio. It was much as she remembered it, only more spacious and without all the picnic guests.

When they got to the library, Anton motioned her to the couch, while he drew up a chair nearby. "Do you remember that, before I left for New

York, I ordered you to take a day off?"

She glared at him. "You don't have any right to tell me what to do—or not to do—with my free time. I took that as a suggestion."

"Well, I'm here to see that you take me up on my. . . suggestion. I'm giving you an afternoon free of responsibility. I want you to enjoy yourself here. . .as a gesture of my appreciation for your conscientious work."

"That's completely unnecessary," she retorted. "My salary is ample compensation for what I do for you."

He ignored the remark. "Feel free to use the pool or the beach, or simply relax here with a good book." With a wave of his hand, he indicated the floor-to-ceiling library of leather-bound volumes. "If you need me, a servant will know where to find me."

He got to his feet and was about to leave when something seemed to occur to him. "Oh, yes, there's something else." He drew out some familiar-looking papers from the inner pocket of his suit coat, unfolded them, and laid them on the table. "Give this some thought this afternoon. I'll be taking the contract to Len this evening. There's a pen on the desk."

With that, he turned abruptly and left the room.

So that was why he had brought her here! He expected her to sign Len's contract. What was he up to, anyway? One minute, he was accusing her of having ulterior motives about modeling; the next, he was practically demanding she sign on the dotted line!

A tap on the door intruded on her thoughts. Maybe Anton had forgotten something. "Yes?"

It was a maid, bringing lemonade and light refreshments. *Even the house staff is well-trained,* Amber thought, certain she wasn't the first woman he had brought here under false pretenses. Probably all the servants were accustomed to Anton's romantic escapades. Not that she was his most recent conquest. That would be Gina!

Suddenly realizing that she was a prisoner in this isolated place, Amber felt a sense of panic. She had to get out of here! But she had no car, no way to get back to the cottage.

The maid was still in the room, arranging sandwiches on a plate.

"Please," Amber began, "could you tell me how to find the bell tower?" Maybe from there, she could see a way out. At least she might be able to think more clearly. Anton had told her that when he needed relief from his mother's suffering, he'd often gone there.

"Yes, ma'am. The tower room is always unlocked. My husband, Mitchell, sees to that. Just go up one floor and take the stairs at the end of the hall. That will lead you to the tower. There's a beautiful view from those windows."

So Mitchell was her husband. Amber thought she had detected a glimmer of curiosity in the woman's glance. No doubt Mr. Mitchell had overseen the episode with Anton on the beach after the picnic and had told his wife about it. Feeling her cheeks flush, Amber thanked her and hurried from the room, absentmindedly carrying the tote bag with her.

The bell tower wasn't difficult to find. As Mrs. Mitchell had said, it was right at the top of the second flight of stairs.

Amber creaked open the heavy door and found a small, squarish room, bounded on three sides with benches, a huge bell suspended from the ceiling. The large clapper would undoubtedly make a sound that could be heard for miles. She resisted the urge to ring it.

In each of the three walls was an arched opening. To the right, a tree-studded area stretched as far as the eye could see; through the arch directly in front of her, was a view of the formal gardens at the back, the pool, and tennis court. To the left, in the distance, shimmering under the mid-afternoon sun, was the ocean, the rays of light glancing off the waves like small explosions.

She thought of Anton, wondering if he had found the peace he'd been seeking here, or out there, on the beach. No doubt his mother had hoped that in this place of solitude, with the evidence of God's creative work all around him, her son would turn to the Lord for comfort. Poor woman. She had died with her prayers unanswered. Amber felt pity and pain tearing at her, then a surge of anger at the man who left nothing but misery in his wake.

She stared at the vast expanse of water across the rocky shoreline. It drew her like a magnet. Strangely, she didn't fear the ocean as she did the lake that had claimed her parents' lives. A swim would do her good. Maybe on the beach, with the sound of the surf blocking out all the angry words she and Anton had exchanged, she could hear the Lord telling her what to do—about the contract, about Anton, about her life.

She left the tower and found Mrs. Mitchell on the way down. "I think I spotted Mr. Pasetti's private beach from the bell tower. It looked so lovely and peaceful, I'd like to go for a swim. But I'm not sure how to get there."

"It's through the gardens, ma'am, past the pool and tennis court to the left. You'll see it. But watch the steps going down from the terrace. They can be dangerous."

In one of the guest rooms, Amber changed into the swimsuit Anton had brought for her. It was not exactly the type of suit she would choose. Good thing he'd never see her in it. She wrapped the cover-up securely around her, then headed for the beach.

The steps Mrs. Mitchell had mentioned were steep and narrow, and Amber was careful making her way down. At the bottom, she realized that the beach was actually a cove, walled in by perpendicular cliffs. Stretching to the far horizon was the ocean, silver-tipped waves swelling toward the shore. She stood for a moment, drinking in the stillness. Only the cry of a gull and the rhythmic ebb and flow of the waves against the coastline disturbed the serenity. It was a pocket of peace in the midst of all the confusion of the past few days.

She breathed in deeply, feeling the tension in her muscles beginning to ease. A stiff sea breeze tugged playfully at her beach wrap as if daring her to feel the kiss of the sun on her skin. She loosed the ties and dropped the cover-up onto the rocky beach.

Running to the water's edge, she exulted in the sensation of wind-whipped hair, glad she hadn't tied it back. It was glorious! Wind in her face—like the brush of angels' wings—and warm sand beneath her feet. *Thank You, Lord,* she breathed, losing her cares as easily as she had shed the cover-up. *I know You have the answers. Just give me the patience I need.*

She dashed into the water—not as icy as the mountain streams back home, but brisk and invigorating. With her face tilted toward the rain-washed sky, brilliantly blue and almost an ache to the eyes, she missed seeing a huge swell rolling toward shore. Before she knew what had hit her, she was knocked off balance and pulled under by a strong current. Struggling to find her footing, she came up gasping and choking, sea-water streaming from her drenched hair.

From the beach, the sound of masculine laughter brought an after-shock. Anton!

"When you run headlong into the ocean, don't expect to win!" he called, still laughing. "And watch out for the undertow. It's strong this time of the afternoon."

"How. . .how long have you been standing there?" she sputtered, accepting his hand as he waded out to lead her to shore.

"Long enough. This is my private beach, you know, my retreat from the rat race." He offered her a towel. She grabbed it gratefully and covered herself, rubbing vigorously to shake the chill. "You're one of very few who have ever been here."

"Oh. . .I'm sorry. No one told me I shouldn't—"

He stopped her with an uplifted hand. "Now that you are," he leaned over to pick up the cover-up she had dropped on the beach, "maybe we'd better protect that skin. Models have to be especially careful in the sun."

Hurriedly she finished blotting herself dry and slipped into the wrap, fastening it securely around her waist. "I'm not a model."

"You didn't sign?"

"No."

There was a stony silence between them, with only the sound of the surf and a seabird or two calling to each other above the cliffs.

His jaw flexed. "Well, we can't stand here." He eyed the water rising to fill half the beach. "The tide will get us soon." The tide was advancing rapidly, making pools in the rocky indentations before rolling back out to sea.

He strode over to an area against the cliffs where he had only recently been sitting, she guessed. She followed reluctantly.

He turned to face her, his expression grim. "I suppose you know that Gina will be offered the contract if you refuse to sign."

Amber nodded, acutely conscious of her bedraggled appearance—hair slicked back, face washed clean of makeup. Even here, in this deserted place, she couldn't escape the flawless image of the beautiful redhead.

"She's flying in tonight from New York. Her contract with Len is up for renewal. Tomorrow she expects to be told whether Len wants her for the new campaign, or whether he's signed. . .a new model."

Amber lifted her chin. "Then tell her the contract is hers. I made my decision before you brought me here." She could feel the sparks shooting from her eyes.

For a moment, he didn't respond. Then a slow grin split his face. He looked ridiculously boyish. "You're irresistible when you're angry, you know." His expression shifted, and something unfamiliar flickered in his eyes.

His words were charged with tension when he spoke again. "You may not be a model. And today you're not a secretary. But you are. . .a very desirable woman."

She was suddenly aware of his nearness—the massive shoulders, the bare chest, the strong jawline. She could not look away. A storm of emotion swirled inside her. Like the strong ocean currents, she felt herself drawn into the undertow. She was helpless, powerless.

Almost against his will, it seemed, Anton backed away. "But then. . . Ken, is it? is the one true love of your life. . .and you've never gotten over him."

Amber's breath caught in her throat. How could she answer him without exposing her newly discovered feelings?

Anton shrugged. "You're suspicious of me—not without justification, I must admit—but I do know the honorable thing to do." He quirked a brow. "You're either a true innocent, or you're playing a very convincing game. And not even I can decide which it is."

"I don't play games, Mr. Pasetti. I've told you before." The shadows loomed darker as the sun sank toward the sea. How could she be so ambivalent—despising him one minute, wanting him to crush her in his arms the next?

He narrowed his gaze. "Oh, I think you may be playing the most dangerous game of your life. Gina says you're determined to be more than my secretary." He cocked his head as if trying to gauge the effects of his next words. "She thinks you want to be. . .my wife."

Amber exploded in a volley of words. "How could she say something like that? I've never done anything to make her think. . .and why would I want to be your wife? I don't even like you, Mr. Pasetti! You're arrogant, egotistical. . .and cruel!" Shaken to the core, Amber turned and ran across the rocky beach, now covered with water.

His laughter mocked her, ricocheting off the cliffsides. "And don't forget. . .immoral and godless!"

A wall as hard and impenetrable as the rock walls fell between them. Her tears blinded her, and she hurried toward the narrow steps. How could things have gotten so out of control? Even God seemed as remote as this secluded cove.

Finding the path, she rushed up, her bare feet slapping against the slippery wooden steps. She was out of breath, as much from anger and frustration as from exertion. The man was maddening! If she never saw him again, it would be too soon! Just a few more steps. . .

Her last thought was of Anton before she lost her footing and felt herself falling.

Chapter Twelve

Gina swept into the office, red hair flaming like fire in a shaft of sunlight pouring in through the reception room window. "Is Anton alone?"

Amber looked up. "I'll buzz."

The woman's green eyes were coolly calculating today. "Don't bother. After all the time we spent together in New York. . ."

The implication was clear. But in the next minute, as Amber turned her head to press the intercom button, Gina gasped. "What happened to you? You look awful!"

Automatically, Amber reached up to touch the tender flesh under her right eye. She winced. It was still swollen and horribly black and blue, despite her efforts to camouflage it with makeup this morning. "Oh. . .it's nothing. Just ran into. . .a little problem." Gina was the last person she'd tell how she'd ended up with the world's biggest shiner!

"Well, whatever it was, you sure got the worst end of the deal. Too bad." Gina flounced past the desk on her way into Anton's office, throwing Amber a smile that was more condescending than concerned.

Amber flinched when the door clicked shut behind the woman. Her headache was only slightly worse than the ache in her heart. Already Gina would be gloating. Probably she was in Anton's arms right now, celebrating her triumph.

After what had happened at his house last night. . .

Amber recalled her nasty spill down the cliffside steps, hitting her head on the way down. How humiliating that, after the stormy scene with Anton on the beach, she'd ended up sprawling at the bottom of the steps at his feet! But when he'd helped her up and checked her over for serious injury, there had been only the one spot, reddening around her eye.

"The angels caught you," Aunt Sophie would have said. Amber believed it. How else could she have escaped such a fall with nothing more than a black eye?

She was pretty sure that Anton was counting his blessings, too. Good thing for him she hadn't signed that contract for Len's line of eye makeup. Now Gina would have clear sailing.

Amber was pouring herself a second cup of coffee when she decided to take a breather. It was about time for her morning break anyway. She'd just ask Charis to send a replacement a little early, then she'd beat a hasty retreat to the older woman's office at the other end of the hall. No need to put herself through the torment of seeing Gina and Anton coming out of his office together—if they ever did.

"Come in, dear." Charis didn't look up from some papers on her desk until Amber took a seat, at eye level. "Oh, my! You poor darling!" Charis exclaimed the minute she saw her. "Anton told me about your little accident, but I wasn't prepared to see you looking like the victim of a train wreck."

Amber gave a wry grin, then grimaced in pain. "I know I'm a mess. But it could have been a lot worse."

"Have you been putting ice packs on that eye?" Charis rose to come around her desk.

"That. . .and beefsteak, too. Mitchell and his wife, Edna, couldn't have been nicer. Anton even insisted on calling in a doctor. But I'm fine. . .really. No broken bones. Only this monster."

Charis took Amber's face in one hand, tilting her head to study the injury. "What a shame. But there's no real damage done. Nothing that a little more concealer couldn't fix."

"Oh, I'm not worried. The doctor said it would be as good as new in a couple of weeks. It's just that. . ."

Charis leaned back against her desk, arms folded over her chest. *She looks regal today in royal blue,* Amber thought, *like a queen.* "Yes, Amber?"

She resisted the urge to let the whole ugly truth spill out. Her lack of love for Ken, who was the right kind of man for her. Her disturbing feelings for Anton, who was anything but right for her. Her—yes, she might as well admit it, if only to herself—her jealousy of Gina's hold over him. And now, even if she wanted to sign Len's contract. . .

Like the surf rushing over the rocky shore and washing back to sea, she let her thoughts ebb away.

"Well, if you haven't anything to tell me," Charis began, "I have something to tell you."

Amber jerked to attention.

"We really want you to reconsider Len's offer, dear."

Amber was stunned. Charis couldn't mean what she was saying. Not with this face looking like something out of a horror movie!

"There's more to it than the eye makeup line alone." Charis rose once more, her silk dress rustling as she moved over to a window and looked out over the city skyline.

"A colleague. . .in the clothing business. . .has seen your photographs, thinks you have the wholesome, innocent look she needs for a new line and wants you for a fashion spread. . .in Paris."

Amber was barely able to catch her breath. Paris! The ultimate escape. A place to lose her memories, to find herself. Was this the answer to her prayers? "Paris? But my job. . .my eye—"

Charis turned to face her. "Anton is willing to release you for the project. The two shoots won't take more than a month at most, and Len could design his campaign around the Paris theme. As for your eye. . ." She cocked her head and gave a mysterious little smile. "Do you remember the old movies starring a blond by the name of Veronica Lake? Her signature hairstyle was a side part, with hair swinging forward to cover the right side of her face."

Amber was still speechless, though her mind was whirring with the speed of a Pentium III 733. Maybe she could get away long enough to forget Anton Pasetti.

"And there's always Len's great cosmetics," Charis was saying. "He carries the best concealer in the business, you know."

Concealer. . .The truth burst on Amber with all the intensity of the San Diego sunshine. Secrets. . .Ken. . .she owed it to Charis to tell her about that episode in her life—even if she was as confused as ever about Anton. "Before you decide whether or not you really want me for this assignment, there's something I have to say."

❧

On the way to lunch, there were murmurs of sympathy from practically everyone in the building. Even the women who had hated Amber for outdoing them in her Mexican outfit were now coming up to offer their condolences. And why not? With this eye, she was no threat to anyone!

It was only after Ron fixed her up with a black patch that made her look like a gun moll or a female buccaneer that the women began to ignore her again.

"They can't stand it when someone else takes the limelight," Kate muttered, moving through the line. "You'd think they'd be happy you weren't killed in that fall!" She frowned at a group leaving the cafeteria, no doubt talking about Amber. "Uh-oh! Don't look now, but here comes Miss You-Know-Who."

Amber couldn't resist.

"Hi, you two," Gina said brightly. "Mind if I join you?" Not waiting for a reply, she set her tray down. Removing her birdlike meal from the tray, she placed it on the table and sat. "How can you girls eat that fatty food?" she asked, wrinkling her nose.

"People who work hard need the energy," Kate snapped.

"Work?" Gina scoffed. "You don't know what work is! Try sitting under hot lights with the cameras grinding away. Try having your hair shampooed half a dozen times a day."

Amber continued munching on her chicken salad sandwich.

"But," Gina added in a snide tone, "I suppose Amber will soon learn—now that she's a model."

So Anton told her, Amber thought. *Wonder if he knows why I signed that contract—that I can't take being in the same office with him, that I'm tempted to love him when I know I can never have him.* "I'm not a model yet, Gina. In the meantime, I'm still a secretary."

"Lamarr Cosmetics doesn't think so. Anton doesn't think so." Gina was breathing hard. "And a signed contract, the one Charis's other little secretary delivered while I was in his office, says otherwise!"

Amber stiffened. She didn't want to tangle with Gina over this. "Look, Len had those photos taken on a whim. I'm no model and I don't want to be."

"Ha! As if you didn't worm your way into landing that contract behind my back, while I was in New York!"

"Oh, come off it, Gina," Kate put in defensively. "Can't you be satisfied with the shampoo commercials? There's enough to go around in this business."

Gina shot her a withering look.

"Just a minute." Amber held up a hand. "I didn't ask for the contract. Just what are you talking about?"

"Oh, Anton told me all about it. How you've been cozying up to the Lamarrs, playing tennis with Len, seeing him in his home. Said Len was intrigued with a certain air about you. . .like you're hiding some deep, dark secret that's just perfect for his new campaign." She stabbed a piece of lettuce with her fork. "What I think you're hiding is your scheming and conniving to get what you want!"

Kate came up out of her seat, eyes flashing. "That's not true!"

"Oh, really?" Gina returned her scorching look. "Well now, how would it seem to you if you went away with your boss and heard nothing but talk of his 'dedicated, efficient little secretary,' who was grieving her little heart out over a lost fiancé—and then came home to find out that not only had she taken your job but she was trying to take your man!"

"Of all the rotten things to say!" Kate began. "Amber is not like that at all. You're the one who would stoop to anything to get what you want!"

Amber moaned.

Gina arched a well-groomed brow. "I know a few tricks, but your little friend here uses them. She used her grief to play on Len's and Anton's sympathy, for one thing." She darted an appraising glance at Amber. "Frankly, I don't think you're suffering at all."

Suddenly Amber had had enough of being sweet and patient. "Listen, you. . .you don't know the meaning of love or grief, because you don't have a heart! I did grieve for Ken and I loved him, though not as much as he wanted or deserved." Amber rushed on, her volume increasing. "I wore the engagement ring out of respect. But I've put the whole sad thing behind me. What's wrong with that? Why should you assume I'm putting on some—" She broke off, horrified to see Anton coming into the cafeteria.

Gina did not miss the direction of her gaze. "So you say you don't play games? I know the truth. You want Anton for yourself, don't you?"

"I don't have to stay here and listen to this!" Amber grabbed her purse and, leaving her half-eaten lunch on the table, rushed from the cafeteria, Gina's mocking laughter trailing her all the way out the door.

৯

Anton paused at the threshold of the reception room door, eyes wide. Amber had never seen him shaken—except maybe at that moment at the bottom of the steps when he'd thought she might be seriously injured— or dead! Now he seemed able only to stare before walking slowly past her desk, his eyes riveted on her new hairstyle.

After lunch, Amber had fled again to Charis's office in tears to vent her frustration over Gina's latest accusation—although she carefully avoided mentioning that the redhead was on the right track. Amber was attracted to Anton, but she was fighting it with everything she had in her. Besides, Layla was still in the picture, and a woman couldn't win over the memory of a lost love. Not that she was hoping to win. Oh, she didn't know what she was hoping! She only knew she always felt better when she was with Charis.

With the older woman's help, Amber had removed the eye patch Ron had playfully created out of construction paper. Then, with Charis's help, she'd parted her hair on the left, swept it to one side, and allowed the silky strands to fall over her face. The effect was amazing! The black eye was completely covered, while the lift at her hairline on the left cast the planes of her face in a whole new light. Charis had been delighted. "Just wait until Len sees this! His 'Woman of Mystery' campaign will be the hottest thing he's ever done!"

It was only seconds after Anton reached his inner office that he buzzed for Amber. She set her phone to transfer all incoming calls to voice mail, grabbed her laptop, and reported dutifully, taking her usual chair beside his desk.

"You won't need to take notes, Amber."

Her startled glance at him revealed the granitelike mask of his expression. What was this all about? Some glitch in the contract already?

After a moment, he swiveled his chair back, stood, and turned to look out the window. "You'll be leaving for Paris next week, for the fashion shoot and the cosmetic layout."

So soon? She permitted only a small intake of breath.

"We'll have some details to clear up before you go. Would you. . .go out with me this weekend?" His tone held a dare—or was it the first trace of humility she'd ever observed in him?

She didn't know what to say. Was this business or pleasure? She had no wish to torture herself further. But she would soon be out of here. Maybe this would be her last chance to try to live her Christian witness in front of Anton—after she'd just blown it in the cafeteria. Could she do it? *Lord, help me.*

"Well?" he asked, turning around to face her. As on the day of her interview, the sun was slanting through the window at that peculiar angle that blinded her and cast him in the shadows. "Will you go with me?"

He was probably hoping she'd refuse—to prove she had no designs on him. But until the plans were actually finalized for the Paris shoot, she was still his secretary.

"Yes, sir. Of course. What's the occasion?"

He narrowed his gaze curiously. "Celebration of your new career."

She stiffened. So this was to be "personal." "All right," she told him, looking him in the eye. "I'll need to know when and where."

He seemed to be surprised at her answer. "O—of course. Dinner," he said, returning to his chair at the desk. "An elegant place on the ocean front. Quite formal."

"What time?"

"I'll call for you at seven. . .if that would be agreeable with you."

She nodded. It was pretty satisfying to see him groping for words for a change. "I'll be ready."

He rose, still staring at her as if he couldn't believe what he'd just heard. "Then I guess that will be all. . .for now."

Amber stood, shut her laptop, and without another glance his way, left the office. But the minute she was out the door, she was wondering why she'd ever agreed to such a crazy idea!

❧

On Friday afternoon, after she had gathered her belongings at work and left early, Amber laid out her outfit for her dinner date with Anton. At Charis's insistence, she had accepted the loan of a stunning sleeveless, scoop-necked sheath they'd found in Wardrobe. "It's that delicious shade of hot pink that looks so good on you, Amber."

"But the back. . ." The back dropped away to a deep V, exposing Amber's California tan.

"It's completely modest, dear," Charis had assured her. "Don't worry. We wouldn't let a Pasetti model out in just any old thing—especially not this Pasetti model." She had rummaged in a jewelry drawer and come up with a string of faux pearls and matching pearl-and-diamond earrings. A pair of barely-there sandals, studded with glittering stones, completed the ensemble.

Amber felt a hint of panic. What was she doing, going out with a man who had the ability to take her breath and spin her head and her heart every which way but loose? There was much more preparation to be done before she'd be ready to meet Anton Pasetti. And so she prayed.

She prayed in the shower. *Lord, please clean me up on the inside, too. Help me get rid of all the ugly feelings I've had about Gina. And, Lord, keep me pure. . .even in my thoughts about Anton.*

She prayed as she was dressing. *Clothe me in Your beauty, Lord—kindness and gentleness. Help him see You in me. Teach me how to be a friend to this man who needs You so much.*

She prayed as she was drying her hair and brushing it out to camouflage her right eye, now a sickening yellow-green. *Thank You, Lord, for sparing my life that night I fell. I could have broken my neck! Was it for this moment? To share my faith one last time with this bitter, angry man?*

When she was ready, Amber took one final look at herself in the floor-length mirror on the back of the bathroom door. "Not too bad on the outside. At least, that eye doesn't show. I just hope my insides are ready for this."

With a final desperate prayer for guidance, Amber went to answer Anton's knock. *Help, Lord!* The man was devastatingly handsome in his black tux and starched white shirt, a bow tie knotted perfectly at his throat. *Send Your angels to protect me, as You did the other night. But this time, send them to protect me from myself!*

Chapter Thirteen

"If anyone ever had the Pasetti look. . ." For a moment Anton seemed speechless. "In a word, Amber, you're. . . perfection!"

His gaze was openly admiring as he took in her evening attire—from the top of her satin-smooth hair, draped over one eye, to the tip of her rhinestone-studded sandals.

She caught her breath, praying that she wouldn't betray her thudding heart. "I might say the same for you, sir."

He quirked a brow. "Sir? Since when have we been so formal after hours?"

"Until I leave for Paris, I believe I'm still your secretary. . .Mr. Pasetti." Amber picked up a light wrap that Charis had found for her. *"In case you two take a moonlight stroll on the beach,"* Charis had said with a knowing look. "I'm ready."

He took a step forward, arms outstretched. For a moment, she was afraid he meant to take her in his arms. But something in her one uncovered eye held him at bay. He stared hypnotically, then backed away. "There's something. . .different. . .about you tonight," he mumbled under his breath. "I'm not quite sure—"

"The new hairdo," she supplied.

He shook his head wonderingly.

"The outfit then? Incidentally, it's straight out of Pasetti Wardrobe. Charis—"

"Keep it. It's exactly right for you. . .but, no. . ." He shook off whatever seemed to be troubling him and glanced at his watch. "We'd better be going. Our reservations are for seven."

His touch was restrained as he escorted her through the front door of the little cottage, then taking her keys from her hand, he turned and locked up behind them. He handed her into the front seat of the Mercedes as if he were afraid she might break.

There was little conversation on their way into the city. Anton kept his eyes on the road except for an occasional glance at Amber, that expression of puzzlement still in his eyes.

With the ocean on one side and the moon riding low in the sky on the other, Amber drifted through the night at his side. God was watching over them. Angels hovered around them. She could feel the peace. She only wished Anton could feel it, too.

ॐ

At the restaurant, an upscale beachfront structure with an elegant nautical decor, the maitre d' showed them to a corner table overlooking the ocean. On the way through the crowded room, Amber noticed heads turning and whispered conversation. With his picture often in the society pages of the paper and news of the agency in the business section, Anton Pasetti would be recognizable anywhere.

In the center of the skirted table, tall candles flickered in a crystal candelabra. Overhead, brass chandeliers sparkled with a thousand tiny subdued lights, mirrored in the vast expanse of glass walls and water beyond. An orchestra played music from another era, while well-dressed couples danced to the haunting tunes. *It's a scene straight out of one of the slick magazines featuring Pasetti models,* she thought. And catching sight of the reflected image of herself and Anton in the window-wall next to their table, she couldn't help feeling that, tonight at least, the two of them could qualify for some cover.

No sooner had they been seated than a waiter appeared. With a flourish, he presented them with oversized menus tasseled in gold.

"Eddie," Anton greeted him. "I see you're back. And how is your mother doing after her surgery?"

"Oh, she's much better, Mr. Pasetti. And she asked me to thank you for. . .well, you know what you did for us." He ducked his head in embarrassment, then seemed to remember his place and spoke up briskly. "And what will you. . .and your dinner guest be having tonight, Mr. Pasetti?" The young man gave Amber a curious glance before stepping aside to wait discreetly while Anton studied the choices.

No doubt he had come here many times before, probably with Gina or some of the other models, Amber guessed. She was thoughtful as she watched the handsome man so intent on making just the right selection. He did everything with such panache. She couldn't help admiring that trait—not to mention his legendary acts of benevolence. He was always doing something nice for someone, usually someone who couldn't afford it—like the waiter's mother.

For a moment, she wavered in her resolve to keep her distance. Then she recalled something she'd heard in a sermon once: "Good deeds will not earn the reward of heaven without a personal experience with Jesus Christ." Anton Pasetti was not a believer. He'd said so himself. She steeled herself against his charm, his human kindness. And when he glanced over the top of the menu with that dazzling smile of his, she was ready for him.

"Please order for me," she said, once more in control of her fickle emotions. "I'm sure I'd enjoy anything you choose. You have exquisite taste."

"Yes. . .I have, haven't I?" His gaze warmed, lingered on her eyes, her hair, her lips. The man got to her, and she very nearly weakened again. How could he affect her so deeply without even so much as a touch? She should never have agreed to come to this romantic place. *Lord, keep me strong!*

She was relieved when he turned to the waiter and handed him the menu. "Then we'll have the crab bisque for starters, Eddie. And the lobster with shrimp as our entree."

To avoid further awkward moments, Amber shifted her attention to the moonlit beach, the waves rolling in to caress the shore. Even the elements seemed to be conspiring against her. "Um, the tide is coming in, I see. Does the waterline ever reach the restaurant?" she asked, then blushed. It seemed an inane question.

He shook his head. "Unless there's a storm, or in the unlikely event of a tidal wave. Nature seems to know her limits."

Amber wondered if she knew hers. A storm was raging within her at this very moment. Allowing herself to be in Anton's company tonight— even if she would be safely out of the country by tomorrow—was probably a big mistake. It was one thing to pray for protection from temptation, but quite another to deliberately plant oneself in the middle of it!

She was more than relieved when the food was served and they could turn their attention to the exotic dishes. Since crab was not usually included in her weekly grocery budget, she was prepared to enjoy the experience. She savored each spoonful of the delicate, creamy bisque.

But when Eddie brought in the main course, served on domed silver platters, and he whisked off the covers, Amber gasped. "Oh, Anton, I've never eaten lobster before!" she confessed. "How—"

He chuckled. "Don't worry. The shell is for decoration only. All the work has been done for you."

With her fork, she tested the dish—the meat of the lobster cooked in a rich sauce and stuffed inside the imposing shell—and found it to be flaky and tender, easily removed with a flick of the wrist. She had to giggle. "When you ordered lobster, I figured I'd have to wrestle the thing for my dinner!"

By the end of the meal, she was completely relaxed—for the first time since leaving the cottage. Dessert was mousse a l'orange, followed by a special coffee that Anton favored. Lulled by the music, the good food, and her companion's strangely respectful demeanor, Amber was not prepared for his next suggestion.

"Let's get out of here," he said abruptly, wiping his mouth and refolding the napkin. He rose, stretching out his hand as if expecting her to read his mind. "We have some business to attend to."

"B–but. . ." As far as Amber knew, she had wound up all the loose ends at the office before she left. Her replacement knew how to access all files on current contracts, where to find supplies, how to contact her in Paris if anything came up. "Where are we going?"

"You'll see." He inserted a hundred-dollar bill in the leather folder Eddie had left on their table, came around, and took her firmly by the arm, steering her through the tables of diners still lingering over their meal or dancing to the haunting melody of "Blue Moon."

It was an oldie, but as the singer crooned the words into a microphone, the message was as new as tonight: "Blue moon, you left me standing alone. . .without a dream in my heart. . .without a love of my own." It followed her all the way to the car, onto the freeway, and up a familiar, winding road. She wondered if the words were somehow prophetic.

⁓

When Amber stepped out of the Mercedes in front of Anton's estate, she shivered. The air was considerably cooler here, and the mist was rising above the cliffs, threatening to obscure the house and grounds. It was a lovely, eerie sight. Surreal. Much as the evening had been.

Anton was at her side in an instant, covering her bare shoulders with the wrap she had brought. "You're cold. Let's skip the beach and go inside."

"This shawl. . .it isn't mine, either, you know," she replied, stumbling over her explanation, as if to hold him at bay with words. "It belongs to the Pasetti Agency. Just as I do. . .for one more night. But after that, I won't be your secretary—"

Anton smiled. "Amber, Amber, don't fret. I'm not going to harm you. Just trust me."

Trust him? Now that's the last thing she would do. But she should hear him out. Maybe he really did have a little more business to discuss. Maybe it had something to do with her trip tomorrow.

He led her inside and up the stairs to his study, where they had talked once before. He struck a match and lit the fire that had already been laid, then lowered the lights. She sat down stiffly on a chair, putting as much distance between them as the room would allow.

Anton took off his tuxedo jacket and threw it over the back of the couch. "Now that you're leaving, I think it's time we were honest with each other."

He wanted to be honest? The biggest con artist of all time? She felt her eyes widen. Her lashes grazed the hair falling over her face, and she pushed the strands back over one ear, no longer concerned about her appearance.

"I have an idea that you've been able to put your fiancé's death behind you while you've been with us, that you're no longer grieving. Am I right?"

She nodded slowly.

"You no longer love him." It was a statement, not a question.

"I really don't see what business it is of yours. . ." The look on his face silenced her, and she shook her head.

Anton rose and paced in front of the fire. Then he turned to face her. "I'll have to admit I had other plans for us tonight. Oh, you would have resisted, but I intended to pull out all the stops." He looked deep into her eyes. "But there is something about you tonight, something I can't put my finger on. . .that changed my mind."

Amber let out her breath in a soundless sigh, unaware that she'd been holding it. *Thank You, Lord.*

"Still, I'd like. . .I need to tell you about. . .Layla."

She leaned back against her chair, watching the strong line of his jaw flex and relax. What more could he tell her than she already knew? Charis and Len had confided in her from the first about the sad loss of their only daughter. She even knew that Anton and Layla had planned to marry.

He dropped down onto the couch and stared into the fire. "She was young and beautiful. . .and driven." It seemed to Amber that at that moment, the years fell away and he was in the past—with Layla. "I was in my early twenties; she was nineteen. We were," he paused, searching for the right words, "very close. We were both enamored of ourselves, the glamour, the possibilities for success. We felt nothing could stand in our way. Mother was running the business then. . . ."

There was a long pause while he contemplated the fire. Then he rose, drove his hands into his pants pockets, and hunched his shoulders. Standing there like that, he looked young and vulnerable. Amber's heart went out to him. "She used me. . .used me to buy herself a contract from my mother, to make a place for herself in the business! And I fell for it."

He sighed, long and deep. "Oh, Layla came back to me. . .between jobs. . .when she wasn't doing some movie or TV commercial—bit parts mostly. She had everything: beauty, guts, determination. She could have made it on her own, but she chose to take a shortcut." The memory seemed overwhelming. "Or maybe she just enjoyed playing around, wielding her power over men." He let out a bitter laugh.

"We aren't sure if her drug overdose was accidental, or if it was because she finally saw the futility of it all. A film producer she had decided to marry jilted her, and she didn't get the contract she was after."

Drug overdose? Amber was stunned. Len and Charis hadn't shared that part of the story. "I'm sorry, Anton. . .so sorry. You must have loved her very much."

"No, I didn't love her," he blurted, with such a tortured look on his face that Amber shivered in spite of the warmth of the fire. "I don't think either of us was mature enough for real love. But her death was a blow to me. For several years afterward, I spent a lot of time abroad, handling our businesses in Paris and London. Then Mother got sick."

Amber didn't think she could stand much more. Seeing Anton like this. . .but he went on. "The next few years made me face up to my responsibility, take over the reins. I've tried to run the business as I think Mother would have run it." Tears glimmered in the silvery eyes. "Because of her—her standards, her values—I try to be as honest with others as I expect them to be with me."

I know what he's going to say now, Amber thought. Hoping to shut out the imagined sound of those words, she cleared her throat. She'd say it for him and get it over with. "You're in love with Gina."

His harsh laugh was a jolt. "Gina and I are. . .honest with each other," he began, neither admitting nor denying what Amber had said. "I have some. . .plans for her. But I'd never tell a woman I loved her if I didn't mean it."

He hurried on. "Gina makes no pretense about what she wants, either. . . personal or professional. And I make no pretense in letting her, or anyone else, know they can advance with my agency only if they please my clients. There are no contracts based on one's. . .compatibility. . .with the owner of the company."

It took a while for the words to sink in. Then Amber felt the color storm to her face. "You still think I. . . ?"

She jumped to her feet and walked over to the heavy scarlet draperies covering the sliding glass doors to the balcony. Parting them, she saw her own reflection in the glass. With her hair falling over her face again, she looked like a stranger, the gray mist outside swirling around her image. Maybe it was all a dream. . .a nightmare! She'd surely wake up and find that none of this had happened.

"I'm not blaming you, Amber," he said amiably. "I understand completely. I believe you're a true innocent. . .pure, untouched. And I'm enough of a gentleman to leave that alone. I'm simply offering you some sound advice that could save you a lot of trouble in the future, particularly in Paris. I'm trying to say that my experiences with women like Layla and Gina have taught me how important career advancement can be to a woman. It won't work with me, not anymore. But some men wouldn't hesitate to take advantage of you."

Amber was mortified! How could she have had feelings for this impossible man who never believed a word she said? He had his own mind made up that all women were devious, and nothing she could say ever seemed to dent that stubborn insistence.

"I just want you to know, Amber, that if you have your heart set on modeling—as a permanent career—Pasetti Agency will back you and work for you. I'll hire another secretary, and we'll issue a long-term modeling contract."

He was still talking. Would he never stop? "When you get back, I'd be willing to escort you to places like the one we visited tonight—places our clients frequent—so they can get a look at you. I have no doubt you'll be a very successful model for Pasetti Agency. That innocent look will take you a long way. It'll be a refreshing new slant on selling in an industry that's seen everything else. I'm afraid we're all pretty jaded by now."

When she didn't reply, he kept on. "I know how much you enjoyed tonight," he said. "The glamour of it, the clothes, the attention. You seemed to light up. That mysterious sadness was gone. In fact, tonight you were a very different person, all aglow, lovely."

He didn't understand. Would never understand. Her head whirled like the mist outside. She couldn't hear anymore. She didn't belong here. She had to get away. Back to the cottage. Back to the real world. "Please. . . take me home. I have some more packing to do."

He frowned. She could see his jaw clench again. "Very well. Anything you say." He was all business again. "I had hoped we could come to terms, but apparently you aren't ready to open up to me." He narrowed his gaze sharply. "Just keep in mind what I've told you. The offer stands."

She jumped up and got her wrap before he could reach her, then preceded him down the stairs and out the massive front doorway. Mitchell was nowhere in sight. No doubt Anton had briefed the staff ahead of time.

The mist clung to her face, mingling with the tears that were beginning to trickle down her cheeks. She braced herself. *No time for that, Amber.* As Aunt Sophie would say, "The Lord never closes a door that He doesn't open a window." Apparently, Anton was a closed door. No, make that a slammed door. He didn't even understand the basic reasons for the differences between them. She'd just have to keep looking for that open window. . .and praying for Anton's soul.

Neither of them spoke all the way back to the cottage. The car moved swiftly through the murky night, making hazy circles in the fog. The full moon that had been clearly visible earlier was hidden from view. *Just like so many things about my life,* Amber thought.

She tried not to notice when Anton did not take her arm as they walked across her backyard. Nor did he ask for her key, but let her fumble with the lock herself. He waited, rigidly, near the door as she made a hasty inspection and returned to give him the all clear.

But he seemed reluctant to leave. "I hope you won't allow anything I've said tonight to harm our working relationship. You're a very valuable employee, Amber. . .more now than ever."

She shook her head. Of course she was more valuable. Models brought in more dollars for the agency than mere secretaries. The flood that had been threatening to break loose was just behind her eyelids.

"You'll be all right?"

"Of course," she answered, not daring to look at him, hoping he'd leave before she made an idiot of herself.

He stepped back and, with his hand on the doorknob, turned once more. "Have a safe flight. . .and may God go with you. . .and keep you safe."

That was all it took. The minute he was out the door, the dam broke, and she leaned back against the door and released all the tears she'd been holding back.

"Lord, why? Why does it have to end this way?"

Chapter Fourteen

Red roses were waiting in Amber's plush hotel room when she arrived on Monday afternoon, Paris time. The card read simply: "All good wishes, Anton." This time the long-stemmed beauties marked the beginning of a truly new career, if she decided she wanted it, and the end of a relationship that was over before it had begun.

She was too tired to register any emotion. The famous jet lag she'd heard so much about, probably. Not only that, but she was still drained from her last painful encounter with Anton.

On the plane, she had had time to do a lot of thinking and praying. It seemed symbolic somehow that she was running away from yet another heartache—this time with wings. Still, the distance would give her some space to gain perspective on the whole thing. And God was still in control. . . even if He sometimes seemed to operate on a different timetable.

She unpacked her Bible and set it on the dainty nightstand. Knowing absolutely no one in the city, there would be plenty of time to read. Maybe she could find some guidance for the future, when all this was over and she was back home in North Carolina.

The jangle of the telephone jarred her from her thoughts. Who could that be? Someone back at the office must be needing something. For a moment, she found herself hoping it was Anton, checking to see if she'd had a safe flight.

Shaking off the memory of his mellow baritone, she lifted the receiver. "Hello. Amber Jennings."

A familiar masculine voice greeted her.

"Ron? Ron Jordan? Is that you? What's wrong? Something at the office? Did I leave—" Rattled, she broke off to catch her breath.

"Hey, hold it! Nothing's wrong. And I'm not at the office. I'm here. . . right here in Paris."

"Here? In Paris?" she squeaked.

"In the same hotel, room 412. I arrived yesterday. So I'm all over my jet lag and ready to show you the enchanted city."

Amber's brain felt numb. "But, Ron, what are you doing here?"

"Same thing you are. The 'Innocence in Paris' shoot. Anton thought I'd be great as your male counterpart. My blond looks, your brunette beauty. You know, wholesome, clean-cut guy meets girl next door. Nostalgia's in—or had you forgotten?"

She reached for her briefcase and pulled out the fax Anton had given her just before she left and scanned it again:

> Anton, your Amber Jennings is perfect for our "Innocence in Paris" collection. We must contract for her immediately. She has that fresh, innocent appeal we're looking for. Every woman in the world will want to look just like her. Once again, you've proven to be a genius, dear boy. Fly her to us!

Amber had been stunned. His Amber Jennings! How could Anton have pretended to resent her posing for Len, then use those very photos to "sell" her to some client—and without even asking her permission! She was still furious with him.

"Amber, are you there?"

"What? Oh, yes. Sorry, Ron. I'm still in the clouds, I think."

"Well, why don't you take a nap, then put on one of those knockout dresses Charis lined up for you, and let's go out for a late dinner."

"Sure," she replied noncommittally. "Sounds good. I'll give you a buzz when I wake up."

Amber kicked off her shoes and finished her unpacking, hanging the clothes in the full closet and putting away the undergarments and makeup, all courtesy of the Pasetti Agency. Not a scrap of clothing and none of the accessories she'd brought belonged to her. Even from a distance, Anton still controlled her. And now, he'd sent Ron. She wouldn't be surprised if that had been planned by the boss, too, simply to keep an eye on her!

Speaking of eyes, she ought to check on her bruise before she went out in public. The "Veronica Lake look" was beginning to be a nuisance.

In the bathroom, she was startled to find an unusual piece of porcelain plumbing. She'd have to ask about that. Leaning over to look in the gilded mirror over the basin, she examined her eye. The bruise was fading nicely. But she could definitely use some sleep. She washed her face, then padded back to the bedroom in her stocking feet.

Plumping the pillows, she pulled back the brocade bedspread and lay down. She was asleep almost before her head hit the pillow, her last troubled thoughts of Anton.

✿

"We've missed April in Paris," Ron quipped when he came by her room to pick her up for dinner, "but May isn't half bad. There are flowers everywhere." Spotting the roses in the tall vase on the *écritoire*, he grinned. "I see you already have a sample."

She smiled, but didn't explain, and turned to lock the door behind her. When she turned around, Ron was standing very near. "You're gorgeous tonight, Amber. Love your new hairstyle. And that dress—wow! Green is my favorite color, you know."

She glanced up to see if he was kidding. "Ron. . .it's blue. . .periwinkle, to be exact."

He shrugged and grinned. "Oh. . .did I also tell you I'm color blind?"

In spite of her exhaustion and her preoccupation with Anton, Amber giggled. "Where are we going for dinner?"

"Surprise," Ron said, leading the way to the elevator at the end of the corridor. "It isn't Maxim's, but Anton said you'd love it. Said he wanted your first night in Paris to be spectacular. So just relax and enjoy the ride."

Puzzled, she followed him into the elevator. When she had first arrived at the Richelieu, she had been too tired to notice much about her surroundings. But now she took in the splendor—French furnishings complete with elegant gold leaf, ornate mirrors, and massive arrangements of fresh flowers adorning every available surface in the lobby.

Outside, Ron carried on a brief conversation with the liveried doorman, and a limousine drove up.

"How did you manage that?" Amber wanted to know. "I didn't know you spoke French."

He patted his coat. "Handy vest-pocket dictionary. But I didn't order a limo, I asked for a taxi. Must have been Pasetti's idea." He frowned a little, then shrugged. "Oh, well. We might as well travel in style; he can afford it. My French might have gotten us to the restaurant, but after that. . ." He spread his hands.

Feeling more lighthearted than she had felt in quite some time, Amber laughed as he settled her in the backseat of the limo and ran around to slide in beside her. She still couldn't believe she was in Paris! From a small town in North Carolina to the streets of the world's most romantic city in only a few months! She ignored the twinge of regret that she wasn't here with someone more special than good old Ron.

Leaning forward to take in the sights as the driver made his way through the crowded streets, Amber could see that the city sparkled. No wonder Paris was known as "The City of Lights." It practically vibrated with life and motion. There were people everywhere—window-shopping along the wide boulevards, sitting at sidewalk cafés, strolling in one of the fabulous gardens they passed. The sight of a couple openly embracing near one of the fountains brought back another scene—Anton's rooftop garden. Could she never escape the thought of him?

"We'll have plenty of time to do some sight-seeing in the next few days," Ron was saying. "Our first fitting is not until day after tomorrow, although Madame Collette wants to meet us at two. She promised we'd be through by three, and the shoot doesn't start until next week. So. . .*ma chérie*," he leered playfully, twirling a make-believe moustache, "I will haff you all to myself. I will not let you out of my sight. I will be your personal tour guide. Trust me."

She couldn't help laughing. "And I'm to trust your French?" With a shock of hair falling over one eye and that fake accent, he seemed more like Peter Sellers in one of those old *Pink Panther* movies. "Sorry, Ron," she said. "You'd be more believable as a Swiss ski instructor."

They were still laughing when the driver pulled over to the curb in front of a quaint building with an awning extending over the sidewalk. A doorman sprang to open the door. "*Bonsoir*, monsieur, mademoiselle."

Amber took his hand and stepped out, feeling like a celebrity. Apparently Anton hadn't spared any expense. But he'd do the same for any of his models. Didn't Gina always have the best? And when Ron mumbled another phrase in French, the only word she could make out was "Pasetti."

They didn't need the dictionary for the rest of the evening. Apparently, the Pasetti name was the key that unlocked all the golden doors. Inside the restaurant, they were shown to a corner table, where three uniformed waiters appeared instantly. One was holding a bouquet of red roses, which he presented to Amber; another trundled over an iced bucket of not champagne, but Perrier; still another produced a large menu, then spoke in startlingly flawless English, "If I may be so bold, may I recommend the speciality of the house: filets de sole Cardinal and scallop salad with truffles?"

Amber and Ron looked at each other and gave a helpless shrug. "Bring it on," Ron ordered.

The rest of the evening proceeded without a hitch. It was as if Anton himself were orchestrating the entire event and was standing by, somewhere in the shadows, to be sure they had the best of everything. Amber could almost feel his presence. Still, when she glanced up occasionally to look through the window, it wasn't two dark heads reflected there, but Ron's blond one beside hers.

Noticing her sudden silence, he spoke up. "You do recognize those tall spires over there, don't you? That's the Notre Dame Cathedral located on the Ile de la Cité. I think that's why Anton chose this particular restaurant. He knew you'd like—" He broke off as if disgusted with himself, and speared a forkful of sole. "We'll have lots of time to explore the city. Besides," he cocked his head, grinning at her, "I have another surprise for you. . .something you're really not going to believe!"

Later, at a little sidewalk bistro, when they met up with Kate and Jim, Amber was stunned. "What are you two doing over here?"

After hugs, Kate gave a sheepish grin. "I was going to tell you, Amber, really I was. . .but everything happened so fast. . .and you were so busy getting ready for your shoot. . .and," the words tumbling out rose to a shriek, "Jim and I are married!"

Amber could only gasp. "Married? But when. . . ?"

"Day before yesterday. I'll tell you all about it later. It was just that Daddy was suddenly transferred to another base, and the wedding had to be rushed up, or you know you would have been my maid of honor. As it turned out, it was just a simple ceremony with only the family. But, Amber, the best part—"

"Let me tell her." Jim, who had been standing by quietly, broke in. "Mr. Pasetti is giving us this honeymoon trip. . .so we could be here to help out with the cosmetic shoot week after next." His grin shifted to a stern scowl. "But let me warn you. We plan to make ourselves scarce until we're actually needed. After all, this is our honeymoon."

"Hey, pal, congratulations!" Ron clapped his friend on the back. "This is news to me, too. But don't worry, we aren't likely to be running into you. It's a big city, and we have a few plans of our own."

There was lots of laughter and catching up over café au lait. From the corner of her eye, Amber could see the amused smiles of passersby, overhearing their chatter. To them, it must appear that the two couples were rendezvousing, both pairs giddy with the excitement of being in love.

She took a moment to watch Ron as he filled their friends in on their schedule for the next two weeks. He was extremely attractive—those perfect, even features, his face so animated as he talked. Still, as Aunt Sophie had often said, "I hear married folks say it's not looks that count—though it doesn't hurt any to get yourself a good-lookin' one. No, the man you marry better be your best friend, someone who can make you laugh, 'cause you're going to be spending an awful lot of time together!"

Well, Amber hadn't had a better friend than Ron. . .not since Ken. Ron kept her in stitches. She hadn't laughed so much in ages.

"So," he was telling Jim and Kate as Amber shook off her thoughts, "we'll stay out of your way if you'll stay out of ours."

Now, what did he mean by that?

"Hey, wife," Jim said, helping Kate up, "it's one o'clock in the morning. We're still trying to adjust to Paris time, you know—"

"And Amber needs her beauty sleep," Ron added, then amended, "What I mean is, she's exhausted from her trip, and tomorrow is a big day. So. . .we'll say adieu," he scrambled for his pocket dictionary, "or is it au revoir?"

Kate giggled, and Amber got to her feet, suddenly overwhelmed with all that had happened in the past few days. "Ron's right. I do need my beauty sleep. I'm still fighting some swelling in this eye." She touched the area where makeup had concealed most of the fading bruise. "I don't need bags, too!"

With another round of laughter and the promise to get together at the first shoot, Ron hailed a cab. All the way back to the hotel, he joked about the surprise wedding and their unpredictable friends.

At her door, he made a mock bow and kissed his fingers. "Mademoiselle, Paree is nossing compared to your beauty. I would like to book every available moment of your time while we are here, *s'il vous plaît*."

When he straightened, though, there was no trace of levity in his expression. "I mean it, Amber. I'd like the chance to let you see that I'm not just some goofy guy with a crush on the latest Pasetti star." He flexed his jaw. "Tonight might have been compliments of the great Anton Pasetti. . . but the rest is on me. I want us to get to know each other better on this trip. . .much better."

His eyes held hers in a steady gaze, and she couldn't look away. "I'd like that, too," she whispered before unlocking the door and stepping aside.

Long after she was in bed, her mind churned. Maybe this was what it was all about. Maybe this was why she had come halfway across the country—to San Diego—and now halfway across the world. She and Ron. Was he God's best for her?

❧

The next week passed in a blur. Anton had arranged a session at Carita, one of the city's finest beauty salons, for a facial, manicure and pedicure, and hairstyling. For the fashion shoot, it was decided that Amber's eye had sufficiently healed to wear her hair pulled off her face in a fresh, natural style. "*Très ingénue,* mademoiselle. *Très naturelle,*" the stylist murmured. "Makes the eyes appear wide and vulnerable, *non?*"

From there, Amber was introduced to Madame Collette, the couturiere who had designed the line of clothing she would be modeling.

"*Très belle!*" Madame exclaimed the minute she saw Amber, which Amber correctly translated, "Beautiful!" But when the woman, a tiny wisp of a thing with hair piled on top of her head, exploded in a volley of French phrases, Amber lost her. From the smiles of the staff looking on, she assumed they were pleased.

"Enchanting, *ma chérie,*" Madame said in passable English. "So right for my collection. Our Paris models in the haute couture houses have the. . .what shall we say? . . .the seductive look. But you. . .there is such innocence. . .such purity. *Mais oui,* I know what it is. . .it is the look of a Botticelli angel!"

There were long afternoons and evenings with Ron, too. Times when they could get away to take in all the city had to offer. Since both were on an expense account and wanted to be fair to the agency, they used a cab for only those attractions that were not within walking distance. They browsed through the stalls of the booksellers, strolled the Luxembourg Gardens, ate lunch in a bistro beneath the Eiffel Tower.

At one of the boutiques, Ron insisted on buying her a vial of real perfume, *L'Heure Bleue,* "for women who are romantic, sensitive, refined, and feminine." She brushed it on the pulse point at her wrist, and he lifted her arm to sniff, then dropped a kiss on the spot.

I'm beginning to like this guy, she admitted to herself. More than she would have believed possible. More than she had intended.

❧

On Sunday morning, Amber found Ron waiting for her in the lobby. "I know we didn't discuss this last night, and I hope you don't mind," he began on an apologetic note, "but I knew you'd probably be looking for a place to worship. Right?"

She blushed and didn't know why. Her faith was very important to her, and almost everyone back at the agency knew it. "Yes. I'd planned to take a cab to one of the churches. We haven't visited any yet and. . .well, today seemed like the right time."

"Then, allow me. I have an idea I know just the place." He offered her his arm, stepped confidently through the front doorway, and ordered a taxi in fluent French.

"I'm impressed. You've been practicing."

"Just the most important phrases," he gave her a searching look, "but I'm saving some of those for later."

She wasn't surprised when the driver crossed one of the many bridges leading to Notre Dame Cathedral. Amber hadn't had such a grand place in mind. She'd been hoping for a smaller, more intimate place, where she could drop into a back pew and pray quietly while the Parisians worshipped. But this was thoughtful of Ron, who was obviously making a noble effort to do the right thing.

Inside the great Gothic building with its twin towers, there was a steady stream of spectators. The two rose windows, dating back to the thirteenth century, were magnificent, and remarkable sculptures depicted Christ at the Last Judgment and other sacred works. It was all very interesting, but the vast interior was cold and impersonal. Amber felt separated from God rather than closer to Him. *In fact, it seems dark and oppressive in here,* she thought, and she was eager to get back out into the sunshine.

But before she stepped through the door leading outside, Ron pulled her into a secluded corner of the cathedral. "There's something I need to tell you, Amber."

This wasn't the fun-loving man she'd come to know. This was a much more serious Ron.

"I've been a Christian since I was a boy," he shuffled his feet, looking down, "but I must admit it's been a long time since I've put my faith into action. . .like you seem to do without thinking about it twice. Until you invited me to church at the beach, I hadn't darkened the door since. . ."

well, that's another story. It's not the politically correct thing to do in this industry, you know." He looked up, gazing at her intently. "But it's different now. You've helped me see what's really important. . .no matter what people might think."

Amber nodded, feeling she had no right to be hearing Ron's confession. This was too personal; it was something that should be shared only with the woman. . . It was all moving too fast. . .much too fast. She didn't want to hear anymore. But he wasn't through.

"*Je t'aime.* Translation, in case you haven't been doing your homework; I think I'm falling in love with you, Amber."

Until this moment, she had thought she had put Anton completely out of her mind, out of her heart. But it was no use. *Why couldn't he be here, saying these words?* "Not now, Ron. This isn't the time. Please, could we go? It's chilly in here."

She had prayed for Anton Pasetti every day. But she hadn't counted on loving him so much it hurt.

Chapter Fifteen

It was just as Gina had said.

Modeling was hard work. Long hours under the hot lights. Holding a pose when your back was aching. Looking into Ron's blue eyes when it was Anton's dark gray ones Amber was seeing. It was all she could do to keep that fresh-faced glow when her spirits were about as low as they had ever been.

She had never prayed so hard in her life. Just about the time she'd thought she was beginning to make some sense of everything that had happened, she'd discovered that she was her own worst enemy! That Anton had never been far from her thoughts. And that she could never love Ron in the same way. Was she rebelling against all the Lord wanted for her? She'd tried to let it go, but the more she prayed for Anton, the more her thoughts and feelings followed.

Still, something was working. At least, Madame Collette was pleased. "She has zee face of an angel," she would say to anyone who would listen.

Amber was always embarrassed by the woman's remarks, but when she would blush, Madame would emote even more. "Do you see? How pure. . .how untouched she is! Most women today haff forgotten how to blush."

The "Innocence in Paris" line was a sensation. At several fashion shows, Amber modeled the latest day and evening attire for the "wholesome, natural girl" and swimwear for "the innocent." The results of the grueling photo sessions appeared in the Parisian papers, calling her "a stunning new find."

Amber was relieved when the fashion shoot was over. That meant Ron would be returning to San Diego soon. Not that he'd given up on her. That day in the cathedral, when she hadn't been able to hide the truth, she'd seen the pain in his eyes.

But he had rebounded quickly. And by morning, he was at her door with a rose between his teeth, begging her to give him another chance. "*Je t'adore*, Amber. You are zee only woman in my life!"

She hadn't wanted to hurt him, but she'd had to tell him she wasn't ready to make a commitment. It had been painful for them both. So

Charis and Len's arrival the following week was a welcome reprieve.

Madame Collette repeated her sentiments to the Lamarrs. "She is all yours. . .at least for zee moment," Madame said with a secretive smile. "But I haff zee plan. . .I shall fax Anton and we shall discuss it."

When Kate and Jim showed up to assist with the shoot, Kate was ecstatic. "Oh, Amber, Paris is the most perfect place for a honeymoon. We'll never forget it, will we, darling?" She looked at her new husband as if he were a chocolate éclair, and she could easily devour him in one mouthful. Lucky Kate.

Amber had to fight back a feeling of jealousy. She was probably destined to be alone for the rest of her life. Even her aunt, who had responded to her postcards, was on the verge of "taking the leap after all these years." Lucky Aunt Sophie.

With Kate and Jim assisting Charis, Len's shoot went well. But about the only positive thing Amber could find was that the "haunting" look they needed for the "Woman of Mystery" line could be called up at a moment's notice. All she had to do was think of Anton, and the photographer got exactly the shot he was after.

Because of the chemistry that was flowing, the shoot took practically no time at all, much to the delight of everyone concerned. Kate and Jim were eager to get back to San Diego and begin their new life as husband and wife. Len and Charis had important business to attend to.

"I really can't be away from the office another day," Charis confided. "Amber, darling, you must know how very pleased we are with your work. Your professionalism has saved us a great deal of time and money."

"Yeah, but there goes my tennis partner," Len cracked. "She'll be so much in demand now that we'll never see her."

Just as they were packing up the equipment to be shipped back to the States, Madame Collette appeared on the set with the look of a cat eyeing a bowl of cream. "Ah, *chérie*, there you are! It appears dear Anton has released you to me. . .just as I had hoped."

Amber was shocked. "W–what?"

"You are my inspiration! I must have you near me to complete another line of designs. Zey will be a masterpiece—the *pièce de résistance*—the crowning achievement of a lifetime! I will call it—'Angelique'!"

Len and Charis were equally stunned. "What are you talking about, Collette?" Len demanded, instantly defensive. "Amber has a contract as a Pasetti model. And, more than that, she has a life of her own to consider. How could Anton do a thing like this without consulting her?"

Madame Collette smiled. "Oh, don't fret, *mon ami*, I shall do what is right by her. I shall pay her much more than she would receive anywhere else in zee world! Besides, with my 'angel' to inspire me, I shall complete zee line quickly. . .say no more than seex months."

"Six months!" The three dropped their mouths.

"She shall have zee best accommodations and plenty of time to enjoy our beautiful city, *non?* What woman would not love such an arrangement, eh?"

Suddenly, everything seemed clear to Amber. There was no place for her back home. Her best friend was married now. Aunt Sophie and Uncle Jack would probably follow suit pretty soon. And Anton had let her go—without so much as asking her opinion! No secretarial job. No modeling contract. What did she have to go back to?

Before Charis or Len could object further, Amber spoke up. "I accept, Madame Collette. When do you want me to begin?"

❧

Amber wasn't quite sure how Aunt Sophie would take the news that she was going to stay on in Paris. Her aunt hadn't been too keen about it in the first place. "I've heard that city is full of all kinds of sin and perversions," she'd warned. "Just don't forget your upbringing." But now that she had Uncle Jack to think about, she hadn't corresponded lately.

Kate was delighted. "Aren't you the lucky one?" she wrote. "Now you'll get to see all the places you missed. Kick back, friend, and enjoy. You deserve it!

"As for Jim and me, we're more in love every day. We're planning to celebrate our first anniversary in Paris—at the same small hotel where we spent our honeymoon. It's quaint, charming, and well off the main thoroughfares. You might want to check it out. If so, be sure to give the proprietors, Monsieur and Madame LaRue, our love. They're such dears."

With Kate's directions, the place wasn't hard to find, and Amber soon moved out of the Richelieu and settled into her new routine. The LaRues were everything Kate had said they were, and more, a French version of Aunt Sophie and Uncle Jack. She felt right at home.

She was expected at Madame Collette's shop for only a couple of hours a day to sit for sketches. Later, as the garments were developed, she would have to be measured and fitted once again. For now, most of her days were free to absorb the ambiance of the city. If she was lucky, she might even be able to put Anton out of her mind once and for all.

But no matter where she went—shopping in the boutiques that lined the wide avenues, spending an afternoon in one of the famous museums, stopping for croissants and café au lait at one of the sidewalk bistros—it took only a glimpse of a strong profile or a dark head to bring the images flashing back.

There was an occasional letter from Ron. "Just to remind you that I'm still around, waiting for you back in sunny California. Be good. . .and remember—*je t'aime.*"

&

Soon after becoming a resident of the little hotel, Amber discovered a chapel nearby. It was centuries old and covered with ivy, but the interior had been restored back during the war, she learned, and a few people from the neighborhood, most of them elderly Parisians, had volunteered to clip back the weeds and clean the vestry, then gathered to pray from time to time.

As the season subtly shifted to autumn and the leaves turned, she began to drop by more and more frequently to soak in the peace and to pray for guidance. When Madame Collette's collection was finished, Amber hadn't the slightest idea of what she would do. Always, though, after coming here to the chapel, she left with a sense that God was working out the details of her life. . .if she only had patience to wait on Him.

And always, always, she prayed for Anton. If she could do nothing else, she could ask God to protect him, to make him happy with Gina, to heal his heart and save him from his own foolishness.

&

By the end of November, Madame Collette was putting the finishing touches on her new collection. "Ah, this is my best work. I shall have a. . . how you say? . . .a preliminary showing—with you as zee only model, of course. We shall begin with a little reception in my salon for only my best *customairs* and their daughters, home for the holidays. They will see you in my enchanting designs. . .and beg their *mamans* for a new frock. And you, chérie, will be dazzling in *blanc!*"

"*Blanc?* White?"

Madame beamed. "Yes—*blanc*, ivory, *crème*. And now you know my secret." Her pale eyes danced. "All the garments in this collection will be white—velvets, wools, satins. White. . .like the snow! Ah, I can see it now!" She clasped her hands together. "In the midst of winter's bleakness. . .the light! Perfection! Brillant! Even I have never been so inspired." She laughed with delight and gazed at Amber fondly. "It is you, Angelique, who inspire me."

❧

On the afternoon of the showing, after the final presentation—a magnificent bridal creation in satin and lace—Amber headed for the dressing room to change. She was exhausted. She'd made eight changes: a silk gown and peignor set; loungewear in brushed velvet; a worsted wool skirt and cashmere turtleneck, worn with high-heeled kid boots. . .ending with Madame Collette's masterpiece.

She lifted the long satin skirt and hurried into the room. The sooner she got out of this heavy dress, the better.

At the dressing table, she removed the tiara and veil and was pulling out the pins in her upswept hairdo when she heard a knock at the door. "*Entrezvous*, Madame."

But it wasn't Madame Collette. Amber's eyes locked with a familiar pair of smoky gray ones. "Anton!"

"Put on something warm. I have a car waiting."

She came up out of her seat and turned to face him. "Just a minute! How dare you show up after all this time and start ordering me around! I'm not your secretary. I'm not a Pasetti model. I'm not on your payroll at all," she hesitated at the smile tugging at his lower lip, "or am I? Have you and Madame Collette been conspiring behind my back?"

His silence spoke louder than words before he went on. "Ah, Amber, I'm relieved to see that you haven't changed at all. You still look glorious when you're all heated up like that." His gaze swept the wedding gown. "You always did go in for those high-necked affairs, didn't you? All right, all right," he backed off, seeing the fire in her eyes. "I'll rephrase my invitation. When you've changed, would you do me the honor of accompanying me to dinner? There is a matter of some. . .urgent business that must be handled. . .and only you have the answer."

She sighed, skeptical. She'd been expecting something like this. No doubt the new secretary hadn't been able to locate a file or a contract. "I should have my head examined. . .but I'll go. Give me a minute."

"Just remember," he grinned, flashing white teeth, "I'm not a patient man."

Hurrying back into the wool outfit and boots, Amber grabbed a hooded ivory greatcoat and joined him in the salon. Without another word, he led her outside to a sleek, low-slung car at the curb. A few flakes of snow drifted out of the sky, and their breath frosted in the cold air.

They passed now-familiar sights, but nothing registered. Only the man seated beside her in the little sports car filled her senses. He was so close she could touch him, yet he was completely beyond her reach.

He turned in at a French café. "It's small, but the food here is excellent. I doubted that you would eat before the showing."

She nodded, not trusting herself to say a word.

They ate their meal in silence. The food, delicious as it might have been, tasted like sawdust in her mouth. Over coffee, Anton spoke softly, kindly, allowing her time to unwind, briefing her on office happenings in her absence, painting pictures in broad strokes. There was one major omission. Gina. What about Gina?

He sighed. "I have another offer," he said. "Another contract."

"Really? I'm sure Gina would be available." Amber couldn't resist the dig. "That is, unless she's too busy with her duties at home."

"At home? I wouldn't know anything about that. She's currently in New York, making the first of three movies. Her contract reads that she'll be tied up for the next five years. Seems she's wanted to act all along."

Amber couldn't stifle a gasp. "But I thought. . ."

He shrugged. "I suppose I know what you must have been thinking. You despise me, don't you, Amber?"

The expression in Anton's eyes broke her heart. But she had to be firm. Even without Gina in the picture, they were worlds apart. "I don't despise you, Anton. But I think I understand you. Business always comes first, then pleasure. After that, everything—and everyone—else. I believe that's really why you never married."

He looked down at his cup, tracing the rim with his finger. "You're right about so many things. . .but not everything. When I was younger, I was too busy pursuing pleasure. Then there was Mother's illness, and afterward. . .I was too busy trying to keep the company going. After Layla. . . well, for so long there was no one who came close to capturing my heart for more than a short time. And, strange as it may seem to you," he looked up and the dark eyes shimmered silver in the candlelight, "I've always believed that marriage should be a lifetime agreement, don't you, Amber?"

When she didn't answer, he added, "You do believe it. That's why you couldn't go through with the marriage to Ken. . .or Ron." He smiled when she looked up in surprise. "Knowing you as I do, I don't think you'd ever agree to marry a man unless you loved him completely."

Amber's head whirled. The guillotine operators didn't have anything on this guy. In fact, being beheaded would be far easier than having to sit here and listen to this. She wondered what satisfaction he could possibly derive from torturing her.

"And now that your obligations to the Pasetti Agency—and Madame Collette—have come to an end, I want to offer you a contract I hope you won't refuse. I promise it will bring you everything the agency and I personally have to offer. It's a marriage contract, Amber. Can you forgive me for hurting you? For being a world-class jerk?"

"Wh–what?" She couldn't believe her ears. "I don't understand. You don't love me, Anton. And even if you do, I can't—"

She could not bear the humiliation. From somewhere inside her, anger and hurt surged up. "You can't run my life for me. I'm through with the Pasetti Agency. I'm through with you. Love and marriage are far more than a piece of paper! But you wouldn't understand anything about that!"

He smiled sadly. "Of course I love you, Amber. I've loved you ever since the day you came to my office, looking like a scared little rabbit, but so determined to make a new start. I've loved you even when I was so angry with you I could have drawn and quartered you. . .or swept you off your feet with kisses and caresses." He paused, adoring her with his eyes. "I hardly dared believe that someone so lovely could be just as lovely on the inside. You seemed too good to be true. And, I must admit, the businessman in me was almost convinced, at times, that you were just another conniving female, jockeying for a career, but with a little different twist."

In spite of herself, Amber was fascinated. "I. . .I know how confusing that must be. Working with Madame Collette has taught me a great deal. And I've seen for myself that some people will do anything to get ahead."

"But there's more, Amber." He reached across the table and covered her hand with his own. "Since you've been away, I've made a commitment. . .to the Lord."

She jerked her hand away, blinded with tears of fury and indignation. "Now you really have gone too far with your games, with your pretending! And you almost had me believing that you—how could you lie about something so important?!"

He shook his head. "Please. . .there's one more stop we need to make."

He didn't touch her, but allowed her to struggle into her coat and follow him out to the car. They drove through the crowded streets, taking several turns until they emerged into a quiet neighborhood, by now endearingly familiar. To Amber's amazement, he pulled the car to a stop in front of the ivy-covered chapel where she had spent so much time, shed so many tears.

He opened her door and she got out reluctantly. "I don't see what—"

He silenced her with an uplifted hand. "Just give me a chance to explain."

He led her inside the now-deserted building, illuminated by candles flickering in front of the altar. She knew the little chapel by heart, could have found her way in the dark. She sat down at the back, ran her hand over the pew, worn smooth with time.

The moon through the stained-glass windows filtered onto Anton's upturned face. "I've had so many doubts, so much anger in me. But I wanted to believe. . .that God could take my pain from me, could forgive all the terrible mistakes. . .sins I've committed. But this industry is full of people just like me. They spend their lives, their money creating an illusion."

He turned to gaze down at Amber. "Until you came along, I had little evidence that faith really changes anyone. . .that it works, that it's real."

Amber held her breath. Was this the indomitable Anton Pasetti—a man willing to confess his faults? Willing to ask God to change him?

"I know now that the only real world is the world where God makes all things new. My mother tried to teach me. . .bless her heart. Charis and Len tried, too. And then God sent you. I've been going to the mission church, Amber, looking for whatever it was that gave you the courage and faith to start over. I found it. . .or rather, I should say, I found Him. But it was you who opened up that whole new world to me."

There was a very long pause before Anton continued. "Well, now you know the whole truth. I don't blame you for turning down my marriage proposal. I'm not nearly good enough for you. But I could send you to Rome, where you might find some good man. And don't forget Ron. He's waiting patiently back home in San Diego. As for me, I can understand why you could never trust me again. I've hurt you too much."

Amber rose to stand beside him in the aisle. Moonlight spilled over the pews, drenching them in a golden glow. "Yes, you did hurt me, Anton. . . but you had your reasons. God knew it was for the best. Otherwise, we might both have missed His best plan for us."

She saw the cool mask slip over his features again and hurried to finish what her heart leaped to say. "I think God knew what had to happen to bring us together. . .for the rest of our lives."

Almost as if in disbelief, Anton studied her features. "Darling, are you saying what I think you're saying?"

"Oh, Anton," she whispered, snuggling in his embrace, where she belonged, "I love you and, more than anything else in this whole new world, I want to marry you."

He held her as if he were afraid she might vanish into the night, as if she were some priceless object in the Louvre. "Are you sure, darling? Very sure?"

She pulled away just enough to look up at him, and cocked her head. "About that lifetime contract. . .where do I sign?"

The Fruit of Her Hands

Jane Orcutt

JANE ORCUTT lives in Texas with her husband and two sons. *The Fruit of Her Hands* was Jane's first book published with **Heartsong Presents**. She is now a multipublished author.

Dedication

To Kay Wiesmann and Carol Thomson—excellent wives, mothers, and sisters.
To Bill, Colin, and Sam for their love and patience.
Thank You, God, for the promise of Isaiah 42:3.

Chapter One

"Whatever happened to peanut butter in a kid's lunch, anyway?"

Grumbling, Henry Steelman jerked open cupboard doors, searching through the cans. Brian had asked for chicken salad, and chicken salad it would be.

A quick glance at the gold wristwatch elicited a groan. Tardiness was frowned on at the bank, and Clayton Fitzhugh probably wouldn't accept lunch making as a valid excuse, even from one of his officers.

"Aha!" Eager fingers gripped a can emblazoned with a smiling cartoon hen. "Gotcha, Miss Clucky! Now, if I can just find the mayonnaise. . ."

Thirteen-year-old Brian slammed past the kitchen's swinging door. "Can you put some egg in it? Last time it was awful! Just chicken and mayonnaise!"

"Sorry." Henry fumbled with the can opener. "You know I'm not used to cooking."

He laughed. "I never thought of chicken salad as *cooking* before."

Henry winced. How embarrassing. The kid was right, of course. No doubt he was even more skeptical about what was on the menu for dinner.

The opener slipped off the can and clattered to the floor. Exasperated, Henry sighed. "Can't you just buy your lunch?"

"Sure." Brian pushed back through the doorway. "But we used to get good lunches before."

Before. Henry leaned against a counter. Yes, before they'd all had it better. Better food, a cleaner house, the kids' homework done on time. . .

Henry smiled wistfully. "Spouses just shouldn't die."

When Leslie was alive, things had been different. Mornings had been pleasant affairs with lightly seasoned poached eggs, crisp turkey bacon, and exactly one and a half mugs of coffee stirred with a dollop of cream. Leslie knew all the family's favorite foods and all the daily, quirky schedules.

Les never would have forgotten that Brian had soccer practice on Tuesday afternoon or that Cindy's ballet lesson finished at five o'clock rather than five-thirty. Les would have known that Brian liked eggs in his chicken salad sandwich. Or how to make chicken salad in the first place.

Henry stared at Miss Clucky, feeling a smile rise at the hen's absurdity. Life did go on. They'd muddle through, somehow. Pastor Reynolds counseled it would take a long time to get over the shock.

Henry snapped a banana from the stalk, then absentmindedly reached in the knife drawer. Just a quick breakfast today. A big business lunch was always nourishing.

The banana peeled easily, and Henry chopped the banana into three neat sections. With the last stroke, the knife cut into flesh. Blood oozed from the wound and dripped over the pale yellow fruit.

"Can't *anything* go right around this house?" Tears sprang from weary eyes, smearing expensive mascara.

Eight-year-old Cindy burst into the kitchen, and her eyes widened with shock. "Mom, you're bleeding!"

Henry smiled weakly, reaching for a paper towel. She moistened it under water and wrapped her injured finger. "I'll be all right, honey." She drew herself up on three-inch-high Italian heels, shaking shoulder-length brown curls with resolution.

&

Henry entered the main suite of First Houston Bank's Personal Trust Department at exactly one minute after eight, walking with purpose and confidence. *This* was her world, the one where she fit and moved with ease. She'd known ever since she was a little girl that she wanted to work in a big office building just like her daddy. She'd worked hard to get where she was today. Les's death hadn't left the family financially destitute, but now more than ever, Henry needed to advance in her career. A vice presidency would mean greater security.

"Mornin', Henry." Joe Preston leaned out of his office. "You watch the football game last night?"

"Sure did," Henry said, suppressing a grimace. She'd meant to clean the bathtubs, but an interesting fumble had occurred in the middle of the second quarter to turn the tide of the game.

"Good morning, Mrs. Steelman." Louise, Henry's secretary, held out several envelopes. "These came for you late yesterday."

"Thank you. Anything exciting happen after I left early?"

"I'm afraid not." Louise smiled. "How was your daughter's ballet class?"

Henry pretended to study the mail. "It seems the class was over at five and not five-thirty like I thought. I not only missed seeing her rehearse, but Madame Corkly was ready to lock up by the time I got there. Cindy was pretty upset with me."

"That's a shame. You know, my mom keeps telling me that the kids are only young once. I hate when I miss something exciting like Tommy's first steps."

Henry shrugged, sifting through the mail. "Why don't you stay home with him, then?"

Louise lowered her eyes. "I'd love to but I have to work. We couldn't make it on Mark's salary alone. Maybe when he's through getting his master's degree. . ."

She trailed off and a smile reappeared. "I'm lucky I have my mom to watch Tommy. Someday I'll be home with him. It'd be nice if I had a househusband who—"

The mail stilled in Henry's hands and she froze, waiting for the inevitable backpedaling.

"Oh, Mrs. Steelman, I'm sorry. I forgot your husband. . .well, that is, that he. . ." She bit her lip.

Henry smiled. Usually the pussyfooting annoyed her, but she knew the young woman well enough to recognize sincerity. "I don't mind talking about him, Louise. Really."

"I. . .I'm sorry. I thought it wasn't polite to mention someone who's dead."

"I wish somebody *would* mention him. Les was the world's best husband, and I still want everybody to know it." Henry sighed. "But until I see him in heaven, I've got all kinds of work here on earth to do."

"Oh. . .oh. . .yes, ma'am." Louise backed toward her desk. "I didn't mean to keep you."

Henry smiled a farewell and passed the bustling cubicles of the clerical pool on her way to her own small office. She closed the door behind her for a few moments of privacy. Already exhausted, she plopped down in the swivel leather chair as though it were the end of the day instead of the beginning. She had barely stowed away her purse before someone rapped on her door then opened it without invitation.

Clayton Fitzhugh, manager of the bank's personal trust department, stormed in. A stern-looking man in his late fifties, he ran the department as a captain ran a ship. And right now Henry felt his exasperation like a pointed sword at her back, forcing her to walk the plank.

"You were late again, Mrs. Steelman. Our hours start at—"

"Eight o'clock sharp. I'm sorry, Mr. Fitzhugh, it's just that—"

Clayton braced his palms against her desk. "You've been here how many months, Mrs. Steelman?"

"Eight, sir."

"And in what capacity were you hired?"

"Trust officer, sir." Henry had the absurd inclination to stand and click her heels.

"And what's the next step on the promotional ladder for you?"

"Vice president, sir."

Clayton straightened. "Do you think it's wise to waltz in late every day? Or to leave early? Do you see the other officers doing this?"

"No, sir, but they're all men. They have wives who take care of—"

"No excuse!"

Henry jumped back in her chair and the casters squeaked.

"I will *not* give you special privileges because of your gender. Either be here on time or don't be here at all!"

"But, sir, my work is always done on time. And our customers always have good things to say about—"

"No excuse!" Clayton whirled and stomped out. Arms full of manila folders, Louise slipped through the doorway just before the door banged shut.

Henry exhaled a whoosh of air. "I guess you heard that."

Louise nodded, solemn.

Henry sighed. "I ought to be able to do all this. Other women do. It's a good thing I'm not ready to date."

"How will you know when it's time?"

"I've been wondering that myself, but I haven't met any man I like well enough. Brian and Cindy have made friends since we moved to Houston, and I think it's time for me to do the same. Outside of my sister, Mary Alice, I don't even know many other women."

"What about your church?"

Henry grinned. "As a matter of fact, I signed up to attend a cooking class there. My church is between the University of Houston and Rice, so we offer basic cooking classes for students. My first lesson is tonight."

"You mean. . .you really don't know how to cook?"

"I can barely boil water," Henry said cheerfully. "But lately my kids have looked a little thin, so I figured it was time to do something about it."

"Well. . .good luck," Louise said skeptically, pushing the folders across the desk.

Henry took the first one off the top and grinned. "Thanks. I'll need it."

Chapter Two

"Sorry to leave you with the cleanup," Henry said, waving at the pots and dishes stacked in the sink. "But if I don't make tracks, I'll never get to the church by seven-thirty."

Mary Alice eyed the mess and smiled breezily. "Don't worry about a few dishes, Sis. Just be sure to get there on time. I'm for anything that will help you learn how to cook."

"So are the kids." Henry grinned. "One bite of my meat loaf, and Brian clutched his stomach as though he were reenacting the stabbing of Julius Caesar. I don't think he was half-kidding, either."

Mary Alice headed her toward the door. "You'd better hurry. It's already seven, and you never know about downtown traffic."

Henry slung her purse strap over her shoulder and checked herself in the hallway mirror for suit wrinkles. Hopefully, no one would notice that spot of tomato sauce on her lapel. Maybe if she—

"Go!" Mary Alice gave her a more persistent shove and opened the door. "Have a good time!"

"I will. The kids are already doing their homework, and I told them they could have a snack later. Don't forget to—"

The door banged shut, cutting off her last instruction. "Guess she's tired of looking out for us," Henry said. She shrugged, unlocking her late-model four-door car.

As she drove from the suburbs to downtown Houston, Henry thought about her younger sister. Mary Alice had always enjoyed baking and cleaning house. No one in the family was surprised when she and her high school sweetheart married and immediately started a family.

Henry and Les had also married straight out of high school, but they had Brian just after they both graduated from college. Eight months pregnant, Henry had waddled across the stage to accept her business diploma.

She eased the car into one of the few available spaces in the church parking lot. That was nothing unusual. The church had a variety of evening classes for members and the community. Henry had already volunteered to help organize a food distribution program as soon as things were more settled at home.

She entered a side door, anxious to finally discover the mystery of cooking. Lots of people at the bank thought it was relaxing and even listed it as a hobby on their job applications.

Henry smiled. "Imagine doing something for fun that can be done just as well at a fast-food restaurant."

She rounded the corner to the kitchen. Examining the class roster outside was a tall, well-built man in a stylish gray suit.

Henry sucked in her breath. *My, my!* Was he really that good-looking or had she suddenly reopened her eyes to the male species?

As if he felt her stare, he turned and flashed her a bright smile. "Ah. There you are. I was afraid I was late."

"Excuse me?" Had they met before and arranged to meet here? Surely she would have remembered.

The stranger gestured at the kitchen, where younger men and women nervously examined pots and cooking utensils. "I was afraid they'd be mostly college age, and I was right. Everybody else has checked off their names on the list, but I see there's another man signed up."

"We're supposed to sign in?" Henry stepped closer to the sheet.

"Aren't you Vera Fabbish, the instructor?"

"The instructor?" Henry laughed, fishing a pen from her purse. "No, I'm afraid I'm one of the lowly students."

"But the only other name on the list is—"

"Henry Steelman." She checked off her name with a flourish then extended her hand. "Don't feel bad. People always mistake the name for a man's."

He looked her up and down. Bewildered, he shook her hand. "What's a *woman* doing at a beginner's cooking class?"

"Same thing you are, I guess," she said cheerfully. "Trying to learn how to master the basics."

"*Master?* You must be at least thirty years old. Are you telling me you don't know how to cook?"

His remark about her age deflated her usual good nature. "Thanks for the compliment. I'm thirty-five."

"Look, Miss Steelman. Just because—"

"It's *Mrs.* Steelman. And no, I can't cook. Good-bye."

Henry turned into the kitchen, flashing fake smiles at the other students as she strode to the farthest end of the room.

Rude man! Why were some people surprised when a woman didn't know how to cook? She certainly wouldn't insult him if he didn't know how to change a tire!

"Hello, hello!" a female voice boomed. "What a crowd tonight! You all flatter me with your presence."

Henry turned in time to see a corpulent, older woman in a multicolored flower muumuu enter the kitchen. A hot pink ribbon swept up her gray-streaked dark hair, and her warm eyes flitted from student to student as she nodded her greetings. In her left hand, she gripped the class roster. The other hand was in constant motion—shaking hands, touching a shoulder, ruffling the hair of a preteen. She called everyone by name, and everyone returned her greeting with enthusiasm.

"Tom, Paula, good to see young newlyweds. You can't live on love alone, you know. Even the first year of marriage. Ha–ha! Andrew, Steve, Mark—"

She stopped at Henry. "I don't believe I've met you, dear. I'm Vera Fabbish. Are you here with one of your children?"

Henry's smile felt weighted. "No. I'm here on my own."

Vera leaned closer. "Good for you!" she whispered. "Don't ever be afraid to try something new." She winked and moved on to the next student.

While Vera finished her rounds, Henry noticed that Rude Man had skulked inside and loitered near the door.

"At least I had the courage to march right on in," she muttered.

Vera took her place at the head of the stainless steel island, where she had a view of the entire class. "Who's here to learn how to cook?"

Silence. Everyone looked at each other, perplexed at the obvious question.

"Good." Vera beamed, leaning her palms on the counter. "Because this class isn't about cooking. It's about taking care of the ones we love and even those we don't. And sometimes," she grinned mischievously, "it's about just plain taking care of ourselves."

She straightened. "We all have to eat, right? Some would argue that it's not how fancy the food but how it's served. I agree. Jesus fed thousands of people with bread and fish, and I'll bet it was the best meal they ever ate."

"Did I wander into Pastor Reynolds's Bible study by mistake?" someone cracked.

The room laughed, Vera right along with it. "All right. I'll get off my soapbox. Let's start with a few questions so I can get a general idea of the class's experience. Who can bake a turkey they'd be willing to feed their in-laws?"

A few hands raised, Henry's and Rude Man's not among them.

"All right. Who can bake a casserole—of any kind—that they'd be willing to feed their immediate family?"

More hands shot in the air. Henry glanced away. Her eyes met then darted from Rude Man's, whose hand stayed at his side.

"Who can bake a potato, even in a microwave oven?"

All hands raised except Henry's and Rude Man's.

"Make a grilled cheese sandwich?" Vera said hopefully.

With a confident smile, Rude Man raised his hand. Henry studied the tomato spot on her lapel.

Vera looked at her. "Dear, can you butter bread?"

"Yes."

"And slice cheese?"

"Of course!"

"And you do know how to operate a stove top?"

The others burst into laughter. Henry managed a grin, wondering how much longer she could endure being the butt of the class's jokes. Even Rude Man laughed, the nerve of him!

"Quiet down, everybody," Vera said, motioning with her hands. "The point is that all of us have the skills to cook. We just don't always know how to put them together to come up with something palatable. And that's why we're here. Like everything else in life, cooking takes practice. Which we'll do here away from your homes, prying eyes, and disapproving taste buds."

A few people shot Henry apologetic glances, which she returned with a smile. Rude Man studied his nails. The corners of his mouth twitched.

"For this class, we'll work in teams of two," Vera said. "The goal is to encourage each other, not to tear down. If I hear one word of criticism, the offender will be forced to eat his own cooking!"

Her hot pink hair ribbon dangled over her ear as she squinted at the roster. "When I call your name, pair up along the counter here."

"Just like Noah's ark," someone mumbled.

"Andrew and Shelly—Tom and Grace. . ."

Henry noticed she rattled names off the list, not making any effort to match people who had obviously come to class together.

"Henry Steelman and. . ." Mrs. Fabbish squinted. "I can't read the signature, but the initials are R. M."

Henry stopped in midstride to the counter. *Rude Man? It couldn't be! Wouldn't that be a joke!*

"I guess that's me," a deep voice said behind her.

Henry turned, heart sinking at the sight of the handsome man's—*Rude Man's*—smirk. He took his place beside her, extending a hand. "I never got to introduce myself. I'm Rick Montgomery."

"Mr. Montgomery," she said coolly, clasping his hand in her best business handshake. His eyes crinkled at the corners.

"Good. That's settled." Vera beamed at the paired-off class like a proud matchmaker. "The first order of business is aprons. Then I'll arrange you all in your places and we'll start with breaking eggs."

Someone groaned. "That's not cooking!"

"Young man," Vera said sternly, "there's an art to cracking an egg and telling if it's fresh or not. Good cooks need to know both. Shelly, please pass out the aprons. Meanwhile, let's take our places."

Vera spaced the couples evenly down the counter, side by side. Henry and Rick didn't even look at each other as they dutifully tied large canvas aprons behind their necks and waists.

Henry finally glanced up. She'd seen Les wear an apron a thousand times, but never over a business suit. She laughed.

"What's so funny?" Rick smiled faintly.

"You! Instead of the Galloping Gourmet, you look more like the Bounding Businessman!"

Rick's smile deepened. "You don't look too realistic yourself with your own suit. Are you in cosmetics sales or something?"

Henry's laughter died, and she straightened. "I'm a bank officer."

Rick raised his eyebrows.

Vera set a crock of eggs between each couple and an empty bowl in front of each student. "Most people make their mistake by whacking the egg against the bowl like they're opening a can of biscuits. Tap the egg's circumference on the table, like this, then ease it open over the bowl."

The egg's contents dropped into the bowl without a sound. Vera set aside the shell. "Now each of *you* try," she said. "And remember, no wisecracks!"

Rick grinned at Henry. "Ladies first?"

"Age before beauty?"

He laughed. "I'm thirty-seven. You've got me there." He reached for an egg.

Henry noticed how tan his hands looked. His long, slender fingers curled around the egg in an oddly protective gesture and rolled it delicately in the curve of his palm. He had the hands of an artist or a musician, smooth and expressive.

He gently tapped the egg against the counter.

"It works!" Rick peered at the egg in his bowl, then proudly held up the even shell halves. "And not a speck of eggshell in the bowl."

He rested his hand near Henry's bowl. "Come on, it's your turn."

Unnerved, she picked up an egg. Her fingers shook as she tried to tap the egg on the counter. She carefully lifted the broken egg over her bowl.

Halfway there, the egg slipped from her grasp and plopped right on the back of his hand. She stared at the mess, mortified.

"Hey!" Rick swiped at the sticky blob with his apron.

Henry snapped to life. "I'm sorry! Let me help." She grabbed the hem of her own apron and knocked over his bowl. The puddle of goo headed in a dangerous stream for the edge of the counter, but Rick caught it with his apron. He rubbed the sticky edges together, then glanced up, smiling. "Yuck."

"Yuck is right," Henry said, embarrassed. "I am so sorry."

He propped an elbow on the counter and studied her. "It's okay, Henry. I've cleaned up my share of my own messes. Before she died, my wife always said I couldn't crack an egg. I guess you and I have that in common."

Henry forced a crooked smile. "Actually, we have a lot more. I'm a widow."

He stared at her a moment, then cleared his throat. "I'm sorry about how rude I was earlier. Will you let me make it up to you by going out for coffee with me after class?"

"Well. . ." She cocked her head, pretending to consider. "I really don't know you that well, Mr. Montgomery."

"What do you want to know? I'm a Houston native, I like golf, I—"

"Oh, save it for your coffee later!" Vera broke in. "Right now you're supposed to be cracking eggs." She turned to Henry. "He's been a member of this church all his life and that's recommendation enough, dear. You'll go with him, won't you?"

Henry held up her hands in mock surrender. "I guess I don't have a choice now!"

Vera's gaze traveled from the counter's gooey remains to their soiled aprons. "Not if you want to pass my class," she said dryly.

Chapter Three

"You're not going to insist on driving, are you?" Rick said as they walked out to the parking lot. "If you handle a car the way you crack eggs, I'd better make sure my insurance premium is paid up."

"No." Henry recognized his teasing tone. "This was your idea, so you're in charge."

Rick unlocked the passenger door of a maroon minivan in dire need of a wash. Henry squinted in the dim light then smiled. Someone had traced a heart in the grime on the passenger door.

The inside, however, was surprisingly clean, much tidier than the usual clutter Brian and Cindy managed to leave behind. The upholstery and dashboard gleamed as if straight from the sales lot. Henry sniffed, imagining she smelled fresh leather. Rick probably used the vehicle for professional purposes.

"New car?" she said as he started the engine and backed out.

"Last year. I bought it right after my wife died."

Henry stared down at her hands, starting when the windshield wipers clicked on and thumped downward. The windshield was covered with a light mist, a typical Houston wet spell that couldn't rightfully be called rain.

The minivan pulled up to a red light. Gathering her courage, Henry turned. "About your—"

"About your—"

They laughed, and Henry again noticed the corners of his eyes crinkled. The lines were endearing, proof he had a good sense of humor. He'd probably laughed a lot until his wife died.

"You first," she said quietly.

"No, you."

The light changed and the car eased into motion again. Henry pretended to study the windshield. "I'd like to hear about your wife. I usually appreciate the chance. People are always afraid to talk to me about my husband."

"I know what you mean. Once the funeral was over, hardly anyone ever spoke Nancy's name again."

Henry nodded. "It's especially hard for the kids."

Rick pulled the minivan into a parking space at the bookstore. He shut off the engine and gave her a curious stare. "How many children do you have?"

"Two. Brian's thirteen and Cindy's eight."

He shook his head. "I had no idea."

Before Henry could reply, Rick stepped out and reappeared at her side. He opened the door then frowned. "I hope you don't take this as an insult."

"Why would you think that?"

His gaze flickered over her suit as she stepped out. "You're the career type."

"I'm still a woman."

Rick's eyes twinkled. "I hadn't forgotten."

Henry's high heels clicked as she and Rick made their way across the wet asphalt and into the bookstore. Bright lights, classical music, and the aromatic fragrance of brewed coffee jolted her senses. Rick led the way to the café counter, and they paused to consider the list of exotic coffees and desserts.

"Hungry?" he said.

Henry made a face. "After cracking those eggs? No way!"

"Two hazelnut coffees, please," Rick said to the teenage girl behind the counter.

"Cream and sugar is at the next counter," the girl said indifferently, pouring coffee into thick mugs.

"Thanks." Rick counted out money then handed Henry her coffee.

She took a tentative sip of the steaming liquid. "Ummm."

Rick leaned against the counter, watching her. He smiled. "I'll bet you usually take cream."

Startled, she lowered her cup. "How'd you know?"

"All good executives do." He grinned. "At least the women. Men act like they have to prove something. They usually drink theirs black."

Henry ambled to the near counter. She used a light hand to pour cream, then held out the small pitcher. "And you? Do you have something to prove?" she teased.

"Me? No way." Still grinning, he took the pitcher and added a few drops to his cup. "I'm just an architect."

Henry took a long swallow to hide her pleasure. So he *was* artistic, after all. "What do you design?"

"Office buildings, mostly. My most recent work was the Stanhope Building."

"Really?" She looked at him with new respect. "I read how it won several awards. It's right next door to my bank."

"Then you must work at First Houston."

"Personal trust. I handle estates." She sipped her coffee. "At least the business aspect wasn't a surprise when Les died."

Rick's eyes glowed with sympathy. "Your husband?"

Henry nodded, tightening her grip around the mug. "He's been dead a year, come January. The kids and I moved down here from Nebraska. My sister's my only living relative, and I wanted to be near family."

"It helps. Fortunately, my parents still live here. Still go to the same church, even. They help out, but you know how difficult it is with kids."

Henry set her mug down with a thump. "You have children?"

Rick's mouth curved upward. "Does that surprise you?"

"I didn't make the connection. The minivan was so clean; I thought it was used to carry architectural projects or something."

Rick laughed. "*Or something* is more like it. I have four children."

"*Four?*"

"Graham's fifteen, Rachel's fourteen, John's nine, and Clara's two."

"My, my." Henry lifted her cup and took a long swallow. And she thought she had it rough!

"They're good kids," Rick said. "Graham and Rachel especially pitched in to help out when Nancy died."

Henry softened. "What happened to her?"

Rick toyed with his plastic stirrer. "The doctors found the cancer when she was pregnant with Clara, but there wasn't much they could do. She went fast after the baby was born."

"I'm so sorry," Henry whispered, absentmindedly laying a hand over his. "It must have been very difficult."

Rick glanced down. Embarrassed, she drew her hand away, but he clasped it in his own. "What about your husband?" he said gently.

"Car accident. He was going to the store, and he got hit by a drunk driver. He died before they could get him to a hospital."

"At least I had some warning," Rick murmured.

"I don't suppose it makes the pain any easier to take. Sometimes I miss him so much, I think about going to the backyard to scream my head off."

"Me, too."

Henry drew a deep breath to steady herself. It'd been a long time since she'd fallen apart, and she wasn't about to do it here—in the middle of a bookstore—with a near stranger. But he seemed to understand her grief.

"The worst," she said tentatively, "is that I feel like it's my fault."

"How do you figure that?"

Henry studied their clasped hands. "Les was a home-based freelance writer. He loved the whole domestic bit—cooking, cleaning, PTA meetings, car pools—everything. So I worked at an office and he took care of the home front. But if I'd been the homebody, maybe that accident wouldn't have happened."

Henry felt the pressure of Rick's hand increase. "That's ridiculous. You were doing what you enjoyed and so was he. Would you want him to feel guilty if you had been hit on a downtown street during your lunch break?"

"N–no."

Rick's hazel eyes shone warmly, gold flecks dancing. The crinkles had reappeared in a smile of sympathy.

"Finish your coffee," he said. "I'll be right back."

Henry obediently lifted her mug, swallowing the lukewarm liquid. Rick released her hand and headed for the book rows on the other side of the coffee area. She watched as his brown head disappeared among the stacks.

She swiveled her stool around to face the counter. What was wrong with her, anyway, to pour out her heart like that? She didn't have to make a fool of herself just because she and Rick had both lost a spouse, went to the same church, and couldn't cook!

Henry drained the mug and drifted outside the low iron rails separating the café from the bookstore. She glanced through several bargain coffee-table art books while keeping an eye out for Rick.

He soon reappeared, carrying a bag. To her surprise, he withdrew a hardback, placing it in her hands. "I want you to have this. It helped me a lot after Nancy died. I still read it occasionally when I feel down."

"*Blessed Are Those Who Mourn.* I've enjoyed several of this preacher's books already, but I've never heard of this one."

"I think you'll find it helpful. Read it, then get back to me. We can talk some more."

She felt the warmth of gratitude. "Thank you. That's very thoughtful."

Rick smiled. "We'd better get back. Graham and Rachel may have lost their good humor about baby-sitting, and your kids probably want to see you some more tonight, too."

Henry laughed. "They like to see me, but not anywhere near the kitchen. I made a meat loaf tonight that may turn them both into vegetarians."

Rick's eyes warmed. "Then you'll just have to be sure to come back to cooking class next week, won't you?"

They rode back to the church in companionable silence. At the lot, Henry pointed out her car, and Rick pulled up alongside.

"Be careful on the way home. There are a lot of kooks in this city."

Henry's fingers gripped the spine of the book. "Thank you, Rick. For the coffee, the book, and most of all, the sympathetic ear."

"Anytime," he said softly.

He stared at her a moment, and her heart lurched. Surely he wouldn't kiss her!

Her heart fell back in place. The thought was more appealing than she liked to admit.

Rick leaned back against his door and smiled. "Why do you call yourself Henry?"

She grinned, relieved the tension had broken. "My real name's Henrietta."

Without waiting for a reply, she opened the door.

Chapter Four

Mary Alice peered at her sister through a singed, bottomless, copper teakettle. "Tell me again how this happened."

"I decided to use some of that potpourri you boil in water. You remember that autumn-scented stuff we both got at the mall?"

Mary Alice nodded. "Go on."

"Well, just before breakfast last Saturday, I mixed some with water in the teakettle. Just like the directions said."

"Uh-huh."

"And I put it on the stove."

Mary Alice quirked a brow. "Did you set the burner on high?"

"Of course not! I put it on low."

"And then. . . ?"

Henry sighed. "And then later when I went to heat up some soup, I accidentally brushed my hand against the burner. Did I show you the blister I got on my finger? It popped just yesterday, but—"

"The teakettle?" Mary Alice prodded.

"Oh. Well, after I got through dancing around because of the blister and holding my finger under cold water, I remembered the kettle. I picked it up, but the bottom stuck to the burner. It could have happened to anybody!"

Mary Alice closed her eyes as though sending up a prayer for patience. "What time did you remember the kettle?"

Henry shrugged. "Dinnertime."

Mary Alice groaned. "You left it on the stove all day?"

Henry grinned. "I guess so."

"You *guess* so?" Mary Alice waved the pot at her sister. "You could have started a fire!"

"But I didn't!"

"No, but you sure did over here." Mary Alice stepped from the kitchen to the fireplace in the living room. She tapped a foot next to a burned spot in the rug. "What happened here?"

"Oh, that." Henry waved her hand. "The kids and I were watching the football game Sunday, and I decided to build the first fire of the season. But apparently I put too much wood on the grate, because in minutes we had an absolute blaze."

"Did a spark jump out?"

"No. The fire was so big, I decided to take out one of the logs with the tongs."

Mary Alice covered her face. Her shoulders shook.

"It's not that funny!" Henry put her hands on her hips. "I tried to make it to the porch, but the burnt end of the log fell off. If Brian hadn't been there to stamp it out, the hole would have been even larger!"

Mary Alice lowered her hands. "You don't just need a man. You need a *fire*man!"

"Very funny," Henry mocked, her voice rising in exasperation. "And please stop laughing!"

"I'm sorry." Mary Alice wiped away a tear. "You did ask me here to watch your kids, not to criticize."

"Yes," Henry softened, giving her sister a tentative smile. She grabbed her purse and headed toward the door. "I'll try not to be so late this time."

"Don't worry about that," Mary Alice called cheerfully. "If Rick asks you out for coffee again, by all means go."

Henry shut the door firmly and turned back to her sister. She narrowed her eyes. "What do you know about Rick?"

"I hear the talk. And you've obviously changed from your business suit to a very feminine dress. Come on, Henry, the least you could do is tell your own sister before I have to hear the gossip at church."

Henry groaned. "What gossip?"

"You two were seen heading out together for coffee after your first class last week. It seems you're cooking partners." Mary Alice grinned. "Or should I say you're *cooking?*"

Henry ignored her sister's teasing. "Who told you about the coffee?"

"April."

"April. . .April. . ." Henry failed to remember that name from her class. "April who?"

"April Logan. She heard it from Carole Swanson."

"Carole?" Again Henry drew a blank.

"She heard it from Mary Black—"

"I don't know any Mary!"

"Who heard it from Vera Fabbish."

Henry groaned. "Not Vera!"

Mary Alice winked. "You'd better watch out. The lady not only knows how to cook, she's the world's best manipulator. She'll have you and Rick married before you know it."

"That's ridiculous!"

"Vera grew up with his parents," Mary Alice said. "Apparently, Rick's only recently started coming back to church."

Henry softened. "Because of his wife?"

Mary Alice nodded. "He and Pastor Reynolds talked for several months, and now Rick wants to be an active member again."

Henry shook her head. She didn't have any business listening to this! She crossed her arms. "Is nothing about the man safe from gossip?"

Mary Alice's lips twitched. "You'd better move fast. He's not seeing anybody. Yet."

Henry gasped in exasperation. "Oh, really?" She yanked open the door. "Well, tell Mary and Carole and April. . .and whoever else. . .not to hold their breath."

Mary Alice laughed. "Henry!"

"*What?*"

Her sister smiled. "I hope you're holding yours."

"Dreamer!" As if she had time for a man!

❧

Rick was already aproned and arranging cooking utensils when Henry sidled up to the counter.

"Sorry I'm late, partner." Henry drew on an apron, tying it behind her neck. "What's on the menu tonight?"

He smiled. "Pumpkin pie. Since Thanksgiving's next week, Vera liked the idea."

"Mmm. Pumpkin pie is my favorite part of the holiday." She fumbled with the ties at her waist. "Wouldn't you know it? I think I've managed to knot this."

"Here. Let me."

Henry turned around and felt the warmth of Rick's hands on her back as his fingers worked nimbly at the knotted canvas. As he bent his head, she caught a whiff of cologne. She closed her eyes. A wave of nostalgia washed over her as she identified the scent. It wasn't what Les had usually worn, but it smelled clean and masculine.

He fastened a tight bow, and she turned back around. His gaze flickered over her apron and the soft blue dress underneath. "What happened to the suit?"

Henry glanced down, feeling like a high school girl. "I. . .uh. . .thought this might be more comfortable."

Rick's eyes warmed. "You look—"

Vera Fabbish appeared from nowhere and laid a hand on each of their shoulders. "How was the coffee?" she boomed.

All other conversation stopped and the rest of the class turned their way. Henry was certain her ears glowed red.

"The coffee was fine," Rick said casually.

"Good. Good. Now let's get to that pie." Vera winked at him, then waddled to the head of the counter. "Attention, everybody. Let's begin. First, you take. . ."

Henry and Rick worked together, following Vera's instructions. Occupied with measuring, mixing, and stirring, they didn't have any further time to speak. They'd scarcely poured the batter into the pie shell and congratulated themselves on their success when Vera whisked the completed pie from their hands.

"We'll bake all of these overnight and use them in the church's soup kitchen tomorrow," she said, lining up the pies by the oven.

"Is that what happened to all those eggs we cracked?" someone called out.

Vera nodded. "They made great scrambled eggs the next morning."

"Probably not my eggs," Henry whispered. Rick laughed and Vera shot them an approving look.

"Even your eggs, Henry," she said warmly. "Except the one you gave to Rick as a manicure."

Everyone laughed, and flush with the apparent success of their pie, Henry laughed along with them. This cooking business wasn't so bad, after all. Now she could bake something that at least *looked* edible.

Vera waved her hands. "Class dismissed. See you next week."

Henry reached behind to untie her apron, but Rick was already loosening the bow. "Can I interest you in another discussion over coffee? Or do you need to get back to your kids?"

She turned. "I'd love some coffee. I finished that book you gave me."

"Great." He smiled. "That gives us a topic to start with."

The drive in the still unwashed minivan was more animated than their first. They discussed not only the book, but a current spy movie, Pastor

Reynolds' Sunday sermon, and the merits of business lunches at several downtown restaurants. Rick told her about his architectural work, and she proudly related her accomplishments at First Houston while they waited in line for their coffee.

"My job has been good therapy since Les died," she said. "And I'm working hard to get a vice presidency."

He handed over a full mug, and they settled at the counter. "Why?"

Henry thought for a moment. "Security."

"Financial, you mean?"

She nodded as she sipped. "It's not just the money, though. It's the position. With two kids to raise and put through college by myself, I have to make sure I'm indispensable. That way, the bank can't ever fire me."

Rick stared at his mug as he swished the plastic stirrer in his coffee. "Don't you ever want to get more involved with your kids? Do PTA stuff?"

"I spend time with them. We play ball together, go to church—the same family bonding as everyone else. We just get together in the evening and on weekends like most single-parent families."

Rick still didn't look up. "If you didn't have to work, would you?"

"Yes." She laughed. "You already know I can't cook. I'm sorry to say the rest of my domestic capabilities are also sadly lacking. Even if I could manage, I don't think I'd be happy wrangling dust bunnies all day."

Rick didn't say anything.

When he dropped her off at her car, he still seemed quieter than when they'd first left. Henry took his silence for end-of-the-day weariness; she, however, was sorry to see the evening end.

"Thanks again for a wonderful time."

He smiled faintly. "Guess I'll see you next week. You did a good job on that pie tonight."

"*We* did a good job."

Rick cleared his throat and opened her car door. "Be careful driving home."

"I will."

He carefully shut the door. Smiling to herself, Henry started the engine. For the first time in a long while, she felt happy.

≥∴

The next few weeks passed slowly, even though work kept Henry busier than ever. She handled not only her own customers, but several others from overburdened coworkers.

Yet every time the phone rang, she scrambled for the receiver, only to hear about another estate crisis.

Why didn't Rick call?

Sitting at her desk, she nibbled on the end of her pen. She'd certainly thought she and Rick had something going, but apparently he didn't think so. He was exceedingly polite and even joked with her while they stumbled through each class, but he never again offered to take her out.

She opened another folder with determination. So he wasn't interested. She'd never become a vice president by mooning over a man like a love-struck girl.

A knock sounded at her door. "Mrs. Steelman?" The door swung inward and Louise appeared with an apologetic look. "I'm sorry to interrupt, but there's a woman to see you who claims she's here about the Montgomery estate."

Henry leafed through the folders on her desk, bewildered. "I'm not handling any Montgomery estate."

"She's awfully insistent. If you don't mind my saying so, I think you should speak with her."

Henry glanced at the stack of folders and sighed. "All right. Send her in."

She quickly scanned her desk for neatness and then she rose. Before she could adjust her suit jacket, a large figure swathed in a bright blue Mexican housedress swept into the office and firmly closed the door in Louise's face.

"Vera Fabbish!"

"Sit down, dear." Vera motioned at Henry's chair then plopped herself in an opposite seat. "We've got some talking to do."

Perplexed, Henry sat. "What estate—"

"Rick Montgomery." Vera pulled her chair closer. "That man needs you."

Henry leaned back in shock, then straightened. "I hardly think that's any of your—"

"It's plenty of my business and then some!" Vera nodded for emphasis then pulled a handkerchief from her large vinyl purse to mop her neck. "Boy! It's really sticky outside. Even for December. Even for *Houston!*"

Henry gripped her pen for patience. "About Rick?"

Vera popped the handkerchief back in her purse. Leaning forward, she lowered her voice. "He's crazy about you."

"Crazy? About me?" Henry laughed. "We're not even what you could call friends! We're just in the same cooking class."

"Oh, you think that's all, do you?" Vera's mouth curved in a superior smile. "Don't tell me you haven't noticed the way he looks at you...the way he makes excuses to get closer to you. Why, at the last class, even I could see from clear across the room how he held your hands."

"He was just showing me how to hold the cleaver." Henry hated to admit it, but she *had* felt a tingle.

"Then how do you explain the fact that he told his parents he met someone at his cooking class he wanted to date?" Vera smiled triumphantly as though she'd just baked a perfect soufflé.

Henry's heart lifted hesitantly. "He said that?"

Vera nodded with authority, blinking like an owl. "He said that."

Henry's heart crashed. "But we only went out twice for coffee. Surely he must have meant someone else."

"There isn't anyone else." Vera leaned forward. "But I have it on authority he won't ask you out because you're not domestic enough. He doesn't want to get serious about someone who isn't. He knows you can't cook. And he's heard rumors you can't keep house, either. Something about a copper kettle and a burned rug?"

Henry jammed the pen back into the holder. He'd avoided her because she didn't like keeping house? Because she wasn't Betty Crocker?

She struggled to keep her voice low. "I have a good job. I take good care of my kids. I *love* my kids. Isn't that what counts?"

"You don't have to tell me. You just have to convince Rick."

"*Convince* him?" Henry rose and flattened her palms on the desk. "I don't have to convince him of anything! I'm not some helpless female from the nineteenth century who needs a man to take care of her! And I don't need his caveman attitude!"

Vera stood. "But, dear, I'm here to help you. I wanted to offer you cooking lessons on the side. Maybe some housekeeping tips, too."

"I like the man, but I'm not auditioning to be his maid. So you can tell his parents or April or *February* or whoever else is in your gossip group that I'm not interested!"

Vera sighed, clutching her bulky purse. "All right, dear. I was hoping it would work out, but apparently not. Don't let what I've said destroy your friendship, though. You two really do work well together. Out of all my students, you and Rick have shown the most improvement."

Henry's anger dissipated like steam from a hot pan plunged in ice water. "Really?"

"Really." Vera nodded. "Good-bye, dear." She shuffled out of the office.

Deflated, Henry slumped to her chair. Imagine, all those people trying to throw her into Rick Montgomery's arms. And worrying that she didn't have the domestic skills he needed!

Henry straightened the items on her desk with unusual interest, swiping at a layer of dust. "It doesn't matter. If Mr. Montgomery is interested in love, he'd better call a housekeeping service!"

Chapter Five

"I give up," Mary Alice said, laying down her fork. "What is it?"

Henry's face fell. "Tuna casserole."

"This is tuna?"

"Benjamin!" Mary Alice poked her husband in the side.

"I thought it was chicken!"

Brian giggled along with his cousins, Caroline, David, Robert, Stephen, and Alison. "You did it again, Mom," he said, brandishing a fork.

Cindy slid out of her chair and stood next to Henry. "I like it," she said solemnly. "Especially the potato chips."

"Thank you, Cindy." Henry gave her a quick hug.

"But Dad always crunched the chips in the tuna casserole, brainless." Brian made a face at his sister. "You're not supposed to just throw them on top!"

"You're the brainless one. Brainless Brian, brainless Brian!"

"That's enough!" Henry said. "And, Brian, if you didn't like the casserole, why'd you have two helpings?"

Cindy snickered and returned to her chair. Henry flashed her a disapproving look, but she inwardly smiled at her daughter's defense. At least somebody appreciated her attempts.

Mary Alice sighed. "I wish we weren't going to Ohio for Christmas. It doesn't seem right to leave you three alone."

"We'll manage," Henry said. "You need to be with your mother-in-law. After all, she's in a nursing home, and she especially needs family this time of year."

Mary Alice bit her lip. "Can't I at least fix you a dinner in advance? Something you could heat up for Christmas Eve and Christmas Day?"

"Nonsense! Vera showed us how to fix a turkey and green beans. We'll have a Christmas Eve feast that can't be beat!"

"Yeah. Literally."

"Brian!"

"Excuse me." He threw his napkin down and bolted from the table. He dashed down the hallway for his room. They heard the door slam, followed by a radio's blare.

Benjamin gave Henry a pointed look. "That boy needs disciplining. His attitude will just get worse as he gets older."

Henry collected plates with more force than necessary. "He's not a horse I'm trying to break. He's just a teenage boy trying to understand why his father had to die so suddenly."

"Of course he is," Mary Alice said soothingly, casting her husband a reproving glance. "But he is growing up, Henry. He hates it when you send me over here to baby-sit for him and Cindy. He's big enough to take care of them both. He is thirteen."

Henry stopped short. "I hadn't noticed how much he'd grown up. We've spent the past year just trying to cope with everything."

She set the plates down. "I need to talk to him right now."

Henry followed the radio's screeching electric guitar down the hall. As usual, Brian's door was closed. Hand poised to knock, she stared at the "No Trespassing" sign as if for the first time. Why had she let her son hide in there so long? She and Cindy were resilient enough to nurse their hurt alone and together, as needed. Somehow, she'd ignored Brian's veiled pain.

She knocked on the door, then pounded with her fist when she knew she hadn't been heard. "Brian? Open up. We need to talk."

"Go away!"

"Brian, please open the door. I don't care what you said about my cooking. I want to talk to you about something else."

The music abruptly clicked off and the door opened a crack. Eyes red, Brian stared at her through the sliver of space.

"Either let me in or you come out," she said quietly.

He stepped back, shrugging. "Whatever."

"Thanks." She stepped into his private lair. Dirty clothes littered the floor, and a half-eaten sandwich moldered on the cluttered dresser. Henry pushed down her dismay. A reprimand could come later.

She casually pushed aside several pairs of blue jeans and sat on the unmade bed. "It's been pretty difficult for you since Dad died, hasn't it?"

Brian scuffed the toe of his sneaker at a pile of dirty T-shirts. "I still miss him," he said grudgingly. He offered a bleak smile. "I'm sorry I've teased you about your cooking. I know you're doing the best you can. It's just. . ." He turned away. "It's just not the same. Nothing's the same."

"It'll never be like it was when your father was alive," Henry said. "Not just the cooking, but everything. If we all pitch in and do the best we can,

I think one day we'll find ourselves happy again."

Brian turned back. "You're not happy? I know you miss Dad and all, but you're always so cheerful. And you never cry. I thought I was the only one who couldn't handle it."

Henry smiled. "I'm happy because I still have you and Cindy. And I cry, but not when you're around. I didn't want you to know I was still having trouble, too. Maybe that's our problem—not telling each other how we feel."

She cleared her throat. "Speaking of which, your aunt tells me you've been upset about her staying with you and Cindy when I go to cooking class."

Brian straightened. "I'm big enough to look out for us. We don't need Aunt Mary Alice to baby-sit!"

"No, I guess you don't." Henry stopped herself from ruffling his hair. "When my cooking classes resume after the holidays, we won't call her anymore."

"Can I get paid for watching Cindy?"

Henry grinned. "No. But I'll be glad to pay you for doing extra chores around the house, like painting or cleaning screens."

"Aww, Mom!"

Rising, Henry glanced around the room. When had the Donald Duck posters turned into movie heroes, the curtains from trains to a sedate solid color? She could remember Brian passing from elementary school to junior high, but when had he changed, too?

"This will be a rough Christmas," she said softly. "And I'm taking some extra time off around the holidays. The three of us can start new traditions this year."

"I'll still miss Dad." Brian sniffled once, then tentatively put his arms around his mother.

Henry kissed his wet cheek and held him close, grateful for the hug. "So will I, Brian," she murmured.

≈

They missed him more than they could have possibly predicted. They missed not only his presence, his laughter, his singing Christmas carols off-key, but his ability to place the star on the top of the seven-foot-high tree.

Henry stretched on her toes, but she lost her balance and fell into the tree, knocking it over. After disentangling herself from the sticky pine branches, she took one look at the puddle of spilled water and wanted to cry. Instead, she blithely asked Cindy and Brian to fetch towels while she placed the star on the tree—still laying on its side—then smugly righted it.

They missed Les when they took their annual drive to see the Christmas lights. He had known all the best neighborhoods and always took the family out for hot chocolate afterward. But Henry couldn't find any good light displays, and she forgot to bring her purse.

The worst disappointment of all occurred on Christmas Eve. Their tradition was to eat their big meal and open presents that night, then help in the soup kitchen on Christmas Day. Christmas Eve dinner was always ham, and Henry thought it fortuitous that Vera had taught the class how to cook a turkey. Maybe the change in menu would be good for the family.

Proud as a new mother, she lovingly basted the bird and shoved it into the oven before breakfast. By noon the turkey still looked raw.

"That's funny." Henry tested with her hand. "It still feels cold." She shrugged. "Oh well, back in the oven!"

Four hours later, the bird had scarcely pinkened in color. Henry's fears mounted, but she kept a cheerful front and turned up the oven's heat.

Two hours later, she was ready to cry. Instead of warm, juicy white meat, the bird could barely be stabbed with a knife.

Cindy tugged at her sleeve. "Mom? Maybe you were supposed to thaw the turkey first."

Henry exhaled with exasperation. "Of course! Any idiot would have known that."

Brian grinned. "What if we start a new tradition by having pizza on Christmas Eve?"

"That's hardly fitting for such a special holiday."

"Please, Mom?" Cindy's eyes shone. "That'd be fun. Like a special treat."

Henry softened at Cindy's pleading. "I guess we could always eat the green beans along with—the green beans!"

She dashed for the stove and flung the lid from the saucepan. Smoke hit her face. She coughed, waving her hand. Blackened mush stuck to the bottom of the pan.

Dismayed, Henry stepped back from the stove. What kind of a mother was she, anyway, to burn half a holiday meal and undercook the other half?

She leaned against the counter, shoulders shaking as she suppressed her tears. *Oh, Les, how you'd laugh at me. You used to think it was cute that I couldn't cook, and you joked about being my protector in the kitchen. But it's not funny anymore.*

She felt a hand on her arm. "It's all right," Brian said. "You go get the pizza. Cindy and I'll clean up the kitchen."

"Can I have pepperoni?"

Henry glanced from Brian's face to Cindy's, both lit with hope and the wonder of the season. They obviously didn't care about the menu. Maybe she shouldn't, either.

"They say Christmas is a time to forgive." With a sigh, she reached for her purse.

❧

Henry clutched her red wool coat close as she scurried into the pizza parlor. She'd thought about ordering ahead or even having the pizza delivered, but decided in favor of the extra time alone. She'd nearly broken down in tears there in the kitchen. If she started crying, Cindy and Brian might, too. Then they'd all be miserable.

A bell tinkled as she pushed open the door. At least these people were happy. The jukebox blared "Jingle Bell Rock," and all the employees wore Santa stocking caps and had holly pinned to their uniforms.

"Merry Christmas!" A teenage boy grinned broadly. "What kind of pizza are you ordering to leave for Santa?"

Henry smiled in spite of her gloom. "He's told my family he wants one pepperoni and one cheese. Both medium, thin crust."

"Coming right up. There's coffee by the jukebox while you wait."

Henry shivered, remembering the chill outside. "Thanks."

She wandered to the coffeemaker and poured herself a large Styrofoam cupful. She was reaching for the artificial creamer when a masculine hand covered hers.

"You mean you even drink this poor imitation of coffee?"

Heart thumping, Henry gazed up into a teasing face. "Rick! What are you doing here?"

He shrugged boyishly, handing over the creamer. "The same as you. Waiting for Christmas Eve dinner."

Henry glanced around the restaurant. "Is your family here?"

"No, I ordered carryout just a few minutes ago." He shoved his left hand into the pocket of his overcoat, and Henry noticed his right hand held a nearly full cup of coffee.

She nodded at an empty booth. "Why don't we wait together?"

He smiled in reply, following as she slid across a red vinyl cushion. He sat on the other side of the table, raising his eyes to meet hers.

"How've you been, Henry? I haven't seen you since our last class. I haven't even seen you at church on Sundays."

"I've been going to the early service." She sipped her coffee and shrugged. "And I've been all right."

Rick covered her free hand with his. "The first Christmas is rough."

She bowed her head. "Yes. It's been one disaster after another."

"Want to tell me about it? You're talking to someone who's been there." He paused. "Who's still there."

"It's still hard even after a couple of years, isn't it?"

"Yes." He glanced out the window. "I came here to get away from the kids for a few minutes. I needed some time alone to think about Nancy. Christmas was always special to her."

Henry smiled. "It was for Les, too. It's just not the same without him. Everything's different."

"Even the cooking?" Rick smiled faintly, teasing.

Henry returned the grin. "Especially the cooking. Why do you think I'm here?"

Rick laughed and squeezed her hand. "You're one of a kind, Henrietta Steelman."

Henry felt the warmth of his hand rush through her, a soothing balm to her wounded heart. "You're one of a kind, too, Rick," she said softly. "Not many men would take a cooking class so they could learn to feed their family better."

They fell silent. Rick clasped her hand in both of his. "Why've you been so quiet during the last few weeks of class? You don't strike me as the type to suddenly turn shy."

Henry's pulse raced. "I didn't want you to think. . ."

"What? That you were interested in me?"

Henry nodded. "Vera said you didn't want to date me because I wasn't domestic enough."

He looked at her for a long moment. "Vera Fabbish is a busybody," he said in a low voice. "Will you go with me to the New Year's Eve party at church?"

She felt hypnotized. His hazel eyes made her feel like a schoolgirl all over again. He might as well have asked her to the junior prom.

"I'd love to go," she whispered.

"Montgomery! Your pizzas are ready!"

Rick smiled and released her hand. "I'll pick you up a week from to-night. Seven-thirty."

Henry nodded. They moved to the counter. Rick paid the boy, then reached for his pizzas.

Just before his hands gripped the cardboard, he turned. "Merry Christmas, Henrietta," he said softly, then leaned over and brushed his lips across her cheek.

Before she could react, he pointed at the ceiling above the cash register. Mistletoe hung from the ceiling.

Stunned, Henry tried to compose herself. "Merry Christmas to you, too."

She watched as he ferried the cartons to the door. The bell tinkled merrily as he exited, and she turned back to the cash register with a sigh.

"Your pizzas are ready, too," the boy said, plunking down two cartons. He glanced over her shoulder at the door and grinned. "Did Santa bring you a boyfriend?"

"I'm not sure," she said, still bewildered. "I'm beginning to hope so."

Chapter Six

"You've got a date!" Dreamy-eyed, Cindy stared at Henry's reflection in the mirror.

"A minivan just pulled up in the driveway," Brian yelled from the front hallway.

"It's not really a date, Cindy," Henry said, rising from the vanity stool. She checked herself in the mirror a final time then reached for her evening bag. Funny. Her hands were trembling. "It's more like a. . .a. . ."

"He's getting out of his car!"

Henry took a deep breath and patted her hair. Cindy tugged at her hand. "Come on!"

"He's coming up the walk!"

Henry rounded the corner and saw Brian peering out the front door's peephole. Cindy bounced on the toes of her sneakers. "Mom's got a date! Mom's got a date!"

"Cindy," Henry said sharply. "It's not a—"

The doorbell rang.

Everyone froze. Brian pulled back from the door as if in shock, and Cindy's squeaky shoes silenced. Henry nervously smoothed the skirt of her crepe dress. "Open the door, Brian."

He threw her a tormented look, then yanked open the door.

"Hi. You must be Brian."

"Yeah," he mumbled, stepping back. He shot Henry a killing glance.

Henry stepped forward. "Come in, Rick." Her voice seemed an octave too high.

Rick entered, smiling. He held out a long-stemmed yellow rose. "A belated welcome to Texas."

She accepted the flower, inhaling its fragrance with appreciation. "How lovely. And especially this time of year. Thank you."

His dancing eyes met hers, and she inhaled sharply. Under his opened black coat, he wore a stylish light charcoal suit. Freshly polished black shoes complemented the outfit. His gaze flickered over her as well, and she was glad she'd chosen the simple elegance of a basic black dress and pearls.

Rick cleared his throat, turning to Brian and Cindy. "Did you two have a good Christmas?"

Cindy nodded. "I got a new Barbie doll."

"My daughter, Rachel, has a whole collection she's outgrown. But I'm sure she'd love to have you come play with them at our house."

Henry warmed at Rick's overture. Not only was he kind, he was suggesting the two families should get together.

"This is Cindy," Henry said, stepping beside her daughter. "And this is Mr. Montgomery. He's in my cooking class."

Cindy beamed. "Hello, Mr. Montgomery."

"And Brian."

Brian stared down at his shoes.

"Hello, Brian." Rick held out his hand. Startled, Brian glanced up. He gulped, then extended his own hand.

Cindy jammed her hands against her hips. "What about me? Mom says even women should learn how to shake hands. It's good business."

"Oh, is it?" Rick cocked an eyebrow at Henry, who hid a smile behind her rose. Rick made a serious face and extended his hand to Cindy. "How do you do, Miss Steelman? It's a pleasure to make your acquaintance."

"I'm very well." Cindy pumped his hand once and simultaneously nodded. "Thank you."

Smothering a laugh, Henry retrieved her coat from the closet. "Mr. Montgomery and I have to leave now. There are snacks on the counter and the number of the church is by the phone. You and Brian may stay up until midnight, then off to bed."

Brian straightened. "I'll take good care of Cindy. We'll watch the video you let us rent."

Rick took Henry's coat from her hands and held it up behind her. "Allow me."

She eased her arms into the sleeves and shrugged into the coat. He straightened the narrow collar, then his hands drifted downward to linger on her shoulders.

"Thanks," she murmured. The pressure from his hands unsettled her composure. He didn't seem in any big hurry to release her. She could almost feel him lean against her, could feel his lips near her hair.

Henry turned. Rick gazed down at her with a slow-spreading smile.

"Are you ready?" he said, taking her hand.

She nodded. "Have a good time, kids."

Rick turned to Brian and said soberly, "I'll take good care of your mom."

Brian nodded, straightening even more at the man-to-man assurance.

Rick kept a hand at Henry's elbow as they crossed the flagstone path to the driveway. When they reached the van, she burst out laughing.

He frowned. "What's wrong?"

Henry pointed, even though she knew it wasn't mature. "Your van. It's washed!"

"My father gave me a book of car wash coupons for Christmas."

Henry laughed. "I'll miss the heart on the door."

"That was Rachel's handiwork. She was mooning over some boy at school." He grinned. "You didn't think I drew it, did you?"

Flashing him a teasing glance, she shrugged. "How do I know what new architectural design you might be considering?"

Laughing, Rick shut the car door after her.

Warm yellow lights bathed the outside of the fellowship hall. Henry was pleased the parking lot was full. All the adult Sunday school and community classes had been invited, and judging from the loud party chatter, many people had chosen to share the festive occasion. In just a few short hours, it would be a new year, with new possibilities and hope.

She smiled and Rick squeezed her hand. "Happy?"

She nodded. "It's been a long time since I've been to a party."

He studied her a moment. "Me, too," he said softly. "Too long."

They stepped up to the welcome table where a teenage girl took their coats for safekeeping. They had barely set foot inside the hall's doorway when Vera Fabbish broke away from a small knot of conversationalists.

"Well, look who's here!" her voice trumpeted as she advanced on them. She wore a tight black dress studded with iridescent sequins. A large, live poinsettia bloom perched behind her ear as though it had taken root at the back of her neck.

"Hello, Vera." Rick bent over and kissed her powdery cheek. As he straightened, she giggled, flushing, and turned to Henry.

"Isn't he a wonderful man? His parents are over there, dear. I know they'll be glad to meet you."

Oh, no. Henry had known people would whisper about her and Rick, but she hadn't realized his parents would be present.

Rick leaned closer. "Don't worry," he whispered, taking her hand again.

He flashed a dazzling smile at Mrs. Fabbish. "Are you here alone?"

She fanned a ring-studded hand and giggled again. "Good gracious, boy. I'm here with *all* my friends!"

Rick laid a hand over his heart and rolled his eyes heavenward. "Surely there must be someone special? Mr. Graves the janitor, perhaps?"

To Henry's amazement, Vera flushed crimson. Her mouth opened and closed like a catfish, but no sound came out.

"Don't worry." Rick smiled, then leaned forward. "I won't tell," he whispered dramatically.

Vera's complexion returned to its natural color, and she drew herself to her full five-foot, four-inch height. "Richard James Montgomery, you'd better *not* breathe a word to anyone or I'll. . .I'll. . .tell your mother! Mr. Graves just doesn't know yet that I. . .I. . ."

"Adore him?" Henry put in, linking her arm through Vera's. "How will he know unless you tell him?"

"Well, I. . ."

"Of course," Rick put in, flanking Vera on the other side, "I suppose two well-meaning friends could speak on your behalf if you're shy."

Vera glared. "Don't you *dare!* "

Afraid any laughter would be construed as an insult, Henry pulled away. "We're only teasing, Vera. Please forgive us."

"We just want to see you happy," Rick added.

Vera glanced from him to Henry. "Seems to me I see two people who are awfully pleased with themselves," she grumbled. "Picking on a poor, defenseless old woman!"

Henry laughed gently. "Vera Fabbish, the day you're old and defenseless is the day I'll become a. . .a. . ."

"Cordon bleu chef?" Vera suggested mildly.

Henry laughed again. "Exactly!"

Rick took Henry's arm to guide her away. "Have a good evening, Vera," he called over his shoulder.

Still chuckling, he led Henry to the punch bowl, where they accepted two full glasses from the server. Henry sipped from hers, noticing the crinkles hadn't faded from around Rick's eyes.

"You *are* awfully pleased with yourself, aren't you?" she teased. "How'd you know about Mr. Graves?"

Rick laughed. "My mother told me. I really do want to see Vera happy.

The woman's had a sad life. She never married and had kids of her own, so she tends to take people under her wing. Whether they want it or not."

"She's certainly taken a personal interest in us. She came all the way to my office to offer me extra cooking lessons and housekeeping tips."

"To snare me?" Rick asked, grinning.

"Something like that." Henry dropped her gaze to her punch.

She glanced at the few people clustered around the punch table, then backed away to the wall. Rick followed, smiling quizzically. "What?"

Henry set her glass on the windowsill. "We might as well set things straight right now. I'm sure that what Vera said was true. You're probably more interested in dating a domestic woman. Not someone who's all thumbs, and brown thumbs, at that."

Rick set his glass beside hers. He stretched out his hand as though to touch her, then glanced around and dropped it at his side. "Look, Henry," he said quietly. "You've jumped ahead of me, but you might as well know my intentions. I had some time to think these last few weeks. I do want to date you. I want to get to know you better. You may not be Betty Crocker, but you have a lovely woman's heart. You care about your kids, your job, and other people. Most of all, you laugh at yourself when you make mistakes and you keep trying. That's a very rare gift. Especially for someone in the business world."

His hazel eyes locked with hers as he moved closer, and she felt rooted to the floor. The room's conversations eddied around her, dropping to an indistinguishable hum.

"Since we're *setting things straight*, I'm going to give you fair warning," he continued, his voice low and husky. "I intend to kiss you at the stroke of midnight, Henrietta Steelman, from the first chime to the last. And I *will* see you again—as often as you'll let me—during the coming year. If you have any objections, say so now."

Henry's mouth went dry and her palms damp. What was wrong with her composure tonight? She was a career woman!

"Henry?"

She forced herself to breathe. "I want to see you, too, Rick," she whispered.

He held out his hand, smiling. "Good. Now that everything's straight between us, are you ready to mingle?"

Henry smiled and placed her hand in his. "Lead on."

And he did. Straight to his parents. Henry's stomach had barely righted itself when he led her across the room to a well-dressed older couple. She knew immediately from the family resemblance they were Mr. and Mrs. Montgomery.

"Richard!" The man clapped a hand on Rick's shoulder. "So you made it, after all!" He smiled warmly at Henry, glancing from her then back to his son.

"I told you I was coming. And that you'd get a chance to meet—"

"How do you do, my dear?" The silver-haired woman interrupted, taking Henry's hand. "If we depend on these two, we'll never get acquainted. I'm Mary Montgomery."

"It's a pleasure to meet you, Mrs. Montgomery." Henry smiled at the woman's warmth. "I'm Henrietta Steelman."

The woman squeezed Henry's hand once more before releasing it. "Please call me Mary."

"Only if you'll call me Henry. Henrietta was my great-aunt's name."

"Henry?" Mr. Montgomery chuckled. "That was the name of my first business partner. It's a good, strong business name."

"Henry's a good businesswoman, Dad." Rick turned to her, smiling. "This is my father, Allen Montgomery."

Allen chuckled, pumping her hand several times. "The pleasure's all mine. Rick's been moping around the house for weeks now. Even the children have started to complain."

Mary smiled. "Have you met Rick's children, Henry?"

"No. We haven't known each other long."

Mary drew Henry aside, turning away from Rick and his father. The men started a spirited business discussion.

"Rick's been moping because of you, dear," Mary said softly. "He finally confessed when I pried it out of him."

She paused, her eyes warm. "I hope you don't think I'm interfering by telling you. It's just that Rick's been so unhappy since Nancy passed away. When he first mentioned you, his face lit up like it hasn't for a long time. You're the first woman he's been interested in since she died."

"I feel the same way, Mary."

Rick wrapped an arm around each woman. "Hey, you two, no secrets!"

Mary playfully swatted her son on the shoulder. "No secrets, indeed. This is New Year's Eve. You two go chat with somebody closer to your own age. Have a good time. You don't want to stick around the old fogies."

Allen winked at Henry. "Besides, I think I saw Vera Fabbish coming this way. She claims she threw you two together. If you don't hurry, she'll start crowing and won't leave you alone all night."

"We already ran into her," Henry said.

Rick smiled. "She'll probably steer clear of us for a while."

Mary's face fell. "You didn't tease her about Mr. Graves, did you? Oh, Rick!"

"We only offered to help her budding romance by letting the poor man know her feelings. After all, she's meddled in our relationship already. Maybe it's time we helped her out."

"Don't you dare!" Mary took another swat at Rick, this time less playful. "Vera Fabbish is one of my oldest, dearest friends. If you upset her, you'll have to answer to me!"

Rick laughed and held up both hands. "All right, Mother. We promise to be good, don't we, Henry?"

"Yes, ma'am," Henry said solemnly, nodding.

Rick moved closer and casually draped an arm around her shoulder. "But we'll take your advice and make the rounds. See you two later."

"Good-bye, dear." Mary smiled at Henry. "It was lovely meeting you. Don't wait for an invitation. Come over to the house anytime."

"Thank you, Mary," Henry said. "It was nice meeting you, too, Mr. Montgomery."

"Allen. And the invitation goes double with me."

Henry and Rick chatted with fellow cooking students and their respective Sunday school class members, even making new friends. Though the church had three services every Sunday morning, people welcomed strangers like lifelong friends. Henry wondered how long it would have taken her to meet Rick if they had never signed up for the cooking class.

Several times during the night, she surreptitiously glanced at her wristwatch. Her stomach danced every time she remembered Rick's promises for midnight. Would he really kiss her in front of all these people? How tongues would wag!

By eleven-thirty, Henry and Rick sat at a large table. They had managed to avoid Vera all night, but she must have forgiven them. With a big smile, she plopped down in the chair next to Henry.

She glanced at Henry, then Rick, who was involved in a discussion with the man seated next to him. She peered at Henry's watch and grinned. "You know what happens at midnight, don't you?"

Henry nearly choked on her punch. "Wh–what?" How could she have overheard their conversation?

Vera drew back in apparent surprise. "Why, we sing 'Auld Lang Syne,' that's what!"

"Oh, that!"

Vera eyed her suspiciously. "What did you think I meant?"

"I wasn't sure." Henry shrugged innocently. "I thought maybe the church had some special tradition."

Rick leaned forward. "What's this about tradition?"

"Vera and I were discussing midnight traditions. Do you know any?" Rick winked at her.

Eleven-fifty. Someone brought out party hats and blowers. Eleven fifty-five. One of the servers filled all the glasses with punch for toasting. Eleven fifty-eight. Everyone pushed back from the table.

Rick lazily took Henry's hand and eased her away. "Come on, Henry. Let's—"

"Where do you two think you're going?" Vera clamped a hand on their arms. "You'll miss the party!"

Henry's stomach dropped. "But, Vera, we—"

"Nonsense!" She steered them back to the table. "I wouldn't dream of letting you miss the fun."

Miserable, Henry forced a smile.

"Everybody lift your glass," Vera commanded, raising hers.

Rick raised his glass and smiled apologetically at Henry. Disappointment knifed through her, not only from the lack of the kiss, but from the expression on his face. He might kiss her good night at her door later, but it wouldn't be the same as at midnight.

"Oops!" She wobbled on a high heel and bumped into Rick. Punch splashed his shirt, and her eyes widened. "Oh, Rick, I'm so sorry!"

He dabbed at the spot with a napkin. "It's all right. It's—"

"Come on!" She grabbed his hand. "Excuse us, everybody! If we don't get the punch out right now, it'll make a permanent stain."

"But you'll miss the midnight celebration!" Vera wailed.

"Can't wait, Vera." Henry tugged at Rick's hand. "Let's go!"

They escaped through the maze of people, who ignored their departure in favor of the countdown. "Ten. Nine. . ."

Heels clicking against the linoleum, Henry pulled Rick down several well-lit halls to the darkened kitchen.

"Slow down!" Rick said. "It's just a little punch!"

She pulled him into the kitchen. Dim light spilled in from the hall and across the steel counters. Henry's heart pounded as she pulled him to the back of the room.

Even in the shadows, she could see his face switch from confusion to understanding. He laughed. "You deliberately spilled that punch."

"You weren't going to kiss me in front of that mob, were you?"

Rick's laughter died out. He moved closer, his voice lowering. "It crossed my mind, but no, probably not. Especially with Vera watching us like a hawk."

They heard muffled shouts and blowers.

Rick pulled her close, then cradled her face in his hands. "You're a special woman, Henry," he murmured as his face moved closer. "Happy New Year."

"Yes. . .Happy New Year," she echoed just before his lips pressed against hers.

The pounding in her ears drowned out the faint strains of "Auld Lang Syne." She was certain her heart beat in sync with each stroke of midnight. But just when she thought the minute was up, Rick pulled back, only to kiss her again.

At last he broke the kiss, but he dropped his arms around her to pull her even closer. She encircled his waist with her arms. How different it felt to be with another man than Les, yet how right. Rick had revived the heart she'd thought had stopped for good, the heart she'd thought could never love again.

"Would it frighten you if I said I'm falling for you in a big way?" he said softly.

Henry pressed her cheek against his shoulder, reveling in the scratch of his wool jacket. What a safe, masculine touch.

"I'd be frightened only if you don't want to hear the same from me," she murmured. "I never thought I'd be so happy again."

"I didn't, either." His hand stroked her hair, and he nuzzled his cheek against her forehead. "This is why I wanted to kiss you at midnight. I want to begin the new year with you. I have a feeling this is going to be a great year."

"A *great* year," she echoed, raising her face for another kiss.

The kids were healthy, the bills paid, and now she had Rick. She'd work harder to get that vice presidency, then life would be complete.

Chapter Seven

"And Mrs. Redwine called, and Mr. Tate, and. . ."

Henry absentmindedly accepted the pink telephone message slips from Louise, only half-listening to the secretary. She'd been back at work two weeks since the holidays, since New Year's Eve, and her heart still soared whenever she thought about Rick—which seemed to be all the time, lately.

"Then there's the Sampson estate." Louise plopped down a huge manila folder on the desk, jarring Henry back to reality. "You have a lunch date with Mrs. Sampson."

Henry blinked. She and Rick had planned to eat together. "Lunch? With Mrs. Sampson?"

Louise nodded, her blond curls swaying. She sat down tentatively, glanced over her shoulder, then quietly shut the door.

"Is everything all right, Mrs. Steelman? I know it's none of my business, but you've been in a fog since New Year's."

Henry grinned, leaning back. Ordinarily, she sat ramrod straight in her high-back executive chair. But now she slumped casually, tempted to cross her ankles on top of her desk. She giggled at the thought and covered her mouth with steepled fingers.

Louise stared. "Mrs. Steelman?"

Henry picked her feet up and spun around in the chair. "Whee!" She giggled again, then burst into outright laughter at Louise's stunned expression. "I've always wanted to do that."

"Mrs. Steelman, are you *sure* you're all right?"

Henry steadied herself with a hand on the edge of her desk. "I'm fine," she said, smothering a final chuckle. "I'm. . ." She giggled again, covering her mouth. "No, I'm not fine. My stomach's in knots. How can I sit here and read through a stuffy file or concentrate long enough to have a business lunch?"

Louise gave Henry a sideways glance, a smile curving her lips. "It's that man you've been seeing, isn't it?"

Henry's face fell, all humor gone. "How'd you know?"

Louise shot her a smug look. "I'm a secretary, remember?" She grinned and shoved another stack of pink squares across the desk. "I especially notice when the man in question—Mr. Montgomery—provides me my job security. It's a good thing the voice mail is broken."

Henry picked up the slips and fanned them out on the desk. "He called this many times?"

Louise nodded. "And that's just from this morning when you were in the meeting with Mr. Fitzhugh! Each time he left a one-word message."

Henry fingered the four slips. The message from nine-ten said merely "Steelman;" nine-thirty, "mine;" nine-forty, "Henrietta;" ten o'clock, "be." Henry put the slips in logical order. "Be mine, Henrietta Steelman," she whispered.

Louise grinned. "The second time he called, he apologized for taking up my time."

"Be mine?" Henrietta whispered again. "What does that mean?"

Louise rose. "Sounds pretty serious." She paused. "Do you want me to come up with an excuse to cancel your lunch date?"

The door burst open, and Mr. Fitzhugh angrily stepped inside. He glared from Louise to Henry. "What's this about canceling lunch with Mrs. Sampson?"

Henry put on her business face. "Nothing, Mr. Fitzhugh. I just told Louise I had a bit of an upset stomach, and she wondered if maybe I should skip lunch and go home."

"Well?" Mr. Fitzhugh thundered.

Henry rose, resting her fingertips on her desk for support. "I'm fine, Mr. Fitzhugh. There won't be any problem with my lunch plans."

"Good! The Sampson estate is one of our most important. I would hate to have to give it to someone else because of your *stomach* problems."

He gave her one final glare, then turned on the cowering Louise. "In the meantime, let the executives decide the fate of their own day, Mrs. Johnson."

"Y—yes sir," she whispered, eyes filling with tears.

Mr. Fitzhugh harrumphed one more time, then stomped out of the office. Louise leaned against the door, pressing her knuckles against her mouth. Henry moved swiftly from behind her desk to the secretary's side and laid an arm across her shoulder.

"Don't worry, Louise," Henry soothed. "He's just blowing steam."

Louise sniffled. "I'm sorry, Mrs. Steelman. I didn't mean to get you into trouble. I just thought you might want to have lunch with Mr. Montgomery instead."

Henry handed Louise a tissue. "He'll understand. I forgot all about this lunch date, that's all."

Louise blew her nose then drew a deep breath to regain her composure. "Thank you for covering for me. Mr. Fitzhugh probably would have fired me if you hadn't helped me out."

Henry grinned. "He'd probably have fired me, too. I don't think the man allows his employees to have a personal life."

❧

"Richard Montgomery," the deep voice said.

Henry smiled into the receiver. "Is this the Richard Montgomery who leaves women cryptic messages?"

Rick laughed. "Just certain women. Is this one of them?"

"Are you auditioning for a harem? When you said, 'Be mine,' I didn't realize it meant being one of a collection."

"It doesn't. To the best of my recollection, I haven't asked a girl to be mine since I had a crush on Suzie Knox in fourth grade."

Henry laughed. "And did Suzie accept?"

"Nope," he said cheerfully. "Turned me down flat for Pete Reston."

Henry's smile slipped. "What did you really mean by that message?"

She heard a chair squeak over the phone, indicating Rick had leaned back. "Why, I want you to be my girl," he said softly, his voice still retaining the hint of a tease.

"And what does that mean?"

"What do you want it to mean?"

"I'm not sure."

"Henry, you know I'm crazy about you," he said softly. "So crazy, all I can do is think about you. About your soft brown hair, your expressive gray eyes, the way your laugh turns husky when you're really happy, the way you walk in those skinny little heels. . . . What more can I say?"

Henry swallowed hard. "Say you'll pick me up tonight for the cooking class."

"And dinner afterwards?"

Henry shook her head, then realized he couldn't see her over the phone. "I can't. It's a school night."

"Say you'll have dinner with me this weekend, then. At my place. You can meet my children."

Henry smiled. "Are you doing the cooking?"

"Yes, ma'am. Barbecue," he said proudly. "I operate a mean outdoor grill. It's the inside stuff I can't handle."

"It's a date then."

"Good. What time should I pick you up for lunch?"

Henry shifted uncomfortably. "I can't make it today. I forgot I have a business lunch."

"Oh." He put a lot of disappointment in that one-syllable word.

"Maybe tomorrow?" she said hopefully.

"The rest of the week is out. I have to go west of town every day to a construction site. I don't like to design from my office and never get a feel for the whole project."

Henry felt a rush of admiration. That was one of the things she admired about Rick. Part of the reason for his hard-earned respect in the architecture world was his refusal to sit in an ivory tower.

"I'll pick you up tonight," he said. "We might as well set Vera's tongue to wagging by showing up together for the first class of the new year."

"We do owe her the pleasure," Henry agreed, "after the way we teased her at the party."

The chair squeaked again over the phone. "Seven o'clock, then, Henry," he said softly. "I'll count the hours."

⋙

That evening, Henry scurried around the house to get ready. She hadn't been able to leave the office at five o'clock, and the laundry was behind schedule. A clean, unfolded pile collected wrinkles on her bed, the dryer hummed with another load, and water rushed in the washer over yet another.

Brian had to be nagged to clean up his room; Cindy spilled an entire glass of milk at dinner, and dirty dishes piled up in the sink like a stoneware Tower of Babel.

"Brian, rinse off the dishes, then make the lunches for tomorrow. Cindy, you're big enough to run the vacuum cleaner. Clean up the living room and the den. I'll get the bedrooms and hallways later."

"But, Mom, I have a science project due tomorrow!"

"And I have Girl Scouts tonight! Don't you remember? Betsy's mom is picking me up."

Henry held a hand against her throbbing head. "We have to get organized around here! We can't take care of this house, eat, and have time for all our activities when I don't come home until six-thirty."

Brian shrugged. "Why don't we get a maid? At least then we wouldn't have to worry about cleaning the house."

Henry stopped in her tracks. "You know how I feel about that. It's. . .it's *lazy* to have a maid, that's what it is!"

Brian shrugged again. "Maybe so, Mom, but it sure would help."

Staring at the pile of clothes on her bed, Henry sighed. Somewhere in there was the red sweater she wanted to wear tonight. Rick said he liked the way the color blended with her hair, and he hadn't seen the sweater yet. She lifted a wrinkled blouse. There didn't seem to be much point in digging through the pile; the clothes had sat neglected in the dryer for two days.

She sifted through the few occupied hangers in her closet. Too summery, too heavy for the warm day, too bright, too dark. . .nothing seemed right for this evening.

Henry slumped on the bed beside the pile. "I give up. We'll just have to get a maid until things settle down."

"Hooray!" Brian called from the hallway.

"Neat," Cindy said, grinning. "I thought only rich people had maids."

"We're hardly rich." Henry shifted a few wrinkled clothes through her hands and sighed. "Just desperate."

⁂

"You're going to hire a maid?" Rick's voice was incredulous.

"It makes a lot of sense. I can afford it, and it will help out around the house. Then I'll just have to worry about cooking and making sure everybody's where they're supposed to be at the right time."

Rick's jaw tightened in the glare of oncoming traffic. "Nancy never once asked for a maid, and she was busy with four kids and more volunteer work than she had a right to be."

Henry bristled, then relented. She'd been tempted to compare Rick with Les, too. "I'm not Nancy."

Rick sighed, groping for her hand while he kept an eye on traffic. "I'm sorry. You're right."

As they entered the church, they saw a large cardboard sign announcing the formation of the Bread and Fish program. Henry had volunteered to help get it started, but so far no one had contacted her.

"Looks like the soup kitchen's going to get a little competition," Rick said.

"It isn't supposed to compete. It's designed to reach out to the community," Henry said. "Rather than others coming to us, we're going to help people where they live. The homebound as well as the homeless."

Rick smiled and opened the door for her. "Sounds like a good idea. I'd like to help."

When they walked into the kitchen, the room burst into applause. Henry shrank back against Rick in surprise. Clapping the hardest was Vera Fabbish, who stepped out from the group with a wide grin on her face.

"Our class romance," she said proudly, bobbing her head at Henry and Rick. Henry smothered a giggle; Vera's hair was trapped in a sparkly silver cafeteria server's net, which contrasted with her pseudo-gold lamé dress.

"Hooray for Rick and Henry!" someone yelled.

"Calm down," Rick said, grinning. He casually put an arm around Henry and someone else whistled.

"We're just happy for you, dears," Vera said, drawing them to their appointed spot at the counter. "Prudence Standish told me how she caught you two coming out of the kitchen together after midnight on New Year's Eve."

She narrowed her eyes. "I wondered why you two were in such a hurry to get away when we toasted in the new year. I should have known it wouldn't be like Henry to worry about a little stain."

Rick sensed Henry's embarrassment and came to her rescue by lifting a green bean from the pile in front of them. "What are we learning to cook tonight? Or are we going to eat these raw?"

Schoolteacher serious, Vera took her place of authority at the head of the counter. "You learned how to cook green beans before Thanksgiving. Tonight we're going to take it a step further and make everyone's favorite green bean and mushroom casserole."

A few groans sounded around the room. "My mother bakes that for every holiday!"

Vera flashed a smug smile. "There's a reason for that, dear. It's not only easy to make, but *most* people like it. Now, we start by snapping the beans. . ."

∂⊛

Brian dropped the clean laundry on the couch. He sighed in disgust as he plopped down on the opposite end, then flipped on the television with the remote control. Stuporous, he sat in the darkness without turning on the lamp.

Cindy came through the front door, waving at the station wagon pulling away from the curb. "See you later!" The driver honked in reply and Cindy closed the door. She frowned at Brian in the darkened room.

"How was your old Girl Sprouts meeting?" Brian never took his eyes off the blaring set.

Cindy hugged her handbook with both arms. "We're going to go camping soon. At least. . ." she paused. "I guess most of the girls will."

Distracted by a commercial, Brian glanced up to see his sister's tears. "What's the matter, Cinder-face?" he said gruffly.

Cindy sniffled. "It's supposed to be a father/daughter camp out. I guess I can't go."

Brian made a face. "Maybe what's-his-name will take you."

"Mr. Montgomery? Why would he do that?"

"Are you brain-dead?" Brian snorted. "He's probably going to marry Mom."

Cindy's face turned white. "You mean he'd be our dad?"

"That's usually how it works." Brian turned back to the television and flipped channels aimlessly, shrugging. "I guess it could be worse."

"But I don't want another dad!" Cindy dropped the book to the floor and burst out in tears. "I want Daddy back!"

Brian gulped, then jabbed the channel button of the remote control. As he rapidly switched channels, he gradually increased the volume. The television's blare alternated feverishly between rock music, a sales pitch, and suggestive dialogue, gray-white light flashing in syncopation against the darkened room.

The harder Cindy sobbed, the faster the channels changed. The volume increased to ear-splitting level. Cindy screamed and covered her ears. Brian threw the remote control to the carpet, and the television mercifully shut off.

Brian jerked to his feet and balled his fists at his sides. He glared at his wailing sister. "Grow up, Cindy!" he yelled, then stomped to his room.

Chapter Eight

Henry smiled uneasily through the screen door at the teenage boy standing on the other side. He balanced a toddler on his hip, ignoring the little girl's tugs at his hair.

With effort, Henry increased the smile on her face. "Hi! You must be, um. . ." She cast about in her memory. "Graham?" She smiled at the girl. "And Clara?"

The boy continued to stare. The girl continued to ignore Henry, laughing as she tugged at her brother's curly brown hair.

Anxious, Henry tried to peer over the boy's shoulder without being obvious. Why didn't he invite her in? Did he think she was a salesperson?

"I'm Henry Steelman," she tried again. "Your father's expecting me. He invited me for dinner."

The boy flipped his hair back with a toss of his head and shifted the toddler higher. "Oh, yeah," he said flatly, pushing the screen door open with the toe of his sneaker.

"Thanks." Henry stretched her smile to its limits.

Boy and toddler faded down the hall without a backward glance. The door nearly slammed in Henry's face, but she squeezed through at the last moment, the side banging her blue-jeaned hip.

"Great," she muttered under her breath, rubbing the tender spot. "I'll probably have a bruise by tomorrow."

The words echoed in the empty hall. Henry glanced up and her eyes widened. Judging by the entryway alone, Rick's dwelling could appear in the pages of an interior decorating magazine.

Italian marble gleamed underfoot, flanked by muted green walls with white trim. On closer inspection, Henry discovered that the hall's only framed print was a limited edition—the first of one hundred—signed by a famous modern artist. She wished she'd paid more attention when her art appreciation class had studied his work.

"Wow," she murmured, turning slowly. What had Rick thought about the humble art book prints hanging in her own front hall?

"Henry? I didn't hear you come in."

She whirled around, her heart jumping.

Rick stood at the end of the hall, clad in typical weekend griller attire: a tall white chef's hat and a chest-to-knees canvas apron. He held a messy two-pronged fork in his hand. One look at his getup and Henry's heart dropped back in place. She burst out laughing.

"I happen to cook better in this outfit, thank you," he said haughtily. He bent over and whispered in her ear, "You have to do it, you know."

Bewildered, she drew a blank. "Do what?"

Rick pointed proudly at the words on his apron front. "Why, kiss the chef, of course."

Henry laughed and stepped closer. Rick's face sobered under the tall hat, and he wrapped an arm around her. "Come here, you. I've been waiting for you all week."

"Mmm," she whispered in reply, drawing her arms around his neck. "Me, too. I've been—"

Her words died in her throat as his lips met hers, and his free hand pressed against the middle of her back.

Warmth rose inside her, the warmth of love and hope. And with it, an unfulfilled dream to not only capture a love as fine as the one she'd lost, but to surpass it.

With this man. This incredibly handsome, brilliant, artistic man.

Who even now was dripping barbecue sauce down her back.

"Uh, Rick," she murmured, placing her hands on his chest.

"Mmm?" He bent for another kiss, pulling her closer.

She squirmed in his embrace, then seeing that she wasn't gaining his attention, placed her lips next to his ear. "The fork," she whispered in her best seductive voice. "It's dripping sauce on me."

His eyes flew open, and he jerked away to arm's length. "Oh, Henry, I'm sorry!" He turned her around. "Great. All down your back. And this is a silk blouse, isn't it?"

Henry tried to suppress a smile. "It *was* a silk blouse."

"I'm so sorry!" He brushed at the glob but only succeeded in spreading the stain.

"For once, you made the mess." She laughed. "Don't worry about it, Rick."

"Send me the cleaning bill." He clucked his tongue. "Such a waste. It's a beautiful shade of red. And that print. I'll bet you can't find another one like it."

Henry smiled to herself. Men. What did they know about mail-order catalogues? She waved her hand. "Forget it. But maybe we'd better see if we can put some water on this thing to take care of the major damage."

"Better yet, I'll get you another shirt. Rachel's would be too small, but you can wear one of my sweatshirts."

Henry's humor instantly faded. "I wanted to look nice to meet your family."

He smiled warmly. "They're going to love you." He paused. "Just like I do."

Shocked, Henry forgot about her attire. "You love me?"

Rick nodded. "I think ever since you held out your hand and introduced yourself as Henry Steelman at that first cooking class." His expression sobered. "But maybe I shouldn't have said anything."

She wrapped her arms around him. "How could I not love you back? You're a sensitive, caring man who feels as passionately about his family as his work."

"And you. Don't forget that."

Heedless of her sticky blouse, Rick pulled her closer. She stood on tiptoe, and this time her lips met his first.

"Ahem."

They broke apart, and with guilty expressions, turned.

Graham shook his head. "Dad, you'd give me all kinds of trouble if you caught me in a lip lock like that."

Henry rolled down on her heels. Rick cut his eyes at his son, then pulled Henry forward. "Graham, this is Henrietta Steelman."

"Yeah," Graham said, smirking. "*Henry,* right?"

"That's right." Henry smiled and held out her hand. "We met at the door, but how do you do, Graham?"

He stared at her hand in disgust. "Dad said you were the career type."

"Graham!"

Henry lowered her hand. "That's all right, Rick. He's entitled to an opinion."

"But he—"

She turned to Graham. "What do you do for a living, Mr. Montgomery?"

"Come on. I go to high school."

"Think about how hard it is for your dad to keep your household together. He has a career. I have a career. We work to take care of our families."

"I have a job," Graham said defensively. "I work in Dad's office during the summer."

"I'm glad to hear it." She gestured at the sophisticated decor. "You have a good life here, Graham. A lot of people are lucky just to have three square meals a day. But don't forget your father works hard to earn his money. Just like I work to support my family."

"Henry's very talented at what she does," Rick said. "It would be a shame to hide that light under a bushel."

His words softened and swelled inside her. "Thank you, Rick."

Graham shifted from one foot to the other. "Yeah, well, if we're done, I'm heading out for the mall."

Rick's face darkened. "No, you're not, young man. I told you this was a special dinner tonight. I want all of you to meet Henry—"

"I met her."

Rick glared. "And get to know her better."

Henry smiled at Graham. "That's all right. I know what it's like when your parents' friends come over and you're expected to visit."

"No," Rick said firmly. "I told him about this, and he will stay to eat."

"Fine." Graham turned on his heel. "But I don't have to like it!"

❧

Rick offered Henry one of his sweatshirts, and she changed in the guest bathroom. As she rinsed her stained blouse in the sink, she eyed the expensive wallpaper, claw-foot tub, plush rug, and brass fixtures. Even the bathroom was more tasteful than her home.

She was still chuckling as she emerged into the cool, ivory-painted hallway. Rick waited at the end of the hall, smiling, chef's hat and apron gone.

"I made Graham finish grilling. For punishment." He grinned, encircling her waist with an arm. "Now come meet the rest of the family. I'm sure they'll be more receptive."

"I hope so."

She matched his stride as they passed more ivory walls and the leather furniture in the den. She felt Rick's gaze and glanced up.

"You look very. . .fetching. I don't think I've ever seen my shirt look better."

"What, this thing?" She glanced down at the light blue sweatshirt and celebrity walkathon logo.

"Uh–huh." His gaze flickered over her again, and he tickled her waist with his fingers.

The back door slammed open, sliding glass protesting in its tracks.

"Dad! We need—"

The girl stopped short. Her face changed from excitement to shock. She stared at Henry and Rick, then at her father's arm firmly wrapped around Henry's waist.

"Rachel." Rick released Henry and gestured. "This is Mrs. Henrietta Steelman. Henry, this is—"

"Yes. Rachel." Henry stepped forward and extended her hand. "How are you? I've heard so much about you from your father."

Rachel shook Henry's hand without enthusiasm, keeping her gaze downcast. "It's nice to meet you, Mrs. Steelman."

Henry sought to put her at ease. "Please call me Henry."

"Wachel! Wachel!"

Two-year-old Clara toddled through the open door. Clutching a plastic shovel, she was covered with dirt from her baby-fine brown hair to her frilly dress and patent leather shoes. A grin lit her face from ear to ear.

Rachel's expression was contrite. "I'm sorry. I know you wanted Clara all dressed up, but she wanted to play in the flower bed."

Rick laughed and scooped up the dirt-smudged little girl. "That's all right. It's too lovely a January day to worry about nice clothes. Henry, meet my youngest daughter, Clara."

Henry smiled at the glow of adoration in Rick's eyes as he gazed at the little girl. Then she remembered that his wife had died not long after Clara was born. The child must sometimes be a painful reminder, as well.

Henry lifted the little girl's soft, small hand. "Hello, Clara," she murmured.

Clara beamed. "Hey–wo." She stretched out her arms to Henry. "Daddy, cwoser!"

Rick laughed. "Sure thing. Come meet the pretty lady up close."

Clara studied Henry with a child's curiosity, apparently deciding whether to trust this stranger. Henry held her breath, hoping the little girl would rule in her favor. Her arms suddenly ached with the memory of holding a child, and she fleetingly wondered if she might someday have a chance to hold one of her own—a baby—again.

Laughing, Clara stretched out her arms.

With a smile, Rick relinquished the girl, barely able to restrain her from jumping out of his arms.

Henry gently hugged the child. "Will you be my friend, Clara?"

Clara nodded her head solemnly and broke into another smile. Henry hugged her again, then when the girl didn't resist, added a quick kiss on top of her head.

"I think she likes you," Rick said softly. A slow, warm smile spread across his face.

Henry glanced up and caught Rachel's eye. The girl had a sad expression on her face, but her gaze held no malice. Henry thought she saw tears in her eyes, but Rachel swiped her hand quickly across her face.

"Graham says the barbecue's almost ready," she said. "I'll go get John from Timothy's next door, then we'll be ready to eat."

"You already set the table?" Rick shook his head. "I don't know what I'd do without you, Rachel. You sure keep things humming around here."

Rachel shot Henry another haunted look, then jerked her head. "If you'll excuse me, Henry, Dad."

She bolted from the room and out the front door.

Clara cooed, entranced with Henry's dangling gold earrings. With a puzzled expression, Rick turned back. "What got into Rachel?"

Henry sighed. "The same thing that's wrong with Graham, evidently. They know how much you like me, and they see me as a threat."

"A threat to what?"

Clara laughed as she swung Henry's earring back and forth.

"A threat to the memory of their mother," Henry said softly.

Rick laughed. "That's ridiculous! You couldn't replace Nancy. You're nothing like her!"

Henry winced, hoping her face didn't reveal how much his words stung. He made it sound as though she couldn't measure up.

She set Clara down, and the little girl toddled to the back door. "You should tell all of your children that I have no intention of replacing Nancy," Henry said quietly.

Rick reached for her hand. "I didn't mean anything by that. I certainly didn't mean to imply that you and I. . .that is. . ."

He broke off, his face turning red. "Oh, come on," he mumbled. "Let's go eat."

※

Henry wiped the last of the sauce from her mouth with a napkin, then leaned back with a contented sigh. "You barbecue some wonderful spareribs, Rick." She glanced across the table. "You, too, Graham." He didn't even look up from his plate.

"It's our specialty," Rick said. "Steaks and chicken are fine for beginners, but it takes a skilled chef to baste the ribs just right, then barbecue them to perfection."

"They were the best, Dad," nine-year-old John piped up. He smiled at Henry, sitting at his side. "Didn't you like the potato salad?"

Henry leaned over, warmed that the boy had taken an instant liking to her the moment they met. "I loved the potato salad," she confessed in a whisper.

"I made it," Rachel said.

Henry smiled. "Will you give me the recipe?"

Rachel shrugged, dropping her gaze to her plate. "I guess."

Silence fell over the table. Henry bit the inside of her lip. Graham had been quiet for the entire meal, sullen, picking at his food. Rachel hadn't contributed much to the conversation, either. Her attitude had been respectful but reserved, as though Henry were a visiting schoolteacher.

John had chattered from the moment they'd met and even taken her by the hand to seat her. He insisted on sitting beside her. Already won over, Clara happily smashed potato salad in her high chair.

"What's for dessert?" Rick rubbed his hands together. "A good meal should always be followed by an even better dessert." He paused. "Didn't Vera Fabbish say that?"

The children giggled. Even Graham cracked a smile. Perplexed, Henry looked from one face to another, waiting for an explanation.

Rick finally stopped chuckling. "Ever since I started the cooking class and Vera found out who my parents were, she's taken it upon herself to visit us regularly. She usually brings a casserole or two as an excuse, but I think she really comes to sit on our sofa and dispense advice."

John's giggles turned into a fit of unbroken laughter. "One day, she was wearing shorts and stayed so long, she got stuck to the leather!"

Henry hid a smile behind a hand. Rick gave her a mock stern look, turning the expression on the others. "I thought we agreed we wouldn't discuss. . ." His shoulders shook, and his face twisted with mirth until he gave in to a full-fledged chuckle. "She means well."

Rachel's faint smile faded. "I'll get dessert."

Henry smiled and rose. "Let me help."

"No," Rachel said sharply. She squared her shoulders and lifted her chin as she swept past Henry. "I can manage."

Henry sat back down. Rick flashed her a thankful smile, tempering Rachel's rebuff.

Graham yawned loudly. "Can I go now?"

"But—"

Henry laid a hand on Rick's knee to still his protest. "It's all right," she said softly.

Rick sighed. "Fine, Graham. You may go."

"Thanks." The chrome leg of his chair scraped against the tiled floor as he pushed back and left the room. They heard the front door slam.

Rick's face darkened. "He really should have stayed."

"He's a teenage boy," Henry said softly. "It'd be hard enough for him to sit still even if I were just your business associate."

Rick's eyes gleamed. "I'm glad you're not."

Smiling, Henry shyly turned her face. Rachel entered, her arms laden with a tray full of ice cream and pound cake. She glanced at her father and Henry, then paled.

Clara pounded a fist against her tray. Without a word, Rachel placed a small bowl in front of her. Clara scooped up a frozen lump with her hand, and Rachel silently continued to pass out bowls.

Henry lifted the spoon to her mouth. The frigid ice cream sent a sharp rush to her head and chest, but she swallowed with delight.

"Homemade!" she said when she regained her breath. She smiled at Rachel. "Did you make this yourself?"

Rachel nodded. "It was Mom's favorite. Tutti-frutti."

Henry idly stirred her ice cream. "My husband used to make this a lot, Rachel," she said softly. "It was kind of you to remind me of him, too."

Rachel reddened, then lowered her head until her long hair hid her face.

John stared at Henry's bowl. "Hey! You're making soup!"

Henry smiled, not missing a stroke with her spoon. "I like my ice cream this way. It makes a frosting to drizzle over my slice of cake, you see?"

John peered into her bowl as Henry spooned ice cream on top of her cake. His eyes widened, twinkling. "Neat! I want to try that." He turned to his father. "I hope you bring her home more often."

Rick smiled at her. "I'll do my best."

Henry lingered at the Montgomerys' for another hour. She admired Clara's cheerful nursery, decorated in primary colors and dancing bears. One by one, the little girl pulled toys off a low shelf to play with Henry and Rick. Henry had forgotten how much fun it was to play with a toddler, and several times she again saw a warm light in Rick's eyes when their gazes met over the little girl's head.

Henry grinned at the nuclear fallout sign adorning the closed door to Graham's room. John grabbed her hand and pulled her into his own room, its walls ambiguously covered with ninja character posters and cross-stitched children's verses. He was still at that in-between age, not a little boy anymore, but not yet a teenager.

When Henry politely asked, Rachel somewhat grudgingly showed her her room. As tasteful and clean as the rest of the house, it was decorated in matching Victorian prints from the bedspread to the bay-window curtains to the wallpaper. Henry recognized the classic mark of a famous British designer.

"What a lovely room, Rachel," she said softly. "I always wanted a cushioned bay window when I was a girl. It seemed like a great place to dream."

"Rachel designed the room herself," Rick said. "We moved into the house about a year ago."

Henry glanced from the desk to the bed to the dresser. Unlike her own room, there wasn't a sign of clutter anywhere. "You're a very tidy person," she said with a smile.

Rachel shrugged, eyes downcast, as she fiddled with the doorknob on the closet door. "I like things to be neat, but Mrs. Brewster does most of the cleaning."

"Mrs. Brewster?"

"The maid," Rick said. "She comes at least once a week. Sometimes twice."

Henry said her good-byes to Rachel then stuck her head in John's room. He and Clara were absorbed in a mock battle of plastic figures. They both returned her farewell hastily, then went back to play.

Rick put an arm around her and led her to the front door. He handed her a plastic bag with her soiled blouse. "I'm sorry I ruined it."

"That's all right." She twisted the plastic ends into a knot and bit her lip. "You never told me you had a maid."

"Does it matter?"

"Well. . .yes. You didn't seem too pleased when I told you I was thinking about getting one."

Rick sighed, spreading his hands out wide. "Henry, I have four children."

"And I have two. Do maids have a minimum offspring requirement for their employers?"

"No, but. . ." He broke off, letting his hands drop helplessly.

"But I'm a woman," she finished. "Is that it? I'm supposed to not only know how to run a house but enjoy doing it?"

He sighed again, looking sheepish. "No, I guess not. I've worked with women on a professional level and never thought about it before. The women I've known on a personal level were all homemakers. By choice."

"This one isn't," Henry said, slightly miffed.

Rick stepped forward, pulling her into a warm embrace. "Right now, all I know is that I'm in love with you, and you're in love with me. That ought to be enough to make up for a multitude of differences."

Henry closed her eyes as his lips covered hers, but her heart quivered. Even if Rick wanted her in his life and could overlook what he perceived as shortcomings, two of his four children couldn't.

Chapter Nine

Mary Alice stared as she shoveled pasta into her mouth. Henry set down her own fork, smiling. "What? Do I have tomato sauce on my face?"

"Mmmff," Mary Alice mumbled, swallowing furiously. "You just look different. I can't get over it. You're glowing. And you've given up those uptight businesswoman's suits."

Henry glanced down. "This *is* a suit."

Mary Alice took a final swallow, then a drink of water. "Yes, but it's much more feminine than what you used to wear. Instead of black and gray, you're wearing real colors. Red, blue, green—happy colors."

She sat back in her chair and folded her arms. "You're in love!"

"Shh!" Henry brushed a finger against her own lips, certain that her sister's voice had carried halfway across the Italian restaurant. "Why didn't you just go on television and announce it?"

"I knew it!" Mary Alice's eyes shone as she leaned forward. "Come on. Tell me all about it."

"There's nothing to tell." Henry picked up her fork and poked at her spaghetti to avoid her sister's gaze. "Rick and I enjoy each other's company. That's all."

"Uh-huh." Mary Alice smirked. "Come on, Henry. This is your little sister here! The one you used to tell about each and every one of your boyfriends!"

Henry glanced up. "This is different. With Les, I knew it was the real thing. But now I'm older and not so certain."

"It was Vera Fabbish," Mary Alice said, nodding. "Didn't I tell you that woman would throw you two together?"

Henry smiled. "I don't know if she can take all the credit, but she's certainly done her best."

"So when's the wedding?"

"Mary Alice!" Henry struggled to cover a smile at the thought. "Rick and I have only known each other a few months. You're being a bit hasty, don't you think?"

"It's never too early, especially if you want a June wedding. That's only four months away. And as your future matron of honor, let me warn you that I have a busy schedule."

"Oh, really!" Henry dipped her fork to twirl the pasta, then shoved it in her mouth to avoid further conversation. Common sense ruled that her sister was premature in her speculations, but a portion of Henry's heart longed for a storybook ending.

She swallowed quickly, glancing at her watch. "Look at the time! I've got to get back to work by one o'clock or Mr. Fitzhugh will fire me. I've taken on three extra estates just this week. I think that man is trying to overload me with work. Instead of dangling that vice presidency, I think he's secretly hoping I'll quit."

"Why don't you?" Mary Alice shrugged, a gleam in her eye. "When you marry Mr. Famous Architect, you won't have to work."

"Not you, too!" Henry groaned. She fished in her purse for her wallet and tossed some bills at her sister. "Be a lamb and take care of the bill, will you? I've got a five-block walk back to the office."

"Sure, sure." Mary Alice smiled. "You'd better practice walking, all right. You'll need it when you walk down that long aisle at church."

Henry flashed her sister a look of exasperation then headed for the door.

⁂

Pastor Oliver Reynolds smiled at the group assembled around him on folding chairs in the fellowship hall. Rick squeezed Henry's hand. They smiled at each other, remembering the New Year's Eve party.

"I think everybody's here, Oliver," Vera said. She took a seat beside the pastor.

"Good." Once again, he beamed at the group of twenty. "Thank you all for giving up a weeknight to meet here to plan the Bread and Fish program."

"It's about time we got this thing going," Vera said, nodding. "This community needs more than the soup kitchen can provide."

"Exactly. So what we propose is to work out a food distribution program to take directly to the people. What that involves is up to the people in this room."

A young woman from Rick and Henry's cooking class raised a hand. "Does it have to be hot meals?"

"It could be," Oliver said. "Or it could be canned goods delivered on a regular basis. That's what we're here to decide."

"Maybe we should start by placing someone in charge," Vera suggested.

"That's a great idea," Oliver said. "I'll be on hand to help out in any way, but we need a leader."

Vera rose to her feet. "I nominate Henrietta Steelman."

An approving murmur rippled through the crowd. Henry blinked. "Me?"

Rick squeezed her hand. "Why not?" he whispered. "You'd be great at it."

Oliver raised a hand to quiet the room. "Anybody else have a nomination or want to volunteer to head the program?"

Silence.

Lowering his hand, Oliver smiled at Henry. "Looks like you're elected." He stood and gestured at his chair. "Come on up here and take charge. I'm just an interested observer from now on."

Embarrassed, Henry cast a quick glance at Rick. He gave her a warm smile of reassurance, and she took the empty chair.

Vera leaned forward. "I know you can do it, dear." She winked.

"Well. . ." Henry gazed out at the faces. Some she knew and some she didn't. What should she say?

She straightened her shoulders. This was just another business delegation. And for a good cause, too.

"All right," she said warmly, feeling the keen sense of responsibility. "The first thing we need to do is decide how we want to operate. I'm sure we all have our individual ideas, but let's make the discussion as brief as possible. As I see it, we can either deliver groceries, prepared meals, or a combination of both."

"Meals on Wheels already delivers hot meals," Rick said. "We might just be duplicating their service."

"Good point," Henry said, furrowing her brow. "And the plus side for groceries is that it would be more a matter of money than manpower." She grinned. "If you'll pardon the expression, ladies."

The room laughed. Henry rubbed her hands together, excited. Leadership was one of her strong points, and she hadn't had a chance to use that gift in her church. She enjoyed assigning tasks by ability and giving the individual creative freedom to solve the dilemma. Nothing gave her greater pleasure than to see the pride on someone else's face from a job well done.

"Excuse me."

A woman timidly raised her hand at the back of the room. She stood up slowly, and a shy smile etched its way across her face. "I'm Polly Faradon. I. . .I'm new to this church."

"She works in the soup kitchen," Vera said. "Jumped right in from the first day she joined the church."

Henry smiled at the pleasant-looking blond, judging her to be in her mid- to late-twenties. "What's your idea, Polly?"

Polly cleared her throat, glancing nervously around the room. "As Mrs. Fabbish says, I work in the soup kitchen occasionally, and a lot of times there's food left over. Sometimes we use it the next day, sometimes not. Couldn't we use some of the food we prepare in the church for this program? And besides," she continued in a rush, "I, uh, like to cook. I'd hate to just shell out money or shop at the grocery store. I'd much rather make something and take it in person."

Rick nodded. "A serving heart," he murmured as Polly hastily took her seat.

Henry pushed down a twinge of guilt. The woman did have a point. "Polly, make a list for the next few days and see what kind of food we have left over from the soup kitchen. Also, work on some ideas for what we could prepare, either here at the church or in our own homes. I'll work on a budget and securing funds."

Mind racing, she closed her eyes in concentration. "Hmm. Let's divide into two teams. Those who are more interested in cooking can work with Polly. Everybody else can work with me. We'll get someone to work with both teams." She opened her eyes. "Vera?"

"I'd better work with Polly, dear. I know that kitchen pretty well. I wouldn't be much good at raising money."

Henry glanced at the other faces, then her gaze fell on Rick. "How about you?" she asked. "You've even spent more time in the kitchen lately thanks to the cooking class."

Rick laughed along with the rest of the room. "I'd be honored to accept the position as committee liaison," he said, bowing his head as though receiving knighthood.

"Good. That's settled," Henry leaned back, pleased. Things were progressing even better than she'd expected. With a little dedication, they'd have this program up and running in no time.

As Henry asked for volunteers to work with Polly, Rick smiled and winked at her. Her heart warmed, and she looked forward to the coming days. Not only would she be able to serve the community through the Bread and Fish program, she would also have another excuse to spend time with Rick.

≈

Clayton Fitzhugh tapped a finger against one stack of several folders lining Henry's desk like an ancient city wall. "Why aren't these done?"

Henry glanced up, hoping her eyes didn't appear as red as they felt. She'd stayed up late last night, trying to catch up on work. "I'll be finished with them before lunch, Mr. Fitzhugh."

His eyes narrowed. "Hmmph! You'd better be!"

The door banged shut behind him. Henry was certain she saw the window vibrate.

She closed the folder she'd been working on and set it aside. Pulling another one from the stack, she glanced at the desk clock. Eleven o'clock. Judging from the work yet to accomplish, lunch wouldn't come for another four hours.

Reaching for the telephone, she rubbed the bridge of her nose. Henry cradled the receiver against a shoulder with her chin, smothering a yawn as she dialed.

"Rick Montgomery."

"Hi," she managed to say before she smothered another yawn in her palm.

Rick laughed. "Am I keeping you awake?"

"No." She frowned, irritated. Did he have to joke? "I can't make lunch today."

Rick groaned. "But we were going to talk about Bread and Fish!"

"I know that," she said sharply, tapping a pencil against her desk. Relenting, she softened her tone. "How about tonight?"

"Tonight I'm getting together with Polly Faradon. She and I are supposed to hammer out some details."

"Well, there's always class tomorrow night." Henry skeptically flipped through her daily planner. "No, wait. I have to meet with a customer. I can't even come to class."

Rick groaned again. "Henry, we have to get serious about this program. It's never going to get off the ground if we don't get everything straight."

Henry curled her fingers around the edge of her desk. "I realize that," she said in a low voice. "I'm trying to make time. Look, I've been mean-ing to get you and your kids over to meet my kids. Why don't you all come for dinner Saturday night? The kids can get acquainted, and we can talk about the program over dessert."

"Well. . ."

Despite her edginess, her lips curved in a smile. "Is it my cooking you're worried about?"

"Actually, I was thinking about the kids. If your children are as stand-offish as mine have been lately, we're in for an interesting evening."

Henry smothered another yawn. She couldn't remember the last time she'd said more than a few words to her kids.

"Both Brian and Cindy *have* seemed out of sorts. I hadn't noticed until you mentioned it just now, but they haven't been their usual selves. Brian's been even moodier than normal."

"He hasn't been very pleasant when I've come to pick you up. I think he's having the same reservations about me that my kids seem to have about you."

"But Cindy? I thought she liked you."

"Even she's seemed cool to me the last few weeks."

Henry rested her chin over the mouthpiece and closed her eyes. *What more, Lord?* Work was a shambles, her family had turned into strangers, the food distribution was lagging behind in schedule—

"Henry? Are you still there?"

She smiled. "Just barely."

Rick laughed softly. "After dinner tonight, take a hot bubble bath and forget about everything for at least an hour. Promise?"

"Promise." Henry smiled. "What would I do without you in my life, Rick Montgomery?"

"Someday soon I hope you'll be wondering what to do with me *in* your life," he said. "Permanently."

Henry let the implication set in. "Do you mean that?" she whispered.

"Yes, Henry," he said in a deep voice. "I'll call you later tonight. After the kids have gone to bed and you've had your bath."

Henry felt a shiver course up her spine. "Okay," she whispered. "Bye."

She replaced the receiver, then turned back to the folders.

28

That night after a long soak in the tub, Henry got ready for bed and decided to study her Bible while she waited for Rick's call. Remembering his words from the morning, her mind wandered to the proverb about the excellent wife. No doubt Rick had read that passage, too.

Henry frowned as she studied. The unnamed biblical woman seemed like some sort of Super Mom: She spun wool, searched for food, rose early in the morning to feed her household, and worked until late at night. She also helped the poor, sewed her own clothes, sold her handmade garments and belts, spoke words of wisdom, taught kindness, and never had a spare moment. And because of this, her children and her husband praised her name.

"Whew!" Henry marked her place with a finger and closed the book. "Talk about your Type-A personalities. Nobody can live up to that!"

She leaned back against the propped-up pillows and glanced over at the phone, then at the clock. Eleven-thirty. Rick should have phoned by now.

"He and Polly must have gotten into a good discussion," she mumbled, sliding down against the pillows. She yawned, covering her mouth with a fist. She barely had the energy to set the Bible aside and turn out the light before her eyes closed.

Just before she fell asleep, she had a fleeting image of the excellent wife. And for some reason, the woman seemed very shy and had blond hair.

Chapter Ten

Mary Montgomery set down her china cup. "I'm glad you could meet me for lunch, Henry."

"Thank you for inviting me." Henry glanced around the elegant tearoom, located in one of Houston's finer hotels. A string quartet played softly in the corner, and dutiful, hushed waiters attended wealthy diners at pale-covered tables.

She sighed. "It's good to get away from the office."

"Rick said you'd been spending an inordinate amount of time working lately. Are you sure you want to have him and the children for dinner on Saturday? They're quite a crew to cook for." She leaned forward, whispering, "Not to mention, if you're like me, I always leave the housecleaning until the last minute!"

Henry chuckled and Mary straightened with a smile. "That's better, dear. You've been so somber all through lunch. Is something troubling you?"

Henry lowered her gaze to her linen napkin. She brushed a soft edge with a fingernail, hesitating.

"Henry? What's wrong?"

Henry met Mary's gaze. "Tell me about Nancy."

Mary looked puzzled. "What do you want to know, dear?"

"What she was like. Was she funny? Was she serious? Did she dress in the latest fashion? Did she prefer butterscotch or chocolate topping on her ice cream?"

"In other words, everything."

"Yes."

Mary smiled sadly. "Nancy was a sweet, cheerful girl when she married Rick, and she grew into a lovely, generous woman. Taking care of her home and family was second only to her faith."

"But she never worked outside of the home?"

"Not for money. But after John started kindergarten, she volunteered extensively."

Henry twisted her napkin around a finger. "Rick's home is very important to him, isn't it? It's immaculate."

Mary's lips twisted in a wry grin. "A little too immaculate, if you ask me.

He may have a maid to pick up after everyone, but he's hard on the kids when it comes to taking care of that showplace. Nancy appreciated her lovely home, but she wanted it to be comfortable. Livable."

Mary laid a gentle hand on Henry's arm. "Why all the questions?"

Henry drew a deep breath. "Rick and I are. . .talking seriously about our relationship."

Mary's face filled with joy. "I'm so pleased. You strike me as a perfect match for Rick."

"Wait a minute. You sound like my sister." Henry grinned. "We haven't actually said anything about marriage. I've got a career to manage, and I'm not sure if I'm the type of woman who's wanted by Rick and his kids."

Mary smiled sympathetically. "God made us all different but equal, Henry. I'm surprised a woman of your independence and confidence would even question your worth."

"It's not that," Henry said, searching for words. "I know what my strengths are. . .as well as my weaknesses."

She shifted in her chair. "Les—that was my husband—he loved and accepted me for who I was. Not for who he wanted me to be. He teased me about my klutziness around the kitchen and the house, but he also was my biggest cheerleader. He was content for me to have the limelight, so to speak, while he took care of things in the background."

"And Rick?"

Henry laughed. "Rick admires me, too, because we're so much alike. We're both ambitious go-getters. As long as we're dating, it's all right. But if we were married. . .well, I wonder how content he would be to have a wife out front with him. A wife with a hectic schedule. After all, we'd have six children in our family."

Mary shook her head, casting Henry a stern look. "Don't change a thing about yourself. You're wonderful just the way you are. Rick thinks so, too. Love always finds a way."

Henry grinned, feeling optimistic again. "I hope so."

❧

Brian looked up the number of the maid who'd cleaned the house for the past few weeks, then dialed. It was a shame she didn't speak English. None of the Steelmans spoke much Spanish, but Mrs. Maldonado had come highly recommended. Rick Montgomery usually came over when there was interpreting to do. *He* spoke Spanish.

Brian tapped his foot until the other end of the telephone line clicked. "Uh, *Señora* Maldonado? Uh, *soy* Brian Steelman." He made a face, holding the excited chatter from the other end of the phone away from his ear. "*Sí. El hijo de Señora* Steelman. Um, *mi madre. . . dice. . .no venga la casa en el sabado. ¿Porqué?* Why doesn't she want you to come?"

Brian hastily filtered through the limited Spanish he'd acquired from the classroom and playground to come up with an excuse.

"She's sick! Yeah, she's, uh. . .*mi madre está. . .*" What was the word for sick? *Em, en,* something. What had Chuy Mendoza said when his mother was ordered to bed?

"*¡Encinta! That's it! ¡Mi madre está encinta!* "

He heard a pause on the other end of the line, then a rapid succession of Spanish. Mrs. Maldonado's voice rose to a fevered, imploring pitch. Brian held the phone away from his ear again, grinning at his apparent success. She was probably telling him how sorry she was and recommending a hearty bowl of chicken soup or something.

"Uh, *Señora* Maldonado. I have to go. Uh, *gracias. Adiós.*"

Brian hung the phone up, silencing the chatter. Feeling smug, he leaned against the desk and folded his arms. "That ought to take care of things."

Cindy walked into the room, Barbie doll and box in hand. "Who were you talking to?"

Brian flashed his sister a self-satisfied smile. "Mrs. Maldonado. She won't be able to clean house in time for the stupid dinner on Saturday."

"We'd better tell Mom. That's two days from now. Maybe she can find somebody else."

Brian pushed away from the desk. "Don't you get it? If the house is a mess, ol' what's-his-face won't want to marry Mom."

Cindy bit her lip. "She sure does like him, though."

"Oh, come on, Cinder-face," Brian snapped. "Do you want him to replace Dad? Mom doesn't spend enough time with us as it is, what with her job, that cooking class, and that guy. Besides, he's got kids already. Four of 'em! Do you want more brothers and sisters?"

"It might be nice to have a sister," Cindy said wistfully.

"It wouldn't be the same. Listen, don't say anything to Mom about Mrs. Maldonado. Do what I say on Saturday, and that man won't be taking Dad's place, okay?"

Cindy scuffed a toe against the carpet. "Okay," she mumbled. "What do I have to do?"

Brian's grin stretched from ear to ear. "Here's the plan. On Saturday morning, you suddenly remember. . ."

હ

Henry stared in disbelief at her daughter. "What do you mean you have to take cookies to a Girl Scout meeting this afternoon? This is Saturday!"

"It's a special cookie contest," Cindy said calmly. "They have to be home-made cookies."

"Sweetheart, couldn't you have remembered yesterday? I planned to be in the kitchen all day cooking for our dinner tonight. Rick and his kids are coming."

Cindy shrugged. "I'm sorry, Mom."

"Can't we just buy some and pretend we made them?" Henry asked, desperate. "I don't have time—"

"I can make them by myself. I'll make sugar cookies. They're easy."

Henry cast a dubious glance at her daughter. "Well, okay. And if you make a mess, Mrs. Maldonado can clean it up when she comes at two o'clock."

"Okay, Mom," Cindy said cheerfully. She moved slowly around the kitchen, taking her time in finding an apron and collecting ingredients.

Henry felt a dull throb in her head. She stared at her watch, tension gnawing her stomach. Eleven o'clock. The Montgomerys were due to arrive at six-thirty. She could start dinner at three o'clock while Mrs. Maldonado finished cleaning up the house. For now, she could clip those hedges out front. She'd been meaning to trim them for a long time, but just hadn't had the time.

She glanced down at her frayed jeans and favorite sweatshirt with its cutoff sleeves. She was certainly dressed to do yard work. As she headed to the garage for the hedge clippers, she smiled. Maybe the outdoor work would relax her.

હ

"Mom!" Brian called out the front door. "Are you ready to take me to Adam's?"

Henry paused with hedge clippers in hand, then wiped her forehead with her wrist. "Adam's? I don't remember anything about your going to his house today."

"I told you several days ago."

"But he lives across town! It'll take an hour to get there and back. Not to mention picking you up." Henry sighed, shoulders sagging. "All right. Come on."

An hour later, Henry winced as she passed the shrubs while pulling the car into the driveway. The hedge was horribly lopsided where she'd stopped working. She glanced at the car's clock as she eased into the garage. One o'clock. Thankfully, Mrs. Maldonado would be here soon.

"Cindy, I'm home," she announced as she entered the kitchen. "How did your—what happened in here?"

Henry stood stock-still, surveying the empty kitchen. Sugar littered the floor like sawdust, and dripping water formed a sticky puddle below the silverware drawer. Flour dusted the counters, and chocolate chips dotted the kitchen floor like a Hansel and Gretel trail.

"Cynthia Renee Steelman!" Henry planted her fists on her hips. "You have three seconds to get in here!"

"Coming, Mom," Cindy said meekly, appearing from the bedroom hallway. "I'm cleaning it up. Honest! You should have seen it before."

Henry closed her eyes and let out a long breath. The dull throb in her head had lodged itself directly behind her eyes. "What happened?"

Cindy bowed her head. "I spilled the sugar."

"I see. And the flour?"

"I was lifting the bag from one counter to another, and. . .well, I didn't know it was already open!"

The pressure behind Henry's eyes increased. "And the chocolate chips?"

"The bag spilled." Cindy looked up hopefully. "You aren't mad, are you?"

Henry sighed. "No, I'm not mad, honey. Accidents happen. Let's start cleaning up. What we don't finish, Mrs. Maldonado can take care of."

Guilt flashed briefly across Cindy's face, but she quickly turned her head. "Okay, Mom."

They worked for an hour, Henry nervously consulting her watch every five minutes. She wanted everything to be perfect this evening, and so far nothing had gone right.

She left Cindy with the last of the cleanup and wandered the rest of the house taking inventory. Bathtubs with rings, unmade beds, towels thrown everywhere—what a wreck. She should clean first so the maid could find room to clean up!

Two-thirty. She frowned. Where was Mrs. Maldonado? It wasn't like her to be late.

The telephone rang. "Don't back out on me, Mrs. Maldonado. Please!" she muttered, then lifted the receiver. "Steelman residence. Henry speaking."

"Mom! Where are you? You're supposed to come get me!"

"Brian!" Henry slumped to her bed, holding her tired head in her hand. "You're ready to come home now? Can't Adam's parents bring you? I'm kind of in a jam here."

"They're going out soon. The other direction from our house."

Henry sighed. "All right. I'll be there as soon as I can."

An hour later they pulled into the driveway. Henry reminded herself to finish clipping the hedge. It looked as if a dinosaur had taken several bites out of it.

"Why didn't I call a professional?" she berated herself out loud as she got out of the car.

"Oh, yeah." Brian's voice was unusually cheerful. "Speaking of professionals, Mrs. Maldonado called yesterday and said she can't come."

"*What?*" Henry slammed the car door. She winced and closed her eyes against the increased pounding in her head. She lowered her voice. "What do you mean she can't come?"

Brian shrugged and entered the house. "I guess something came up."

Henry stood in the garage, alone. "She can't come today," she whispered. She had the absurd urge to giggle.

"Mom!" Cindy stuck her head through the door. "Are you all right?"

Henry let out a deep breath and pressed her head against her hands. "Sure, sure."

She squared her shoulders. Henry Steelman never gave up. They'd get this house in tip-top order yet!

❧

Rick pulled the minivan up to the curb and shut off the engine. Four pairs of young eyes stared out the windows at the Steelman home.

Graham smirked. "Nice hedges."

"I think they look cool!" John said with awe.

Clara babbled with excitement from her car seat next to a quiet Rachel.

Rick cleared his throat and picked up a spring bouquet from the seat. "Are we ready?"

A mixed chorus of groans and cheers answered, and then they crossed the distance to the front porch. After he straightened a child's collar here and pressed down a cowlick there, Rick rang the doorbell.

Graham sniffed the air. "Something smells funny."

Rick frowned. Henry had gotten better at her cooking. He'd seen it himself at class. Surely she wouldn't have—

The door opened suddenly, and Henry appeared. Rick did a double take. He'd never seen her looking less than professional, but here she was in a cutoff sweatshirt and frayed jeans. Hair straggled limply around her face and shoulders, and flour dotted her clothes.

"Come in, come in!" she said with exaggerated cheerfulness. "You'll have to forgive the house. We've had kind of a situation today."

"Hello, Henry." Rick bent to kiss her floury cheek as the children filed solemnly past them into the house. He held up the bouquet. "If you'll bring me a vase, I'll put these in water."

"Sure." Henry looked dazed as she accepted the flowers. "Cindy! Brian! The Montgomerys are here."

She turned back to Rick. "You really will have to forgive the mess. It's been an interesting day."

Graham sidled up to his father. "Dad, the place is a wreck," he said. "You should see."

"I'm sure it's not a wreck. Now apologize."

"No, he's right." Henry took Rick's hand. "Let me show you."

She led him to the kitchen. When she pushed open the swinging door, his mouth dropped.

Dirty pots and pans lined the counter. A skillet on the stove was filled with grease and what appeared to be the charred remains of chicken drumsticks. A bowl of. . .glop was the only way to describe it, stood sadly next to a blender full of more unidentifiable liquid.

Henry opened the refrigerator and pulled out a covered bowl. "We're having salad for dinner. At least that's something that doesn't have to be cooked."

Brian and Cindy appeared in the kitchen, but hung back. Henry gestured at her children for the benefit of the Montgomerys. "This is Brian and Cindy."

She pointed one at a time to Rick's children. "And this is Graham, Rachel, John, and Clara."

"Hi," Brian and Cindy mumbled together. The Montgomery children continued to stare.

"Take them to your rooms to play," Henry said to her children. "Rick and I need to talk."

Graham and Rachel led the way, John and Clara trailing behind. Graham shook his head, letting out a long whistle as he eyed the kitchen. "You two better do more than talk."

"That's enough, Graham," Rick said sternly. He watched them file past, waiting until they were out of earshot.

Alone at last, he turned to Henry. She clutched the salad like a life preserver, a goofy grin plastered on her face. He gently pried the bowl from her hands and put his arm around her. "What happened?"

"Everything, Rick." She gestured around the shambles of a kitchen. "Cindy had to have cookies; Mrs. Maldonado didn't show up; Brian had to go across town. I didn't have enough time to cook the food, trim the hedges—"

"Whoa! Sounds like you've had a busy day."

"I have," she said in a small voice.

Rick stared down at her face, disturbed to see her lips tremble. Not once had he seen her come close to crying. Not even on the anniversary of Les's death.

He wrapped his arm around her. "It's all right. We'll clean it up together."

"That's the problem," she murmured. "Someone's always having to help with my messes." Her shoulders shook and tears welled in her eyes. "This house business is just too much for me to handle."

Rick drew her against him, suppressing a smile. "It's just been a bad day, Henry. We'll both have lots more of them. Let's order some Chinese food and forget it."

He broke the embrace to tip her face up for a kiss, but she pulled away and reached under the sink for a rag and the spray cleaner.

❧

Brian switched on his radio to an alternative rock station. He wasn't too fond of the noise, but he figured Graham Montgomery, being older, would approve. He didn't want to catch any flak. Brian was feeling so guilty that he just wanted to be left alone.

Graham flopped down in a beanbag chair and pawed through a stack of music magazines. He pulled one out. "You like this group?"

Brian shrugged. "I guess so."

Graham glanced up. "What's eating you? That mess your mom made?"

"She didn't make it."

"Yeah?" Graham laughed. "Well, who did?"

"I did." Brian's face reddened. "Because of your dad."

Graham stopped laughing. "What's wrong with my dad?"

"I don't want him to be my father!"

"Well, I don't want your mother for my mom, either!"

"Good!"

They glared at each other. An ultrahigh guitar riff blared from the speakers. Graham winced. "Can't you change that racket to another station?"

Brian flipped the radio off.

Graham laughed, settling back in the chair. "So tell me how you arranged that fiasco out there."

Brian told him, and Graham nodded grudgingly. "I've pulled some sneaky schemes, and that was pretty good. If I had to have a new brother—but I'm not saying I want one—you wouldn't be half bad."

"Thanks." Brian warmed at the older boy's approval, feeling some of the sting from his guilt lift.

Chapter Eleven

Rick and Henry had nearly finished cleaning the counters and dishes when the doorbell rang.

"Must be the Chinese food," Rick said, straightening over the broom. "You'd better help, Henry. There's probably a couple of bags."

She followed, and he opened the door to a short Hispanic woman with snapping eyes. "Mrs. Maldonado! What are you—"

She shook her finger at him, then Henry, and burst into a tirade of Spanish. Henry shrank against the wall. She'd never seen the woman so agitated.

Rick help up his hands. "A little slower, *por favor, Señora* Maldonado. *No comprendo.*"

Mrs. Maldonado continued to babble, gesturing from him to Henry. Rick listened attentively, then burst out laughing.

"What's she saying?" Henry said, bewildered.

Rick laughed so hard that Mrs. Maldonado stopped chattering and stared. He wiped his eyes, the last chuckle fading. "I can't quite make out all the words, but apparently she's either saying that you're a live oak or that you're pregnant."

"Pregnant! *¡Sí! ¡En cinta!*" the woman insisted. Her expression softened, and she clasped her hands together in an imploring gesture. "*Señora, Señor, por favor. . .el bebé. . .*"

Her words ran into a babble again. Rick's amusement tapered to a smile, and he put an arm around the woman and murmured softly in Spanish. She glanced at Henry with an expression of relief. "Ah, *Señora, perdóname. Perdóname.*" After one last mortified stare, she backed hastily out of the door.

Henry felt her face warm. "She thought I was pregnant! No wonder she wouldn't come clean today. She thought. . ."

She glanced at Rick, who studiously looked away. "It's all straight now," he mumbled. "Let's get back to the kitchen."

❧

But despite the dismal evening's comic relief, Henry's mood refused to be dispelled. She had wanted the evening to unify the two families, to introduce the children to each other and see if the two households could cement. The day's catastrophes had blunted her optimism, however, and she wished the Montgomerys would go home.

Oddly enough, the children seemed to get along, if not beautifully, at least passably. Rachel, Cindy, and Clara set up a Barbie dream world in Cindy's bedroom, and Henry's heart warmed at the sight of Rick's teenage daughter sprawled on the floor alongside the younger Cindy.

Even Graham and Brian amiably discussed music and cars. Henry didn't hear any more sarcastic cracks from Graham, and once she even caught him looking at her with something like sympathy.

After dinner, the children took over the living room to watch television; Rick and Henry retreated to the kitchen.

"You're awfully quiet tonight," he said as they rinsed dishes. "Are you still upset?"

Henry bent to stack a plate in the dishwasher, then picked off a soft noodle. "I'm just tired," she said. Her head still throbbed.

"We were supposed to talk about the Bread and Fish program tonight."

Henry flipped the dishwasher closed and spun the dial to wash. She folded her arms and leaned against the counter, all business. "Where should we start?"

Rick put his hands on her shoulders and led her to the table. "Sit down first. You look worn out. I'll make some coffee, then we can talk."

She watched him bustle around the kitchen, finding the coffee filters and coffee without any help. He measured the ground beans and poured water to drip.

He smiled at her as he retrieved coffee cups, and she felt her heart do a flip. Their first real conversation had occurred over a cup of coffee, and the smell of hazelnut coffee brewing reminded her of the cozy intimacies of marriage. It was the commonplace things she had loved about being a wife: the first cup of coffee in the morning, the late-night conversations about the kids. . .even the arguments over the monthly bills.

She turned her head, eyes misting.

Rick set a steaming cup in front of her then peered at her face. "Are you crying?"

She blinked the tears to the back of her eyes. "No."

Rick sat across the table, then took her hand. "What's wrong?"

"It's nothing." Forcing a smile, she lifted the cup to her mouth to hide her face. "Tell me about your meeting with Polly."

Rick set his cup down, all smiles. "That woman is a wonder. She's a whiz with the leftover food from the soup kitchen, and she has the best decorated apartment I think I've ever seen. She has excellent taste."

Henry's hands tightened around the cup. "You went to her apartment?"

"Vera went with me." He quickly swallowed his coffee. "Polly has some good ideas for the program. She wants to start a knitting group to make afghans and scarves. She also volunteered to head up a group to tidy houses. Cleaning, painting, stuff like that."

"Those are good ideas," Henry said in a small voice.

"And she sews, too. She makes the cutest baby clothes. She showed me some she'd made for her niece, and—where are you going?"

Henry turned back, hardly aware she'd gotten to her feet. "Bathroom," she mumbled. "Why don't you check on the kids?"

She made her way down the hall to her bathroom, at the far end of the house, then locked the door and collapsed on the chenille mat. She leaned against the cold tile wall and pulled her knees to her chest. Wrapping her arms around her legs, she rested her forehead against her knees.

She wouldn't cry. . .she wouldn't.

How foolish she'd been to think she could juggle her family, her job, community service, and a man in her life. She felt like one of the kids' old rubber dolls whose arms and legs could be stretched to unreasonable lengths before snapping back.

Or breaking.

Soft knuckles rapped at the door. "Mom?" Brian said in an anxious voice. "Are you okay?"

Henry raised her still-dry face, sighing. She couldn't hide in the bathroom like a child. She'd have to untangle the knotted yarn of her life later.

"I'm fine," she said, rising. "I'll be out in a minute."

"Okay." Brian didn't sound reassured, but Henry heard his carpet-muffled footsteps retreat down the hall.

She glanced at herself in the mirror, groaning at her puffy eyes and red nose. A lot of good it had done to suppress the urge to cry. Except for the lack of tears, she looked as if she'd been bawling her eyes out.

After splashing on cold water, Henry dried her face. She examined herself in the mirror and groaned again. Her face looked better, but now the grungy sweatshirt and blue jeans drew her attention. What a sight she must have been when she opened the door to the Montgomerys!

Feeling guilty for abandoning her company for so long, she quickly changed into a pair of black leggings and a baggy sweater. She pulled her hair back with a barrette and applied fresh makeup.

"Well!" Rick's gaze swept appreciatively over her when she reappeared in the kitchen. "You must be feeling better."

"A little," she admitted.

Laughter erupted from the living room over the sound of a board game in progress.

"It's amazing." Rick shook his head. "I never would have thought it possible so early, but the kids seem to have hit it off." He paused. "Brian was concerned about you, though. He came in here looking like he wanted to talk to you about something."

Henry frowned. "He didn't say anything."

Rick glanced at the living room, then smiled. His eyes gleamed, and his voice was soft as he took her hand. "Come on, Henry. The kids are busy. Let's sit in the den for a while. Just the two of us."

Henry swallowed. Funny how Rick made her feel like a teenage girl who wanted to hide with her boyfriend from her parents. He made her forget she was supposed to be the parent. "If one of the kids came in, what would they think?"

He smiled, drawing her closer. "They'd think the truth. That I'm crazy in love with you. And they'd know it was true because I would be kissing you. Like this."

He curved a palm under her jaw and bent to kiss her. His lips brushed hers gently, testing, then became more insistent, more passionate.

It was foolish. She didn't have time for romance. And their relationship couldn't possibly work. If they married, they would have six children to raise. *Six?* She couldn't take care of two! Rick might forgive her for one night of bedlam, but not a lifetime. He couldn't see down the road to the endless piles of dirty laundry, messy kitchens, and ruined meals.

She broke away, breathless. "I. . .I think maybe you'd better go."

A slow, teasing smile spread across his face. "Do you think so?"

"Y—yes." She forced herself to turn away. "I'm glad things went well with Polly. Let me know what else happens, all right?"

She could feel his stare like heat on her back. "Henry, what's wrong tonight? Why are you giving me the rush? The kids are quiet; we've already talked about the ministry. This should be our time." She felt his hands on her arms. "Our time to dream. There's so much I want to say."

Henry closed her eyes against temptation. "It's been a long day. Thank you for coming over. And for the flowers."

He sighed. "All right, Henry. I'll round up the kids and head out. Then you can get a good night's rest."

"Rest. Sure," she said vacantly, tilting her cheek to accept a final peck. "That's all I need."

≈

The casters on Mr. Fitzhugh's chair squeaked as he leaned forward. Evidently trying to draw out the moment and make Henry squirm, he drummed his fingers against his leather desk blotter and squinted.

Like some sort of self-satisfied toad, Henry thought, fighting the urge to smile. Instead, she lifted her chin, her regal posture a result of childhood ballet lessons. The business world set great store by body language, and she knew all the tricks.

"Well?" he barked, evidently tired of the showdown. "Do you think there's any reason to justify your secretary's behavior?"

Henry clenched her fists in her lap where Mr. Fitzhugh couldn't see them. "Louise is a top-rate secretary," she said firmly. "I gave her permission to take the afternoon off because her little boy was ill."

"*You* gave her permission?"

"Yes, sir. She's under my direct supervision. As are several other people in this department." Henry paused, taking courage. "That's what you hired me to do."

"A decision I've had occasion to question, especially since I have my eyes open for a new vice president." He cleared his throat and shuffled several folders. "I'll let this indiscretion pass this once, but next time I won't be so lenient."

Henry took little satisfaction in her own reprieve. "And Louise?"

Mr. Fitzhugh leveled cold, fathomless eyes. "She's cleaning out her desk."

Henry jumped to her feet. "Sir, I—"

"That will be all," he said, handing her the folders. "I suggest you call a temporary agency until you can find a suitable replacement."

"Louise is the best secretary in the office. If you fire her—"

"I said, '*That will be all.*'"

Henry wavered, pressing the folders between her arm and body to keep her hands from shaking. How dare he! How *could* he!

She clenched her teeth. Nothing she could say would get Louise's job back, and Henry needed that vice presidency for her own security. "Yes, sir," she said, then turned on her heel.

Outside his office, she leaned against the wall, collecting energy. Tears stung the back of her eyes at the thought of the young mother without a job. Would her husband have to leave graduate school to support his family?

Louise walked toward her, a cardboard box cradled in her arms. She smiled bleakly.

"I'm so sorry," Henry said. "I feel like this is all my fault. I should have known Fitzhugh would get angry if you left early."

Louise shuffled the box to one arm and laid a hand on Henry's shoulder. She cast a furtive glance at Mr. Fitzhugh's office. "To tell you the truth," she whispered, "I'm glad it happened. I don't want to work for a man who puts business over family. And something will come up. God will provide for us."

Henry put an arm around her to give her a hug. "You have my number, Louise. Call me if you need anything. Anything at all. I'd be glad to give you a recommendation."

Louise smiled. "Thanks."

Henry helped Louise distribute the box more evenly in her arms. "You've been a great secretary. . .and a good friend."

Louise's smile widened. "You, too. I'll be praying for you and Mr. Montgomery."

Henry's heart sank at the mention of Rick. She forced a smile, then trudged down the hall.

"Henrietta?"

She turned back. Louise was smiling warmly. "Don't ever forget that a family's love is a precious treasure."

Henry nodded and returned to her office.

Chapter Twelve

Cindy and Brian worked silently at the couch, folding clean laundry to the shrill noise of an early evening game show. Neither cast a glance at the television or each other but concentrated on rolling socks and stacking T-shirts.

Cindy sat down, sighing. "When did Mom say she'd be home? I'm starving!"

"She said she'd be home by six." Brian grimaced, glancing at the clock on the VCR. "It's already past six-thirty now."

The phone rang and he lifted the receiver. "Hello? Oh, hi, Mom."

Cindy straightened over the clean piles and clutched a stack of T-shirts.

"Okay," Brian said, rolling his eyes. "We'll watch for her. . . . Yeah, I love you, too." He replaced the receiver then kicked the sofa.

Deflated, Cindy slumped. "She's not coming for a while, is she?"

Brian turned back to the laundry, automatically stacking clothes according to owner. "Aunt Mary Alice is going to bring us something to eat."

"Again?" Cindy pounded her fist against a stack of clothes. "Why can't we have a mom who stays at home? Or at least a mom who *comes* home?"

"Be quiet, Cinder-face."

"You and your stupid plan to keep her away from Mr. Montgomery. He may not be Dad, but at least if she married him, she might be home once in a while. And I liked Rachel. She was nice to me! She said she liked me, too!"

Cindy snatched up her clothes and fled from the living room. Brian grabbed the clothes he'd folded and followed in the wake of his sister.

"Yeah. Me and my stupid plan," he mumbled.

❧

Rick paused, and Henry's fingers tightened around the phone receiver. She could imagine the look on his face.

"You can't come to class tonight, Henry? That makes. . .how many weeks in a row?"

She sighed. "I know. I don't like it, either. I miss Vera and everybody else."

"How about me? You won't go anywhere with me, and you haven't even called in the last few days."

Henry blinked, swiveling in her chair as though she were avoiding his face. "I'm sorry. It's just that Mr. Fitzhugh has been breathing down my neck, and with Louise gone, there's been even more work to do. I have to work hard so I'll be in the running for a promotion. You know that."

She heard Rick sigh. "Henry, exactly how much does a vice presidency mean to you?"

"How can you ask that?" she said, hurt. "I need to get ahead so I can raise my family. You know how work is. You have to work hard to get ahead."

"But there has to be a line somewhere."

She pressed her thumb against a pencil. "I can't worry about some imaginary line. I have a job to do." She drew a deep breath. "You're just angry because I haven't had time for you lately."

"How much time have you had for Cindy and Brian?" he countered. "I'll bet you've been neglecting them, too."

The pencil snapped in her hand. "That's none of your business. I can't help that I'm a single mother and have to spend a lot of time with my work. Lots of women do it."

"But you don't have to," he said softly. "You could give it up today, Henry. Our kids seem to get along, and you know I love you."

"Business is my world, Rick," she murmured. "I'm secure here. Not with the washing machine and dishwasher stuff at home."

"You could learn. Nancy always said running a house was just like running a business, only much more rewarding."

Henry laughed. "Shuffling dirty laundry, cleaning out bathtubs, and cooking dinner? There's no monetary compensation for that."

Rick was silent a moment. "Some things you do just out of love, Henry. You ought to know that."

Henry cleared her throat. "Look, Rick. All this talk isn't getting my work done, and I have a dinner appointment with a customer."

"Dinner? You're not even eating with your kids?"

She bristled. "This is the only time I have. I'll be home later to help them with their schoolwork."

"Sure, Henry," Rick said, then let out what sounded like a frustrated breath. "I'll give your regards to Vera at class. Why don't you call me later tonight after the kids go to bed? We can talk some more."

"I don't think I'll have time," she said curtly. "Good-bye, Rick."

She set the receiver down without waiting for a reply, then put her head in her hands.

❧

Henry bustled into the exclusive restaurant, checking her watch for the umpteenth time. Traffic had been terrible. As her car crept through the congestion, she'd wondered where everyone else was going. Were they on their way home to family? Off on a date? Or maybe, like she, they had business.

"Business," she mumbled under her breath, glancing at the lush surroundings. "This is a place for people in love, not for people to discuss an estate!"

"Mrs. Steelman?"

Henry turned. A slight, white-haired woman with a warm, wrinkled smile stood beside her. Henry automatically held out her hand for a proper greeting and put on her professional face. "How do you do, Mrs. Smithwick?"

Mrs. Smithwick clasped Henry's hand with both of hers, disdaining protocol. "I've secured us a lovely table over here, my dear. And I hope you don't mind, but I took the liberty of ordering coq au vin for us both. I'm sure you don't want to spend an evening with an old woman."

Nonplussed, Henry followed the woman's lead to a secluded corner table and took a seat. "Sorting through an estate so soon after your husband's death is a painful process, Mrs. Smithwick. We'll spend as much time as necessary."

Mrs. Smithwick smiled patiently as though Henry were a rambling child. "What about you, dear? Won't Mr. Steelman miss you at dinner tonight?"

"My husband is dead, Mrs. Smithwick, which is why I understand how important estates are. It's terrible to have to—"

Mrs. Smithwick leaned forward and covered Henry's hands with her own. "I'm so sorry. And you're so young. Were you fortunate enough to have children?"

"Why, yes. But about your—"

"And how old are they?" Mrs. Smithwick folded her hands in front of her.

"Brian is thirteen and Cindy is eight." Henry cleared her throat. "Now, if you'll—"

"But why aren't you home with them, dear? We could have met anytime at your office or in my home. Don't you want to be with your children?"

Henry leaned back, sighing. Why did everyone seem to question her love for her kids? Couldn't they see she was just doing her job? Just trying to make a living?

"Mrs. Smithwick," she tried again, shifting in her chair as though digging in for battle. "My children are quite capable of taking care of themselves for a few hours. And we're here to talk about your husband's estate. Not my personal life."

"Nonsense!" Mrs. Smithwick waved a hand. "I insist you go home right now. We can talk later. My only problem is deciding what to do with my money. My husband left me far too much for my own good."

Henry smothered a grin. Never had she heard any of her customers complain about being left too much money. "Maybe you could start a foundation," she suggested. "Perhaps distribute a regular amount to the charities of your choice."

"A wonderful idea!" Mrs. Smithwick's face lit up. "Just wonderful! You must be a woman who's interested in charities herself."

Henry cringed inwardly, remembering the Bread and Fish program. She hadn't given it much attention lately. "As a matter of fact, my church is starting a food outreach program. I'm the coordinator and in charge of raising money. Would you be interested in hearing more about the program and consider making a donation?"

Mrs. Smithwick's eyes warmed, and she patted Henry's hand. "That's a good girl. I prefer to talk about what I can do with Robert's money rather than the amount. But let's meet another time, shall we? You've already sold me on the idea. I just need to hear the details and write you a check."

Henry smiled, relaxing. "Thank you, Mrs. Smithwick. I'd be grateful to meet another day."

"Call me Mildred, dear. And scoot on home."

Henry gathered her purse then rose. "But what about the dinner? You said you'd already ordered."

"Don't worry about that." Mildred winked. "I'm a big eater."

Henry laughed. The woman couldn't weigh a hundred pounds. "All right, Mrs—Mildred," she amended. "May I call you tomorrow to arrange another meeting?"

"I'll be delighted to hear from you again." She waved her hands. "Now shoo!"

❧

Spurred by Mildred's comments, Henry determined not to miss another dinner because of work. She discovered that if she got to the office by six o'clock, she could leave at five. She also wanted to renew her efforts at the Bread and Fish program and get back to the cooking class.

A day before the next class, she and Rick drove to Polly Faradon's apartment to discuss her group's efforts. The program was near completion, and Henry was excited about seeing it in action.

She also hadn't seen Rick all weekend, due to the volume of work she'd taken home, but they'd talked several times on the phone. He still disapproved of the extra hours she spent with her job, but he seemed pleased she'd made an effort to cut back. Henry promised herself she would make a date with him for the weekend.

They held hands as they stood outside Polly's apartment. As he knocked on the door, Rick smiled warmly at Henry, the March sun no competition for his expression. She thought her own heart would burst with hope; she had missed being with him.

Polly opened the door, a smile lighting her own face when she saw Rick. "Hello! It's good to see you. And Henry! Won't you come in?"

"How've you been, Polly?" Rick said as she shut the door behind them.

"Busy as ever." She grinned, tucking stray blond hair behind her ear. "But pleased with the results. My group is very dedicated to this project."

She gestured at the sofa. "Have a seat. I'll bring out some lemonade."

"I'll help," Rick said, following her to the kitchen.

Henry sank into the overstuffed cotton sofa, amazed at the spotless white material. Polly would probably have kids so well-behaved they'd never even spill a crumb or leave smudges on the glass coffee table.

She glanced around the room. Rick was right. Polly did have a well-decorated apartment. With white cotton-covered chairs to match the sofa, a rattan and glass table and mirror, and hanging ferns, the apartment looked like a tropical paradise. Henry thought guiltily about the one straggly ivy in her living room and resolved to water and feed it more carefully.

Polly emerged from the kitchen, bearing a tray with tall, thick glasses filled with lemonade.

Henry accepted one and took a sip. "Mmm. Delicious. And these glasses are so unusual. Are they imported from Mexico?"

"No." Polly glanced away modestly. "I blew them myself."

Henry nearly choked on her lemonade. "You did?"

"I studied with a glassblower several years ago."

"Isn't that great?" Rick said. "She's such an artist. Wait till she shows you the clothes she's made. And the afghans she and her group have knitted."

"I like to make things," Polly said, blushing. "It's nothing."

"Nothing?" Rick set down his glass on a woven coaster. "It's wonderful! Our church is fortunate you joined when you did. Your group's work is going to put the personal touch to this program."

Henry forced a smile and a murmured agreement. Rick's eyes shone like a kid who'd discovered buried treasure, his admiration for Polly more than evident not only in his words but his expression. Henry's palms grew damp against the heavy glass. She set her lemonade down on a coaster identical to Rick's. Polly had probably woven those, too.

"Shall we get down to business?" Henry said abruptly, flipping open her leather notebook.

Polly's shy smile fell. "Can't it wait a while, Hen?" Rick said. "This is a good chance for you to get to know Polly. She's been dying to talk to you."

"Yes, Henry," Polly said quietly. "I feel I know you already. Rick talks about you all the time."

Sure, Henry thought. *He probably tells you how I ruin holiday dinners and scorch pots and pans.*

"I'm sorry, Polly," she said in her most businesslike tone, "but I can't chat today. Maybe another time."

"Oh. S—sure," Polly said, her expression hurt.

Rick glanced quizzically at Henry then settled next to her on the couch and related details of Polly's group. Henry scribbled furious notes.

❧

On the way home, neither Rick nor Henry said a word. He pulled up outside her house, and they stared at the warm glow emanating from behind the drawn living room curtains. Henry rested her elbow in the van's window, open to the spring breeze.

She felt Rick's palm, warm and soft, on her cheek. "Why do I get the feeling lately that I'm losing you?"

Henry managed a weary smile. "I've had a lot on my mind." She put a hand on the door. "And now the kids no doubt need help with their homework. Thank you for taking me to Polly's. I learned a lot."

"Did you, Henry?" he murmured, sliding closer. His fingers curled behind her neck as his face lowered to hers.

"Y—yes. I—"

Rick brushed his lips against hers, silencing her words. The trembling in her stomach intensified, and despite her better sense, she wrapped her arms around his neck.

"Rick," she murmured as he bent his head again, this time for a kiss more passionate than the last.

How had she fallen for this man? They were too much alike, she and he, both of them cut for business talk and action. They worked well as a team, but a husband and wife needed to be more than good decision makers. A home had to have not only heart but someone to manage the day-to-day aspects of living. Rick might want to learn to cook for his children, but he would never be Les. And even if she wanted to give up her career, Henry could never equal the love Nancy had put into maintaining a home.

Rick needed someone like Polly, whose hands and heart could fulfill his life's dreams. Whose confidence and energy could help him raise not only his own children but more of their own. Who was all the things an excellent wife should be.

Henry pulled away quickly, averting her face. "I have to go in," she whispered.

Rick smiled patiently. "But, Henry, I—"

"Thank you again." She blinked as she fumbled with the door handle.

"Good night," he called softly as she scrambled out of the van in blind haste. "I'll call you tomorrow."

Henry forced back a sob, striding up the walk with her head low.

Chapter Thirteen

The next evening, Henry stood outside the church and stared at the glass doors. She had come to love the building for more than its wood and stonework. It represented a pillar of stability, a framework of fellow believers who had seen her through some rough emotional times.

She sighed, shoulders slumping. No doubt now she would have to find a new church home.

"Henry!"

She turned, managing a bleak smile. Vera Fabbish waddled toward her in a bright pink and turquoise wind suit, material swishing. She panted under the weight of a large cardboard box in her hands.

"You're here awful early for class," she said, huffing up. She stared at the door, then back at Henry. "What's the matter? Did that old coot Graves leave it locked again?"

Ordinarily, Henry would have smiled at the woman's pretend anger at her secret beau, but she wasn't in the mood for teasing. "No, Vera. I've been waiting for you."

Vera flashed her a puzzled glance and shifted the box in her arms. "Come inside and we'll talk, then. Can you hold the door open?"

Henry complied. She let Vera pass, then waited, holding the glass door open.

Vera stared back at her. "Come on, Henry. We can talk in the kitchen."

"No, I. . ." Henry's hand gripped the door tighter. "I just wanted to tell you that I won't be coming to class anymore. I couldn't phone; I had to tell you in person. To thank you for all your help."

Vera set the box on the floor with a thud. "You're dropping out of my class? But the session will be over in a few weeks! And the best part is the graduation dinner."

"I. . .I know," Henry said, losing courage under the woman's hard gaze. "But I just don't have the time anymore to come every week, and—"

"It's Rick, isn't it?" Vera put her hands on her hips. "You're backing out because of him. Did you two have a spat?"

Henry's heart constricted, rising to her throat. "No spat," she said softly, then touched the woman's shoulder quickly before releasing her hold on the door and stepping back. "Good-bye, Vera. Thank you."

The door swung shut. Vera gaped through the glass and Henry fled for her car.

≥•

Henry stared at the pile of pink telephone message slips on her desk then glanced at the clock. Rick had called every fifteen minutes since eight o'clock, and it was now ten-fifteen. She'd left the answering machine on at her house last night, and each time she'd heard his voice pleading with her to pick up the phone, she thought her heart would break.

The last message he'd left at her office said in no uncertain terms that if she didn't phone him back, he would call Mr. Fitzhugh and demand to speak to her. Henry sighed, knowing that she was only putting off the inevitable.

"Hello, Rick," she said quietly when he picked up his phone.

"Hello, yourself," he said in a puzzled tone. "What's up, Henry? I missed you last night, and Vera said something about your not coming to any more classes."

"That's right," she said softly. "I don't have the time anymore. You know how busy I've been."

Silence. "Henry, you're not sick, are you? When Nancy first found out she had cancer, she wouldn't tell me for weeks. But I could tell something was wrong from the way she—"

"I. . .I'm fine."

Rick's sigh was audible. "Thank God."

Silence again. "I need to get back to work," Henry finally said.

"Good. Because you're getting off by six o'clock tonight, and I'm taking you for a drive."

"I don't have time to—"

"I want to show you a project I'm working on just outside of town," he said. "It won't take long, I promise. Bring some work home to do later, but say you'll go with me. I'll treat you to dinner and have you home by eight o'clock."

"Well. . ."

"If you don't say yes, I'll call Mr. Fitzhugh!"

"All right."

"Good!" Rick sounded pleased with himself. "I'll pick you up outside your building to save time, then drive you back to your car when we're through. And Henry?"

Her heart quickened. "Yes?"

"I love you."

"I. . .I have to go, Rick. I'll see you tonight."

She hung up before he could reply, then turned back to the mountain of folders.

❧

Henry gazed out the van's window as they exited the westbound freeway. The office complexes and mini-malls lining the transportation artery of Houston receded to quiet neighborhoods with sidewalks, parks, and playgrounds. Suburbia.

"I thought you only designed office buildings," she said, frowning.

"Not always," he said cheerfully, turning right at a stop sign. He waved at a young girl lugging a box of fund-raising candy.

"Then what—"

"Here we are," he announced, pulling the van to a stop at the end of an undeveloped cul-de-sac.

Henry stared out the window at a large concrete slab with various pipes sticking up like candles on a mutant birthday cake. The heavily wooded area showed signs of recent clearing to make room for the foundation.

"Come on." Rick smiled. "I can't wait to show you."

He was at her side of the van to help her out before she could touch the door handle. Whatever this project was, it certainly meant a lot to him.

Rick encircled her waist with his arm as they plodded the bare earth. The foundation seemed to grow larger as they approached, and Henry's curiosity piqued even more.

"Well?" Rick asked proudly as they stood in front of the barren cement. "What do you think?"

"I. . ." She turned to him, eyebrows drawn together. "What is it? It's so big. Is it a convenience store?"

He gave her a tender look. "Look here," he said softly, gesturing down. "But watch out. It's still wet. The crew just poured it today."

Henry stared down at the concrete. There at the edge, etched in cement was a large heart. Inside was the inscription R. M. + H. S.

Rick reached in his pocket and pulled out a small, square box. Opening the lid, he held it toward her. A large diamond surrounded by sparkling sapphires nestled in the black velvet.

"For you, Henry," he murmured. "I want to marry you. I want you to be my wife."

Stunned, she gestured at the foundation. "The house. . .you're building it. . .for us?"

He nodded, smiling. "Seven bedrooms, Henry. Plus a study for you and a study for me. We'll all have plenty of room." His voice dropped to an excited murmur. "And God willing, more children to fill it as the older ones move away."

He drew her into his arms, apparently not noticing her shock or the shudder that ran through her. Nuzzling his chin against her hair, he pressed her face against his shoulder. "I love you so much. You've made me so happy. We'll have a wonderful life together, and—"

"No," she mumbled against his shirt. She raised her hands to his chest, blindly pushing herself away.

Rick grasped her arms gently, giving her a blank stare. "No?"

Henry shook her head. "I can't. You're such a wonderful man. . ."

His jaw tightened, and he dropped his arms. "But you won't marry me."

Unable to speak for her clogged throat, she shook her head again. She wrapped her arms around herself, stifling a sob that welled inside her stomach.

Rick snapped the box shut and jammed it back into his pocket. He turned away in frustration, running his fingers through his hair. He stared at the grove of oaks lining the property then spun back around.

"Why? Is it your precious job? Are you afraid I'll encroach upon your work time even more?"

A vision of a shy, blond woman ran through Henry's imagination: Polly baking bread for Rick. . .stitching him flannel shirts. . .decorating the new house. . . sewing her own baby clothes. She was the one for him.

"Yes, Rick," she murmured. "You've never understood how much my job means to me."

"I've tried! Isn't there room in your heart for me and your work?"

She closed her eyes so she wouldn't cry. "P—please take me back to my car. It's late."

She heard him exhale loudly. "It *is* late," he muttered. "Too late."

The van's atmosphere during the drive back to town was iron silence. Henry thought she would choke from the heavy, oppressive sorrow hanging between them like a weighted chain. She hadn't been so unhappy since the day the policeman showed up at the bank to tell her Les had died.

Les. She'd loved him for as long as she could remember, a cherished memory like crystal packed in cotton. Then Rick had shown her how to love again, how to look beyond the daily grind to the promise of tomorrow.

But she'd crossed that nebulous horizon and found tomorrow lacking. Would a promotion—even if she got it—make up for losing Rick?

At least he would have Polly. As he should.

"What floor is your car on?" Rick said tersely as he pulled into the dark parking garage.

She told him, and they ascended the ramps. At last she spied her car at the end of the row, lonely and deserted. Rick pulled up alongside, then put the van in park. Henry noticed he didn't jump out as usual to open her door. Her breathing quickened, and she sought for the right words.

"I guess this is it," he said before she could speak.

She nodded stupidly, reaching for the door handle.

He laid a hand on her arm. Her heart pounded faster, and her eyes met his for the briefest of moments.

He dropped his gaze as though scorched. "Have a good life," he mumbled, releasing her arm.

"You, too," she whispered, then fled from the van.

Rick waited until she was safely in her car, then pulled away as soon as her car's engine turned over. His van disappeared down the ramp.

Henry's gaze followed the fading red glow of his taillights, and she leaned her forehead against the steering wheel and cried.

Chapter Fourteen

Henry fiddled with the handle of her teacup and glanced around the luxurious home of Mildred Smithwick. She smiled ruefully at the mantel portrait of Mildred and her late husband.

Mildred leaned forward from her place on the velvet settee. She frowned, following the direction of Henry's gaze. "Something wrong with the picture?"

Startled, Henry jerked back to reality. "What? Oh, no, Mildred! It's lovely. I was just thinking how happy the two of you must have been. How long were you married?"

Mildred carefully balanced her china cup and saucer on her knee. "Sixty-three years," she said with pride. She gazed at the portrait with affection. "Robert always referred to me as his child bride. I felt mighty old at the time, but I was only a girl." She giggled. "Hardly had a lick of sense, either. I hadn't been anywhere but the farthest edge of my daddy's farm in Central Texas."

Henry smiled. "You and your husband must have loved each other very much."

"Oh, my, yes. Robert was a wonderful man. But at the end, he was so sick. It was a blessing to give him back to the Lord."

Henry took a slow sip of lukewarm tea. "It was difficult at first for me to admit my husband had died. I didn't have any warning."

"How did he die?"

"In a car accident. He's been dead over a year now."

Mildred laid a soft, wrinkled hand on Henry's knee. "Is that why you're acting like you feel poorly? When you first came over this afternoon, I thought maybe you were sick. But you've got the look of someone who's pining for a lost loved one."

"In a way, I am." She turned from Mildred's knowing eyes, finding it easier to speak to the wall. "A few months ago I met a man at church. . . someone I thought was very special. He. . .well, he thought I was special, too."

"But he broke off with you?"

"No, he asked me to marry him, and I refused."

Mildred's face fell. "But if you cared for him, why?"

"We're just not right for each other. We're too much alike."

Mildred pursed her lips. "Pardon me for saying so, dear, but that's the feeblest excuse I've ever heard for turning down a marriage proposal!"

Henry felt her face flame. "We're both too involved with our careers," she said. "And since we would have six children between us—not to mention any future children—someone needs to stay home to—"

"Wait a minute!"

Henry blinked. "I beg your pardon?"

Mildred smiled sweetly. "I said, 'wait a minute,' young lady. In this age of day care and maids, are you trying to tell me you turned down a marriage proposal because neither one of you wants to defrost the refrigerator?"

"Well, it's not quite like—"

"And you can't tell me, Henrietta Steelman, that you truly like your job."

Henry frowned. *Did* she like her job? Or had she been so busy she hadn't realized the work no longer satisfied her?

"Close your mouth, dear," Mildred said demurely over the rim of her teacup. "It's not becoming."

Henry clamped her lips together, her face burning. "I need my job," she said with quiet determination. "I have children to feed."

"Even if you married this man you're so obviously in love with?" Mildred murmured nonchalantly into her tea.

"Yes! I would go crazy trying to take care of a house. I like to handle business deals, not mops!"

Mildred set her teacup and saucer on the low mahogany table. "Running a home *is* a business," she said. "Look at the wife in Proverbs 31. She took care of her household, including the servants. Obviously, she didn't do everything by herself. And didn't she consider a field and buy it? She must have been a shrewd businesswoman. The Bible says she brought honor to her husband's name."

Henry considered Mildred's words. Somehow those images had never stood out before, only the wife's duties she herself had trouble with.

"God didn't intend us to be constantly on our hands and knees cleaning," Mildred went on. "He gave us brains, too, to use for our family's benefit. A great deal of intelligence goes into caring for a home, for a family. It's not all car pools and cooking. It's participating in PTAs, just like boardrooms. Planning children's parties, just like business agendas.

Delegating responsibilities to the children, just like employees."

She leaned forward. "But whether we work outside the home or not, we are to love our children and spouses while we can. Having already lost your husband, surely you can see that."

"But—"

"And what about working at home? If you feel you can't last a day without a desk and a daily planner, why don't you find some work you can do out of your house?"

Her face brightened. "In fact, I need someone to run the foundation you've convinced me to start. I plan to do a lot of traveling and charity work, so I don't have the time to consider requests from various agencies who could use my money. I'd also like to start my own charity and give money to needy students or causes. Like your church's Bread and Fish program."

Henry gripped her saucer so tightly she thought the china might snap between her hands. "This is all so sudden, Mildred. I can't just leave my job."

"Why not? It might give you the new perspective you need."

"New perspective? Who says that's what I need?"

"I do! Anybody who would refuse a marriage proposal from a man she's obviously in love with had certainly better get her priorities straight."

Henry set aside her teacup and dragged her briefcase from the floor to her lap. "If you're going to continue to harp on my personal life, it's time we got down to business and settled your own affairs."

"Fine, dear," Mildred said. "I guess you don't need to hear the ramblings of an old lady, after all."

She flashed a sanguine smile and primly pulled the skirt of her fashionable suit over her knees as she edged closer to Henry.

⊱

That night Henry made a special point to get home in time to fix dinner for Cindy and Brian. Using the recipe Vera had given the class several months ago, Henry baked a poppy seed, chicken casserole and scalloped potatoes and fixed a Caesar salad. But by the time she set the perfectly cooked meal on the table, she didn't have the heart to eat.

Cindy and Brian dug in with gusto, even asking for second helpings before Henry had scarcely tasted her own food. She dug trenches in her potatoes and picked at the succulent skin of the chicken, her mind miles away from the table.

Rick.

How was he doing? She'd thought maybe he'd phone—she'd begun to hope he *would* phone—but he was as silent as though they'd never met.

Once or twice she'd even attended the second church service—his usual time—but she hadn't caught so much as a glimpse of him. She even sat in the balcony, hoping for just a look. He either wasn't attending church or was staying well-hidden.

"Didn't you hear me, Mom?" Brian nudged her elbow.

Startled, Henry sat up straight. Two pairs of eyes stared at her, and she flashed a sheepish grin. "I'm sorry, Brian, Cindy. What were you saying?"

Brian's face fell. "I said that I think dinner is a lot more fun with the three of us."

Henry's smile widened. "It sure is. If it takes going in to work at six o'clock, I'll do it. I've missed a lot of dinners with you two, and I'm going to try to make it up from now on."

"What about the cooking class, Mom?" Cindy asked timidly. She exchanged a quick glance with her brother, who quickly dropped his gaze to his lap. "What about Mr. Montgomery?"

Henry set her mouth in a firm line. "The cooking class is over, as far as I'm concerned. And I won't be seeing Rick anymore."

"You won't?" Brian looked surprised. His expression turned serious, a little too quickly, Henry thought. "Oh, Mom," he said, "that's a shame."

"Yeah." Cindy lowered her gaze. "I liked Rachel and Clara," she mumbled.

Henry picked up her fork with renewed purpose, forcing a bright tone. "Well, we won't be seeing them anymore, so it'll just be the three of us. Mrs. Maldonado won't be coming back either, so we'll just have to make do again until I can see about getting another maid."

"I can fold clothes," Cindy said quickly.

"After I wash them," Brian added.

Henry smiled at her children, resisting the urge to rumple their hair the way she'd done when they were smaller. Their eagerness was the best encouragement she'd had lately. Surely it wouldn't be long before she could put her other troubles behind her, as well.

Later, as they settled in to play a spirited game of Parcheesi, more than once she found her mind wandering back to Rick or back to the mountain of work at the office. The children behaved better than they had in a long while. It almost seemed they were trying to make up for her recent heartache.

≈

Henry stared at her desk telephone, mesmerized, subconsciously willing it to ring. Only a few minutes remained until her daily meeting with Mr. Fitzhugh. Shaking her head with impatience, she settled down to the work laid out in front of her.

Paperwork. Meetings to schedule with customers, meetings to attend with her workers, and meetings to endure with Mr. Fitzhugh. A never-ending cycle.

Oh, God, Father, what am I supposed to do?

The phone jangled. Quicker than usual, she picked up the receiver. "Henry Steelman," she said breathlessly, heart fluttering against her ribs.

"Henry. It's Mary Montgomery."

Henry automatically straightened. "How are you, Mary?"

"I'm fine." She paused. "How are you?"

"I'm fine, too."

Henry paused, swiveling her chair around until she stared at the calendar on her wall. "Mary, this is probably as uncomfortable for me as it for you, but—"

"You want to know how Rick is?"

"Well. . .yes." There. She'd admitted it to herself as well as someone else.

"I've seen him in better shape. Graham brought the kids over to my house last night just to get away from him. They said he's been quite grumpy lately."

Henry forced a dry laugh. "I hope he's not taking it out on them."

"He's taking his heartbreak out on everyone," Mary said in clipped tones. "But that's not why I called, Henry. I just wanted to make sure *you* were all right."

Henry's eyebrows drew together. "I'm fine. Work keeps me busy, and the kids—"

"Oh, I'm terrible at lying," Mary broke in. She sighed. "I know it's not my place to butt in, but I wanted you to know just how upset Rick is that you refused to marry him."

Henry gripped the phone. "What's wrong, Mary?"

The older woman sighed again. "He's seeing Polly Faradon."

Chapter Fifteen

"Polly?" Henry's voice came out in a squeak. She cleared her throat. "That's good news. Rick and Polly seem to like one another very much. Polly's a wonderful woman." Her voice dropped to a whisper and she squeezed her eyes shut. "And Rick's a wonderful man."

"My son's a *foolish* man. He obviously did something to upset you. I don't know why—"

A sharp rap sounded at the glass next to Henry's closed door. Startled, she glanced up to see Mr. Fitzhugh glowering through the window as though she were Bob Cratchit and he, Ebenezer Scrooge. She held up a finger in Mr. Fitzhugh's direction to indicate the momentary conclusion of her phone call.

"Mary, I have to go," she said. "Can I call you another—"

"I *did* call you with a real reason, not to throw Polly Faradon in your face. Vera Fabbish asked me to call you. There's a Bread and Fish meeting on Thursday night and she needs you to attend."

"I don't think that would be appropriate, under the circumstances," Henry said. "In fact, I've considered resigning—"

The rap at the window sounded again. This time Mr. Fitzhugh pointed at his watch and glared.

Desperate, Henry leaned closer to the phone receiver, anxious to conclude the conversation. "What time on Thursday?"

"Seven-thirty. Fellowship hall. And, Henry?"

She cast a quick glance at her angry boss. "Yes?"

"Please be there. Don't let Rick keep you away."

"I wouldn't dream of it," Henry said automatically. "Thank you for calling."

She hung up before she could hear Mary's response and leapt from her chair. Mr. Fitzhugh burst through her door, his face and neck still flushed above his stiff white collar and navy blue jacket.

"May I remind you that—"

"I'm sorry, Mr. Fitzhugh. I finished the call as quickly as I could."

"Hmmph. It was a *personal* call, too!" he huffed, folding his arms in front of his chest.

Henry balled her hands into fists. He had eavesdropped!

She drew a calming breath. "I said I was sorry. The call was about a committee that I'm on at church, and—"

Mr. Fitzhugh made a bored face. "I'm only interested in your work for First Houston. Not your personal life."

"No, you're not, are you?" Henry said. A catch lodged in her throat, and she clutched the desk with one hand for support. "You've never cared anything about me, Louise, or anyone else in this office. Do you even know I'm a widow?"

"Well, I—"

"Or that I have two beautiful children growing up faster than the work you throw my way? You know I'll do it just because I want to make vice president. I've risked precious time with my family by trying to please you."

Henry advanced a step and Mr. Fitzhugh backed against the doorjamb. The color drained from his face. Henry's head told her she should back down and apologize, but her heart overruled. She'd lost Rick, but she wouldn't lose her children, too.

She drew a deep breath. "I quit."

Clayton Fitzhugh smirked. "You'll never have a chance at another vice presidency in Houston. I personally guarantee it."

His words drove straight to her heart, seizing her with the impulse to tremble. Instead, she held herself erect and still, sending up a quiet prayer for strength. Instantly, she was flooded with the sensation of rightness. She hadn't felt such reassurance for a long time, probably because she'd been ignoring God, too.

"It doesn't matter if I ever work in a bank again," she said quietly. "That may not be where God wants me, after all."

He laughed. "You'll wind up taking the first low-paying job that becomes available."

"I'll work wherever I'm called, but I know it won't be at the expense of my family."

Henry reached in the trash can for an empty box. Without a word, she loaded it with her coffee mug and pictures of Les and the kids. Mr. Fitzhugh watched with a look of silent disbelief. Henry hooked her purse strap over her shoulder and lifted the box.

Chin high, she made her way to the door, then paused and turned. "I'm sorry I couldn't be the automaton you wanted, but I'm more sorry you don't understand the importance of love and family. I hope it doesn't take you much longer than it already took me."

She headed for the elevator.

Once in her car, she drove from the garage's stifling darkness into the warm glow of the spring morning. Driving in midday downtown traffic seemed dreamlike. Normally if she were on Texas Street, she'd be on foot, delivering a sensitive document or searching for a quick, greasy lunch.

Only when she left the stair-stepped Houston skyline behind and hit the Loop did she realize she was clutching the steering wheel like a novice driver. Laughing, she let out a long breath and eased her posture and grip.

"Face it, Henrietta, you're a free woman. You may not be eating for much longer, but you've finally left the clutches of that man. Mildred was right. You really *didn't* like that job. Now you'll have much more time to be the mom to Brian and Cindy you need to be."

Her conscience twinged. Before, it had always been a matter of not being able to cook for her kids; now it was an issue of not even having the money to feed them.

She shook off her fear with resolution. "Okay, God, I'm going to trust in You and not lean on my own understanding. You lead the way and I'll follow."

She pulled into her driveway and braked, staring at the brick structure she called home. Funny how different the house looked in the middle of a weekday. It looked much more expensive. Would God truly provide food, mortgage, and all the other necessities of life?

Henry pressed the remote and smiled as the heavy garage door slowly raised. "Just for today, I really am going to consider the lilies of the field," she said, grinning. "It feels good to be free."

❧

Cindy and Brian gaped, their backpacks sagging from their hands as they stood outside the bathroom. "Mom?"

Henry raised up from where she bent over the tub and waved a soapy hand in greeting. "Hi, kids! How was school? Give me two hours to finish both bathrooms and vacuum, then I'm taking you out to celebrate. You pick the place."

"Celebrate what?" Brian said warily.

Henry winked. "I think I'll save that for dinner. Now off with you, and finish your homework so we can take our time tonight."

Two hours later, they pulled out of the driveway, the children still puzzled and Henry still cheerful. "Where do you want to eat?"

Brian glanced at Cindy, then shrugged. "Pizza?"

"Pizza it is!"

When they pulled up to the pizza parlor, her enthusiasm fizzled into uncertainty. For the second time that day she remembered Rick. The last time she'd been here was Christmas Eve.

"Come on, Mom, what's the surprise?" Cindy tugged at Henry's sleeve.

"Let's order first, then I'll tell you," she said as she slid across the booth's vinyl upholstery.

While Cindy and Brian selected music for the jukebox, Henry fingered a paper place mat. What would Rick have thought of her quitting? He'd thought she worked too much, but would he think her irresponsible for abandoning a steady income?

Brian and Cindy took their seats. "We ordered at the counter, so tell us what's going on."

Henry smiled crookedly. "I quit my job."

"You *what?*"

"I quit. Mr. Fitzhugh was absolutely impossible, and I realized I was tired of not spending time with you. I'm sorry I've ignored you both."

Cindy looked guiltily at Brian, then back at Henry. "We thought maybe you'd agreed to marry Mr. Montgomery," she said softly.

Henry felt an ache in her heart, not only for herself but for the hurt expression on her daughter's face. That was peculiar; she'd thought Cindy and Brian didn't like Rick.

"No, honey. I thought you understood that Mr. Montgomery and I aren't seeing each other anymore."

"Oh," Cindy said in a small voice, lowering her eyes. She slumped her elbows on the table and fixed her gaze on the chrome napkin dispenser.

Brian cleared his throat. "Why aren't you seeing him anymore?"

"We're just not suited for each other, Brian. Mr. Montgomery—Rick— needs someone more domestic than me."

"You sure looked domestic enough this afternoon," Brian muttered, glancing at Cindy. She raised her eyes and exchanged a guilty stare with her brother before both heads bowed.

Henry frowned. What was wrong with these two?

Cindy glared at Brian. "Well, if you're not going to tell her, I am!"

"Tell me what?"

Brian sighed, dragging his gaze to meet Henry's. "We deliberately messed up that Saturday-night dinner with the Montgomerys."

Henry drew back in surprise, speechless.

"We didn't want you to get married to him!" Cindy piped up, her expression earnest. "But that was before we got to know his kids. And he *has* always been nice to us." She glared at Brian again. "I don't care what you say!"

"He wasn't so bad," Brian conceded, then added, "neither was Graham."

Perplexed, Henry studied her children. "What do you mean you messed up the dinner?"

"We figured if he could see you weren't good around the house, he wouldn't want to marry you," Brian said. "I called Mrs. Maldonado and told her you were sick so she wouldn't clean."

"So *that's* why she didn't show up! But she. . .Brian, you know Mrs. Maldonado doesn't speak English. What Spanish word did you use to tell her I was sick?"

"*En. . .en. . .*" He squeezed his eyes shut in concentration.

"*Encinta?*"

Brian looked relieved. "Yeah, that's it."

Henry suppressed a smile. "That means pregnant! Mrs. Maldonado thought I was pregnant."

"Oh."

" 'Oh' is right." Henry's smile widened. The two little wretches had certainly gone to a lot of trouble. "Did you two also plan that little cookie mess in the kitchen?"

Brian and Cindy nodded.

"And that sudden need to go to Adam's was a ruse to keep me from cleaning house?"

Brian nodded again, sheepish.

Henry leaned forward on her elbows, trying to keep her voice stern. "That was a very selfish thing you both did. I'm hurt that you wouldn't even tell me how you felt about Rick. Did you think I would marry a man you two didn't like?"

Brian and Cindy glanced at each other. "Well, you weren't exactly always at home," he said. "And we figured if you married him, you'd have even less time for us."

Henry considered his statement in the light of two children who had lost their father the past year and their mother to a busy career. Her heart flooded with compassion, and she said a silent prayer of thanks that her eyes had finally been opened. How foolish she'd been.

She laid a hand on a shoulder of each child. "That's going to change. I have to find another job to support us, but I promise I'll never let it come between me and the two of you again." She paused. "And as for you two trying to keep Rick away, I forgive you for that."

Cindy and Brian glanced at each other, then turned relieved expressions to their mother.

"Thanks," Brian said. "I'm sorry we didn't try to talk to you, Mom. And I'm sorry for the stupid stunts we pulled."

"Yeah," Cindy echoed, "me, too."

"Then it's forgotten." Henry leaned back, making way for the server to set down their pizzas. "Come on, guys, dig in!"

Chapter Sixteen

Henry combed her hair with her fingers and drew a steadying breath as she entered the church building. Light from the lengthening spring evening filtered into the empty corridor, and a flickering fluorescent bulb lit the way to the fellowship hall.

Before she could take more than five steps, the door opened behind her. With a knowing sense of dread, she paused. A lively conversation between a deep voice and a higher-pitched female one abruptly halted, and two sets of footsteps hushed against the carpet. The weighted door banged shut against the frame.

"Hello, Henry," Rick said.

Henry pasted a smile on her face. "Hi, Rick. Polly." Hopefully her voice sounded steadier to their ears than her own.

Polly's normally serene face looked mortified. "H—hello, Henry. How are you?"

"Fine, thank you." She bobbed her head, the fixed smile feeling as solid as one of Vera's sponge cakes.

Polly drew a short breath. "I'm glad we're having this meeting tonight. I. . .I mean, so that we can talk about the program." She glanced at Rick as though for support. He kept his eyes fixed somewhere beyond Henry, who could see his shoulders raise once as though he'd drawn a long breath.

Polly flushed. "Excuse me, but I have to go to the ladies' room. I'll meet you in the hall." Her low-heeled pumps swished against the worn carpet as she scurried in the opposite direction.

Rick and Henry stared at one another for a long, awkward moment. She desperately tried to think of something to say, but drew a blank.

Face expressionless, Rick took the initiative. "How have you been?"

"Fine." Her insides turned to jelly. "And you?"

"The same." He paused. "How's your job?"

Henry's heart leapt to her throat. If she told him, maybe he would—

"It's fine, too," she heard herself say calmly.

Silence. Henry straightened. "I guess we'd better go in."

Rick stared as though searching her eyes. He finally broke the gaze and glanced down the hall. "You go ahead. I'll wait for Polly."

Henry cleared her throat. "I'm anxious to hear what you and Polly have done."

He turned his gaze back to her.

"I mean about the food program."

She wanted to run down the hall—or straight out of the building—but she forced a steady gait down the hall. Why had she been so shocked to see Rick and Polly together? Mary Montgomery had warned her.

Vera Fabbish met her in the doorway of the crowded room. "Hello, dear," she said above the hushed conversations. "You haven't returned my calls about the program lately. I was beginning to think you'd dropped off the face of the earth."

"I'm sorry," Henry said, feeling genuine regret. "To be honest, I thought about resigning and I didn't want to face you. I didn't want you to be disappointed."

"Disappointed? In you?" Vera's dangling silver coin earrings jangled against her neck as she laughed. "Nonsense. I didn't take any offense about your dropping out of my class, if that's what you're thinking. And if you're truly too busy to handle the food program, I'd understand."

Henry caught a choking whiff of gardenia perfume as Vera leaned closer. "But if you dropped out of my class or this program because of a certain young man," Vera whispered, "why, you're right. I *would* be disappointed. You're too smart to let a little heartache stop you."

Henry tore her gaze from the older woman's knowing eyes. "Thanks for the vote of confidence," she muttered.

Vera straightened. Her coral-colored lips parted and curled upward. "Then you'll be at my graduation dinner for the cooking class!"

Henry glanced nervously at the door just as Rick and Polly entered. "Well, I. . ."

Vera planted her fists against green spandex hips. "Two weeks from Saturday here in this hall."

Henry cut her eyes at Rick and Polly. They moved through the crowd, chatting comfortably. Polly would probably show up on Rick's arm for the graduation dinner, as well.

She swallowed hard, then squared her shoulders. She might have lingering feelings for Rick, but just to prove to him, Polly, and Vera—everyone, if not herself—she'd go to the dinner and have a good time. Vera Fabbish *had* taught her how to cook, after all.

She took Vera's hand. "I'll be there. Should I bring something?"

Vera's eyes gleamed. "Just yourself." She turned away to speak to Pastor Reynolds, then tilted her head with a final aside to Henry. "And wear something nice. It's a formal dinner."

Henry shrugged, then took her place at the podium. She cupped her hands around her mouth to be heard over the room's din. "Attention! We're ready to start."

All eyes turned forward and everyone found a seat. She waited until they had settled comfortably on the metal folding chairs, then smiled warmly. She noticed out of her peripheral vision that Rick and Polly were in seats up front, on her right.

"Thank you for coming and for your hard work," she said. "I'd like to give a report on my committee, then we'll hear from Polly Faradon's."

She paused. "But first let's open with a prayer." She bowed her head, squeezing her eyes shut to force her attention on God instead of the man sitting down front.

"Father, thank You for the love You have given us and that we can return that love through the corporate body of this church. Bless the fruit of our hands, Lord, and use it as You see fit. Amen."

"Amen," the crowd murmured.

Henry raised her head, inadvertently catching Rick's gaze. For a moment their eyes held. The room receded, and Henry could see—*knew*—he still loved her. She wanted to push the podium aside and fling herself in his arms to babble her regret and confess her own love for him.

Polly leaned over to whisper something in Rick's ear. Henry blinked, then glanced out over the crowd. She cleared her throat and clasped her hands behind her back for support. She dug her fingers into her wrists as she watched Polly and Rick share whatever information they had between them.

"I've been in contact with a fairly wealthy widow interested in supporting our organization," Henry said. "She's also asked me to speak to several of her friends. If they're interested, we'll raise even more money. I've also spoken with the heads of several homeless shelters, runaway centers, and other churches to help get out the word about our services."

A murmur of approval rippled through the crowd. Henry forced herself not to look at Rick. He would probably be displeased with her businesslike approach to the situation. She didn't have a tangible product to show for her efforts, only good intentions and promises.

"That's all I have," she said, deflated. "Polly, I turn the floor over to you."

"Thank you, Henry." Polly rose, then made her way to the podium. She, too, clasped her hands behind her back and timidly told of her group's work of potential menus and clothing sewn. Henry only halfheartedly listened. She'd already seen Polly's handiwork.

When the meeting was over, Henry made her escape as quickly as possible. As she inserted her key in the car door, she heard hurried footsteps. Polly and Rick stood behind her.

"I didn't get a chance to tell you what a great job you've done," Polly said breathlessly. "I don't know how you manage to speak so well or to find the courage to ask people for money."

Henry shrugged. "Thanks, Polly. It's nothing."

"No, it was wonderful, Henry," Rick said. He started to touch her shoulder then drew his hand back. "That was good work. You have a real knack."

Henry turned the key before tears formed in her eyes. "I'll see you at the next meeting," she murmured, then whipped open the car door. She saw Rick and Polly walk toward his minivan, and she gunned the engine.

❧

"What's the matter with Mom?" Cindy whispered as she and Brian rinsed dinner dishes.

He glanced at the living room, where Henry read the paper. "You mean, why has she been reading the same page for thirty minutes?" he whispered back.

Cindy nodded. "Do you think she misses Mr. Montgomery?"

"I know she does." Brian grimaced. "She hasn't moped around the house this much since Dad died."

Cindy scraped a plate under the running water then handed it to her brother. "Maybe we could call him."

"No way. I ran into Graham Montgomery, and he said his dad's been miserable, too."

Brian wiped his hands on a kitchen towel, contemplating. He cast another glance at the living room, then smiled. "You keep an eye on Mom. I'm going to make a phone call."

Cindy sighed with exasperation. "Haven't you had enough scheming?"

"We got her into this mess, and it's up to us to get her out. Just keep her in that room, Cinder-face. I'm going to check with someone who's older and sneakier."

"Who's that?"

Brian grinned. "Graham Montgomery."

⋟⋞

"Henrietta!" Mildred Smithwick said over the phone. "How lovely to hear from you."

Henry grinned. Why had it taken her so long to accept the gift that had been dropped in front of her? "This isn't strictly a social call. I wanted to know if that job offer you made me a while back is still good."

"You mean the foundation directorship? Why, yes! Are you interested?"

"Only on condition that I can work out of my home. I'd be glad to attend lunches and appointments, but I'd like to do the paperwork out of my house. I can get my own computer and fax and modem and—"

"Slow down!" Mildred laughed. "I didn't realize running a business these days took so many modern conveniences!"

"It does." Henry smiled. "One other thing, though, and for this I'd be willing to take a pay cut."

"What's that, dear?"

"I'll need a secretary. I'm a terrible typist."

"Do you have anyone in mind?"

"I most certainly do. My ex-secretary from the office. The last time I talked to her, she was still unemployed. She has a little boy and would be glad to work at home, too. We can probably exchange information through our computers without ever leaving the house."

Mildred's tone turned serious. "Tell me your salary at First Houston."

Henry named a figure and felt her stomach twist when Mildred didn't immediately respond. "That's more money than I can spend, Henrietta," she finally murmured. "Especially with a secretary, too."

"I thought so." Henry paused. "Can you afford two-thirds? Between me and the secretary?"

Mildred considered. "I think the foundation can survive that." She paused. "If you can."

Henry smiled at the receiver. "Believe me, it'll be worth it. And I know Louise will think so, too."

"Good. Then invite the young lady over to my house tomorrow, and we'll discuss the details. Meanwhile, we'll write the foundation's first check to the Bread and Fish program."

"You're a dream come true, Mildred."

The older woman chuckled. "I was just about to say the same for you, Henrietta Steelman."

Chapter Seventeen

Hair in curlers and clad in her terry-cloth bathrobe, Henry deliberated in front of her closet.

"Wear the black dress, Mom," Cindy urged. "The one you wore on New Year's Eve."

"Not that one." Henry rifled through the hangered clothes. "Vera said the dinner was formal, but I couldn't."

"Why not?"

"You're too young to understand," Henry muttered.

"It's your prettiest dress!"

"And it reminds me of a marvelous night, Cindy. Besides, Rick's already seen me in it. A lady tries never to wear the same dress twice in front of a man."

"I thought you said you weren't seeing him anymore. Do you care whether he notices?"

Henry paused with her hand at the shoulder of a severe gray suit jacket. *Was* she hoping to capture Rick's attention?

"Nonsense!" she said, as much to herself as Cindy.

"Then you'll wear it?"

Face hidden, Cindy kneeled to study the closet's line of shoes. If Henry didn't know better, she'd say her daughter was smiling.

Henry sighed. She didn't have much of a choice. "I'll wear the dress." She peeled back the cleaner's plastic, rejoicing that the dress was clean.

She frowned. That was funny. She thought she'd hung it back in the closet right after wearing it New Year's Eve. Getting clothes to the cleaners had always been a problem.

Henry scooped up the plastic from where she'd tossed it on the floor. Maybe a dated bill would jog her memory.

"I think the shoes with the little black straps would look nice," Cindy said, holding up a preferred pair.

Henry ran the plastic wrap through her hands.

"Looking for something, Mom?" Cindy leaned against the closet door.

"The cleaning bill. I don't remember taking this dress in."

Cindy shrugged. "You took it in back in February, I think."

"I don't remember." Henry frowned. "And as much as this dress meant. . ."

She trailed off, exasperated. What difference did it make? The dress was clean. The last few months had been so hectic, it was a wonder she even knew where her closet was.

"Here." Cindy shoved the shoes in her hands. "Get dressed, then come out and show me. Then I'll watch you put on your makeup."

Henry smiled, smoothing the dress between her hands. "You can help me brush out my hair, if you want, too."

Cindy beamed at the offer to help make her mother glamorous.

By the time Henry was ready to leave the house, every curl and every flake of powder had come under the scrutiny of Cindy's critical eyes. Her daughter talked her into emulating a celebrity hairstyle they'd seen.

"The magazine was right. It's definitely sophisticated and alluring." Cindy stepped back from arranging the last soft curl. "Guaranteed to turn heads."

Henry laughed, twisting her neck from side to side to see the upswept style's full effect. "I don't care about turning heads. I just don't want people to remember how my cooking used to turn stomachs."

Brian slouched against the door frame. "You don't do that anymore, Mom. You've gotten a lot better."

"I've learned more than how to cook," she said. "Mostly that I'm lucky to be able to stay at home now. A lot of moms need jobs, inside or outside their homes. What matters most, though, is that family comes first."

Brian ducked his head. "Aw, Mom. Did you have to get so mushy?"

Cindy glanced at her brother, then back to Henry. "You'd better get going, or you'll be late."

Henry smiled. "Thanks for all the help, Peaches. I don't know why you made such a fuss over me. It's just a silly dinner. But I feel better all dressed up."

Cindy led her by the arm toward the garage. "You look great. Have fun."

"Yeah," Brian mumbled, unsuccessfully trying to look disinterested. "Have a good time."

The careful attention to her fashion lifted Henry's spirits considerably, and by the time she arrived at the church, she was singing along with the radio.

She glanced around as she shut the car door. That was odd. There were only two other cars in the lot—Rick's and Vera's. She looked down at her wrist then remembered she hadn't worn a watch. Was she early?

The corridor was silent and eerie as she made her way to the fellowship hall. She clutched her handbag, eyeing her own shadow with skepticism.

"Behave yourself, Henrietta," she muttered. "There's nothing unusual about. . ."

The fellowship hall was dark and empty.

Henry didn't even bother to flip the light switch. Obviously no dinner was scheduled to take place here tonight. She must have gotten her dates mixed up.

Disappointed, she slunk back down the hall. Just as she put her hand on the glass door, she heard voices in the kitchen. Curious, she followed the noise, wondering what Vera and Rick were up to.

As she drew closer, she could hear the confusion in Rick's voice. "But Graham said you were interested in buying the ring."

Henry leaned against the door frame. She recognized the small velvet box he held out to Vera, who suddenly turned.

"Henry!" She bustled to the doorway. "I'm so glad you could make it. Come in, come in."

The large, hot pink bow at the back of Vera's head bounced as the woman nodded vigorously. She wore an equally loud pink chiffon dress, covered with a white ruffled apron. Henry smiled. Any other cook would have at least a minute stain on an apron that white. Not Vera Fabbish.

Rick tucked the box into his jacket pocket. Henry recognized the suit as the same one he'd worn on New Year's Eve. Out of all the well-tailored suits she'd seen him wear, why did he have to wear this one tonight?

Rick's expression was puzzled. "Hello, Henry. What are you doing here?"

She took a step forward, closer to the steel counter where he stood. "Even though I didn't finish the class, Vera invited me."

She glanced around. "By the way, where is the rest of the class?"

Rick chuckled, folding his arms across his chest. "I was beginning to wonder that myself."

Click.

They whirled around to the door. It had shut firmly, and they heard a key turn.

"What—" Rick stormed forward and turned the knob. It refused to budge.

"Hey!" He pounded on the door. "We're locked in here."

Suspicion mounting, Henry glanced around. "Where's Vera?"

"Why, she's right—" Rick turned. His mouth dropped in shock, then he quickly recovered. He chuckled. "That crafty old woman."

"What?" Henry strode toward him, heels tapping a staccato across the linoleum. Had everyone gone crazy?

Rick raised laughing eyes. "Don't you get it, Henry? She's thrown us together so we'll patch things up."

Henry felt heat rise to her face. "That's ridiculous."

"Is it?" a voice called sweetly through the door. "It's what the two of you want, you ninnies."

"Vera," Rick warned, "enough is enough. Let us out."

They heard a sharp laugh. "Not on your life, mister. Your kids and I went to a lot of trouble to arrange this, so you might as well at least enjoy the meal I prepared for you."

"Our kids?" Henry called. "Were they in on this?"

"It was their idea. It seems they now like the idea of having a new mom or dad."

"Wait till I get my hands on Brian and Cindy," Henry seethed. "If they think I'm going to forgive them for interfering again. . ."

"What do you mean, interfering again?" Rick said.

She sighed, shoulders slumping. "The night we ordered the Chinese food for all the kids. Remember what a fiasco the day had been for me? My kids were behind all that. They wanted you to think I was a lousy housekeeper so you wouldn't want to marry me."

Rick laughed. "I'm afraid their stunt had the wrong effect. I wanted to marry you even more!"

Henry's heart thumped against her chest. "You did?" she whispered.

Rick's eyes shone, warm. "Yes, Henry. You looked completely frazzled, but you accepted it all with grace. I knew that night you would be a wife equal to any challenge life threw us."

Henry felt her heart rise then sink again. She turned away. "Polly would be better for you."

"Polly!"

She nodded, unable to speak.

Rick gripped her arms, and a shudder of pleasure rippled through her at his touch. She tried to pull away in embarrassment, but he held her firmly.

"You think Polly would make a better wife?"

"I thought she was what you wanted. What you needed."

Rick turned her around, raising her chin with a gentle hand until their eyes met. "I could never feel for Polly what I feel for you, Henry," he said softly. "I told you before I thought you were a special woman, and I'll always think that."

Henry felt tears glistening in her eyes. She wanted to look away, but his hazel eyes glowed with sincerity, revealing his hurt.

"I thought you didn't need a businesswoman for a wife," she whispered.

Rick's hands clasped her shoulders, but his eyes never left her face. "I need *you*," he whispered. "Just as you are. The gifts you have as a businesswoman are just as important as Polly's gift of crafts. We all have different talents, Henry. It's what we do with them that counts."

He dropped his hands and turned away. "But I guess you'd rather spend your time at the office than with a family."

Henry laughed through her tears, joy bubbling in her heart. "I quit my job," she said. "I'm going to be the foundation director for the woman who's funding the Bread and Fish program. I'll be working at home so I can spend more time with my family."

"What happened? You loved your job. You wanted to get ahead."

She shook her head. "Not anymore. Mr. Fitzhugh put so many demands on me and treated everyone in the office like robots instead of human beings. I quit not long after you and I stopped seeing each other."

Rick smiled tenderly, touching her face. "And you refused to marry me because of Polly?"

Henry nodded. "Then when your mother told me you were seeing her. . ."

Rick shook his head. "I took Polly out for dinner one night because she wanted to talk about you. She heard we'd broken up, and she wanted to make sure she wasn't the cause. Leave it to my mother to use that to try to get you to call me."

"But at the last meeting you and Polly were together!"

Rick laughed, his eyes dancing. "She had a flat and asked me at the last minute to pick her up. She doesn't care for me, Henry. At least not like you think. She told me I remind her of her older brother." Rick moved closer, his voice lowering. "Not someone who would ever kiss her. . .not like this, anyway."

He bent his head and gently captured her lips with his. Her head swirled and her heart danced. His arms tightened around her, pressing her closer, and his lips moved to her temple.

"I thought I'd lost you, Henrietta. If I ask you again, what will you say?" he whispered against her ear.

A shiver of pleasure rippled through her. "Try me," she murmured dreamily.

"Will you marry me?" he whispered. "Will you walk beside me, before God, as my beloved in His eyes?"

"Yes," she said softly. Her arms tightened around him in a firm embrace. "I will."

They held each other, motionless, savoring the moment. Henry knew the emotional intensity wouldn't last through every moment of their married life, that they would know sorrow and disagreement as well as joy and peace. But as long as they held each other's honor as securely as they now held each other, as long as they listened to the God who had brought them together, the depth of their love could only increase.

"Hmmph!" On the other side of the door, Vera cleared her throat. "It's about time you two got things worked out. Why don't you give her the ring?"

They laughed. Rick withdrew the velvet box and gently placed the diamond on her finger.

"I'll be adding a gold band to that," he said. "But promise you won't make me wait. We've already been apart too long."

Henry nodded, smiling.

"Let us out now, Vera," Rick called. "We need to break the news to the kids."

"No need. I already phoned them while you two were busy spooning. But I *did* cook you a fine dinner. You'd better eat before it gets cold."

Henry glanced at the empty counter. "Where is it?"

"Start with the oven."

Rick and Henry looked at each other with a shrug, then did as Vera suggested. Rick opened the oven door to reveal a succulent steak. He withdrew the platter and plucked a note sticking out under the sirloin.

" 'This meat is for the strength you must have to withstand the times of trouble in life,' " he read aloud. " 'Go to the first shelf in the pantry.' "

Henry opened the door and took out a covered dish. She removed the lid to find two steaming, baked potatoes. " 'These potatoes represent the sustaining life of your love, a necessary staple of any marriage,' " she read, smiling. " 'Go to the top of the refrigerator.' "

Rick pulled down a chafing dish from the refrigerator. Inside were small, braised onions. " 'These are to remind you of the tears you must occasionally shed, of the weeping that comes before joy,' " he read from the note attached to the handle. " 'Look in the microwave.' "

Henry opened the microwave door, pulling out a covered casserole dish. Inside was a bed of steaming green beans, laced with several pats of melting butter. " 'These signify the tenderness with which you must each always regard the other. Look in the refrigerator.' "

Rick opened the door and pulled out a French silk pie, covered with delicate shavings of chocolate. He gently loosened the note taped to the side of the pan. " 'This pie represents the sweetness of words and actions for which you should strive.' "

Henry took the pie pan from his hands and set it beside the other food. She swallowed a lump of emotion. "Vera went to all this trouble. . .the kids went to all the trouble. . .just to get us back together," she said, awed.

Rick turned the piece of paper over, frowning. "What comes after dessert, Henry? It says, 'Look under the sink.' "

"The sink? Ugh!"

Together they bent to open the door. Rick withdrew a small fire extinguisher and turned with a grin. "You want to read the note?"

Henry plucked the note from the nozzle, laughing, then wrapped an arm around Rick.

" 'In case Henry cooks.' "

A Matter of Faith

Nina Coombs Pykare

NINA COOMBS PYKARE is a native resident of northeastern Ohio and has five grown children and seven grandchildren. Although *Matter of Faith* was her first inspirational romace, Nina has been writing novels for twenty years.

Dedication

For Patrick

Chapter One

The small auditorium looked even smaller, filled as it was with excited chattering children. Rachel Peterson tucked a stray wisp of brown hair behind her ear and sighed. Directing the children's theater was never an easy task, but auditions were almost unmanageable. Trying to decide which of five hopeful little girls would get to play the part of Cinderella was a job for a high-level diplomat, not a tired secretary. And trying to find one ten-year-old boy willing to even pretend to kiss a girl was even more difficult.

The peal of one particular voice reached her ears, and she smiled and straightened her shoulders. After all, this was a work of love. She hadn't gone into directing the children's theater for her own amusement, but for the sake of eight-year-old Abby. After Peter's death. . .

A shiver stole over her as she remembered the horror of that phone call, of the futile trip to the hospital where Peter already lay dead. There hadn't been a chance to say a proper good-bye to the man she had given her love and her life to.

She wrenched her thoughts back to the moment.

Almost two years had passed since that horrible night. The nightmarish quality of life without Peter had gradually lessened.

"Mrs. Peterson, Mrs. Peterson." The small boy at her side was persistent. She recognized him as Tony Howard, the boy she had finally persuaded to take on the role of Prince Charming.

"Yes, Tony?"

His freckled face was almost pale, and the green eyes beneath the shock of unruly sun-bleached hair held actual fear. "What is it?" she asked, putting more patience into her voice than she felt.

"That scene. . ." He stumbled over the words and looked down at his feet. "The fellers say I've got to really kiss her." The words came out in a rush. "At the ball, I mean. And Mrs. Peterson—" He looked up, his eyes wide with appeal. "I can't kiss a girl!"

The anguish in the young voice was real, so Rachel swallowed a chuckle. How differently he would feel in a few short years. She sank into a nearby chair. "Listen, Tony. What did I tell you?"

The small shoulders straightened. "That I only have to dance with her," he replied in tones of distaste. "And at the end hold her hand. That the kiss is just pretend. I just have to sort of lean toward her."

Rachel nodded. "And that's the way it will be. I don't lie, Tony. That's all you have to do."

His worried gaze searched her face. He seemed satisfied. "Yeah. Okay."

"Tony?"

"Yeah, Mrs. Peterson?"

"You know the other boys will tease you more if they see they can get to you." She had a sudden inspiration. "Besides," she went on, giving him a mischievous smile. "You know, when we do Sleeping Beauty, you won't be playing the prince."

Tony was a bright child. His eyes sparkled as he got her drift. "You mean some other feller will have to kiss her awake!" he exulted. "Thanks, Mrs. Peterson. That'll keep them from pestering me."

"You're welcome, Tony." She leaned back in the chair for a moment of precious rest and watched him move away from her. A sudden ache rose in her throat. She and Peter had wanted a large family. But there was only Abby.

Abby came up beside her. "Momma, I wish I was going to be Cinderella."

Rachel managed a smile. "I know, punkin. But remember what I told you when I took this job. I have to be fair and let everyone have a turn at the big roles."

Abby nodded. "I know that's what you said. But the lady who did this before you always gave her daughter a big part. The kids told me."

Rachel put her arm around Abby's shoulders. "Did they tell you how they felt about it?"

Abby's brown eyes twinkled. "Yes, they didn't like it. They didn't like the lady, and they didn't like her daughter." Abby was silent for a moment. "Is that why you're fair? So people will like us?"

Rachel gave her a gentle squeeze. "Not really. I'm fair because that's what God wants. People who have power over others should always be fair."

Abby made a face. "But lots of times they aren't."

Rachel was afraid her smile showed some of her weariness. "I know. But we don't take our rules for behaving from other people."

Abby grinned. "I know. We take them from God."

Rachel felt a rush of energy. How blessed she was to have a lovely little girl like Abby. *If only Peter. . .* She pushed the thought away.

"Well," she said. "We've got to get on with these auditions." She stood up and clapped her hands. In a moment, the hubbub around her had lessened enough so that she could be heard. "Boys and girls, the next audition will be for the ugly stepsisters. Will those auditioning please come up to the stage?"

As Abby took her place, Rachel's gaze sought out the other girls. The boys had their foibles about kissing and that "mushy" stuff—though actually, there was never any real kissing in the productions she directed—but the girls were just as bad. When she tried to cast a witch or anyone ugly, the girls all hung back. All but Abby, who was trying to make things easier for her.

"Isn't there another girl out there who'd like to play one of the stepsisters?" This time she didn't use the word ugly, but her plea seemed to have little effect. The girls had gathered in a chattering group, all avoiding her glance. *Whichever one I choose will be unhappy with me,* she thought sadly, *but Cinderella had more than one stepsister.*

"Mrs. . ." A trembling voice wavered from the back of the auditorium.

"Peterson," Rachel supplied automatically, searching for the owner of the voice. She found her, a small, golden-haired child, whose pale face shone in the auditorium's dimness.

"Mrs. Peterson." The voice took on a little strength. "I would like to be one of the stepsisters, please."

The girl cast an appealing look at the tall man next to her. Rachel gave him a second's appraisal. She saw a very attractive man, pale blond hair, broad shoulders, sun-darkened face.

She turned her attention back to the girl. "Of course. Won't you come up here?" Her questioning look asked for a name, but it was the big man who supplied it, not the diminutive figure making its way up the aisle. "Karen Hendricks."

"Have you performed before, Karen?"

"Yes, Mrs. Peterson." The small voice was firmer now. She was gaining confidence. "I've been in holiday pageants at school."

Rachel nodded. "I see." She bent over the table and, selecting several large cards with dialogue printed on them, handed one to each girl. "Let's see what the two of you can do with this scene."

Though these were the only two willing to play the stepsisters, she would go through the audition process. It was, after all, good practice for the children. She turned toward the seats. "Let's quiet down now and listen."

The silence that followed this request startled her, accustomed as she was to the constant buzz of sound from these youngsters. She saw then that the big blond man had moved up and taken a seat at the end of the front row. Far more children were looking at him than at the girls on the stage.

"Abby," Rachel directed, "you can begin. Read the part numbered one. Karen, yours is numbered two."

"Yes, ma'am."

A very polite child, Rachel thought, leaning back in her chair. But there was obviously something amiss in her relationship with her father. The girl gave him one almost pleading glance and then turned back to the card she held.

"Just imagine," Abby cried, contorting her face into what she must think was ugliness. "The prince is looking for his sweetheart." Abby's sigh was heartrending. "But what a strange way to choose a bride. By trying on a shoe."

Rachel was used to Abby's overzealous approach to acting. There would be time later to calm her down. But what about the shy little girl? Would she be able to—

"I really can't say why a prince would do that."

Rachel straightened in surprise. The girl was good.

"But when the messenger comes around with that shoe, I'll be ready."

"You!" Abby was really getting into the role now. "You're too ugly for anyone to want."

For the merest part of a second, Rachel saw the flicker of pain in the big brown eyes, but Karen's voice didn't waver. "A lot you know," she taunted in a voice whose venom was in odd contrast to the angelic face and golden hair. "Why, your feet are so big you need boxes instead of shoes!"

Rachel interrupted. "That's enough, girls. You'll do very well." She gave the newcomer a smile. Something about this little girl pulled at her heartstrings. "Except, of course, that we'll have to work very hard with the makeup to get you to look ugly."

Gratitude stayed longer in the brown eyes than the fear had. "Thank you, Mrs. Peterson. I wanted this part very much." The child's gaze flicked toward the big man in the front row, then back to Rachel.

"You're going to do a fine job," Rachel assured the child, who was looking almost frightened again. "Why don't you and Abby go off and talk about this scene? It's one of your biggest."

Abby grabbed the newcomer's hand. "Come on, Karen. I know just the place for us to practice."

Turning back to her work, Rachel felt a small inner glow. Trust Abby to take a wounded bird under her wing. But whatever could be wrong between Karen and the big blond man sitting so stolidly in the front row? Rachel threw a surreptitious glance at him and caught an expression that could only be termed grim on his handsome features.

Well, whatever it was, maybe being in children's theater would help Karen resolve it. Rachel turned to the task of pairing off giggling girls and frowning boys for the ball scene. Tony was the only boy at all pleased by this activity. Catching the grin on his face, she knew that life was looking up for him. In the ball scene, all the fellers would have to dance with girls, and worse, hold their hands. Even being told to stand beside Megan Patterson, who was still slightly giddy from being given the part of Cinderella, couldn't dampen Tony's glee at the fact that his tormentors had to share his torture.

With the ball scene cast to her satisfaction and Cinderella, the prince, the king, and the queen all chosen, there wasn't much left to do. Taking the parts of horses and the coachman didn't exempt any boys from being part of the ball scene. An older girl had been persuaded to play the stepmother on discovering that she needn't necessarily be ugly. The role of the fairy godmother had been no problem, of course. All the girls fancied wearing wings and carrying a magic wand.

Finally everyone's part had been assigned. The general hubbub was louder than ever, and Rachel had clapped her hands for silence several times to no avail when that deep male voice went booming out through the little auditorium. "Quiet! Please."

There was no need for the second word. Every eye in the place went to the man still sitting in the front row, and every mouth was wonderfully silenced.

Rachel nodded gratefully toward him. "That's it for today. Pick up your copy of the play and the rehearsal schedule before you leave." She indicated the pile near the front of the stage. "I'll see you next Saturday. And don't forget your hats, scarves, and mittens."

The chatter, when it resumed, was softer than usual. As the children filtered from the auditorium, Rachel sighed and sank again into her chair. For a moment, she was thankful that God hadn't called her to be a schoolteacher. She dearly loved children, but being in charge of so many of them and for so long. . .

She let her eyes close. She was so weary, with a weariness that had not lifted since the day Peter died.

"Mrs. Peterson." The stranger's deep voice, coming from so near her chair, startled her. Her eyelids flew open, and she stared up into a very attractive male face. He had eyes of the same deep brown as his daughter. What a pity that bitterness had marred his attractiveness.

She got to her feet and extended her hand. "Mr. Hendricks. Let me welcome you to the children's theater. And thank you for your help in quieting the mob." The smile she gave him was the same quiet one she gave everyone.

He took her hand in his large one and shook it gravely. "Do you handle these kids all alone every rehearsal?"

He had forgotten to release her hand, and she withdrew it slowly. Strange how some men just radiated magnetism. "I'm afraid so," she said. "The woman who used to be in charge was rather a despot, I'm afraid. She sort of put people off. But I manage."

She turned to look around the rapidly emptying auditorium. "I suppose you're looking for your daughter."

His handsome face, which had seemed almost relaxed, grew tight again. "Yes. I also have some questions."

"Of course." She pushed a stray wisp of hair out of her warm brown eyes. "The rehearsal sheet gives some information." She indicated the one in his left hand. "But what else can I help you with?"

"I want to know if you think my daughter can play this role."

For a moment, Rachel was speechless. In the six months she had directed the theater, parents had approached her with all sorts of suggestions, ideas, and claims of greatness for their little darlings, but no one had ever so much as hinted that a child of theirs couldn't play a part.

She moistened her lips. "I've only just met Karen," she said. "But her reading was very good. I don't see any reason why she can't do the part and do it well. How did she do in the school pageants?"

His face remained stolid. "I didn't see them."

"Oh." She didn't know what else to say and found herself feeling distinctly uncomfortable. She instinctively didn't like the man, a fact which increased her discomfort. She tried not to prejudge anyone, because she believed it was wrong to do so, but this man's behavior was certainly strange, and the child did seem frightened of him.

"I don't think Karen will have any trouble," she repeated. "Now, if you'll excuse me, I'll go look for the girls. Abby probably has them rehearsing scenes."

He only nodded as she turned away, but she could feel his gaze on her as she crossed the stage and went down the stairs toward the little cubicles that served as dressing rooms. What a strange man.

The sound of voices made finding the girls easy. She pushed open a door. "Abby."

Both girls turned toward her. "Hi, Momma," Abby said. "Are auditions over?"

"Yes. And Karen's father is waiting for her."

Though the words were spoken cheerfully, Karen jumped to her feet. "I've got to go." She cast Abby an appealing look.

Abby rose, too, and came to Rachel's side, slipping a hand easily into hers. "I told Karen she can come over after school Monday to practice. That's okay, isn't it?"

"Of course, if her mother allows her."

A flicker of pain crossed the child's face, but Abby answered for her. "Her momma's gone to heaven. Like Daddy."

Rachel suppressed an impulse to take the child in her arms. No wonder she looked so forlorn. "Then she can come if her father allows her."

Abby squeezed her hand in silent supplication. "Will you ask him, Momma? You know how grown-ups are sometimes."

The casually worded request was obviously premeditated, but mindful of the look of concern on Karen's face, Rachel answered lightly. "Of course. I'll ask him to let Karen come over to practice. After all, he doesn't know us very well."

Abby sent her new friend a look that said, *See, I told you she'd help us.*

The big blond man was waiting where Rachel had left him, his face still taut. "I found them, Mr. Hendricks. Just as I suspected, Abby already had Karen practicing."

He nodded. "I'm sure your daughter is an accomplished actress."

"She does all right." Rachel's response was automatic. But why did she feel defensive? She managed to smile at him, though, and to say politely, "We'd like to have Karen come over after school to practice. Abby can help her and learn her own part at the same time."

Her gaze challenged him. *If you're really concerned about your daughter doing well*, it said, *you won't deny her this opportunity*.

For a moment he hesitated. "It isn't far," Karen pleaded, her voice subdued. "Only a couple blocks."

"She can come home with me right after school," Abby said.

Still he hesitated. "I don't want your mother to be bothered."

Abby's usual politeness around grown-ups deserted her. "Bothered? My mother?" she chortled. "She's always asking me why I don't bring more friends home. She likes the sound of kids playing."

And there, Rachel observed, Abby left the matter, trusting her mother to confirm her words. Rachel's little laugh didn't ring quite true, but it was because of the strangeness of this man, not because she didn't want to offer his motherless daughter a haven. "I'm afraid Abby's right," she said. "I like a houseful of children." Was that wistfulness in her voice? "So letting Karen come over would be doing me two favors."

He raised a questioning eyebrow, but she could see that he was beginning to thaw. "How so?"

"It would keep Abby busy. And it would insure that they both know their parts." The smile she gave him was more sincere than the previous one, if still a little nervous. "You've no idea how many children come to rehearsal without having learned their parts. If you think the noise level was bad today. . ." She raised her eyes heavenward.

For the first time he smiled, and his grim face became unbelievably attractive. "All right, Mrs. Peterson, you've made your point. Karen can visit." He turned to his daughter, who, with a grateful look at Rachel, stepped to his side. "And now we'd better get home. Good-bye. And thank you."

"You're welcome." Rachel stared after the retreating figures, the big man and the diminutive girl at his side, the only thing alike about them their golden hair.

Abby's fingers squeezed hers. "I think Karen needs us, Momma."

Rachel didn't reply to this, but she silently agreed. If ever a child looked like she needed a haven, it was Karen Hendricks.

Rachel turned. "And now, young lady, it's time for us to go home, too."

Chapter Two

The next several days, Karen came home with Abby every day after school. Rachel made an extra effort to be cheerful and warm with the girl, who seemed to blossom into an altogether different child when her father wasn't there.

Rachel pondered this one evening during the middle of the week as she put the clean dishes away. Clearly, Karen missed a mother's love, but there must be more to it than that.

As she put the last dish in the cupboard, Abby came into the kitchen. "Momma," she asked, "can we have a talk?"

"Sure. Let's go sit in the living room."

As she followed Abby, Rachel wondered what was bothering her. Several times in the last few days she'd surprised a worried look on Abby's usually cheerful face.

Settling on the couch, she pulled Abby into the circle of her arm. "What is it, punkin?"

Abby sighed and twisted so she could see her mother's face. "I'm worried about Karen."

Relief washed over Rachel. Abby had seemed to cope with her father's death, to be a healthy, normal little girl. But always in the back of Rachel's mind had been a lurking fear. What if the same sort of black depressions that periodically visited her hit Abby? "Why, hon? Why are you worried?"

"Well, I told you. Her momma died."

Rachel nodded. "Yes, you told me."

"Well, that was a couple years ago." Abby frowned. "Her daddy put her to live with her grandma. His job took him all over the world. She hardly saw him at all."

"Wait, Abby." Belatedly, Rachel realized that this information could only have come from Karen's confidences. "Are you sure it's all right to tell me these things? I mean, maybe Karen considers what she tells you to be just between the two of you."

Abby shook her head and looked slightly wounded. "You taught me better than that, Momma," she said. "I asked Karen if I could talk to you. She said it'd be okay."

"All right, then. Go on."

"Karen lived with her grandma for two years," Abby went on. "She only saw her daddy once in a while. He was never at home to come to her school programs."

Rachel nodded. The man had confirmed that much himself.

Abby hesitated and Rachel gave her a hug. "Go on, honey."

"I tried to tell her it isn't so, Momma. I mean, her daddy is big and kind of scary. But he did bring her to the children's theater. And when her grandma died, he got a different job so he could be home here to take care of her."

"What did you try to tell her isn't so?" Rachel asked, wishing she could save this child of hers from the pain of another's hurts and knowing that she couldn't.

Abby swallowed. "She thinks her daddy doesn't love her. And. . .and that he's mad at her because he had to give up his good job." Abby was silent, her little face showing that she shared her friend's misery.

"I see." Rachel was silent for some minutes. *Poor child. Karen must be feeling awful.*

"What can I tell her, Momma?" Abby asked. "How can I help her?"

Rachel suppressed a sigh. "You're already helping her by listening. By being her friend."

"But I want to do more. Maybe if you talked to her daddy. . ."

Rachel's no came automatically and immediately. "I can't do that, Abby. Why, I hardly know the man. Listen." She squeezed Abby's shoulder. "Maybe all Karen needs is some time. After all, she hasn't been around her father much. Give them a chance to work it out."

Abby didn't look entirely convinced. "But, Momma—"

"Listen, punkin. People have to work out their own problems. It's usually not a good idea for other people, even friends, to interfere."

"But Jesus said to love one another." Abby wasn't going to give up easily. "And doesn't loving mean wanting to help?"

"Sometimes," Rachel admitted. "Listen, I understand that you want to help. All I can say is just go on being a friend to Karen. And if there's something I can do, I'll do it."

Abby's face cleared. "I knew you could make it right, Momma." She giggled, overriding Rachel's attempt to interrupt her. "You know, one day at church, I heard the pastor tell someone that with that smile of yours you could charm the lions like Daniel did."

A bubble of laughter formed in Rachel's throat and tangled with the embarrassment that praise always brought with it. "Abby Peterson, it wasn't Daniel who charmed the lions. It was God, who was protecting him."

The unrepentant Abby grinned. "I know, Momma. But Mr. Hendricks is sort of like a lion. And people do listen to you. Even the kids at the theater. And they're hopeless."

Rachel's laughter pealed out. There was no way to outwit Abby. Her faith in her mother was unassailable. *Someday,* Rachel thought with a touch of sadness, *Abby will see that her mother can't do everything.* Rachel thought for a moment of her own mother, so far away in San Diego.

Abby squeezed her arm. "Are there any of those cookies left, Momma? I'm hungry again."

☙

As the month of November moved along, Karen was faithful at rehearsals and a frequent visitor to the house after school. The shorter days and early darkness soon made it impossible for her to walk home, and each time she arrived, she announced the hour at which her father would pick her up. Rachel was always careful to give her time to get ready, aware that Karen feared keeping her father waiting.

It was just after Thanksgiving that Rachel, looking out the kitchen window, noticed that the evening's snow flurry had turned into something approaching blizzard proportions. Momentarily she debated calling someone to clean the driveway. But she rode the bus to work, and she and Abby could walk to church and to the theater, so she just left the car in the garage during bad weather. It was cowardly, perhaps. But she hated to drive in the snow. Peter's accident was always in her mind then. She didn't want to risk bringing disaster into someone else's life—ruining it as hers had been ruined.

Dismissing the thought from her mind, she went into the basement and brought up a load of wood. It was just the kind of night for a fire in the fireplace. There was something cheerful and cozy about that, especially on a cold snowy evening.

By seven, when Karen was supposed to be picked up, the fire was burning merrily and Rachel was curled up in front of it in jeans and an old plaid shirt, studying next week's Sunday school lesson. She liked the people in her class. They had become a second family to her, helping her in every way they could, just as she helped them.

She had called up to Karen that her father would be coming soon, but then she lost track of the time as she considered the parable of the prodigal son. She had to pause for a moment and smile a little. Abby probably wouldn't understand this story. It certainly didn't seem fair that the father should take back the prodigal son and even give him a feast, not after he'd wasted his inheritance and abandoned all his training. But then, God's love went beyond fairness, beyond justice. Though some things seemed particularly unfair, like Peter's—

The pounding on the front door brought her to her feet and she raced to open it. The man who stood there, covered with damp snow, would have looked funny if it hadn't been for the expression of restrained fury on his face. She swallowed her smile. "Mr. Hendricks, I'm sorry. We didn't hear you come in the drive."

"That's because I didn't get in the drive," he said sharply. "At least, not very far." He tried to shake off the snow, but he was no more successful in that than in his effort to mask his anger. "May I come in? The car slid when I made the turn. Now it's stuck. I need to call the tow truck."

Peering past his shoulder through the whirling snow, she saw his sedan tilted at a crazy angle into the front yard. "Of course. Come in."

He shed his boots, coat, and gloves with grim politeness, leaving them by the door. She smothered another smile at the sight of this big, infuriated man stomping about in his stocking feet. He looked different in jeans and a flannel shirt. In spite of his obvious anger, he seemed somehow less frightening.

His voice, as he spoke to the tow truck operator, was calm, but it sank an octave when he said, "An hour's wait?"

He turned away from the phone, obviously trying to preserve his semblance of calm.

"It's all right to yell," Rachel said, taking pity on the man. "But please don't curse in my home."

For a moment she thought her request might bring on the very action she feared, but then the hint of a twinkle appeared in his brown eyes and the beginning of a grin tugged at the corner of his generous mouth. "Why? The girls can't hear me."

"No, but God can." Her answer was automatic, and only afterward did it occur to her that this man was probably not a believer.

His face remained calm, however, and he made no reply.

"Why don't you come and sit by the fire?" she invited. "We'll leave the porch light on. The tow truck place said an hour?"

He nodded. "To be completely accurate, they said at least an hour."

"Then you might as well relax." She gestured toward the living room. "Make yourself comfortable in there. I just happen to have some chocolate cake. And coffee water will only take a minute."

He seemed about to protest, but she turned toward the kitchen anyway. The man drove himself too hard. From the crazy angle at which his car sat, he had swung into the driveway at far too high a speed. No wonder he'd ended up in the yard. Well, he'd have to stay put for a little while now. But whatever was she going to talk to him about?

Too bad they couldn't talk about what was bothering him. But he was a stranger. She couldn't ask him personal questions.

While the coffee water boiled, she cut him a generous piece of cake and herself a smaller one. Arranging the cake and coffee cups on a small tray to carry into the living room, she had a memory of carrying cake and coffee to Peter. For a moment the tears threatened to overwhelm her, but she held them at bay. These moments were coming less often now. And anyway, she had learned to bear them.

Her hand trembled only slightly as she filled the cups, and by the time she got to the living room, she was able to say quite cheerfully, "Here you are."

From the chair that he had pulled up close to the fire, he reached for the coffee and put it on the end table beside him.

"The bigger piece is yours," she said, indicating the cake.

"Thank you. It sure looks good."

He seemed to have overcome his anger, and his dark eyes, as he regarded her, were speculative. "I bet you baked this from scratch."

She laughed lightly. "You lose your bet. I only bake from scratch on rare occasions."

"That theater keeps you pretty busy, huh?"

"Very busy," she replied, at ease now and wondering why she had ever thought this man made her uncomfortable. Karen must be mistaken in what she thought about him. He seemed like a nice man, a man who would be a good father. "The kids take a lot of handling. But it's worth it."

"How did you get into it?"

"When Peter—he was my husband—was killed in an accident, I. . .I didn't want to go on." She was looking into the fire and so didn't see the look of distress growing on his face. "But there was Abby to think about. She loved the children's theater, and so I kept taking her. Then the director quit, and I was the only one willing to take over. It was that simple."

"I see." His voice was low.

She looked at him, surprising an expression of pain on his face. "Abby says you lost your wife."

"Yes." The single syllable held infinite anguish.

"I'm sorry. I know it's very painful. But we have the children."

The hard look returned to his eyes. "You have your daughter. I don't have mine." Bitterness marred his handsome features. "She acts like I'm some kind of stranger."

"She's hardly seen you for several years," Rachel reminded him gently, then wondered if he would ask how she knew so much. But he didn't seem to notice. "These things take time."

"I haven't got forever," he said grimly. "What can be wrong with the girl?"

There were no exploding lights, no voice from heaven, but she knew a God-given opportunity when she saw one. Clearly, she was meant to help this man and his child. "Mr. Hendricks," she began.

His smile returned. "Under the circumstances, perhaps you should call me Steven." He glanced down at his stocking feet, and she couldn't help returning his smile.

She began again. "Steven, I think I can tell you some things that might clear up your confusion."

He leaned forward eagerly, almost spilling the remains of his cake onto his jeans. "If you can help me, Mrs. Peterson, I'll be eternally grateful."

"I can't call you Steven unless you call me Rachel," she pointed out.

"Yes, of course, Rachel." He pushed this aside with a wave of his hand. "What do you know?"

She shook her head. "First, I want your promise that you won't confront Karen with this information. It could be very damaging."

"Promise given," he said, though he didn't look exactly comfortable about it.

She proceeded slowly, choosing her words with care. "It's like this," she said. "Karen believes that you don't love her." Her raised hand held back his protest. "She reasons that this is so because you left her with her grandmother after her mother's death."

He shrugged the broad shoulders under his flannel shirt. "I had to leave her somewhere. I had a chance at a job that required a lot of travel. And frankly. . ." His eyes asked for understanding. "I needed the money. My wife's illness cost a lot. And my mother—where Karen lived—my mother was dependent on me, too."

"But you left that job when your mother died," she pointed out.

His voice grew grim. "Of course I did. I had to be home to take care of Karen. I gave up one of the best jobs in the country," he went on. "I spend half my time driving the kid around, and she thinks I don't love her." He stared disconsolately into the fire.

"She also thinks," Rachel went on, feeling that now that she had committed herself she might as well tell him everything, "that you're mad at her."

His head jerked erect and he stared at her. "Mad at her?" he repeated. "Whatever for?"

"Because you had to give up that good job to take care of her." *And*, she thought, *probably because you look so grim most of the time.*

His face reflected bewilderment. "I miss it, of course. It was an exciting job. But I don't blame the child. What kind of monster does she think I am?"

"I'm afraid she doesn't know you very well. Apparently, she hasn't seen much of you. You told me yourself that you didn't see any of her school programs." She was careful to keep any accusation out of her tone, but his face showed guilt anyway and he hunched forward.

"I knew that was wrong of me. But her mother and I used to go together to watch her. And the memories it brought back—I couldn't handle them. When I was on the road selling, I could keep busy, drive myself till I could sleep at night."

She took a sip of her coffee and nodded. "I think I can understand that." Obsessive housecleaning had been her way out in the early months after Peter's loss.

Steven's face looked haunted. "So my daughter thinks I don't love her and I'm mad at her for having to change jobs. A great start for a relationship." His expression took on that grimness she had first noticed. "What do I do now?"

"You might try a little tender loving care," she said softly. "And giving Karen some time to get used to you again. From what you tell me, you were virtually absent from her life for two whole years. Coming on top of her mother's death as it did, that was quite a loss for her."

"I know." He looked at her with pain-filled eyes. "I've tried to make it up to her. I redecorated her bedroom, bought her new clothes. I let her go wherever she wants to play. I drive her around."

"Mr. Hendricks. Steven." She wanted to make him understand. "Karen doesn't need a new bedroom or new clothes. Or even to be spoiled. She needs a father."

Again his shoulders hunched in that attitude of defeat. "I'm not sure I know how to be a father anymore."

She wanted to lay a comforting hand on his arm. The man needed the touch of another human being. But he was too far away, and besides, he was virtually a stranger. She contented herself with a comforting smile. "We always have the example of God," she said softly.

The expression on his face went from anguish back to bitterness. "Please don't give me any Christian platitudes. I don't have faith anymore. Not after what God did to me."

Shock kept her in suspended silence. One part of her mind searched through her stock of biblical phrases and found several that might help. *"All things work together for good to them that love God."* She could tell him that. Or *"Whom the Lord loveth he chasteneth."*

She moistened her lips to speak the first, more comforting, phrase, to try to lead him back to the God he so badly needed.

But the comforting words wouldn't form, and with a growing sense of horror, she heard a voice in her own head, a screaming mindless voice that repeated his words, *After what God did to me.* Repeated and repeated them. And worse yet, believed them.

The silence in the room lengthened. Again she tried to speak the words of comfort, of faith. But they wouldn't come and, appalled at what she'd discovered within herself, she, too, stared into the flames.

It was the girls, clattering down the stairs, who finally broke the uneasiness that lay heavily in the room. "Mrs. Peterson," Karen cried, coming around the corner from the stairs. "My dad is—" The words died on her lips.

Rachel found herself released from her sense of misery as swiftly as she had been captured by it. With relief, she thrust the whole thing out of her mind. "Yes, Karen. Your dad's here. But the car got stuck, and we're waiting for the tow truck."

"Oh." Karen seemed unable to believe that her father was sitting there, in the Peterson living room, in his stocking feet.

"Shall we go back and practice some more?" Abby asked.

Rachel smiled. Always the little diplomat, Abby had sensed the tension in the room. "I—"

The ringing of the doorbell interrupted her.

"That's probably the tow truck," Steven said, getting to his feet. "I don't know how long this will take." He sent his daughter a smile. "You might as well go back up and play till we get the car out. No use your waiting around down here."

"Yes, Daddy." Karen still seemed in a kind of daze, but Rachel was pleased to see that she responded to her father's smile with one of her own.

Half an hour later, the car was out on the street, warming up, and Karen climbed into her outdoor clothes and joined her father at the door.

"Thank you," Steven Hendricks said. "I'm sorry if I ruined your evening."

"Not at all." Rachel was quick to say the polite thing. "I enjoyed your company." That was not quite the truth, and he seemed to know it. One of those blond brows shot up, and a smile tugged at the corner of his strong mouth.

She felt herself flushing a little. She was not used to telling lies, even polite, little, white ones. But try as she might, she could think of nothing more to say. With an arm around Abby's shoulders, she watched the Hendricks go out into the storm. Surely this had been a God-given opportunity to help the man. Maybe something she had said would be useful to him.

The rest of it—the terrible bleakness in his voice when he spoke of what God had done to him and her own frightening reaction to that—she wasn't even going to think about that. That voice in her head was only some momentary aberration. She didn't blame God for Peter's death. She didn't.

Chapter Three

Gradually Rachel came to believe herself. Whatever it was that had made her feel like that, made her think that she agreed with Steven Hendricks's idea that God had done something terrible to him, it had been only momentary. God did not do bad things to people. It was a person whose carelessness had killed Peter. It was hardly fair to blame that on God.

And anyway, it was not her business to put blame anywhere. She had other things to think of, like Steven Hendricks's daughter.

Karen seemed to be blooming. Her cheeks glowed and her eyes sparkled when she came in after school with Abby. Rachel watched the transformation with a deep sense of inner joy. Karen had obviously found a friend she needed, and Abby was happy too. They were soon letter perfect in their parts as wicked stepsisters, and Rachel often smiled to herself at the sound of girlish laughter drifting down the stairs. *It's a good sound,* she thought, offering a small prayer of thanksgiving that she had been there to offer Karen some much-needed love.

And then, of course, it happened. The Wednesday after Thanksgiving, Karen and Abby came in after school, their faces long, their eyes full of unshed tears.

"Oh, Momma," Abby cried, unwinding her scarf and struggling out of her boots. "Karen's daddy. . ." She came to a stop, clearly not knowing how to go on.

Rachel turned to Karen. "What about your father?" she asked.

Karen swallowed hastily as she set her boots beside Abby's. "He said I can't come here so often. He said. . ." Karen swallowed again. "He said I've been making a nuisance of myself."

The child's big brown eyes reflected her misery. Rachel called up a cheerful smile. "That's nonsense. You're not a nuisance." She watched the misery in Karen's face subside. "Not the least bit. I love having you here. And so does Abby. You know that."

"Thank you, Mrs. Peterson." Karen was still perilously close to tears.

"But," Rachel went on, "since your father thinks you're overdoing it, maybe you shouldn't come so often."

"I don't see why—" Abby began sharply, but Rachel cut her off with a warning look. There was no use railing at Steven Hendricks. He was clearly a troubled man. Their main concern should be Karen and her feelings.

"Your father," Rachel suggested, "must have good reasons for what he does."

She didn't look at Abby, but she sensed her feeling of outrage. "You know, maybe he would like to have you do some things with him."

Karen looked so doubtful that Rachel had to cough to hide a smile.

"He never said so," the child replied.

Now Rachel allowed herself a little smile. "Sometimes people have trouble saying important things. Even grown-ups."

Karen still didn't look convinced, but she did appear interested. "Do you really think—" she began, then shook her head. "He's always so busy." She stopped suddenly, as though remembering something. "But he did say he would help me rehearse." She announced this almost as though she couldn't believe the memory.

"And have you asked him to?" Rachel inquired.

Karen shook her head. "No. I didn't need any help. Abby and I learned it all. And he always seemed so busy."

"Maybe he gets lonely," Rachel suggested. "After all, you've been over here almost every evening."

Karen looked even more surprised by this suggestion.

"I'll tell you what," Rachel said. "You ask him to help you with your part. He'll be pleased at how well you're doing." She smiled in answer to Karen's smile. And then the idea hit her. Of course! Why hadn't she thought of it before? *It was the perfect—God-given,* she thought with a little quiver of joy—*solution.* "And Karen, why don't you ask your father if he'd be willing to come to rehearsal on Saturday and help? Tell him I'd be very grateful."

Karen's smile faded, and Rachel wondered if she'd made a mistake. Maybe having her father there would spoil Karen's enjoyment. On the other hand, he would certainly be there for at least one performance. So it would be better for Karen to get used to him. "Yes," she said aloud, though more to herself than to the girls. "Tell him I'd be very grateful."

❧

The next day's reflection made Rachel considerably less sure of herself. Perhaps she'd been foolish in thinking that the idea had come from God.

That afternoon when Abby came home from school, Rachel was waiting apprehensively. "Did Karen say anything about what we talked about last night?"

Abby tried to smile. It was obvious that she had grown used to Karen's company and was going to miss her.

"She says he's going to help her rehearse, Momma. She's allowed to come here on Mondays and Wednesdays. The other evenings she has to stay home with her father."

Abby's reaction puzzled Rachel. She'd expected much more animosity toward the man. "That will be good for both of them," she said.

Abby nodded. "Yes, I thought so too. Karen really does love her daddy. Maybe this will be the start of their really getting together." Abby's small face crumpled. "But I miss having her here."

"Me, too," Rachel said, opening her arms. "Me, too. But we want what's best for Karen, don't we?"

Abby nodded, her face buried in Rachel's waist. "Every little girl needs a daddy," Rachel said, and then the pain hit, a pain so sharp it was almost physical, the pain of Peter's loss. And her tears came.

"It's all right, Momma." Abby rose to the emergency. "I miss Daddy, but I know he didn't want to leave us." Her arms tightened around Rachel. "And I have you. Karen only has her daddy. And I do want her to be happy."

They stood there for a few minutes, their arms around each other, letting the cleansing tears flow. *Thank God,* Rachel thought, *that I've been given the grace to share my grief with my daughter.* How much more terrible it would be if she hadn't, if she'd tried to save Abby from this very necessary pain.

Their tears stopped about the same time. Abby unwound her arms and sniffled. "I need a tissue."

"Me, too." Rachel took her hand. "There's some in the kitchen. Let's go and wash up. And then," she managed a small smile, "how about baking a batch of cookies? Whatever kind you want. And after supper, we'll play a game or something. We'll do whatever you want."

Abby's smile is like a small miracle, Rachel thought, *a miracle that never ceases to amaze me.*

"Whatever I want?" Abby repeated. "Well, I'll have to think about that."

In the end they made their cookies—chocolate chip, Abby's favorite—and watched a movie on the Disney Channel. And it never once occurred to

Rachel to ask if Karen had mentioned anything about her father's response to the invitation to help at rehearsals.

෯

It was not until Saturday morning, as she stood looking out over the auditorium full of laughing noisy children, that Rachel thought to wonder if Steven Hendricks would take her up on her offer. Probably not. He was, as Karen had said, a busy man.

The noise level was quite high that morning, and she wished she'd sent him a written invitation. She really could use some help.

Well, she'd known something about the job when she took it on. She smiled ruefully. Not everything, of course. It was pretty hard for the mother of one to imagine handling this many children.

She wouldn't get anything done standing there feeling sorry for herself. Clapping her hands, she waited for the noise level to subside somewhat. "Boys and girls." Most of the chatter stopped. A few girls went on giggling in one corner, and two boys were wrestling in the front row of seats. But none of that was unusual.

She raised her voice a tone higher. "Boys and girls. Let's start with the scene where the fairy godmother arrives. Okay—Cinderella, godmother, horses, mice, driver, footmen—on stage. And the rest of you, quiet. Please."

She didn't exactly get quiet, but the called-for actors trooped to the stage. Rachel noticed Abby watching the door, and she wondered if Karen had caught cold or something. But then all her attention was taken up by the children in front of her.

"All right. You boys be quiet till you're called."

"Now, Cinderella, you're sitting by the fire." Megan Patterson dropped to the floor by the pile of logs that represented the fire. "And you're thinking about the ball. Sadly."

Megan tried dutifully to put on an expression of sadness. Rachel backed away, almost to the edge of the stage, to get a better idea of the effect and to see how Megan's voice would carry.

"Careful!" a masculine voice cried behind and below her. Startled, she jumped and almost fell off the edge. She turned. "Good morning, Mr. Hendricks."

"Steven," he said with that disarming smile as he climbed the stairs to the stage. "And I'm here to accept your invitation. What can I do?"

Rachel thought fast. She was really surprised to see him and hadn't given much thought to the matter of what he could do. But she could certainly use his help. She laughed. "Well, if you really want to help, there's one scene I absolutely dread rehearsing."

"Yes. Go on." He looked like he could take on anything.

"It's the ball scene," she explained. "The boys have to dance with the girls."

He grinned. "And they don't like to. Right?"

"Right."

"Okay. I'll see what I can do. I've got Karen's script here. Show me where you want me to begin."

Rachel took the script with a grateful smile. Now she wouldn't have to coax the reluctant boys into dancing with the giggling girls.

"It starts here," she said, showing him the page. "I'll just take Cinderella and the prince off in the corner to practice their lines, and you can have the whole stage."

"You're sure you don't mind?"

"Mind?" Her laughter pealed out so merrily that Abby, across the room, turned to look. "Of course I don't mind; I'll be eternally grateful."

"Fine," he said. "But first maybe you'd better introduce me to the kids. Give me a bit of authority, you know."

"Of course." He was right in what he said, but she knew it wasn't necessary. He already had authority. This man could handle anyone, anyone but his own lonely daughter. But he was here, and surely that was a good sign.

She clapped her hands again, then Steven's shrill piercing whistle rang through the auditorium, and every child turned immediately to look.

"This is Mr. Hendricks," Rachel said. "He's going to be helping us today. Now he wants all the characters in the ball scene on stage." She turned to Cinderella.

"Except you, Megan." She turned back to the seats. "And Tony. You two come with me. We'll go over your lines."

To her surprise, Tony moved quickly, probably because when the other boys were involved in the ball scene, they wouldn't be able to stand around and gawk at him. Or snicker when he professed his undying love for that girl, Cinderella.

The children trooped up on the stage: the boys reluctantly, as though to face torture, and the girls awash in giggles. "Where's the prop man?" Steven asked.

"Prop girl," prompted an ever-helpful Abby. "Here she is. Her name's Shawna."

"Well, Shawna, will you get the record ready while I get these kids into couples?"

"Yes, sir." Shawna returned the smile he gave her and went to the record player.

Rachel didn't watch any more. Steven Hendricks was a competent man. He could be counted on to manage and manage well. She turned to the children in front of her. "Now, Tony, you and Megan have been dancing. She hears the bells chiming midnight and pulls away. We'll start there. Okay?"

"Okay."

"Okay."

"The bells! It's midnight—" Megan pulled her hand from Tony's and turned.

"Wait," Rachel said. "Tony, you've got to hang on to her hand a little harder. Remember, you don't want to lose her."

Tony looked about to say that he'd be happy to do that very thing, but he only nodded. How to make him understand? Rachel puzzled over it. And then she had an idea. "Tony, do you have a dog?"

"Sure. His name's Pickles." Tony watched her, waiting to see what dogs had to do with Cinderella.

"You like him a lot, don't you?" she continued.

"Sure. He's my dog." For Tony that seemed to sum up everything.

"Suppose he was trying to run away and you'd never see him again?"

Tony looked confused. "He wouldn't do that. He wouldn't run away. He likes me."

She took another approach. "What if someone were trying to take him away from you?"

Tony's lower lip thrust out, and he scowled belligerently. "Nobody better try," he said darkly.

"That's it. That's the feeling," Rachel said. "Feel that way about Cinderella leaving you."

From his expression it was clear that Tony couldn't really imagine anyone caring as much for a girl as for a dog. But at least he held on to Megan's hand and managed a more anxious expression as she turned to run off.

"That's better, Tony. Much better." Rachel smiled. "Now let's try it again."

And so the morning went. Almost before it seemed possible, it was noon, and the children were pulling on boots and scrambling for gloves, scarves, and hats. With a satisfied smile and a real sense of accomplishment, Rachel watched them go. The play was finally taking shape. "That was a good rehearsal," she said to Steven Hendricks as he came up, carrying his coat and Karen's. "I wish you could be here every week."

"I don't see why not," he said cheerfully. "I haven't had so much fun in a long time."

"Really? You'll really come all the time?" She could hardly believe her good fortune.

"Yes. If you're sure you'd like that."

The expression on his face was strange. She couldn't understand it. "Why shouldn't I?"

"Well, for one thing, I don't want to get in your way."

Her laughter pealed out again. "Believe me, you won't. You've no idea how difficult it is to get boys this age to dance with girls."

His laughter joined hers. "Oh, yes, I do! I just learned."

Abby and Karen came up then, Abby carrying their coats. "You did very well, girls," Rachel praised. "It's such a relief to me to know that you're perfect in your parts."

"Yes," Steven agreed, his eyes twinkling. "And I think you deserve a reward, all of you."

Startled, Rachel turned to the man beside her. "What kind of reward?"

"How about a big dish of ice cream?"

"I want a hot fudge sundae," Abby cried, her eyes sparkling.

"I want strawberry," Karen said, picking up Abby's enthusiasm.

The girls' enthusiasm decided Rachel. She couldn't bear to disappoint them. She did, however, make a token protest. "But it's lunchtime."

"Then we'll have a sandwich first," Steven Hendricks said. "I know just the place. My treat," he continued, taking Rachel's coat from Abby and holding it out for Rachel to slip into.

"But that's not fair."

"Yes, it is," he said firmly. "How many times has Karen been to your house? How many after-school snacks have you fed her?"

"Lots and lots," chimed in Karen, quite to Rachel's surprise.

"Right," Steven said. "So this treat is mine. It's all settled."

Rachel was too tired to protest anymore, and besides, there was a certain logic to his words. It was never good to make a person feel too beholden. So she allowed herself to be led down the aisle and out the door, the girls chattering happily ahead of them.

The restaurant was a little place. Small and tucked away on a back street, it bore the name of Kitty's. Though it wasn't far from the high school, Rachel had never seen it before.

"I acknowledge that the decor isn't much," Steven said, ushering them into a corner booth. "But the food is great. I guarantee it. And the ice cream—it's absolutely wonderful."

Rachel surveyed the slightly shabby menu. "You have to eat something nutritious first," she warned Abby.

Abby giggled. "I know, Momma. How about a bacon, lettuce, and tomato sandwich?"

Rachel hesitated. "It's so cold outside."

"Then we'll just add a bowl of hot soup," Steven said with a smile. "Will that satisfy your motherly instincts?"

"Yes." She capitulated and joined their laughter.

She hadn't laughed so much in a long time, a very long time, and the fatigue she usually felt after a long morning of rehearsals seemed to have vanished. She didn't quite understand it, but she felt alive and full of energy. Maybe it was because of Steven's help. That had made a great difference. She smiled at him gratefully.

The waitress came to take their orders, smiling at the girls, who were trying to act grown-up and serious but who broke into unexplained giggles every now and then. Steven smiled, too. "First, what's your soup today?"

"Homemade vegetable."

He looked at the girls, who nodded, and then to Rachel. "That should be fine," she said.

"Four bowls of soup then." He looked at Abby. "Still want your BLT?"

"Yes, Mr. Hendricks."

Abby's eyes were sparkling. Oh, Abby was having a very good time.

Steven looked to his daughter. She didn't wait for him to say anything but piped up, "Me, too, Daddy. I want the same as Abby."

His gaze swung next to Rachel. "You, too?"

She returned his smile. "Me, too."

"Well," he told the waitress. "I guess that's it. Four soups, four BLTs. Milk for the girls. Coffee for us." He looked again to Rachel. "Right?"

"Right."

Karen stirred restlessly and looked at her father. She seemed about to say something but couldn't get it out.

"We'll order dessert later." He grinned at them. "Don't worry; I won't forget. I like ice cream, too."

Abby giggled, and Karen joined her. Watching Steve and Karen, Rachel was conscious again of a deep thankfulness. If God meant to use her to help these two get back together, as He seemed to be doing, she was very glad. To help others grow in grace and love could be part of her own spiritual growth.

And she had grown already, she realized suddenly. Now she was able to enjoy this kind of thing, to feel part of the group. When Peter died, she'd lost a vital part of herself. She'd thought perhaps she'd lost it forever. But at least now she'd learned to live with her loss. She could enjoy good times like this without being swamped by old memories. Yes, helping others had unexpected benefits.

Chapter Four

The winter days passed. The week flew quickly by. On Saturday morning, Rachel was a little nervous. What if Steven had changed his mind? That wouldn't be unusual. After all, he was a busy man. To expect a man like that to spend his Saturdays with a children's theater seemed. . .well, strange.

But he did show up, smiling and cheerful, and watched with a pleased expression as Abby and Karen ran through their lines. At Rachel's request, he took over the direction of the stagehands, organizing them and working on the lighting and other effects. She was immensely grateful for his help. She had carried the whole burden for so long, with only a few older children to help her, that now it seemed wonderful to be able to focus all her attention on the actors themselves.

As they stood after rehearsal, watching the children leave, Rachel turned to Steven gratefully. "I can't thank you enough," she said softly. "The theater has become fun for me again."

"You're very welcome," he said soberly. "But I really feel like I should be thanking you. I'm having fun, too."

"Then it's good for both of you," chimed in Abby as she and Karen came up, carrying the coats.

Before Steven Hendricks could reach for it, Rachel took her coat and slipped it on. Turning from Abby, she caught a glimpse of a strange, almost pleading, look Karen was directing at her father. Then he actually winked at the child!

A little embarrassed at having seen this intimate moment between father and daughter, Rachel turned back to Abby. "Well, I guess we've got everything."

"Yes, Momma."

"Well, then, let's go," Steven said cheerfully. "I wonder what the soup will be today."

For a moment Rachel stood silent. One lunch had been all right, but to make it a regular habit. . . Then Abby's hand slipped into hers, and she felt the pressure of pleading fingers, heard the barely audible, "Please, Momma."

"We had such a good time last week," Steven said. "We thought we could make it a regular thing. Didn't we, Karen?"

"Yes, Daddy." The child's eyes were shining. "Please, Mrs. Peterson. We had so much fun."

Rachel hesitated still, but how could she resist the two little faces full of entreaty? Even Steven Hendricks looked anxious, as though he would be disappointed if she refused. The man was lonely, she realized. After all, he hadn't been living long in this neighborhood.

But there was something vaguely wrong with a standing lunch date like this, something. . . It came to her then: the word she was using to think about it. It wasn't a date Steven Hendricks was proposing. She would, of course, have said a definite no to something like that. This was just a lunch to help a lonely little girl and her father get back together.

"On one condition," Rachel said to the circle of waiting faces. "We have to go Dutch."

For just a minute it seemed he would protest, but then he swallowed hastily and said, "You're on. Every Saturday after rehearsals we lunch together." He grinned. "Dutch."

"And no junk food," Rachel added.

"No junk food," he repeated solemnly.

The girls groaned aloud, but their eyes sparkled, and it was clear they were both delighted with the arrangement.

≈

Midway through the next week—a week in which everything seemed to be going well—Abby came home and announced, "I've got to talk to you, Momma."

Rachel put down the potato she was peeling and wiped her hands on a towel. When Abby spoke in that tone of voice, it was time to pay complete attention. "What is it?" she asked, pulling out a kitchen chair and sitting down.

Abby plopped into the other chair. "It's Karen."

"I thought she was getting along fine."

Abby sighed. "I thought so, too. But now she thinks her father wanted a boy. That he wanted her to be a boy."

Rachel shook her head. "Whatever gave her an idea like that?"

Abby frowned. "She says it's easy enough to see. Look at the way he laughs and jokes with the boys at the theater."

"But that doesn't mean anything," Rachel protested.

"That's what I told her, Momma. But she wouldn't listen to me." Abby looked about to break into tears. "And things were looking so much better."

Rachel managed a smile. "Don't worry," she said as cheerfully as she could. "I'm sure it'll work out." She frowned. "Maybe I'll give Mr. Hendricks a call."

Abby's face cleared instantly. "I knew you could fix it, Momma."

"Now, Abby, I didn't say that. I can only try."

Abby's usual cheerful disposition asserted itself. "That'll be enough, Momma. I know it will."

Watching Abby get up from the table and head for the cookie jar, Rachel wasn't so sure. Abby was too young to realize that life was one struggle after another. People would always have problems. They were just expected to solve them.

This problem, of course, had been dumped in her lap. So what was she going to do about it? It did seem that Steven Hendricks ought to know about this newest development. She got up and went back to peeling potatoes. If she called him now, Karen would be there, and he wouldn't be able to talk freely. But she didn't have an office number for him.

Finally, she finished the potatoes and put them on to cook. She'd have to call him at home and arrange to speak to him later. A glance at the clock told her it was after five, so she went to the phone. No use putting it off.

"Hello, Steven Hendricks here."

She swallowed hastily and wondered why she should feel embarrassment. "Ah, this is Rachel Peterson."

"Rachel! Hello! What can I do for you?"

"I. . .I'd like to speak to you. Alone. About Karen. Nothing really serious, but something I just discovered. Will you call me tomorrow at work? Or give me your work number so I can reach you?"

"Where do you work?" Steven asked. Thank goodness, he didn't seem terribly upset. After all, she didn't want to scare him.

"At the high school," she returned.

"Good. That's close to my office. And to Kitty's. How about meeting me there for lunch tomorrow?"

"Well. . .I only have an hour."

"Can't you get someone to cover for you?" he coaxed.

Actually, she could. There were always girls from the secretarial courses around, putting in their office practice hours. And Mr. Wilson wouldn't care if she took a little extra time. He said she spent too many lunch hours at her desk anyway.

"Yes, I guess I could."

"Good. What time's convenient for you?"

She considered. "If we wait till one, the lunch crowd will be gone and it won't be so noisy."

"One it is, then," he replied. "I'm looking forward to it. Good-bye."

What a strange thing to say, she thought as she hung up the phone. He made it sound almost like a date, though of course it wasn't. Probably Karen had been in the room with him, and he didn't want her to suspect what was going on.

Rachel went back to making dinner. It should be simple. She would just tell Steven what Karen was feeling and he would do something to counteract it.

❧

The next afternoon, Rachel arrived at the restaurant flushed and glowing from her walk in the cold air. As she stamped the snow from her boots and unwound the scarf that half hid her face, she searched the room for Steven's familiar figure. There he was, in the far corner, in a secluded booth. She went toward him.

"You look red-cheeked and rosy," he said cheerfully, rising to greet her.

She slid into her seat and unbuttoned her coat. "It's only four blocks, but the wind was a little cold."

"You walked?"

She chuckled at his look of disbelief. "Yes, I walked."

"You should have told me. I'd have picked you up."

She put scarf, mittens, and purse in a neat pile on the seat beside her. "Then I wouldn't have had my beautiful walk. I love walking. It's good for the soul. It's a kind of prayer, I guess."

The smile on his face faded, and for a moment she thought he would turn back into the grim-featured man she had first met. But he said only, rather soberly now, "Shall we order before we talk?"

"Yes, I suppose that would be best." *He's still hurting,* she thought, *hurting so much that even a casual mention of prayer can turn him stern and unforgiving again.*

But he spoke, and she let the thought go. "They make a delicious cream of broccoli soup here, though not on Saturdays," he said. "And their blue-plate specials are usually very good."

"I'll have the soup and a grilled cheese sandwich," she said, realizing suddenly that she had forgotten to lay the ground rules for this meeting. "Separate checks, of course."

"Of course."

She thought she detected a strange note in his voice, but when she looked at him, his expression seemed no different than usual.

He waited until the waitress left with their orders, then said, "Okay, what did you want to tell me about Karen? I thought things were getting better between us."

"I think they are, too," she hastened to add.

"Then what's wrong?"

"Well. . ." Now that the moment had arrived, she wasn't quite sure what to say. "I really appreciate your help at the theater."

He stared at her, perplexed. "I don't understand what that has to do with this."

Rachel sighed. "I'm not doing this very well, I'm afraid. It's just that, well, your work with the boys has been good, so good that Karen thinks you wish she were a boy." There, she'd finally gotten it out.

"That's not true," he said slowly. "Karen looks very much like her mother. I think I told you that. It was one of the reasons I couldn't stand to be around her after. . ."

Across the small table, she looked into his eyes, eyes that still held the anguish of his loss.

"I loved her mother, you see. I loved her madly. We were high school sweethearts. There was never anyone else for us."

Rachel nodded. "Like Peter and me," she mumbled over the lump in her throat.

Steven nodded. "I swear to you, Rachel, it never occurred to me to wish Karen was anything else than the beautiful girl she is. I remember so clearly when she was born. The pain, the joy, the wonder of it." He paused and swallowed.

She saw the unshed tears in his eyes.

"I love my daughter. I love her very much."

Without thinking, Rachel reached across the table and laid a hand on his in a gesture of comfort. "I know you do, Steven. And she will know it, too. It just takes time."

"Yes," he said. His voice was stronger now. "Time is supposed to help with all things. But sometimes I do wonder."

The waitress approached, and Rachel withdrew her hand. After all, her gesture of compassion could have been mistaken for something altogether different. Not by Steven, of course, but by someone else.

"I know you're doing more things with her," she went on between spoonfuls of soup. "And I think that's a good idea. I certainly appreciate your help at the theater, and I don't want you to stop. But maybe you should plan some fun things to do with Karen. Just the two of you."

He shook his head, his gaze meeting hers. "She seems so uptight— almost scared—when we're alone."

Rachel frowned. "I don't understand. She seems very at ease to me."

He smiled ruefully. "That's only when we're with you and Abby. When we're alone, she clams up."

"She had something to do with our Saturday lunches, didn't she?" Rachel asked, remembering the interchange of looks she had glimpsed.

Steven nodded. "The second time," he said. "The first time was strictly my idea." He grinned. "A great idea, too, if I do say so myself."

Rachel smiled. "The girls did seem to enjoy themselves."

"Just the girls?"

She hadn't meant to be rude. "Oh, I did, too. I haven't laughed so much in a long time. Thank you for that."

"If we're going to be giving thanks," he said, "then I'd better do most of the thanking. You've helped me a lot with Karen."

She shrugged, suddenly embarrassed. "A little advice. . ."

"Very good advice." He smiled warmly. "For which I'm very grateful."

She managed a small smile to cover her continued embarrassment. Praise always made her uncomfortable. "I was only doing what I thought I should," she said. "God clearly tells us to help one another." Then she remembered that he didn't like to talk about God. But what she'd said was true. She was only a servant of God. She couldn't pretend to be anything else.

He sobered for a moment, and she was afraid he would say something else, something sharp and painful. But when he spoke, his voice was even. "I guess I've no right to begrudge you your faith, Rachel, just because I've lost mine. But I have to say it. I can't see how you can go on believing in a loving God, not after losing your husband like that."

"I couldn't believe in a God who isn't loving," she said quietly, searching for the right words to help this troubled man.

"That's exactly why I quit believing," he said. "After God took Karen's mother. . ."

She noticed how he avoided saying his wife's name, as though it was still too painful for him.

"But you shouldn't blame God," she said.

"Why not?" he asked. And the quietness of his tone made his question even more bitter.

She searched her mind for something to say, but just as at that first time, she couldn't find anything. Everything she thought of, all the comforting biblical phrases that she knew by heart, seemed flat and empty. She couldn't say them.

She had a sudden sharp and painful memory of people who had tried to comfort her with those same words just after Peter's death and how angry she'd become. She hadn't voiced her anger because she'd been afraid of offending those well-meaning people. In fact, she'd almost made herself sick by turning her anger inward. No, she wouldn't say any of those things to Steven.

"These things happen to many people," she said finally, uncomfortably aware that she wasn't answering his question. "We don't know why." Unconscious of what she was doing, she sighed. "It's not up to us to question God's will. He knows better than we do."

For a moment he stared at her, and her heart pounded in her throat. She felt like the worst kind of hypocrite. How could she explain this thing to him? How could she make him understand it when she couldn't understand it herself? When part of her felt just like he did?

His gaze was still on her face, and he sighed. "I envy you, Rachel." He smiled wryly. "Envy. Another sin to add to my list. I guess it's a good thing I don't believe."

She knew he was trying to lighten the tension with a little joke, but she couldn't joke about sin. Not about something so important.

"Sorry," he said. "I should have known you wouldn't find that funny. But I do admire your faith and your tenacity in hanging on to it through thick and thin."

She was finding the topic too disquieting, so she changed it. "So, what do you think you and Karen can do together?" she asked, in what she hoped was a casual way.

He was not deceived. "Okay, okay. I get the idea. Back to the original subject."

She smiled slightly. "I'd appreciate that." The words were scarcely out of her mouth before she realized how they sounded. A Christian who didn't want to talk about her faith! What was she so afraid of finding within herself? She pushed the thought aside quickly. She wasn't the sort of person to shove her faith on others. The best witness, she believed—she had always believed, she reminded herself sharply—was by example. And she did try to be a good example.

Steven smiled, such a happy smile that it startled her. "I've got a great idea," he said. "A really great idea."

She couldn't help smiling, too. His smile was contagious. "It must be great—from the looks of you."

"Rehearsals are every Saturday morning. Right?"

"Right. Till February. There'll be a little break during the performances."

"Yes. Okay. Well, then, it's simple. Every Saturday after our lunch, the four of us can do something special together."

A thousand protests rushed to her mind. "But that isn't what I meant! I meant just you and Karen. Alone together."

His smile faded. "I told you. When Karen and I are alone together, things aren't the same. Of course she looks relaxed and happy when you see her. You and Abby are there. The rest of the time it's hard going." He sighed. "Just when I think we're doing great, Karen turns quiet and scared again. It's almost like something clicks in her mind and she remembers to be afraid." His look carried entreaty. "When you're there, you and Abby, that never happens. Please, Rachel, will you help me win back my daughter's love?"

He was being unfair. He was asking too much of her. She usually spent Saturday afternoons taking it easy, reading her Sunday school lesson again. She didn't like giving that up, though she knew she could study the lesson in the evening just as well. She didn't go out, after all. And the housework got taken care of during the week after she got home from work.

Still, she was reluctant. She was beginning to—no, she corrected herself, she already—loved Karen a great deal. And she was aware that Karen loved her. One of these days Steven might find a new wife, and that woman wouldn't be likely to appreciate his daughter's love for some strange woman. Or Steven's friendship with that woman.

On the other hand, Steven might have decided, as she had, not to marry again. Then Karen would have no woman to turn to as she grew up. Rachel swallowed a sigh. *"Do unto others as you would have them do unto you,"* she told herself silently. And if it had been she who had been taken instead of Peter (how many times those first terrible days had she wished that!), she would certainly have wanted some Christian woman to be there for Abby.

The answer seemed clear. "Love your neighbor as yourself," God had said. And here was Karen, so obviously needing her love. There was just no way she could say no, or refuse to give what the child so clearly needed. And besides, it would be good for her and Abby to get out more. Her dislike of winter driving and her fatigue after rehearsals had limited them lately. *Strange,* she thought, *the last few weeks I've not only stopped feeling tired after rehearsals—I've actually felt invigorated.*

"Rachel, Rachel. Come back from wherever you are." His voice was soft and gentle, and his eyes, over the rim of his coffee cup, were full of pleading.

"All right, Steven." She managed a little laugh. It didn't quite ring true, but it didn't sound too artificial either. "All right. I was just thinking about what you asked."

"And what did you decide?" His face seemed calm enough, but his eyes had gone opaque, as though he were protecting himself from something.

"I still think you ought to spend more time alone with Karen." His face stayed serene, but his fingers tightened on the handle of his cup. She hurried on. "But if it helps, Abby and I will spend some Saturday afternoons with you."

His breath came out in a great whoosh. "Thank God," he murmured.

Startled by his use of that particular expression, she searched his face. But he didn't seem to know what he'd said. She saw no point in reminding him, not now, not when he was grinning at her like a little boy with a new football.

"Do you like to ice skate?" he asked.

"I don't know," she replied truthfully. "I've never tried. But Abby would, I'm sure."

"Shall we go ice skating next Saturday after rehearsal then?"

"Okay." She glanced at her watch and reached for her purse. "Oh. There is one condition," she said, counted out the money for her lunch. "We go Dutch."

"I can easily afford—"

"We go Dutch," she said again, "or we don't go."

He capitulated with another boyish grin. "All right, you win. We go Dutch."

"Good. See you Saturday."

Chapter Five

During the week that followed, Abby was ecstatic. So ecstatic that Rachel wondered if she'd done the right thing. She'd considered Karen's feelings when she was making her decision, but she hadn't thought about her own daughter. What would happen to Abby if Steven found a new wife? It didn't seem likely—she had to admit that. But these things happened. Men fell in love every day. And for the weirdest reasons. Women, too, of course.

Rachel scolded herself. She was borrowing trouble. She knew that was wrong. Besides, there was no way she could protect Abby from the struggles and pains of life. And even if she could, she wouldn't really be doing her daughter a favor. Living meant struggle. Spiritual growth didn't come to those who'd never faced trouble.

She knew all that, but sometimes when she looked at Abby, her heart ached. Sometimes she thought of the beautiful laughing baby Abby had been. Of the joy she and Peter had felt just looking at her. Being a parent was no easy job. Letting a child step out into the world, not being overprotective, could be very difficult to do.

It was just that sort of thing she was considering when the phone rang on Friday evening. She put down her Bible and picked up the phone. "Hello."

"Hello, Rachel. This is Steven."

"Hello, Steven. How are you?"

"Feeling rather stupid."

A strange choice of words. "Stupid? Why? Is Karen all right?"

"She hasn't been hurt," he said, "if that's what you mean. But she's very upset with me."

Rachel suppressed a sigh. "What happened?"

"She's been so excited all week. About our going ice skating."

"Abby, too."

"And now something's come up. One of our welders has broken down. In Pittsburgh. They need it fixed immediately, and I'm the only one around who knows how to do it. I have to fly out in the morning, so I'll have to miss rehearsal and our ice-skating date."

"That's too bad, Steven. I thought this job didn't mean travel."

He laughed a little harshly. "So did I. But the regular guy for this kind of thing is out West setting up a new plant. And I haven't been on this job long, you know. It's not a good idea to turn down requests like this, especially if you're low man on the totem pole."

"Of course not. Well, we'll just have to wait till next Saturday to go skating. The girls will understand."

"Abby might. I'm not so sure about Karen."

"I'll talk to her after rehearsal. In fact, I'll take them to lunch." The thought struck her. "Where's Karen going to stay?"

"My next question had to do with a baby-sitter," he said. "Can you recommend someone? I don't go out much, and the woman down the street who watches Karen after school is busy for the weekend."

"Why don't you let Karen come here?" Rachel said. "That would help to relieve the girls' disappointment."

"Oh, I can't do that. Karen spends so much time there now."

"And I love it," Rachel said firmly. "Come on. Do me this favor."

"Do you a favor?"

"Yes," she insisted, putting laughter in her voice. "Otherwise Abby will mope around all weekend. And you know how that can be."

He joined her in laughter then. "All right, you win. On one condition."

"What is it?"

"I get to pay for next Saturday. Lunch and the skating. Everything. None of this going Dutch. Agreed?"

"You drive a hard bargain," she returned, still laughing. "But I agree."

"Good. I'll drop Karen at rehearsal on my way to the airport. And her clothes for the weekend."

"Tell her to bring a dress for Sunday school," Rachel said. "Abby likes to dress up."

There was silence on the other end of the line. Now what had she done? Wouldn't he want Karen to go? "We're getting ready for the Christmas pageant," she hurried on, trying to fill the silence. "Karen should enjoy that, don't you think?"

He still waited a moment too long before answering, but the answer came finally. "Yes, I suppose she will."

She swallowed her sigh of relief. She didn't want to offend him, but she certainly couldn't miss Sunday school and church because of him. "Okay. When will you be back?"

"Some time Sunday. I'm not sure exactly. Do you have plans?"

"No." Whatever had made him ask a question like that? "Sometimes Abby and I go to the park, but it looks like it's going to be a real cold weekend. If they want to play outside, they can build a snowman in the front yard."

"Right. Well, if something should come up and you want to take them someplace with you, go ahead. I probably won't get in till dinnertime. Or after. And if I call and you're not there, I'll just call again later."

"Okay. See you Sunday. And, Steven?"

"Yes, Rachel?"

"Have a safe flight." Go with God, she would have said—if she hadn't been so conscious of his lack of faith.

"Thank you. I will. You have a nice weekend."

"I will."

She put the phone into its cradle. Was this the hand of God working in their lives again? More than once in the past weeks, she'd thought about inviting Karen to Sunday school. But knowing Steven's feelings as she did, she'd hesitated to ask him about it. And now everything had been arranged without her having to do a thing except, of course, abide by her faith.

She turned from the phone. "Abby!"

Abby came bouncing into the kitchen. "Yes, Momma?"

"I've got some good news and some bad news. Which do you want first?"

"The bad," Abby replied promptly. "Then the good can make me feel better."

Rachel smiled at her pragmatic daughter. "Okay. Bad news—we aren't going skating tomorrow. Karen's father has to go out of town."

Abby waited, her expression not changing. "That's too bad, Momma. Now what's the good?"

Rachel's smile broadened. "Karen is coming to stay with us after rehearsal. She's going to be here till Sunday evening."

Abby's face lit up. "Oh, Momma! That's great!" She clapped her hands gleefully. "She can go to Sunday school with us. I've been wanting the girls there to meet her."

Abby threw herself into Rachel's arms. "Thank you, Momma. This is even better than going skating."

Rachel returned Abby's hug. "Why are you thanking me?" she asked. "I didn't do anything."

"You asked Karen to come here while her daddy's away." Abby grinned. "I thanked God, too, Momma," she added. She twirled around on her toes. "Do you think Karen can have a part in the Christmas pageant?"

"That would be nice," Rachel said. "But we don't really know if she'll want to keep coming to Sunday school."

Abby stared at her. "Of course she will."

"Well, we'll have to wait and see."

"Yes, Momma." Abby was already halfway to the door. "I'll just go straighten up my room."

Watching her hurry off, Rachel smiled. She'd been very blessed in Abby.

❧

The next morning, Steven stopped by the auditorium only long enough to put Karen's bag down by the coats. "I think she's got the whole house in there," he said ruefully.

Rachel smiled. "No problem. Be careful now."

"I will." Then he was gone, and she turned back to the chattering children.

The morning dragged and dragged. It seemed that everything that could go wrong at rehearsal did go wrong. The boys fought among themselves and made faces and rude noises during the ball scene. The girls got more and more nervous and more and more giggly, until Rachel despaired of ever accomplishing anything, despaired, eventually, of twelve o'clock ever arriving.

When it finally did, she sank down in her chair with a big sigh of relief. How had she managed for so long without Steven's help? Well, she had. She must be coming down with something. That was why everything seemed to get on her nerves. The children were restless, too, no doubt. The weather had been bad all week, and they'd been penned up.

She closed her eyes for a minute. At least the morning was over. And next week she'd have Steven's help again.

"Momma?"

She opened her eyes. "Yes, Abby?"

"Everybody's gone. We've checked all the rooms. The lights are all off. We can go whenever you're ready."

Rachel managed a smile. "Thank you, Abby. I'm ready now. Are you girls hungry?"

"Yes."

Pulling on her boots and slipping into her coat, she thought about the girls. They got along so well together. What a blessing that Karen had come into their lives—or been sent by God to be a friend to Abby.

She followed the girls out into the cold. She was beginning to feel hungry herself.

ᴥ

The rest of the weekend passed quickly, and soon Sunday evening arrived. Rachel built a fire in the fireplace. It was a comfort to her to have a bright, cheery fire there. She settled on the couch with her lesson for the next Sunday. This one had to do with the parable of the man who owned the vineyard.

She thought about the men who had worked the full day and been given the same pay as those who only worked a few hours. On the surface, it did seem unfair, and the complaints of those who'd worked all day seemed justified. But when she thought about it a while, when she looked deeper into the parable, she saw other things.

The early workers had been given what they contracted for. The ones who had started late had trusted in the owner to give them what he thought was right. Was the reader supposed to learn that trust in God brought its own reward? The owner did seem to represent God. And if she went to a deeper level and thought of the pay as the reward of heaven, surely God would make no distinction between those who had always believed and those who came late to their faith.

A sigh escaped, and she turned to gaze into the fire. If only she knew some way to help Steven Hendricks regain his faith. He was still hurting so much from his wife's death. It was hard to get over that, she knew. But to be without faith in God, without the security of knowing His love. . . How did a person live without faith?

People who had never known God. . .she could see that they didn't know what they were missing. But for a Christian, for someone who had always walked with God, to lose his faith—how awful, how despairing that must be. She remembered the pain in Steven's eyes when he spoke of his wife's death, the bitterness in his voice. She sighed again. She had no idea what to do to help him.

Maybe God would work through Karen. The child had certainly loved Sunday school. She had walked beside Abby, her brown eyes wide with surprise at all the friendly greetings and warm smiles. "It's like a big happy family," she'd said on the way home. "I like it. I like it a lot. I'm going to ask Daddy. . ." She paused and swallowed, "to take me every Sunday."

"Good," Abby said. "Just don't forget."

"Oh, I won't," Karen promised.

Frowning slightly, Rachel wondered if the child would get her nerve up enough to do it. Though things seemed to have improved a lot, Karen was still not completely at ease with her father. And sometimes when she spoke of him, her voice or her expression betrayed insecurity.

It's bad for both of them, Rachel thought, staring into the fire. She knew enough of Steven Hendricks now to believe that he genuinely loved his daughter. And she believed Karen loved him. But bad as things might look now, they'd been even worse. It would, as she'd so often told Abby, take time.

Abby. She smiled at the thought of the sturdy little daughter God had blessed her with. Without Abby, she didn't know if she'd have made it.

She rolled down the sleeves on her worn flannel shirt and shivered as the wind whipped the branches of the trees outside the window and whistled shrilly down the chimney. What a bitter winter night. She breathed a prayer for the plane carrying Steven. For all the planes out in this terrible weather. Then she picked up her Bible lesson book and went back to the parable of the vineyard owner. Like all the parables, it took a lot of thought.

The wind hissed around the windows and howled down the chimney, making the flames tremble. She shivered again and wished she knew what flight Steven was on. If only he was home safe. Thank goodness the girls were busy up in Abby's room and didn't seem to notice how bad it was getting outside.

She sighed. There was no use telling herself that God would protect Steven. He hadn't protected Peter. She shuddered, thinking of Peter and that drunken driver. Waves of anger rushed through her. She pushed the feelings away.

"I don't have faith anymore. Not after what God did to me." Steven's words from their first serious discussion echoed in her mind. Was Steven actually being more honest about his feelings than she was? Disturbed, Rachel got up and put more wood on the fire and fixed herself a cup of tea. But activity couldn't drown out the unsettling questions.

Returning to her rocking chair, she took a deep breath to steady herself. She had always prided herself in her ability to look at situations directly, to face the truth squarely. It was time, she admitted, to face her anger about Peter's death.

Tears slid down her cheeks as she confessed to herself and to God how angry she was that Peter had been taken from her. Curled up in a fetal position, she sobbed into her knees so that the sound of her crying wouldn't reach the girls. *God, I am angry,* she prayed silently. *Peter is gone, and I am so tired of doing everything and being everything for everyone. But what can I do?*

Gradually, her body relaxed, and as her tears slowed, she was overwhelmed with a sense of God's love for her. She felt as though He were holding her in His arms—just as so many times she had held Abby.

Savoring the love and security that surrounded her, Rachel realized another important step in her healing had begun. How she wished Steven could have such an experience. *Steven!*

With a start, she jumped from the chair and tore into the downstairs bathroom. She blew her nose, covered her eyes with a cold washcloth to remove any sign of her tears, and prayed that Steven would show up before his daughter realized how late it was getting.

The ringing of the doorbell made her jump. She hung up the washcloth and raced to the door. Her heart rose up in her throat at the sight of the male figure there, then sank back to its normal place as she recognized Steven.

She threw open the door. "Steven! I'm so glad to see you!" She stopped, realizing how she sounded, then stumbled on. "The weather, I mean. It's been so bad." She faltered to a halt again. "You'll have to excuse me," she stammered. "I. . .this weather makes me nervous."

"No problem. I don't care much for it myself." He brushed off snow and stepped into the foyer. He looked around and smiled. "Looks nice and cozy in here." He glanced toward the living room. "I bet you've got a fire in there."

She laughed. Relief at seeing him safe had made her giddy. "Yes, I do. Take off your coat and relax a little. I just put the kettle on for tea."

His smile broadened. "A cup of tea sounds great. It's been nothing but rush all weekend, and then the flight home was delayed." He shrugged out of his coat and unwound his scarf. "It's good to be back." He smiled ruefully. "And to think, I used to actually enjoy this kind of thing." His voice turned thoughtful. "Or think I did."

The sound of footsteps carried down the stairs, and Abby's voice floated toward them. "I told you I heard the doorbell. See? It's your father, and he's all right."

"Daddy." Karen paused halfway down the stairs.

"Hi, honey. I just got in. It was a long flight."

Abby gave Karen a pointed look. Then she nudged her.

Rachel watched, her heart in her throat, as Karen moved hesitantly forward, into the arms that her father opened to her. Rachel swallowed over the lump in her throat as father and daughter hugged each other. Abby's hand stole into hers and, looking down, Rachel saw the shimmer of unshed tears in Abby's eyes. She squeezed Abby's fingers and managed a watery smile. "Now, I've got a full cookie jar," she began.

"Chocolate chip," Abby added happily.

"And there goes the whistle on the teakettle. Just go in and make yourselves comfortable." Rachel directed Steven and Karen, who now stood stiffly, some inches apart, toward the living room. "Abby can come with me and carry the cookies."

She saw the look Abby gave Karen, a look that stopped her from coming after them.

Steven Hendricks slid out of his boots and held out a hand to his daughter. There was only a small pause before she took it. "Let's go see to that fire," he said.

In the kitchen, Rachel exchanged a smile with Abby. Abby piled cookies high on a plate, and Rachel put cups and saucers, cream and sugar, and two glasses of milk on the tray. She fixed her own tea, then filled Steven's cup with hot water and set a tea bag beside it. He could make his tea whatever strength he liked.

Abby went before her into the living room, proudly carrying the plate of cookies. "I helped make these," she said, offering them to Steven. "They're real good, too."

Rachel laughed. "No false modesty here," she said lightly.

Steven had taken a chair near the fire, stretching out his long legs so that his stocking feet reached the hearth. Karen had settled on a stool beside him. She lifted her milk and reached for a cookie. "Take two," Abby said. "Then I won't have to pass them so often."

"We can set them here on the table." Rachel put the tray on the table beside Steven's chair. "Then we can all reach them." She took her own cup and saucer and settled on the couch.

Steven sipped tea and munched a cookie. "These are very good," he told Abby with a smile. "The best I've ever eaten."

Abby giggled. "I know. Thank you."

Steven turned to his daughter. "So, Karen, tell me about your weekend."

"Well, Daddy, rehearsal wasn't so good. The boys were making nasty faces." She made one that set them all to laughing. "And the girls got all silly and giggly, so things didn't go so good."

"I'm sorry to hear that," Steven said to Rachel.

She shrugged. "It happens sometimes. The weather, maybe."

He nodded. "Kids do get ornery when they're cooped up."

"Then we had lunch at our usual place," Karen went on. It did Rachel good to see how Karen smiled at her father.

"It was good. But the most fun was this morning. We went to Sunday school."

Rachel was watching him closely, and she wondered if Karen or Abby could feel the sudden tension in the air. Maybe it was only in her own mind. She hoped so.

"It was great, Daddy. We had a story about a little man who climbed up in a tree so he could see Jesus. He was real short and there were too many people, so he climbed up in the tree. Wasn't that smart?"

Steven nodded. "Yes, it was."

"And Jesus did see him. He even knew his name. Zac. . .Zac—"

"Zacchaeus," Steven supplied quietly.

"Yes, that's it. He was—" She paused and looked at him in surprise. "You know the story."

He nodded. "I remember part of it. But go on."

"I liked the story," Karen continued, her face thoughtful. "It must have been nice to be able to see Jesus like that. To have Him know your name."

"He knows our names," Abby hastened to assert. "And we talk to Him when we pray."

Karen's thoughtful look faded. "Yes, I know. I like that." She turned back to her father. "We talked about the Christmas pageant, too. And, Daddy, I could be one of the angels."

Rachel saw the child was worried. "It wouldn't take much work," Karen went on. "I mean, the wings and halos are already made. And I have a long white nightgown. And practice is on Sunday morning, part of Sunday school. So all I have to do is go there. Can I, Daddy? Can I?"

Steven's face had remained calm throughout Karen's recital, but Rachel thought she saw a muscle twitching in his jaw. "We'll see," he said, his voice flat.

She considered volunteering to pick Karen up, but that probably wasn't such a good idea. If Steven brought her, he would stand a better chance of getting interested himself.

"Sometimes you don't like to get up early on Sundays," he said.

"Oh, I would for this," Karen said eagerly. "I'd get up right away." She smiled wistfully. "It's a real nice place, Daddy. The people are so friendly and nice. And they all know Abby and her mother."

"Yes," Steven said, reaching for another cookie and meeting Rachel's gaze. "I imagine they do."

Though his gaze was on her and his look quite direct, she hadn't the slightest idea what he was thinking. Or what his enigmatic remark meant. Still, she returned his gaze steadily. She had always openly avowed her faith. From the first time he'd set foot in her house and she'd asked him not to curse, through their various discussions on faith, she had made it obvious that she was a believer. What's more, she'd let him know ahead of time that she planned to take Karen to Sunday school. She had done nothing wrong.

He shifted his gaze to the fire again. "Who's directing the pageant?" he asked Karen.

"Abby's mother."

"Of course," Rachel said with a little laugh, saying the words before he could.

Somewhat to her surprise, he chuckled and shook his head. "A glutton for punishment, aren't you?"

She shrugged. "It has to be done," she replied lightly.

His eyes were speculative. "And if it has to be done, you have to do it."

She shrugged. "Something like that, I guess."

Chapter Six

That week sped by, the days flying after each other, and even the Saturday morning rehearsal went smoothly, so smoothly that Rachel could hardly believe the week before had been so bad. She thought about this as the girls went off to get the coats. Did having Steven there really make all that difference? The thought made her somewhat uncomfortable. With their weekly lunches, and now these excursions that she had promised to share, she and Abby were spending a lot of time with Steven and his daughter. Too much time, she was afraid.

The day of reckoning was bound to come. A man as attractive as Steven wouldn't stay unmarried forever. And as she'd reminded herself before, no new wife would want him to continue a friendship with another woman, no matter how platonic that friendship might be.

But perhaps she was worrying too much. Perhaps she should leave all this in God's hands. After all, everything she was doing she was doing to help Karen. Steven, too, of course. But Karen was her main concern. No child should feel unloved. And if she could help Karen understand the truth, help her realize that her father really loved her very much, then she would have done what God seemed to expect of her in this situation.

Steven came up with the girls. "All set?" he asked.

"Yes."

"Good. I'm starving." His gaze sought Rachel's. "It's my treat today, remember."

"I remember." She laughed. "You're not likely to let me forget."

"That's right. I'm not. So let's go."

As they piled into the car, Rachel found herself thinking what a beautiful day it was. New snow had fallen, making the world a fresh crisp white, and the unclouded sky was a brilliant blue. How good life could be. She hadn't thought that for a long time. Since before Peter's—

"Do you want to try a new place to eat today?" Steven asked. "Or shall we go back to our old stomping grounds?"

"Let's let the girls decide," Rachel said. "It doesn't matter to me."

"Well, girls?"

In the backseat, Abby and Karen went into whispered consultation.

Rachel exchanged a satisfied glance with Steven. Hers said, *It's working,* and his seemed to say, *Thank you.*

"We've decided," Karen announced. "We want to go to Kitty's. It's our place, and we like it there."

"Yes," Abby added, "and they know you, so we always get treated good."

They all laughed together. *Ever-practical Abby*, Rachel thought.

"Okay," Steven said. "Your wish is my command."

From the backseat, a flurry of whispers and giggles announced that the girls were enjoying themselves very much.

Rachel smiled and looked out at the snow-garlanded trees. "Isn't winter a beautiful season?"

Steven chuckled. "If you don't have to shovel snow. Or get stuck in driveways. My favorite season is spring, though."

She nodded. "It's the season of hope and resurrection. When life is renewed."

He glanced at her quickly, but said nothing.

"Have you decided if Karen can participate in the Sunday school pageant?" she asked. The question had been lurking in the back of her mind all morning. She might as well get it out in the open.

He was silent for a moment longer, and she wondered if she'd offended him.

"Yes. I've decided to take her. She'll be there tomorrow." He lowered his voice. "I can't very well let my own lack of faith deprive her. God knows—" He winced. "Anyone knows," he corrected, the line of his chin growing grim, "people need all the help they can get in facing life. If there's anything my daughter can have that will help her, I want her to have it."

Rachel reached out to pat his arm. "That's very good of you."

He shook his head. "Just practical. Don't give me credit I don't deserve. I love my daughter. I'd do just about anything for her."

"I know." She patted his arm again before she withdrew her hand.

The girls hurried through their meal, their eyes sparkling with excitement at the prospect of an afternoon at the skating rink. Karen seemed especially cheerful, and Abby positively glowed. Had they overheard Steven tell her that Karen could go to Sunday school? Experience had taught Rachel that children were alert to changes in tone and often heard what wasn't meant for their ears—more often than they heard what was meant for them, in fact.

After lunch, they piled back into the car and headed for the skating rink. "How long since you've skated?" Steven asked as they moved through Saturday traffic.

"On ice?"

"Yes. On ice."

She laughed softly. "I've never skated on ice. And I don't mean to begin today. I just came along to watch."

"What!"

The tone of his voice brought instant silence from the backseat. "What's wrong?" the girls chorused anxiously.

Steven gave her a sidelong look and a little grin before he said somberly. "It's Abby's mother. She just told me she isn't going to skate, and I'm disappointed."

"Momma!" Abby hung over the seat to peer into Rachel's face. "You can't do that. It won't be fun if you just sit there."

"I can have fun watching you," Rachel said. "More fun that I'd have falling down."

"But, Momma. . ."

"Never mind, Abby. Let your mother be." Steven's tone was aggrieved but his eyes sparkled, and Rachel saw what the girls couldn't: the mischief gleaming there. "We have to respect her wishes." He sighed deeply. "Even though that means I can't skate either."

"Why ever not?" Rachel asked, pulled into the game by her own curiosity.

"Why, a gentleman would never behave like that, never leave a lady sitting alone on the sidelines." He sighed again, so dramatically that Rachel almost laughed out loud.

But Abby couldn't see his face. She could only hear his words—and she took them literally. Again she leaned up on the seat, her mouth near Rachel's ear. "Momma," she whispered, "that's not very nice. Or fair. Mr. Hendricks should have some fun, too."

Rachel debated trying to explain to Abby. But how? How could she make Abby understand that what Steven was doing wasn't really lying, that he expected her to see through it, that it was a kind of joke on her? Did Steven really want her to skate? Or did he want to show her that her Christian principles sometimes put her in difficult positions?

She smiled to herself. Well, if he meant to show her that, he was wasting his time. She'd never had any false delusions about her beliefs. Being a Christian, living up to her principles, was no easy job. It never had been.

Subduing a smile, she heaved a sigh at least as big as his. "Well, it doesn't seem fair that Karen's father should have to give up an afternoon's skating just because I might fall down and break a leg."

The girls twittered anxiously, both of them leaning forward to reassure her. "You won't get hurt, Momma," Abby insisted. "It's real easy."

"I haven't been skating for a long time," Karen said slowly. "Since before. . ." Rachel's gaze, going automatically to Steven's face, saw the temporary hardening of the line of his jaw. "For a couple years," Karen finished.

"Please, Momma."

Rachel threw up her hands. "All right! All right! I give up. You win."

The clamor from the backseat covered the sound of Steven's quiet thank you. Why did he find it so important to have her skate, too? Had his upbringing been so strong that he really would feel uncomfortable if he skated when she didn't? Or was he just trying to get her to relax and have some fun? There was no way to get answers to questions like that. This time her sigh was real. She'd committed herself. To change her mind now would disappoint the girls.

Steven paid the admission and took care of renting skates for everyone, his grin reminding her that she'd agreed to let this be his treat. Anxious to get started, the girls grabbed their skates and hurried to a bench. Rachel moved more slowly. She'd always had a dread of sports, of doing physical things where she might make a fool of herself. But the rink was almost full, and most people would be skating themselves. Those few who weren't would be watching someone they knew, not a perfect stranger who could barely stand up. *Maybe*, she thought as she slowly untied a shoe, *maybe if I go around the rink once or twice, the others will get busy and not think about me.* She hoped so.

Steven turned to her. To her surprise, she saw that he already had his skates on. "Here. Let me help." Before she could protest, he had taken her foot and was easing it into a skate. There was something about the gesture that made her very uncomfortable, but before she could figure out how to tell him, he had both her skates laced up. "Are they tight enough?" he asked. "Too tight?"

She tried to laugh. "They feel all right, I guess."

"Are you nervous?"

"Yes." She admitted it freely.

"No need to be," he said. "You'll get the hang of it. You move so gracefully, you're bound to. One of these days you'll be doing double spins."

She had to laugh at that. "I'll be lucky if I can even stand up."

"Nonsense," Steven asserted. "Here, give me your hand."

She shook her head. "No, no. I'll manage."

Steven frowned. "I didn't bring you here to let you spend the afternoon alone. Come on; we'll skate together."

She stared at him. "I. . .I'll pull you down, too."

He laughed then, a laugh that made people nearby turn and smile at them. "No, you won't." He threw back his shoulders. "I used to play hockey. There's nothing you can do to me on the ice that would come near what's happened to me in all-out hockey games. Now, come on."

Still, she hesitated. The skates seemed big and clumsy on her feet. Her knees were weak as water. She wanted to find a hole and hide in it.

"I. . ." she began again.

He shook his head and reached down to pull her to her feet.

"No more excuses," he said. "We're going to skate. Lean on me. Use me for balance. We'll go very slowly."

She knew she was grasping his hand too tightly, but she was afraid to move her feet, and when she did, they felt like they belonged to someone else.

Steven drew her slowly out from the wall. "Here," he said. "Let me do this." His right arm encircled her waist. "Give me your hand." She put her mittened hand in his. "Now your left hand."

That, too, she gave into his keeping. Somewhat surprised, she felt a little steadier on her feet.

"Now," he said, his voice startlingly close to her ear. "Real slow. And together. Left foot. Right foot. Left foot. Easy does it. That's it. Left. Right. Just slide it along."

At first, she gripped his hands so tightly that her fingers grew numb, but gradually some of the tension eased. They made several slow and easy circuits of the rink. Then she said, "I need to sit down. Just for a few minutes."

She turned toward him, forgetting that such a move would put his face so near her own. She turned to the front again, heat flooding her face. "Will you skate for me? Show me what you can do. What was that you mentioned? A double something or other."

"Double spin." He grinned cheerfully. "I think it's too crowded for that in here. Besides," he chuckled, "I'm afraid I'm too rusty to be doing such things now."

"Well, then, just skate around. Backwards, maybe? And do some figure eights like those people are doing out there in the middle." She still didn't turn directly to meet his gaze.

He helped her to a bench and grinned down at her. "I guess I'll have to. A gentleman can hardly refuse a lady a favor."

The girls in their matching red skirts went by, waving. She waved back. "That reminds me. I have a bone to pick with you. All this gentleman stuff—"

His grin got even broader. "I had a very genteel upbringing. But we don't want to talk about that now." He backed smoothly away. "I'll go around a couple times, then come back for you. Okay?"

"Okay." There was nothing else she could say. It seemed clear that he wasn't going to leave her to sit there alone.

She watched him circle the rink. He moved with an easy masculine grace, his long legs swinging smoothly, his lean body twisting easily as he went around those slower than himself. He passed her, smiling. In one smooth easy motion, he turned and skated backward, looking over his shoulder occasionally to make sure that he didn't bump into anyone.

Rachel watched him, smiling. There was such an exuberance in him today, such a joy in life. He was far different than that grim distant man she'd first met.

Karen and Abby sped toward her. Karen appeared to have been skating all her life. Probably they had skated together—Karen and Steven and the wife he still loved. As she still loved Peter. She pushed the thought from her mind. This was not the place for it.

"Momma," Abby cried. "Look at me! Look how good I'm doing."

Rachel smiled. "You're doing very well, Abby."

"It's fun, Momma." Abby grinned. "I saw Karen's daddy helping you. Like Karen helped me."

"Yes, Abby. And you're right. It is fun."

"Of course." Abby's tone held all the confidence of the very young, and Rachel swallowed a laugh.

Steven slid to stop in front of them. "Ready to go again?" he asked.

She was about to say yes when Karen said, "Take Abby around once, please, Daddy. Show her the things you showed me."

Steven looked at Abby. "Would you like that?"

With a sense of shock, Rachel caught a look of pure joy on Abby's face. Her voice was joyous, too. "Oh, yes, sir! If you don't mind."

Steven's laughter was infectious. "Mind? Why I'd love to show you some of the tricks." He grinned at Karen. "See? I told you you'd remember."

He held out a hand to Abby, then smiled at Karen. "Why don't you come too? We'll make it a threesome."

Karen took his hand so fast Rachel knew the child had really wanted to skate with her father herself. Rachel thought about asking Abby to stay with her so that Steven and Karen could skate alone. But that probably wasn't a good idea. Abby was so happy that she hadn't the heart to interfere. Besides, it was likely Karen really wanted Abby along. Hadn't Steven said many times that she was more relaxed with them there?

Rachel watched the three figures circle the rink. The bright red of the girls' skirts flashed by with a speed that dizzied her. But the glimpse she got of Abby's ecstatic face wiped out all her misgivings.

Abby was having a wonderful time. Steven and Karen were acting as a father and daughter should. And she—she was having fun! Her usual Saturday afternoon tiredness hadn't come over her. This skating had been good for all of them.

Four times the three circled the ice. Rachel's heart was warmed by the pleasure on their faces. She gave silent thanks to God for the goodness of the day.

Then the three came back to her. "Time for another lesson," Steven said, laughing. "For you. These two have learned all I can teach them."

Radiant faces turned toward each other, the girls linked hands and skated off. Steven helped Rachel to her feet, his arm going around her waist again to give her support. "You have a fine daughter," he said, linking his hand with hers and skating into the crowd.

"Yes, Abby is a real blessing. So is Karen. She's a sweet child. You're fortunate to have her."

For a moment, the arm that encircled her waist stiffened, then it relaxed again. "Yes," Steven said, as though the thought hadn't occurred to him before. "I am. I really am."

To her surprise, she realized that she was skating without thinking about it. But then she did think about it, and her legs grew wooden again, and she faltered, hanging onto Steven with desperation. "I don't think," she said when she'd recovered, "that I was meant to be a skater."

"Nonsense," he said cheerfully. "A minute ago you were doing fine."

"A minute ago I wasn't thinking about skating," she explained as they moved off once more. "We were talking, and I just moved without thinking about it."

"Then we'll just talk," Steven said, with a smile she could only half see since she was afraid turning her head would unbalance her again. "We'll talk and you can move without thinking about it. Now, let me see. Your favorite season is spring. What's your favorite color?"

"Blue." What was going on in his mind? Did he think she was foolish to worry so about skating? Would he think less of her after today?

What silliness! She was as she was. She'd never tried to be anything else. And Steven was her friend. It wasn't right for her to imagine all these things he might be thinking when the way he was behaving showed that he was accepting her just as she was, including the faith he could no longer hold himself.

"And your favorite tree?" he asked.

"Wait a minute. This has to be a two-way conversation. What's your favorite color?"

"Brown," he said, a strange note in his voice. "A certain shade of brown."

That was a dull color for a man like Steven to choose. And why did he have that peculiar note in his voice? But she was too uncertain of her legs to risk looking at his face.

"Now, your favorite tree?" he repeated.

And so the afternoon passed. Steven skated with her till her legs gave out, then the girls would come and skate with him while she recovered. Then he'd come back and take her out again.

The afternoon was well along and she was thinking with regret that they'd soon have to be heading home, when Steven and the girls stopped in front of her again.

"Skate with me, Momma," Abby pleaded.

Rachel only hesitated for a moment. This was Karen's chance to skate alone with her father. "Okay, but we'll have to go slow."

"I know, Momma."

"You and Karen can go first," Abby told Steven. "Momma and me will follow you."

Watching Steven and his daughter skate away, their faces wreathed in smiles, Rachel swallowed over a lump in her throat. Things really seemed to be working out for the two of them.

"Momma, come on." Abby pulled at her hand.

Rachel got to her feet and took Abby's hand. She felt awkward without Steven's supporting arm. Slowly, tentatively, they moved out onto the ice.

"I wanted Karen to be alone with her daddy," Abby confided. "They're getting along better, don't you think?"

"Yes," Rachel agreed. "I think they are."

"Karen says we're helping them." Abby's face glowed. "Helping gives a person a nice feeling, doesn't it, Momma?"

"Yes, Abby. If we cast our bread upon the waters, it does come back to us." Of course, sometimes helping someone wasn't so pleasant, was in sober fact very unpleasant. But there was time enough for Abby to learn that later.

"Momma?"

"Yes, Abby?"

"Was my daddy like Karen's?"

Rachel swallowed hastily and blinked to hold back the sudden tears. "Don't you remember?" she managed to say finally. "He had brown hair and eyes. Like us."

"That's not what I mean," Abby said. "I know what he looked like. I want to know what he was like. As a person. Did he laugh a lot? I think I remember us laughing. Did he take us places? Did he like to be with us?" Her face was sober. "I'm sorry, but I can't remember."

"Of course we laughed." The memories were not so painful as they had once been. "When you were a tiny baby, we used to kiss your little toes and laugh when you laughed. We went all kinds of place together. To the park, to the zoo, to the beach. We toasted wieners and marshmallows in the fireplace." She had to swallow again, holding back the tears that rose at the thought of what they'd lost. "Your daddy was a very good man. He loved us very much."

"Yes," Abby said wistfully. "I remember that. I just wanted you to tell me about it again. I guess he was a lot like Mr. Hendricks." She glanced toward the benches. "Look, Karen and her daddy are waiting for us."

Rachel suppressed a sigh. Abby might learn the pain of being helpful far too soon. She was becoming fond of Steven—that was easy enough to see. It was natural, too, with her own father gone. Steven was a good man, and he'd been careful not to speak about his questions of faith in front of the girls. There was no harm in Abby's enjoying his company. Except that the time would come when she could no longer have it. When Steven remarried, his new wife would want him to herself. When that happened, Rachel and Abby would fade from the picture. They would have no other choice.

Rachel swallowed another sigh. But it hadn't happened yet. Abby could enjoy what she had now, and since she was just a child, she wouldn't worry about losing it. Not worry, as Rachel was worrying, about handling the pain of that loss.

Chapter Seven

The next morning, walking toward church, Rachel and Abby heard the honking of a car horn behind them. "It's Karen and her daddy," Abby cried as the car pulled over to the curb. "Come on, Momma. We can ride with them."

Rachel climbed into the backseat, breathing a silent prayer of thanks that Steven had brought Karen to Sunday school. If only she could get him to stay there himself. If he could be around the church—well, the people in it—there was a better chance of him regaining his faith.

And then the idea came to her. Right out of the blue. Or more likely, right from God. *Please help me do it right,* she prayed.

"Good morning, Steven. Karen. How are you this morning?"

"We're fine." Steven answered for both them, but he smiled at Karen before he asked Rachel, "And how are you?"

"Pretty good." She managed to inject a little trouble into her tone. Her hand, tightening on Abby's, forestalled protest.

"What's the matter?" Steven asked, glancing at her in the rearview mirror.

"It's no trouble, actually," she said, but she kept her tone troubled. "The Christmas pageant is just a little more than I bargained for. The boys are rather rambunctious, I'm afraid."

The boys had acted up a little last Sunday. She wasn't lying. "I wish I had someone like you to help me. But, of course, you're too busy."

"Oh, I hope not," Abby chimed in, her eyes gleaming. "The boys at the theater are so good when you're there, Mr. Hendricks. People expect Momma to do everything. She gets so tired sometimes."

Rachel shifted a little so that Steven couldn't see her face in the rearview mirror. Since she'd never felt better in her life, this bit about her tiredness seemed awfully close to a lie. But Abby had said sometimes. And sometimes she was very tired. Who, after all, wasn't?

She couldn't help smiling down at Abby. Obviously her daughter had some idea of what she was doing and was trying to help.

Then in the front seat Karen said, "You could stay, couldn't you, Daddy? All you were going to do was go home and read the paper. You can do that this afternoon."

"But that's your time with me," Steven said, his even voice yielding no clues to his feelings.

"I'll give it up," Karen said promptly. "I'd rather you'd come in and help. Abby's momma's been so good to me."

Rachel held back a smile. The three of them really had him boxed in. If he didn't go in and help now, he'd look really ungrateful.

He seemed to realize that. "All right," he said. "I'll see if I can help."

Her quiet thank you was lost in the racket the girls made, but that was all right. It was meant for Someone other than Steven, anyway, and no matter how loud the noise, her Father had heard it.

☙

The day of the pageant arrived, the Sunday before Christmas. Getting into Steven's car—he had insisted on picking them up since he was going anyway—Rachel prayed that everything would work out, that somehow, someway, something would happen to restore Steven's faith.

It was just an ordinary Christmas pageant, centered around the nativity scene. But several of the mothers were experienced at sewing and had volunteered to make animal costumes. So in addition to Mary and Joseph, the Christ Child, the angels, the shepherds, and the wise men, there were several woolly sheep, a cow, a donkey, and even a camel.

It was that camel that worried Rachel most. The camel was the favorite character of all the children. And Nathan and Ryan, the boys who filled the costume, were two of the rowdiest. They could cause a problem. But she reminded herself that she had Steven's help. Everything would go as it should.

When they reached the door to the big hall they used for a dressing room, Steven smiled at her. "I'll check the props. Help the animals get ready."

"Okay." Rachel looked out over the room where children were busy getting into costume. It was difficult getting ready so early in the morning, but the pastor was right to schedule the pageant during regular worship. After having worked so hard, the children deserved a big audience. And when the little ones portrayed the age-old story, who knew what hearts might be touched? Maybe even Steven's. But that was up to God.

She turned to the girls beside her. "All right. Go on over with the angels and help each other get dressed." She looked at Karen's nervous face, Karen who had one of the few speaking parts. "Don't worry, honey," she said. "You'll do just fine."

Karen didn't look like she was convinced, but she managed a little smile and dutifully followed Abby.

Rachel looked around, mentally counting the characters. She heaved a sigh of relief. They were all there. The Holy Family, the angels, the shepherds, and the kings.

She glanced across the room to where Steven should be assembling his odd assortment of animals, but he wasn't there. Then she saw that he and Karen were standing a little apart, deep in conversation. From time to time, Steven shook his head. Karen seemed to be pleading with him. Finally, Steven surrendered and Karen threw herself into his arms and gave him a huge hug.

Rachel smiled and turned to help with a wise man's robe. Whatever Karen wanted, she had managed to ask for it. And to get it. *That*, Rachel thought, *was very important*. A bit of curiosity touched her. What could be so important to the child, could make her plead with her father so persistently, so dramatically?

But there was no time for conjecture. There were burnooses to adjust, Mary's shawl to arrange, crowns to be settled securely on the kings' heads, all the angel wings and halos to be inspected. Last year someone's halo had fallen forward, obscuring a child's eye, and the congregation had barely contained its laughter.

Finally everything was ready. Rachel motioned them all into line in the order in which they would enter the sanctuary When the children's chorus that was to precede their scene began to sing, she signaled the children to be ready.

She looked back at the animals, but Steven wasn't there. Maybe he'd gone out front to supervise the setting up of the stable or maybe just to watch the pageant as a whole. She had no more time to think about it. She'd find out later.

The song ended, and she motioned to the children to follow her toward the door that led into the sanctuary. They filed in and stood silently to one side of the stairs that led up to the chancel platform.

She looked around, but there was still no sign of Steven. Maybe he'd decided he couldn't take it, that there were too many memories here. But that didn't seem like him. He wasn't the type to back out on a job.

She couldn't worry about that anymore. She had to pay attention to the pageant. First, the stable animals climbed to the platform, the cow and the donkey settling into the back of the three-sided building and pretending to munch the hay that lay scattered there. Then the Holy Family took their places. Mary carefully arranged her shawl around the doll that served as the Baby Jesus, and Joseph looked suitably paternal.

The older child who was reading the Christmas story from the Bible took her place at the lectern and began, " 'Now it came to pass in those days, that there went out a decree from Caesar Augustus. . .' "

The pageant progressed nicely. On one side of the stage, the angels made their announcement to the shepherds. Karen's voice rang out, clear and bell-like. " 'Fear not: for, behold, I bring you good tidings of great joy, which shall be to all people. For unto you is born this day in the city of David a Saviour, which is Christ the Lord.' "

The shepherds looked up in awe, then grabbed their crooks and hurried off toward the stable, the sheep moving awkwardly on hands and knees behind them. All of them made obeisance to the Baby Jesus, even the sheep who sniffed loudly at His little feet while Mary watched anxiously.

Rachel almost lost herself in the whole thing. But then the kings started shuffling nervously behind her. She nodded to them and they moved on past, normal mischievous little boys transformed into wise men with gray beards. Wearing robes—which certain fathers might recognize as bathrobes that once hung in their own closets—and cardboard crowns sprinkled with gilt, the kings moved with great dignity, bearing their gifts of gold, frankincense, and myrrh.

Rachel breathed a sigh of relief. The last one had gotten up the steps without tripping over his long robe. But at the top of the stairs, that last one turned and looked back, anxiety temporarily replacing his look of regal command.

Then she saw why. The camel was still waiting at the bottom of the stairs. Nathan and Ryan had gotten cold feet. She edged that way. Funny, the camel looked somehow different.

Then the camel moved, getting up the stairs with a lot of clumsiness. Maybe Nathan, who was in the back half of the camel, was having trouble because he couldn't see. But they'd managed okay in rehearsal.

The kings finally reached the Christ Child, the camel lumbering behind them. His humps wobbled as he moved. Rachel held her breath, hoping the humps wouldn't slide over and hang below his shaggy stomach.

The kings advanced one by one to offer their gifts, and the camel sank, with a grumbling sigh that made the audience chuckle, into a kneeling position, resting its muzzle on its front legs, clearly not interested in anything but rest.

She wondered if Steven had told Nathan and Ryan to make that sigh. It was effective, but still. . .

The wise men finished making their offerings; the girl reading the Christmas story finished and closed her Bible. The whole scene was supposed to freeze until Rachel gave them the signal to leave the stage.

But Karen, who as one of the angels had followed the shepherds to take up a post flanking the stable, leaned over and whispered to Mary. Mary nodded and gestured to Joseph. While Rachel watched in surprise, Joseph got up and took the Baby Jesus from Mary's arms. Then, as the audience stared in surprise, he knelt and offered the Child to the camel's perusal.

There was a moment of absolute silence. It seemed to Rachel that everyone in the church held their breath until slowly the camel's shaggy head lifted. It inspected the Child, and then, as tears rose to Rachel's eyes, solemnly put its head under the Child's tiny feet. A deep sigh moved over the congregation as they released their breaths. And the tableau froze while Rachel counted silently to sixty.

As the children filed down, the congregation got to its feet and began to applaud. Smiling, Rachel allowed the children one bow before she led them out. Her heart was pounding in her throat. What a shame Steven hadn't been there to see! *Perhaps,* she admitted to herself, *perhaps even to have been touched by the camel's act of devotion.*

But whose idea had it been? That was what she couldn't understand. Nathan and Ryan couldn't have thought of such a thing. Not by themselves.

The children scattered as soon as they reached the hall, their voices rising in excited chatter. Rachel moved toward the camel, her gaze still searching the room for Steven's familiar figure.

"Momma." Abby's hand crept into hers; her angel wings whispered softly as they brushed together behind her. "Momma, wasn't it just beautiful?"

"Yes. Yes, it was. But what happened with Nathan and Ryan? Did Mr. Hendricks work this out to surprise me?"

Abby's face took on a strange look. "No, Momma. Not exactly. Let him explain."

"How can he explain anything?" Rachel said, a hint of exasperation creeping into her voice, "when he isn't here?"

Abby smothered a giggle. "He's here, Momma."

Rachel looked around again. "Where? I don't see him."

"Come with me," Abby said and led her across the room.

Rachel paused first to announce, "Remember, children, your parents will be coming back soon. So keep on your costumes a little longer. They'll probably want pictures."

Then she followed Abby toward where the camel sat on the floor, incongruously propped up by its front feet. "I don't want to talk to Nathan and Ryan now. I want to talk to Steven."

"You will, Momma," Abby promised, stopping in front of the camel.

The camel sighed and looked up. "Sorry, Rachel," it said. "I had no idea that was going to happen."

"Steven!" Her knees felt suddenly weak. "Steven, whatever are you doing in there?"

"Suffocating," came the plaintive reply. "How about helping me get this head off?"

"Of course." Though her hands were trembling, she managed to get the thing unfastened and lifted it from him. "Where are Nathan and Ryan?"

He shrugged. "Sick, I guess. They didn't show."

For some reason she wanted to laugh. She tried to smother the urge. "And so you went on in their place."

"It isn't funny," he said, aggrieved. "Karen begged me to do it. I didn't want the pageant to be spoiled for the kids." He grinned wryly. "I've always heard that a good leader shouldn't ask his followers to do anything he's not prepared to do himself."

Hope rose in her heart. "And that last bit, when did you come up with it?"

His face closed. "I didn't. They sprung that on me. I didn't mean to sigh like that either, but it isn't easy for a grown man to go walking around on his hands and knees."

She tried to look properly sympathetic. "Of course not. But you did very well, especially when they presented the Child to you."

He shrugged again. "I couldn't very well spoil the pageant. But when I find out whose idea that was. . ."

She had a mental picture of an interfering angel, an angel who wore Karen's face. Evidently he hadn't been looking that way.

"I think it just happened," she said. That much was the truth. "The children saw that it would make the pageant complete. So they added it." She didn't say what was running through her mind—that his daughter suspected his lack of faith, suspected something, at least, and had done what she could to help him.

He didn't look convinced by what she'd said, but then the door opened and parents poured into the hall. Steven stared at them in panic. "Oh, no! I've got to get out of here!"

"Nothing doing," she said. "You're the star of the show." She lowered her voice. "Please don't spoil the effect by telling them what you told me. That scene was very powerful. Please."

For a moment she thought he might refuse, but finally he nodded. "All right. But I feel like a fool sitting—"

"Mrs. Peterson," the pastor boomed. "The best pageant I've ever seen. Congratulations."

"Thank you, pastor."

"The camel was really unique," he began, then realized that the creature getting to its feet in front of him was that camel.

"Pastor." Rachel held back a smile at the pastor's look of surprise. "This is Steven Hendricks. He works with me at the children's theater. He's been helping with the pageant."

"So I see," the pastor said, his voice full of laughter.

Sometimes the pastor's sense of humor wins out over his Christian charity, she thought, hurrying on. "Nathan and Ryan, you know, the Baker boys? They were supposed to be the camel, but they didn't make it. And Steven kindly took their place to spare the children disappointment."

"I see."

What he saw, Rachel couldn't be sure, but at least he wasn't laughing.

"Well, Mr. Hendricks, welcome to our church." The pastor extended his hand and chuckled again. "Sorry about that. I guess camels can't shake hands very well."

"I'm afraid not." Steven laughed, too, though Rachel could see he was feeling the strain. After all, one didn't ordinarily expect to be introduced to people while wearing a camel suit.

"Well, now," the pastor concluded, "we hope you'll feel at home here. Come back anytime. Maybe become one of us." He beamed at Abby. "We have a great church family here."

Abby nodded in agreement.

"Well," the pastor said, "I guess I'd better move aside. Your adoring public is coming." With another smile, he moved on.

Rachel put a comforting hand on Steven's arm. "He means well." Before she could say more, parents descended on Steven, clapping him on the back, shaking his hand/hoof, and praising his performance.

He replied to them all courteously, smiling and laughing in return. But he either didn't reply to invitations to join the congregation or he turned the matter aside. He did it gracefully, so gracefully that she was sure she was the only one who knew that Steven Hendricks had no intention of coming to the adult Sunday school class, joining the men's group, or singing in the choir. No, in spite of what had happened in the pageant, Steven Hendricks still had no faith.

The looks he gave her from time to time confirmed that. *But one thing still puzzles me,* she thought as she watched the congregation gather around this newcomer and do their friendly best to make him welcome. *Why,* she asked herself, *why if it was all make-believe, if he was only playing a part, why had the camel's act of devotion, its recognition of the Christ Child's sovereignty, touched them all so deeply?*

Chapter Eight

The next week, the rush of Christmas was upon them, and Rachel lost herself in the traditional preparations. On Christmas Eve, while she and Abby were unwrapping the ornaments, Rachel realized with a little sense of shock that she wasn't feeling the pain she'd felt the year before. Time did bring healing.

She hadn't forgotten Peter. She could never forget him or the wonderful life they'd shared. But she could think of him now, of that life, with a sort of joy, with a quiet contentment. At times, at least. Somehow her memories had been transformed. What had once caused her terrible grief was now a source of quiet joy.

The doorbell rang, trilling over the soft hum of Christmas carols from the CD player.

"I'll get it, Momma." Abby hurried to the door.

"Merry Christmas! Merry Christmas!"

Rachel turned from the tree with a smile. How nice of Steven and Karen to stop by to wish them a happy holiday. "Hello," she said as they came into the living room. "Well, don't you look nice." She smiled at Karen, who was obviously proud of her new dress. "On your way to a party?"

Steven shook his head. "No, not exactly. Karen thought that is. . ."

Strange. Steven never stammered. He was always in control of the situation.

Karen slipped a hand into her father's. "We're going to the midnight service at church. I've never been before, that I can remember."

"Abby told Karen that you don't drive in the snow." Again Steven paused and looked uncomfortable. "So we came over early. So you'd have time to get dressed. To come along. If you want to."

"Can I wear my new dress, too?" Abby cried in excitement.

"Of course," Rachel said. "But it's early yet. Come in and help us with the tree." She paused. Steven might have difficult memories of this season, too.

But he smiled and took off his jacket. "It's a lovely tree. Nice and full. We'll be glad to help."

Some time later, the girls went upstairs to get Abby dressed, and Rachel fixed Steven a cup of coffee and put out a plate of cookies. "This should keep you till I get ready." She put them on the end table beside him.

"Thank you," he said, his gaze meeting hers.

"Thank you," she said, feeling a sudden embarrassment. "It was kind of you to do this for us."

"Do what?" he asked.

She lowered her voice, though the girls had gone upstairs and couldn't hear. "I know the midnight service doesn't mean anything to you."

"It means too much," he said bitterly. And for a moment she glimpsed the pain in his eyes. "But I can't deprive Karen of her faith because mine's gone. That's not right."

She laid a comforting hand on his sleeve. "The painful part of the memories will pass, Steven. Eventually there will be only happiness connected to them."

His eyes searched hers as he caught and held her hand. "You really believe that?"

"Yes. It's beginning to happen for me." She returned the pressure of his hand, the hand that clutched hers like a lifeline. "It will happen for you, too. I'm sure of it."

He released her hand then, but his gaze was clung to hers, seeking reassurance.

"I'll be down soon," she said, turning toward the door. "I'll have to find something to match all this finery."

That got a little smile from him. And when she came down later, wearing her white knit dress, he'd regained his composure.

◈

The night was lovely, the air crisp, the snow white. "Like a Christmas card," she said softly, looking at the darkened houses where people slept, the others still lit where preparations weren't finished.

"Yes," Steven said. "It's beautiful."

In the backseat, the girls were quiet, subdued by the lateness of the hour and the specialness of the occasion.

They could see the church from afar, ablaze with light. In the parking lot people smiled at each other, hurrying to get in out of the cold, greeting each other with wishes of happiness for the season.

At the walk, Abby took Rachel's hand. They often walked like that. Then Rachel realized that Karen had taken her father's, and the girls had linked their hands so that they walked four abreast, almost like a family.

But we are not a family, Rachel told herself sharply. Now that Peter was gone, Abby was the only family she was ever going to have. Still, it was good to see the happiness on the girls' faces, to see the reverence with which they entered the candlelit sanctuary. Steven had been very nice to think of this.

The girls sat between them and shared their songbooks. When the first carol began, Rachel was pleased to hear Steven's deep melodious voice. But precisely because it was so deep, so melodious, she noticed when it faltered and stopped. She didn't look at him; her own throat was full, and she could only mouth some of the words.

I was wrong, she thought, tears filling her eyes. Some memories would always be painful, would always call up that longing for a person who would never again be there to love and give comfort. But life had to go on. She blinked back the tears and let her voice ring out. "Joy to the world," they sang. And that, that was the real meaning of Christmas, the joy of the Savior's birth.

After the service, she turned to Steven. "That was lovely. Thank you." She wanted to say more, to tell him that she appreciated what he'd done for her, to tell him again that his pain would pass. But with the girls there, she could only smile and repeat again, "Thank you."

She was fairly sure he'd go directly to the car, avoiding the line that formed to shake hands with the pastor. But they were hardly out of their seats before people came up to talk to him. And while they talked, they moved naturally in the direction of the line.

She couldn't help hearing what was said, the words of welcome, the invitations coming again, thick and fast. And again Steven gracefully evaded any commitment. Her heart was troubled for him. How could he turn his back on all this Christian love and fellowship? She knew its value. She'd learned that after Peter's death when so many people had been there to help her, to see that she had everything she needed, to offer her their love and support.

Steven's bitter reaction to his wife's death, his loss of faith, had cut him off from that, from the comfort and support of the community of Christ. It had left him alone and friendless.

Abby tugged at her sleeve. "Momma."

"Yes, dear."

"It was so pretty, Momma. With all the candles lit." Abby's voice held reverence. "We should do it more often."

Rachel shook her head. "It wouldn't be so special then, honey. Christmas is a very wonderful time. A time of miracles."

"Miracles?" Abby sounded confused.

"Christmas seems to make people nicer and better. For a little while, the world is a better place."

Abby looked puzzled. "But then wouldn't it be better to have Christmas all the time? So people would stay nice?"

Rachel sighed. "It might be better, honey, if it would work. But the specialness would be gone and people wouldn't notice."

Abby nodded slowly. "I think I see. Even people who aren't Christians get nicer at Christmas, don't they?"

"Sometimes," Rachel agreed.

"And sometimes they become Christians."

"Yes, Abby. Sometimes."

Had Abby heard something Steven had said? Or was it just that he didn't go to church? Something had led her to ask these questions. She was smart. She didn't ask questions without good reason.

By this time, they'd reached the pastor and he was shaking her hand. "Good to see you here, Rachel. Very good. I'll be talking to you in a few weeks about the young people's hayride."

"Yes, pastor." She returned his handshake.

"You're looking very pretty tonight, Abby," he said.

"Thank you." Abby smiled proudly.

"And you, Karen." He turned to Steven and Karen. "Is that a new dress you've got on?"

"Yes, sir." Karen looked really pleased. "It's one of my Christmas presents."

"A very pretty one. Good evening, Mr. Hendricks. Glad to see you here." Steven nodded and shook hands. "Thank you." And he moved on.

Following the Hendricks across the parking lot, Rachel realized that in spite of Steven's attitude, she was feeling good. She'd done all she could to help him and Karen. The rest was in God's hands. Surely He would find a way to bring Steven back into the fold.

❧

The Saturday before New Year's, like that before Christmas, there were no theater rehearsals scheduled. Abby was on the phone early, pleading with Steven to allow Karen to come over.

Fixing breakfast, Rachel watched and listened with quiet amusement.

"Yes, Mr. Hendricks." Abby's smile grew. "That'd be fun. Just a minute. I'll let you talk to Momma." Abby handed her the phone, mouthing a silent "Please."

"Good morning, Steven."

"Good morning. How are you this morning?"

"Fine," she said. "At least I am until I know what you and Abby are cooking up."

His laughter was warm and soft. "Abby wants Karen to come over to play. I said she can. I'll pick you all up at noon, and we can go for our regular lunch, then go skating again. What do you say?"

She hesitated. There were a million things that needed to be done in the house. She really should stay home and do them. Just minutes ago, she'd been thinking where to begin and wishing she could call up some energy. "Well. . ."

"Come on, Rachel. You promised to help me." He paused. "Forgive me. I'm sorry to presume so much. You must have other plans."

"No, no. It isn't that. It's just. . .there are things to do here in the house. I was going to clean cupboards."

"You've got all morning to do that," he pointed out cheerfully. Then he laughed. "Want me to stay and help you?"

That made her laugh too. The image of Steven passing the contents of her kitchen cupboards to her was amusing. "No, thanks. I can manage alone."

"Good. We're on, then. Say, if having Karen there will interfere with what you're doing. . ."

"No, no." She laughed again. "It actually helps. It keeps Abby busy." She winked at Abby, who was standing there hanging on her every word.

"Okay, then. I'll drop off Karen, go do my errands, and pick you all up around twelve."

"All right. See you then."

Abby grabbed her in a huge bear hug. "Thank you, Momma. Oh, thank you. It wouldn't seem right without our lunch. And we get to go skating again." She looked around the kitchen. "I didn't know you were going to do cupboards this morning. I can help."

"That's all right, Abby. I can manage myself." Rachel dished up the scrambled eggs and added the bacon. "The toast is in the toaster."

Abby got the toast and buttered it. "All ready, Momma."

"Okay, let's eat." Rachel poured her coffee and joined Abby at the table. Abby looked so happy. It made her feel good herself, though the nagging idea returned, the idea that Abby shouldn't be caring so much. Anything could happen to take Karen out of her life. Steven could marry. He could take a job that required another move. She could go on and on, listing possibilities. Instead, she reminded herself that she and her daughter, as well as Steven and his, were in the hands of God. Whatever happened to Abby, God would sustain her.

ಶಿ

The doorbell rang as Abby finished her toast. She scampered to answer it. "Hi, Karen."

"Hi, Abby."

Rachel smiled at the pleasure in their childish voices. Then, sighing, she gathered up the dirty dishes. Cleaning kitchen cupboards had never been one of her favorite tasks, and this cleaning was long overdue.

She'd start with the bottom one, nearest the sink. If she kept at it, she could have most of them done before Steven got back at noon. She opened the door and got down on her knees.

They'd talked of redoing the kitchen, she and Peter, of changing these old, deep, hard-to-reach cupboards for new ones. But there had always been something else that was more important: Abby's arrival, a different car, a new furnace. And now. . .now she supposed she'd always have these cupboards, just the way they were.

She started taking out the canned goods.

"Here, Momma," Abby said, startling her. "Hand them up to us. We'll put them on the table."

Rachel looked up at the smiling girls. "Karen came over to play, honey. Not to work."

"Please, Mrs. Peterson," Karen said. "At Sunday school, we learned about helping people. About the Golden Rule." She looked around the big old kitchen. "It says to treat other people the way we want to be treated. And I wouldn't want to clean all these cupboards by myself."

"We want to help, Momma. It'll be good for us. Isn't that what you always teach me? To help others?"

With a soft laugh, Rachel gave in. "Okay. But I want to tell you, I think you're two of the nicest girls I know."

Abby grinned. "We're really not that nice. We just want you to skate this afternoon, too. We don't want you to be all tired out from working."

Rachel laughed again. "Okay, I'm convinced. I'll pass the things out. You put them on the table. Try to keep them in order so they'll be easier to put away. And Abby, you get a big empty grocery bag. There'll probably be some things to throw out."

"Yes, Momma."

Abby got the bag and set it open on the floor. Rachel began handing things up to Karen.

"This is like what they told us about at school," Karen said. "The way they make cars."

Abby laughed. "This is a cupboard-cleaning assembly line."

Rachel felt her spirits rising. How could anyone feel sad with such lovely little girls to help her?

"What did you get for Christmas?" Abby asked as Rachel pulled out the old shelf liner and put it in the garbage bag.

"You saw my dress," Karen said. "And I got new boots. A bunch of socks. And a lot of books. My favorite is the Bible story one. The words are a little hard, so Daddy reads it to me."

Rachel stopped wiping the shelves for a moment. From her heart, she sent up another prayer of thanksgiving. Steven was doing all he could for his daughter.

"What's your favorite present of all?" Abby asked, passing Rachel the new shelf paper.

Karen didn't pause for a second. "My daddy said he's going to spend every Saturday afternoon with me. And we're going to do what I want. That's why we're going skating this afternoon. That's what I wanted."

Rachel's hands were steady as the girls passed back the seldom-used dishes in their plastic bags and the canned things she kept in the front. Yes, Steven was doing everything he could to show his daughter his love. Now it was time for her and Abby to see less of them, to move aside. She swallowed a sigh. She'd have to speak to Abby about it later.

With so many hands to help, the cleaning went quickly. At 11:30, the last thing was put away in the last clean cupboard. Rachel went upstairs to take a shower. Funny, she wasn't even tired. In fact, she felt full of energy.

The girls used Abby's bathroom to wash up. When the doorbell rang at twelve sharp, all of them were ready and waiting.

"Well," Steven said, looking at their faces as they trooped past him to the car. "You look like you had a real fun morning."

Karen and Abby burst into giggles. Rachel had to laugh. "I guess it depends on your definition of fun. Karen and Abby insisted on helping me with the cupboards." She gave the girls a big smile. "And I must say the job's never been done faster or better. I feel like a Victorian villain, though, using Karen for child labor."

Steven laughed. "I just wish I knew how you do it. But then, kids always seem more willing to help other people than they do their own parents."

"Not me," Abby protested from the backseat. "I help Momma a lot."

"Yes, you do," Rachel said. "I only hope you didn't put too much pressure on Karen this morning."

"Oh no!" Karen said. "She didn't. I wanted to help. I think we had a real good time, too. We sang Christmas carols, Daddy. And hymns. And we laughed a lot."

"That's good," Steven said, throwing Rachel an amused glance. "They say that laughter is good for the soul."

They laughed through the afternoon—at lunch, where Steven told jokes that had the girls in stitches; at the skating rink, where he clowned it up; and even on the way home.

Watching the Hendricks leave, Rachel was still smiling. It had been a very good day. But she'd have to talk to Abby about the two of them doing something alone on Saturdays. Sometimes, at least.

"Come into the kitchen and help me get dinner," she said, shutting the door and taking off her coat.

Abby started setting the table, and Rachel took out a can of soup. "It's really good to see Karen getting along so well with her father."

"Yes," Abby agreed, "I'm real glad for her."

Rachel turned from stirring the soup. "You know, honey, we shouldn't be doing so many things with the Hendricks. They need time alone."

Abby stopped putting out the silver. "But, Momma, Karen wants us to come along."

"You and I can do things together," Rachel suggested.

"We do lots of things already, Momma." Abby's forehead creased into a frown. "I like to skate."

"We can go skating," Rachel pointed out. "Just you and I."

Abby shook her head. "But it's not the same. Things are more fun with

Karen and her father. We laugh a lot. Like we did today. You and me, we don't laugh when we're alone."

"But Abby," Rachel began. Then honesty made her stop. It wasn't pleasant to admit it, but Abby was right. She hadn't laughed much in the last couple years, not since the accident had changed her whole life.

"We'll talk about it again," she said softly, once more amazed at the truth that could come from the mouths of children. "I'll think about what you said."

Abby seemed satisfied with that. "You know what I think? I think we needed Karen and her daddy. I think helping them is helping us. And I don't think we ought to stop."

While they ate, Rachel thought about what Abby had said. Rachel believed she'd coped with Peter's death. And she had, in a certain sense. But she hadn't seen what Abby was missing. She hadn't seen that Abby needed a male figure in her life just as Karen needed a female one.

Steven was filling a void for Abby. Rachel saw it clearly. She couldn't just close her daughter off from the man. That would be unfair.

Caring about someone, like Abby was beginning to care about Steven, was risky, of course. And she could be hurt. But she already cared enough to be hurt. Rachel sighed. She might as well let Abby have what she could.

And who could be sure of the future? Steven had seemed very much in love with his wife. Just as she'd been very much in love with Peter. She didn't intend to marry again. Maybe Steven didn't either. After all, Karen was no longer in need of a mother figure. She could always come to Rachel.

These thoughts calmed her a little, strengthened her feeling that it would already be too painful for Abby to lose her friendship with Steven. The rest of Rachel's thoughts, the dark pictures of loneliness and despair that invaded her mind when she thought of losing her own friendship with Steven, those she pushed aside. He'd become a good friend. There was no doubt about that—or about the fact that she'd come to care deeply about both his daughter and him.

While it was not a particularly Christian thing to hope that Steven would remain unmarried, it did seem the best chance for her and Abby to go on enjoying his friendship. If it was wrong for her to hope for such a thing, then she was sorry. But seeing how much Abby had come to need Steven Hendricks, how could her mother not want to protect her?

Chapter Nine

The month of January moved along. Every Saturday morning, Steven arrived with Karen to give his help at rehearsals. When that was over, the four of them went to Kitty's for lunch, then ice skating or to a Disney movie or to do something else together—something Karen had asked for.

One evening toward the end of the month, Rachel answered the phone and heard the pastor say, "Rachel, how are you?"

"Fine, pastor."

"I mentioned at the Christmas Eve service that I'd be calling you about this, about the annual young people's hayride."

"Yes," she said. "I remember. I've been expecting your call."

"Well, I was wondering if you'd agree to be a chaperon this year." He laughed a little nervously. "I really do hate to impose on you, but chaperons are getting harder to find every year. Not many people are willing to brave the cold, you know. Especially as they get older."

"Yes," Rachel said, "I suppose that's true."

"Then I can count on you?"

She didn't need to think about it. It was something that needed to be done, and she could do it. If she could, she should. "Yes, I'll be there."

"Thank you. I really appreciate your doing this."

He must have had quite a lot of trouble getting chaperons, she thought, considering the kind of thanks he was giving. "It's all right," she assured him. "I don't mind the cold."

"Good. Then I'll see you at church, Friday night at seven. We're car-pooling from there to the farm."

She hung up and went up to her bedroom. She'd been a chaperon before, though not recently, not since. . . She pushed the thought aside. The cold could be biting. Standing in front of her open closet, she looked over her clothes. How many layers could she put on and still walk?

She'd decided on several sweaters, dug out her wool socks and a pair of long underwear, and was wondering if she could get her mittens on over her gloves, when the phone rang again.

"Hello," she answered.

"Hi, it's Steven. How are you?"

"I'm fine. What can I do for you?"

He chuckled. "I guess that puts me in my place—the guy who's always calling and asking for favors."

"No," she laughed, "that's not what I mean. It's just. . .well, you do always have a reason for calling."

"Yes, you're right. And I would like to ask a favor. I'm going out Friday night. Could Karen stay over with you?"

It had happened. Her heart skipped a beat. It was the beginning of the end. He was going out with someone.

"I'll be out myself," she said, trying to keep the unsteadiness out of her voice. "Chaperoning the church sleigh ride. But there'll be a sitter here. Karen can stay here, too. No problem."

"Thanks," he said. "I'll be there around six-thirty. I'll drop you at the church."

"That'd be nice. Thanks."

She put the phone down and tried to breathe evenly. There were many things he could be doing without having a date. But she didn't believe he was doing them. A man like Steven—who was really attractive, besides being a good person—was bound to attract the attention of women. And these days women didn't have to wait to be asked. They could start things.

She went back to her closet and finished choosing clothes. What Steven was doing Friday night was none of her business. She had her own life to attend to.

≈

The week passed slowly. Many times Rachel caught herself wondering about Steven's date. Had he met someone at work? She'd like to see this woman, know something about her character. Abby had come to depend so much on Steven's friendship. Rachel was worried for Abby's sake. And for his.

Then she scolded herself, remembering how much Steven had loved his wife. This was, after all, a first date, and Steven wasn't a hasty man. Here she was—back to her old habit of borrowing trouble. And after she'd resolved never to do it again.

Friday night came and she put on most of her layers of clothes, leaving the rest to carry with her when she left the house. The baby-sitter arrived, and Rachel welcomed her.

"It's a bitter night for a hayride," Mrs. Collins said, wiping at her reddened nose. "I don't know how you young people can stand it. I just had to walk from next door, and I'm frozen to the bone."

"You just go on into the kitchen," Rachel said. "I told Abby you could make hot chocolate. You can have some with the girls."

Mrs. Collins wriggled out of her ample coat. "You young people have all the advantages. You stay warm in winter. You eat without getting fat."

Rachel motioned her toward the kitchen. Mrs. Collins was famous in the neighborhood for her continual dieting and her just as continual inability to refuse anything sweet.

"I'm expecting a ride soon," Rachel said. "And Abby's friend that I told you about will be coming."

Mrs. Collins moved toward the kitchen. "I'll just go on out then. Now you dress warm. And have yourself a good time."

"Yes, Mrs. Collins."

Having a good time hadn't entered my mind, Rachel thought, looking at the scarves, gloves, mittens, and blanket she had ready. Being a chaperon wasn't a fun job. But since she and Peter had never been on a sleigh ride together, there wouldn't be painful memories. The exuberance of the young people, their obvious joy in life, pleased her. That was how everyone should feel. There was a lot of joy in just living every day, a lot of beauty that could be enjoyed, a lot of pleasure that could be felt, even while trying to live out one's faith. Look at how much fun she and Abby were having while trying to help Karen.

Thinking of Karen brought Steven to mind again. Who was this woman he was dating?

You've got to stop this, she told herself sharply. *It's none of your business.* Of course, she felt some concern for Karen. Not every woman would make the child a good mother.

The doorbell chimed, and she jumped guiltily. How silly. Steven would have enough good sense to think about his daughter's welfare. He wouldn't choose just any wife.

She went to open the door. "Hello, Karen. Hello, Steven."

Abby came running from the kitchen. "Come on. We're making hot chocolate. And we've got peanut butter cookies."

Karen took off her coat and boots. "Bye, Daddy. See you at rehearsal tomorrow."

"Bye, honey."

They hugged, and Rachel and Abby grinned at each other and hugged, too.

Rachel got into her coat and gathered up her things. "I'm ready," she said, allowing herself to notice that this must not be a very fancy date. Steven was wearing outdoor clothes.

He took the blanket and other things. "Okay. Let's go."

She had a little trouble getting into the car. So many layers made bending awkward, but she knew that she'd be glad for every layer, maybe even wish for more.

The church was all lit up, and teens were climbing into cars near the back door. As Steven pulled the car up, Rachel turned to get her things. "Why don't you stay in here where it's warm?" Steven suggested. "I'll go ask the pastor who's riding with us."

She turned back to him. "Riding with us?"

"Yes." Steven's eyes twinkled. "The pastor asked me to be a chaperon. Didn't I tell you?"

Suddenly she felt very silly, and a little lightheaded. "No. . .I. . .no, you didn't."

"Sorry," he said. "I thought I had. I'll be back soon with our share of the kids."

She watched him cross the parking lot. Thankfully, she'd stopped herself in time, hadn't made a fool of herself by asking about his date for the evening.

So Steven was going to chaperon, too. She smiled. No doubt he was as good with young people as he was with little children. Steven seemed able to deal with anyone. He would do a good job. But how had he come to be a chaperon? It wasn't like the pastor to ask someone who wasn't a member of the church community. And people didn't volunteer for a job like this.

Although Steven brought Karen to Sunday school every week, he hadn't been to services since Christmas Eve. There was definitely something unusual going on here. But before she could puzzle over it more, Steven came back across the lot, followed by four teens. Amid a lot of laughter, all four of them piled in the back.

"Hi, Mrs. Peterson. How are you?"

Rachel half turned. "I'm doing fine. It's great to see you."

Heather, Amber, John, and Josh were kids she'd taught in one of her first

Sunday school classes. Seven years ago, they'd been awkward nine- and ten-year-olds. Now they were almost adults, facing an adult world. She smiled at them. "Do you know Mr. Hendricks?" she asked.

John laughed. "Sure. He's the best camel the church ever had."

The others laughed, and Rachel turned a little anxiously to see how Steven was taking this. But he was grinning cheerfully. "You wait, John," he said. "Before too long you'll be married and have kids of your own. Then you're apt to end up in a camel suit—or worse."

John laughed and the others joined him. "I suppose so," he said. "I know my little sister Katie was one of the sheep. She'd have been real disappointed if there hadn't been a camel."

"Yeah," Heather said. "My little brother Cody could hardly talk about anything else. He was the wise man who brought the gold."

"Well," Steven said with a little chuckle, "I wouldn't want to do it again, but I'm glad it went off well. Mrs. Peterson worked really hard on it."

A chorus of thank yous came from the backseat.

By that time, the cars were loaded and began to pull away from the church. "I'll give you directions," John volunteered.

"Good," Steven said. "I'm not too familiar with this part of town."

As the talk flowed around her, Rachel leaned back and relaxed. There'd be theater rehearsals in the morning, and she'd have to get up early. With only a few weeks left till the show opened, there was an awful lot to do. But there was no need to worry; Steven would be there to help.

Amid more laughter and jokes, they reached the farm. They left the car, and she saw John and Heather, then Amber and Josh, take hands. Evidently they were couples, at least for that night. Tears came to her eyes. Peter. There'd never been anyone else for her. Never.

Suddenly Steven was beside her, his mittened hand on her elbow. "It's kind of slippery here. Be careful."

She accepted his steadying hand, just as she'd accepted it at the skating rink. It no longer seemed strange to have him touch her. After all, he was a friend. And friends were there to help each other.

The horses were waiting beside a big, old-fashioned barn, their frosty breath hanging in the cold night air, their hooves stamping impatiently on the frozen ground. Behind them stood the big, wagonlike sleigh, full of fragrant hay.

"Here." Steven's hand tightened on her elbow. "Let me help you up."

"Thanks." She chuckled. "With all these layers of clothes, I'm not sure I can bend in the right places."

"Hey, I know what you mean. I've got on wool socks and long johns and two pairs of pants. And let's see, three or four layers on top. I think we're going to need it all, though."

"It looks like it." She reached the top of the sleigh and half fell onto her knees. She pulled herself forward on the hay, and Steven climbed up beside her.

"Where do the chaperons sit?" he asked.

"In the back, I suppose. Where they can see, more or less."

"Okay. In the back it is." He crawled over the hay, pulling the blankets behind him.

She followed. It was nice having Steven along. He made any occasion fun, and he talked to the teens as the equals they indeed were.

Rachel and Steven settled in the back, a nice cushion of hay between their backs and the end of the sleigh. Steven spread the blankets around them. "There. That should keep us warm."

Turning slightly, she looked up at him. "Yes, but I'm worried about your ears. You can get frostbite when it's this cold, you know."

He laughed and stuck a hand in his pocket. "No need to worry. I've come prepared." He produced a bright orange stocking cap and pulled it on low over his ears. "Feels good," he said. "I wouldn't want them to fall off."

Her laughter was joined by the giggles of the girls settling into the hay in front of them.

"Does your hat glow in the dark?" John asked.

Steven laughed. "You can tell better than me. Wait till we get out of the barnyard light and look. All I care about is keeping my precious ears on my head. You all have hats, don't you?" he asked, raising his voice. "I don't want any frozen anythings on this hayride."

A chorus of affirmations and laughter rose from around them. "Is everyone here?" Steven asked.

There was more noise and calls echoing back and forth. "Wait," Steven said. "I've got a list." He took off a mitten and pulled a list from his pocket. "Whew, it is cold." He shoved his hand hastily back into the mitten and tilted the list toward the light. "We'll do this just like school," he went on with a laugh. "When I read off your name, answer."

A chorus of groans and moans met his mention of school, but the responses came crisp and quick.

Steven finished and tucked the list back into his pocket. "Okay, we're all here. Driver, let's get this show on the road."

The driver clucked to the horses, the runners squeaked across the snow, and the sleigh moved out of the barnyard. It took a few minutes for everyone to get settled comfortably. Then someone said, "Let's sing."

"Yeah, let's. What'll we sing?"

Someone pointed upward. "Look at the moon. How big it is. How about 'By the Light of the Silvery Moon'? Isn't that one of the songs they used to sing on nights like this?"

"Yeah. How's it start?"

"Hey, how do I know? Do I look like a singing star?"

"Say, Steven—Mr. Hendricks, I mean?"

"Steven will do fine. What do you want?"

"You know the song we're talking about?"

"I think so."

"Then help us sing it."

"Hey, do I look like a singing star?" Steven's tone was almost an exact copy of the previous protestor's, and the group burst into laughter.

"Not with that hat on, you don't," John said.

"I like my hat," Steven said, with another laugh. "It keeps my ears warm. Come on, Rachel. You must know the words. Help me."

"I'll try," she said, laughing too.

"By the light."

"By the light," came the echo from around them.

"Of the silvery moon."

By this time everyone was joining in, and the rich young voices rang out over the snow-covered fields. They finished with a great flourish, and the night air was full of the sound of mittened hands clapping.

All kinds of favorites were suggested and sung, from "The Battle Hymn of the Republic" to "Jesus, Name Above All Names" and "Amazing Grace."

Rachel shivered, partly from the cold, partly from delight with the music. Steven's arm went around her, drawing her close to his side. She thought about pulling away—she certainly didn't want anyone to get the wrong idea about them. But it was cold in the sleigh and very dark. The sky was cloudy, and from time to time a dark cloud covered the face of the moon.

Besides, they had blankets up to their chins.

So she didn't move away, didn't indicate she even felt his arm, except to let it draw her closer to the welcome heat of his body. Gradually she grew aware of a deep feeling of comfort and safety.

The singing died away. Then someone pointed out one of the constellations, and that started a round of star naming.

"Warm enough?" Steven asked once.

"Oh, yes, I'm fine. Nice and toasty." But she should be. Nothing but the tip of her nose and her eyes showed. "And you?"

"Me, too. I'm fine."

When the driver took them back to the barn, it hardly seemed possible that several hours had passed.

"Hot chocolate and donuts in the shed," Steven told the group. "Cars will be here to pick us up in fifteen minutes."

When they returned to the church parking lot, Rachel waited in the car while Steven checked to make sure all the kids had rides home. The hayride seemed to have been a huge success. She hadn't heard a single complaint, and the warm sound of laughter echoed in the air.

Finally Steven climbed back in the car. "All rides present and accounted for," he said, shoving the list into his pocket.

"Everyone seemed to have a good time," she said, "in spite of the cold."

He pulled off his stocking cap and shoved it into his pocket. "Yes, I think so. Kids don't seem to mind the cold. How about you? Did you have a good time?"

"Me?" And then she remembered Mrs. Collins telling her to have a good time, a piece of advice, which until that very moment, she hadn't thought of. "Yes, I had a good time, too."

"I'm glad. You need to get out more. Have some fun. Enjoy life."

"I do enjoy life," she said, as he pulled out of the parking lot. "But a lot of it isn't very enjoyable—as you well know."

He looked like he was going to say something else, but then he didn't. Instead he started to whistle "Amazing Grace" half under his breath. A little pool of warmth found a home inside her, and she hummed along with him. In spite of what he'd told her, he was growing more and more involved with the church. Maybe that would help him find his faith again. She hoped and prayed so.

They didn't talk much on the ride home, though they whistled and hummed several songs. She leaned back, enjoying the peaceful beauty of quiet snow-laden trees and houses. And then they pulled into her drive, and he stopped the car.

"Thanks for the ride," she said, digging in her pocket for her keys. Mrs. Collins was probably asleep, sitting bolt upright in front of the TV.

"You're welcome," Steven said. "Thank you for the evening."

She paused, her hand on the doorknob. "Me? Why thank me?"

"For. . ." He paused, and she had the distinct impression he'd changed his mind, that what he then said wasn't what he'd originally meant to say. "Your being there made it easier with the kids."

She stared at him. "You were wonderful with them. Just as you're wonderful with the kids at the theater. You don't have any problems with people."

"Only with the important ones," he muttered, turning back to the car.

He must still be worried about Karen, she thought, watching him fish her things out of the back and come around to join her.

The sidewalk looked a little slippery, and again he offered her his arm. She took it. She was really tired, and tomorrow would be a long day, with rehearsal and everything.

At the door, he put her things down and turned to face her. "Good night, Rachel."

"Good night, Steven. I'll see you at rehearsal in the morning, won't I?"

"Yes," he said, his face strangely serious in the moonlight. "I'll be there."

"You're not worrying about Karen again, are you?"

"No, no. I'm not worrying about Karen." His voice had gone much softer. Was he coming down with something, some sickness? After all, they'd been out for a long time. She hoped he hadn't gotten chilled.

And then, before she had any idea what was happening, he reached out and pulled her to him. She returned his hug, but she was entirely unprepared for the mittened hand that found her chin and tilted her face up toward his. Or for the depths of emotion reflected in his dark eyes. Or for the tender feel of his cold lips on her own.

For one eternal moment, it was as if Peter stood there, as if Peter held her once more. Then realization hit her and she pulled back, out of his arms. "I. . .Mrs. Collins is waiting."

"Of course," he said quietly. "Sleep well. I'll see you in the morning."

"Yes. Good night."

Automatically she picked up her things, fitted the key in the lock, and went in, closing the door carefully behind her. She stood, leaning against the door, her whole body trembling. She had to get control of herself before she woke Mrs. Collins. Nothing so stupendous had happened. Steven was a man, and the hayride had been romantic, with all the teens laughing and sitting in pairs.

Yes, that was it. Steven had just let the atmosphere of the evening carry him away. That was all there was to it. A friendly little kiss. She wasn't going to let one little kiss destroy a perfectly good friendship.

And if she'd felt for a moment like she used to feel with Peter, well, that was only from the shock of it. She and Steven were just friends. Nothing more. No man had ever made her feel like Peter had. No man ever would.

Chapter Ten

"No man will ever make me feel like Peter did," Rachel repeated to herself the next morning when she woke. For a moment she lay silent, reluctant to face the day. Directing the children's theater seemed to have become a job of huge proportions, requiring more energy than she could summon up. The bed was warm and cozy. If only she could just turn over and go back to sleep. Then her mind found and grasped the memory of an elusive dream, and her body went warm with embarrassment.

In a beautiful dream world, she'd been lying in a pair of strong male arms—Peter's, of course. But when she turned her head, filled with joy at his return, it was not Peter's face she saw, but that of Steven Hendricks.

She moved restlessly. Her subconscious mind was playing tricks on her. She frowned. The hayride had been a big mistake. Until then, her friendship with Steven had been safe and comfortable. No disquieting romantic overtones to mar it. If he changed, if he began to think of her romantically. . .

She shivered in the cozy warm bed. Much as she liked Steven, if he did anything so foolish, she'd have to end their friendship. That would be hard on the girls. But she had no desire for a romantic relationship. She loved Peter. She always would.

Finally she dragged herself out of bed and woke the girls. There were only two rehearsals left before opening night. She couldn't miss this one. Steven would just have to understand how she felt. He'd have to respect her wishes.

In the bathroom, brushing her teeth, she scolded herself. She was probably putting too much emphasis on one little kiss. It hadn't been passionate. Friendly was a more accurate word for it. Or maybe tender. And it had been brief. Maybe Steven's friends kissed as hers hugged, spontaneously and with affection, but without romantic intent.

That must be it. She went back to the bedroom and got dressed. She was making too much of the whole thing. She'd known Steven since—she counted backward—since before Thanksgiving. Now it was early February. They'd spent a lot of time together because of the girls. In all that time, he'd never done anything to hint that he regarded her as someone more than a good friend. And that was all she wanted to be to him: a friend.

She'd been foolish, perhaps, taking his arm on the icy walks, accepting its support when they skated, sitting in its shelter during the hayride. But she'd thought of him simply as a friend. She had no romantic interest in him or any other man. All that had died with Peter.

When they arrived at the theater, she was still running the subject over in her mind. What was she going to do if—

"Momma. Mom—ma." Abby's plaintive cry finally penetrated her thoughts.

"What's wrong, honey?"

"Momma, are you sick?" Abby asked. "You've been acting real funny all morning."

Rachel managed a smile. "No, dear. I'm not sick. I've just got a lot on my mind. Opening night is only two weeks away, you know."

"Yes, I know. But—"

She laughed. "I'm okay, honey. Honest. Just a little tired, that's all."

Abby didn't pursue the subject, but she didn't look really convinced either.

Rachel sent the girls off on several errands and tried to concentrate on what needed to be done at this rehearsal. She had to stop this foolishness. Abby was a perceptive little girl. There was no point in upsetting her unnecessarily. Especially over a kiss that probably hadn't been anything more than a friendly gesture.

With a murmur of disgust at herself and her silly ways, Rachel took out her pen and clipboard and began looking over her notes for the morning. First, they should—

"Good morning, Rachel." Suddenly Steven was standing beside her.

She schooled her voice to convey a calmness she was far from feeling. "Good morning, Steven."

"I hope you had no ill effects from last night's excursion," he said cheerfully.

She was about to tell him that he'd had no right to kiss her like that, to ruin a friendship she had come so to rely on, and then she realized that he wasn't talking about the kiss at all. He was talking about the hayride.

"No," she said, finally raising her gaze to his and forcing herself to smile. "No ill effects. Cold weather doesn't seem to bother me."

"Me, either," he returned heartily. "I like winter."

She couldn't help herself. She scrutinized his face. But he didn't look a bit different. He was the same Steven she'd come to rely on.

"So," he said, glancing at the clipboard. "What's the first thing we do this morning, boss?"

This time her smile was real. He wasn't going to say anything about that kiss. He'd probably already forgotten it. "I'm still worried about the ball scenes. Getting those boys to waltz in time to the music and hold onto the girls is a major undertaking."

"So I've noticed. I don't know how you could even try to do all this alone."

"Just stupid, I guess," she said lightly.

"Don't say that." His voice had gone coldly serious, and his gaze locked with hers. "You're a very intelligent woman. Look at how you've helped Karen and me."

"That was my responsibility." She said the first words that came to her mind. Oh, why had he ruined everything by kissing her like that? Now she was so self-conscious she could hardly look at him.

"Is that—" His words were interrupted by the arrival of Abby and Karen. Karen ran to hug her father.

"Is the ball scene where you want to begin?" Steven asked, hugging Karen back.

"Yes," Rachel said. "Tony and Megan can run through their lines, too."

"And us, Momma?" Abby asked eagerly.

Rachel smiled. "Yes, you too. But I don't know why. You're absolutely perfect in your parts."

"Oh, that reminds me." Steven reached down for a bag and produced two pairs of knee socks with separate toes, each toe a different bright color.

Karen looked a little doubtful, but Abby was ecstatic. "Oh, these are wonderful, Mr. Hendricks! Thank you." And she threw herself into Steven's arms and hugged him. Then she plopped down on the floor and pulled on a sock.

Steven smiled. "It's just a thought. I saw them and I thought they might fit. But you're the boss."

"I don't know," Rachel said. "I'm not sure we can get shoes to fit over them."

"We can, Momma." Abby stuck out a foot and wiggled a bright toe admiringly. "Please, Momma, they'll make our scenes a lot funnier."

Abby was right about that. "All right, you can wear them if you want to."

"What about Karen?"

"Let's leave that up to Karen. Maybe she doesn't want to wear them."

"Oh, I do, Mrs. Peterson." Karen took the other pair from her father. "Thanks, Daddy."

Abby pulled at Karen's free hand. "Come on. Let's look in the prop room. I remember seeing some old open-toed shoes in there."

"Don't be long," Rachel said. "We're going to begin the ball scene soon."

"We'll hurry, Momma."

Rachel turned to Steven. "That was very thoughtful. Thank you."

"You're welcome. And while we're giving thanks. . ."

Her heart rose up in her throat. If he mentioned that kiss, if he wanted to change their friendship to something else, she'd say no; she'd send him out of her life even now, now when she needed his help so badly.

"Thank you for asking me to help with the theater." He grinned. "I think a part of me always wanted to be an actor." He looked a little sheepish, but he chuckled. "Though I never intended to make my debut as a camel."

She had to laugh. Relief washed over her in a great wave. "You fulfilled every actor's dream. You jumped to stardom in your first role."

He laughed too. "I think it'll be my last role—if I'm wise. But seriously, Rachel, helping with the theater has meant a great deal to me. And it's helped a lot with Karen, too. You must have noticed how much easier she is with me."

She nodded. "Yes. It makes me very happy."

"But beyond that, beyond Karen, it's meant a lot to me. Personally. It's helped me find myself again. I've begun to enjoy life."

"I'm glad," she said, "very glad. It worked that way for me, too."

His face took on that strange expression again, the one she couldn't figure out. "Have you. . . ?" The clatter of high heels on the wooden floor made them turn to look.

"Shawna has the record ready," Abby said. "We can start anytime. And Karen and I found some shoes. We're going to wear them now to get used to them."

"That's a good idea," Rachel said with a smile. She turned back to Steven. "If you'll call everyone to attention—I can't whistle like you—then we can begin."

Steven whistled, and in a few short minutes the ball scene began to take form. The king and queen, sitting high on their golden thrones, were learning to balance cardboard crowns. Steven positioned couples around the floor so that they could dance and yet not obscure the audience's view of that magic moment when the prince first spotted his bride-to-be from across the ballroom floor.

"The curtain's going up," Steven said. "Music, Shawna. Now, one, two, three. One, two, three. Stay in position. Leave the center open. Remember, the prince has to see Cinderella. And the audience has to see the prince."

The couples twirled awkwardly in two large ovals on the sides of the stage. Rachel made a note. The girls had better start wearing their long dresses so they could get used to the skirts.

"All right, Cinderella." While the music, muted now, continued to play and the dancers continued to move, Megan made her entrance. Megan and Tony ran through their lines, then Karen and Abby came on and did theirs.

When those speaking parts were finished, Rachel left Steven practicing with the dancers and ran the wicked stepmother and the fairy godmother through their more difficult scenes.

Almost before she knew it, the morning was over, and the children were gathering up their things. Now was the time to tell Steven that they'd have to cut down on their Saturday lunches and their skating afternoons. But no words would come. She kept seeing Abby's face, hearing her say they didn't laugh—the two of them alone. Was it fair to deprive Abby of her friendship with Karen and Steven because she, Rachel, felt slightly uncomfortable with him? The answer to that seemed fairly obvious. Abby looked forward to these fun-filled Saturdays and laughed about them often during the weeks that followed.

You're being a real fool, Rachel told herself. Making a mountain out of a molehill. Borrowing trouble again. Doing everything she shouldn't. And it wasn't as if she didn't know better. She did.

Swallowing a sigh, she took her coat from Abby. She couldn't cancel their plans without explaining why. And she couldn't explain why without looking really ridiculous.

Steven didn't act in any way unusual at lunch. The girls were in high spirits, laughing over their new socks and thinking up bits of stage business until Rachel had to remind them that Cinderella was, after all, the star of the play. To which the irrepressible Abby replied, "You always tell me to make the best of every part, Momma," and set them all off into gales of laughter.

By the time they reached the skating rink, Rachel was feeling more like her old self. How silly she'd been to let her imagination run away with her like that.

They got their skates and went to a bench. "I'm getting lots better, Momma," Abby said. "I can go a lot faster."

Rachel looked up from worrying a knotted shoelace. "Not too fast. There are other people using the rink, you know."

Abby giggled. "I know that, Momma. I won't run into anyone or make a nuisance of myself."

Rachel laughed. "I know, honey. Just be careful."

"Sure." Abby and Karen skated off, and Rachel went back to the troublesome shoelace.

"Having trouble?" Steven asked, his shoulder brushing hers.

She straightened, trying to mask her feelings of uneasiness at his closeness. "No. Well, just my shoelace."

"I'll get it." Before she could say anything to stop him, he was kneeling at her feet.

A great wave of embarrassment swept over her. Anyone seeing him like that would think. . . She couldn't finish the thought.

But Steven rose then, her shoe in his hand. "All fixed."

"Thanks." With fingers that seemed to be all thumbs, she grabbed a skate and tried to force her foot into it.

"Wrong foot," Steven said gently, just as she realized it herself.

She managed a little laugh. "Sorry. I get sort of spaced out near opening night."

His smile was grave. "I understand perfectly."

She almost dropped the other skate. Quickly she bent to pull it on, hiding her face in the process. Did he understand? Did he really understand that she was embarrassed to have him touch her, to have him near her? Did he understand how much she wished she could recapture their easy friendship, could go back to the time before his kiss had threatened everything? But there was no going back. There was never any going back. She knew that.

The thing to do now was to concentrate on building a new trust. She couldn't forget Steven's kiss, but she could act like it had never happened. And in acting that way, she might be able to regain some of her old ease with him. Short of breaking off their friendship, it was all she could think of to do.

She put on a bright smile. "All ready."

"Good." He got to his feet with his usual easy grace. "Let's go."

Only then did it occur to her that he would expect them to skate as they always had, with his arm around her. For a moment, she hesitated. But if she refused now, if she made a big thing of not taking his hand, he would surely connect it to what had happened last night. And that would draw too much attention to what was probably an insignificant incident, an incident she wanted very much to forget, wanted him to forget, too.

She put her hand in his and stood up. "Abby says she's been improving. What about me?" she asked lightly.

Steven's answer was equally light. "I'm afraid you'll never make the Olympics, but you are improving."

"Thanks a lot." She hoped her laugh sounded genuine, not as nervous as she felt. Many, many times she'd circled this rink with Steven's arm around her, Steven's strength supporting her. And she had never once considered him as anything more than a friend. To think that one moment, just that one moment, should change everything so drastically.

"Penny for your thoughts," he said, as they glided slowly but smoothly along.

"Afraid I was thinking about opening night. There are so many things that can go wrong."

He chuckled. "And I suppose you've imagined them all a hundred times."

"Just about," she admitted. "It's a rather awesome responsibility."

"You take responsibility very seriously, don't you?"

"Yes, I guess I do." They went on around the rink, his strong arm supporting her. "Is there anything wrong with that?" she asked, hoping to get into a discussion that would distract her, would let her feel as she used to feel with him—safe and comfortable.

"No, of course not." That he took her question seriously was evident in his tone. "But you need to leave some room for fun."

Perversely she asked, "Why? I don't remember the Bible saying anything about fun."

That didn't put him off. In fact, he chuckled. "That's okay, Rachel. Play the devil's advocate and ask me all the knotty questions. I have my answers ready."

"You do?"

"Yes, I do. For example, the Bible does say, 'Thou shalt love thy neighbor as thyself.' Doesn't it?"

"Of course it does," she said, intrigued by his argument. "But what has that to do with fun?"

"It's like this. If you're supposed to love your neighbor as yourself, then you must be supposed to love yourself. Don't you think?"

"Well, I suppose so, but that does sound sort of selfish."

"It isn't," he said. "Not really. If you can't love yourself, it isn't likely that you'll be able to love anyone else. After all, you have to have something before you can give it away."

"Well. . ."

"And no one can be their best self if they never relax. All work and no play not only makes Jack a dull boy, it makes him a sick one. And Jill a sick girl. A little fun, a little relaxation, renews us, sends us out into the world better prepared."

There was sense to his words, of course, but she wanted to keep the conversation going. "I think you have your sources confused," she said with a little laugh. "I don't remember any Jack in the Bible."

He laughed. "All right. Have it your way. I just know that the things we've I've been doing lately have done wonders for me. I feel like an altogether different person."

"I've been feeling better, too," she said, wishing she could pull out of his arms without making him wonder why and knowing that she couldn't. "But I thought it was because I was following through on my Christian responsibilities." She made the words light. She turned slightly to look at his face, grateful that now she could talk about her faith without him getting that stern sober look. Surely that was a good sign.

He smiled. " 'Cast thy bread upon the waters,' " he quoted. " 'And thou shalt find it after many days.' "

"You know a lot about the Bible for a. . ." She paused, suddenly aware of what she'd been about to say.

"For an unbeliever?" he suggested.

She nodded, only vaguely aware that the tempo of their skating had increased. "Yes."

"You're right," he said. "But you have to remember that when I believed, it was wholeheartedly." He smiled, a strange enigmatic little smile. "Like I do everything—wholeheartedly."

She nodded again. She knew what would follow. He had disbelieved just as strongly as he believed. But lately she had been hoping. . . She dared to put some of that hope into words. "And now what are you?"

The arm around her waist tightened slightly, but his tone didn't change. "Now, I'm in-between. Sort of waiting something out."

"Waiting? I don't understand."

"I've prayed for something," he explained. "If I get it, I'll know God's there. If I don't—"

"Steven!" She almost stopped in the middle of the rink, regardless of the people around them. "You're testing God! You can't do that!"

"I don't see it as testing," he said. "But if that's what you want to call it, go ahead. The Bible says, 'Ask, and it shall be given you; seek, and ye shall find; knock, and it shall be opened unto you.' It's very plain. Jesus said all we have to do is ask."

"But—"

"It's not like I'm asking for a new car or a million dollars," he said, amusement in his voice. "I'm only asking for something I'm sure God would want me to have."

"But you can't know," she protested. "You can't be sure that what you want is right."

"Is it right for a father and daughter to have a good loving relationship?"

"Of course." There was nothing else she could say to that.

"Then God must approve of loving relationships. I rest my case."

A wave of relief swept over her. If Steven's renewal of faith rested on the success of his relationship with Karen, then everything should be all right. She sent up a silent prayer of thanksgiving for being allowed to help in that.

"Too much seriousness," Steven said, skating back toward their bench. "It's time for some more silly jokes."

Laughter, Rachel thought with a smile, her misgivings over that kiss almost forgotten as the girls giggled over more of his ridiculous stories; *laughter is good for the soul.*

Chapter Eleven

The next two weeks went by in a whirl of activity. Getting ready for Cinderella's opening night took almost all of Rachel's waking thoughts. Once in a while she felt a little strangeness in Steven's company. But he seemed so entirely his old self that she could only conclude that she'd been right. That tender little kiss had been a momentary aberration. Neither of them would mention it again.

Whenever the thought of it came to mind, she pushed it firmly out. She needed Steven's help with the production. She'd come to depend on him a great deal. And she was grateful she didn't have to break off her relationship with him because of that one bad moment.

If she slept uneasily at night, dreaming strange dreams in which she lay secure in Peter's strong arms and then suddenly found that his face had become Steven's, well, she could hardly blame that on Steven.

It was probably a normal reaction. After all, she'd gotten rather close to Steven emotionally because of helping him with Karen, and that was bound to have some effect on them both.

Opening night of Cinderella arrived. Rachel, half exhausted, scurried around the set, trying to check on everything at the same time. Steven grabbed her hands once as she hurried past him and stopped her. "Hey, there, take it easy. It'll all work out."

She withdrew her hands. She was still a little uneasy about their touching each other. "Yes, I know that," she said with a nervous little laugh. "It's just. . .I'm always a wreck on opening night."

He smiled. "Okay. Okay. Just remember, you're not in this alone. I'm here. Oh, and Karen asked me to check with you. She wants to go sled riding in the park tomorrow instead of skating." He grinned. "We'll need those warm clothes again, won't we?"

The memory of his kiss hit her like a blow, but she forced herself to nod. Her lips seemed frozen and she couldn't shape any words.

"And ice cream after the show tonight," he went on, "to celebrate a job well done."

She wanted to say no, that all she wanted was to go home and crawl into bed and sleep. But she couldn't deprive Abby of a celebration. Or Karen, for that matter. And short of lying and saying she was sick, the kind of subterfuge she'd never allowed herself, she couldn't see any way out. So she nodded again.

When Steven left her on his way to check the props, she pushed the thought of him far back in her mind. There were a million details still to be seen to, not the least of which was shoring up Tony's faltering confidence, since it had occurred to him that a lot of people would be out there watching him make a fuss over a mere girl.

She checked makeup, adjusted crowns, straightened mouse whiskers, reglued the star on the fairy godmother's wand, and suddenly they were out of time.

Cinderella took her seat by the hearth. The curtain went up; the play began.

Rachel watched anxiously from her place in the wings. *You're as bad as any actor*, she told herself crossly. Surely no one could have worse first-night jitters than she had.

Cinderella's opening lines sounded fine, and Rachel relaxed a little. This was Megan's first big role, and Rachel had wondered if she'd have stage fright. But Megan came through like a trouper.

Following Cinderella's opening lines, the ugly stepsisters appeared. *Ugly,* Rachel thought, watching them shuffle on stage in their open-toed shoes, *is an understatement.* Karen's golden hair stuck out in strange points all over her head, and Abby's looked like a cyclone had hit her. Their faces were works of comic art, masterpieces of ugliness.

Abby had said, "We'll be so ugly no one will even know it's us."

Unsound as this reasoning was (for everyone had a program and could read), Rachel hadn't contradicted it. She'd seen the lightening of tension in Karen's face and recognized what Abby was doing.

"We're going to the ball," Abby said spitefully to the wretched Cinderella. "We're going to dance with the prince." And she executed a pirouette that had her tripping over her own feet. The audience loved it and roared approval.

"Yes," Karen went on, after the laughter had died down. "He's looking for a wife." She preened and the audience laughed again. "Remember that, you cinder girl. I'm going to marry the prince."

"You!" Abby's shriek could probably be heard outside the theater. Rachel smiled. They were doing a terrific job, not just with their lines, but with their stage business, too. No need to worry about them. She let her thoughts go ahead to the next scene.

Soon the stepsisters clomped offstage, still exchanging insults. Abby, as the last one out, slammed the prop door behind her. And it promptly fell off its hinges with a resounding crash.

Rachel stood frozen, and Cinderella stared at the fallen door in dismay. Then, while everyone seemed to hold their breath, Abby flounced back through the open doorway. She pointed an accusing finger at the bewildered Cinderella. "Now, see what you've done?" she screamed. "Get this fixed. Right away." And she gave the offending door a kick before she turned and marched out again.

This piece of obviously impromptu action brought down the house, and Rachel slumped in relief.

In spite of her nagging sense of apprehension, the play progressed nicely. The fairy godmother made her appearance in the flash of light produced by magician's powder. The assorted animals that became horses, coachman, and grooms slipped behind the screen and emerged wearing the correct heads. Cinderella was transformed from cinder girl to beautiful young maiden.

As the curtain closed on the pumpkin-coach, Rachel breathed another sigh of relief. If they could only get through the big ballroom scene. If Tony would just look a little upset when Cinderella ran away. If. . .

The stagehands shifted scenery with precision. *Steven's work,* she thought, seeing him across the stage, arranging the couples for the ball scene. Then the curtain went up to the strains of waltz music, and the couples began to whirl around the floor. *A minor miracle, that,* she thought, watching Tony anxiously. He spied Cinderella across the room, and he managed to look surprised. She sighed. Surprise was as close as she could get him to the appropriate expression of delight.

Cinderella was doing better. Her face reflected wonder at this beautiful new world. Tony stopped beside her. "Will you dance with me?" he asked, extending his hand. With just the right amount of hesitation, Cinderella put her hand in his, and they stepped out onto the dance floor to whirl away.

Abby and Karen entered from stage left, their finery some of the ugliest ever seen, and the audience laughed. They knew the comic characters when they saw them. Rachel only hoped that Karen understood that the laughter was appreciation, not derision.

"Who is that thing he's dancing with?" Abby demanded, striking a ludicrous pose. "I can't imagine what he sees in her. Such a simple-looking little thing."

"Funny, I can't remember her name," Karen said, tapping one of the overlarge shoes out of sync with the music, to the audience's delight. "I know I've seen her before, though," she went on. "She looks vaguely familiar. Oh well, what does it matter? Once he gets a look at me, no one else will count."

"That's what you think!"

The girls were doing beautifully. Even the dancers did well. But the big scene was coming up, the one where Cinderella ran away.

Their dialogue finished, Abby and Karen faded into the background. Over the music came the sound of the clock striking midnight. Cinderella stopped dancing and tried to pull free of the prince's hand. "The clock. . . it's midnight. I've got to go."

"Don't leave me," Tony entreated. A little of the tension drained from Rachel. That wasn't so bad. He was trying, at least.

"Don't leave me," he repeated. But Cinderella freed her hand and slipped away among the surrounding dancers. Tony followed her offstage. Moments later he came back, carrying the glass slipper.

"Stop the music," he commanded. As the music halted, the whirling couples froze. Tony climbed the steps to the thrones where the king and queen sat. "The ball is over," he said loudly. "I've chosen a wife."

The king looked properly befuddled. "Where is she? I don't see anyone."

"This is her slipper," Tony said. "I will marry the woman whose foot fits this slipper."

The curtain descended for the scenery change, and Karen and Abby came to Rachel. "You were great," she said, giving them both a big hug. "Stupendous. And, Abby, that part with the door was just wonderful."

"Thank you, Momma. It just came to me." She exchanged a glance with Karen. "Everything's going real good, isn't it?"

Rachel nodded, distracted. "Yes, dear. Listen. I'll talk to you later. Right now, I've got to see Tony and Megan."

The rest of the play went like clockwork. Abby and Karen brought down the house again in the scene in which they tried on the glass slipper and exposed their colorfully painted sock toes.

Catching Steven's eye, Rachel smiled happily. He'd made the whole thing so much easier.

Cinderella came from her ashes, slid her dainty foot into the glass slipper, which was actually a clear plastic shoe, and was borne triumphantly off to the court, where some moments later the prince presented her as his bride, holding her all the while, Rachel was pleased to see, quite firmly by the hand.

The curtain descended, and the applause began. Rachel hadn't needed it, of course, to know that their opening performance was a huge success. A great deal of that credit went to Abby and Karen for their comic routines, but every child had performed well. Tony had outshone himself in portraying devotion to a mere girl, and Megan had made a delightful Cinderella.

And Steven—Steven had been so much help, so very much help. She wondered how she could ever have done it without him. How she would ever direct another play without him. But there was no time to think of that now.

As the children left the stage, she had a smile and a word for each of them. Then she followed them to the green room where admiring parents would gather to praise their little thespians and murmur words of thanks to the director.

Tired as she was, she managed to smile and answer the questions put to her. She looked around the room. Where was Steven? He should be getting some of these congratulations. He'd shared the work. He should share the praise.

Megan's mother came up. "A lovely production," she murmured.

"Megan did very well," Rachel said. That was the truth. It wasn't Megan's fault that her mother, with elaborately made-up face, exquisitely coiffed hair, and clothes from the city's most expensive boutiques, made Rachel uncomfortable.

"Yes, I thought so," Mrs. Patterson said. "All in all, the play was very well done. Though it did appear to me that the stepsisters were a little too prominent."

For a moment Rachel just stared. Then in her calmest voice, she said, "The auditions were open, Mrs. Patterson. All the girls wanted to be Cinderella. Megan got the part over them all. There were only two girls willing to play the ugly stepsisters. It's hardly their fault if their lines are funny." *Or mine.*

"Your own daughter. . ." Mrs. Patterson began.

Rachel took a firmer grip on her temper. "My own daughter didn't try out for the part of Cinderella," she said, "precisely because she's my daughter and that was the part all the girls wanted. As I said before, no one but Abby and her friend Karen were willing to play the stepsisters."

"They did a stupendous job, didn't they?" Steven said from behind her. He'd evidently come up while she was defending the girls.

"Steven Hendricks," Rachel said in introduction, "Karen's father."

Mrs. Patterson's face underwent a strange transformation. "Why, Mr. Hendricks, what a marvelously talented child you have."

Again, Rachel stared. She couldn't help it. Steven's arrival had turned the haughty, demanding Mrs. Patterson into a coy, smiling charmer.

"Yes," Steven said diplomatically. "Aren't we fortunate to have such talented children?" And he moved the woman off skillfully, leaving Rachel to deal with more pleasant parents.

Still, Mrs. Patterson's comments rankled. Rachel told Steven so when he rejoined her later. "Here Abby and Karen take the parts no one else wants, and she behaves like that. It just isn't fair."

"Easy there," Steven said. "You should know by now that the world isn't an especially fair place. We know you did your best. Tonight's performance was a big success. The others will be, too. So just relax and enjoy."

She had to smile then. "Thank you, Steven. You always put things in perspective. Thank you for helping me. I don't know what I'd have done without you."

"You'd have done very well," he said, taking her hand in his. "But I was glad to be a little help."

"A little!" she said, conscious of the warm grip of his fingers on hers but not wanting to pull away and hurt his feelings. "You were indispensable."

A strange look crossed his face, and his grip on her hand tightened. "I wish—" he began. But whatever it was he wished, he never got to finish telling her, as still another set of parents presented themselves to hear her praise their children.

Finally the evening was over. All the children went off with their proud parents. Rachel and Steven, Abby and Karen stood alone in the darkened theater. "We'd better check everything," Rachel said. "Make sure everything's locked up. All the dressing room lights are off."

She turned and was stopped by Steven's grip on her arm. "You're going to sit right here," he said firmly. "I'll check the doors. The girls will get the lights. Right, girls?"

"Right."

As they hurried off, Rachel sank gratefully into a chair. She was tired. Closing her eyes, she willed herself to relax.

A few minutes later, Steven's voice roused her. "That's better. Listen, Rachel. I need to talk to you alone." He glanced around. "Where we won't be interrupted."

All the peace she'd been feeling deserted her.

"I can't," she mumbled. "I'm too tired."

"Not tonight. Tomorrow night. After our sled ride. Will you get a sitter for the girls and go to dinner with me? Please?"

"I. . ."

"Please, it's very important. A matter of faith."

She sighed. When he put it that way, how could she refuse? "All right, but—"

"All done, Momma. Everything's okay."

"Good," Steven said, extending his hand to help Rachel to her feet. "Now for the biggest sundaes in town. We deserve them."

"Yes," Abby agreed, "we do. We got lots of applause, didn't we, Momma?"

"Yes, Abby." Rachel followed them down the aisle. "You were very funny."

"That's good," Abby said complacently. "You know, I think God likes for people to laugh. I think He wants them to. He must be glad we can make them happy."

Turning to look at Steven, Rachel saw that he was looking at her. Abby was right, of course. Laughter was food for the soul. Even a child saw the wisdom of that.

Chapter Twelve

Exhaustion claimed Rachel that night, an exhaustion so deep that nothing could disturb her sleep. But she woke in the morning with an uneasy feeling in the pit of her stomach. For a moment, still half asleep, she couldn't think why. Then it hit her. Steven wanted to talk to her alone. A matter of faith, he had said. Maybe it had something to do with what he'd told her earlier, that day when they were skating—that he had asked God for something and he was waiting to see if he would get it.

That made her really uncomfortable. No matter what he called it, it seemed to her that he was putting God to some kind of test. She'd thought then that he'd been talking about his relationship with Karen. But that seemed really good. It must be something else he wanted to talk about. But what? A matter of faith. What had Steven asked God for? What did he want that he couldn't get for himself? A man like Steven—

"Good morning, Momma!" Abby came bouncing into the room. "It's going to be a beautiful day for sled riding. A beautiful, beautiful day."

Rachel pushed aside her worries and tried to smile. "Yes, honey. It does look like a beautiful day."

Abby plopped herself on the bed and crossed her legs, tailor fashion. "You're not getting sick, are you, Momma?"

"Sick? Me? Whatever gave you that idea?"

Abby frowned. "Oh, I don't know exactly. You've been acting kind of funny lately. Sort of sad. And, oh, I don't know what."

Rachel reached out and pulled Abby into a hug. "I'm just tired, honey. This play was a lot of work, you know."

"Yes, but you had Mr. Hendricks to help this time. That should have made it easier." Abby's childish face showed what she thought of Steven, how much she cared for him.

Rachel swallowed a sigh. "I know, punkin. And it did. But I'm still tired. Don't worry about me, though. I'll be fine."

She glanced at the clock. "Well, enough of this lazy lying in bed. We have things to do this morning."

There was still a pucker of concern between Abby's eyebrows. Rachel threw back the covers. "Last one dressed and in the kitchen has to do the morning dishes!"

"Okay!" Abby bounced off the bed and out the door, her fingers already busy at her pajama buttons.

Rachel started to dress. She didn't like putting Abby off like that, but she couldn't tell her what was really bothering her—this dinner alone that Steven wanted.

It was probably some very simple thing he had in mind, and she was blowing it all out of proportion, like she had that kiss. But she couldn't get the memory of that kiss out of her mind. He'd kissed her once, had thought of her as a woman to be kissed. What had happened once could easily happen again.

And then there were the dreams she'd been having practically every night since then, the dreams in which she lay content in Peter's arms and saw his face become Steven's. She valued Steven's friendship. But to go beyond that. . . She could still remember the pain of losing Peter. She couldn't stand to go through that again.

If what Steven wanted was a change in their relationship, something more personal, she would just have to say no. That would mean putting him out of her life, of course. And out of Abby's. But Abby was strong. She would understand. Rachel would make her understand.

She finished buttoning her shirt and hurried down the stairs.

"I won," Abby cried, looking up from setting the table. "You have to do the dishes."

"Fair enough. Listen, will you put out the cereal? I have to call Mrs. Collins."

"Why, Momma? Where are you going?"

"Steven wants to talk to me alone. We're going someplace for dinner." Rachel tried to sound nonchalant, but for the life of her she couldn't do it.

"Oh. Is there something wrong with him and Karen?"

Rachel looked at her sharply. Something in Abby's voice didn't seem quite right. But her face looked the same.

"I don't know, honey. He didn't tell me."

"Oh."

Abby went on about her work, and Rachel went to the phone. It did cross her mind to pray that their widowed neighbor might be unable to baby-sit, but Steven had said a matter of faith. That couldn't be ignored. And anyway, as she soon found, Mrs. Collins was free and glad to spend the evening with the girls.

The rest of the morning, Rachel hurried about the house, doing a lot of things which later, as she dressed for lunch, she realized amounted to a lot of nothing. Still, she had kept herself busy and hopefully kept Abby from suspecting that anything was really wrong. That was something, after all.

The doorbell rang as she pulled the last heavy sweater over her head. She was dressing warmly because she'd be standing around in the cold. This time she wasn't going to be chivied into doing something she didn't want to do. And in her state of mind, the last thing she needed was to go careening down a hill on a sled. She had enjoyed the skating, though—at least after her first embarrassment was over.

She hurried down the stairs, but Abby was there before her, and Steven and Karen were just coming in. "Momma's not quite ready," Abby said, as Rachel reached the landing. "She had a lot to do this morning."

"Here I am." Rachel forced herself to smile. "Ready to brave the cold." Her smile was stiff. She could feel that. And the layers of clothes made her feel awkward.

But Steven didn't seem to notice anything wrong. He turned to Abby. "Better bring all your mittens and scarves. This snow is the wet kind. And be sure your boots are tight around your pant legs. You don't want to get your feet wet."

"Yes, sir. I will." Abby motioned to the big plastic bag sitting on a chair. "I already put my mittens and stuff in there. Momma's too."

"Good," Steven said. "You're right on the job." He turned back to Rachel. "Well, then, let's go get our lunch and head for the park."

Rachel nodded. It was embarrassing, this feeling of unease she felt with him now. She swallowed a sigh. Theirs had been such a comfortable supportive friendship. She missed that; she missed the friend that Steven had been. That kiss had turned him into a stranger, someone she was almost afraid to talk to.

What had happened to all the good advice she'd been giving herself? All that talk about making a mountain out of a molehill? But everything seemed wrong. Steven didn't say or do anything different, but he seemed different. As Karen climbed into the backseat, she seemed to give Rachel a strange glance. Even Abby seemed to be acting funny. Yet there was nothing Rachel could put her finger on, nothing really that she could say anything about.

I'm losing it, she thought, settling into the front seat. Could she possibly be suffering from some sort of breakdown, some kind of delayed reaction to Peter's death? Then her common sense spoke up. All this speculation was ridiculous, it said. She was just nervous, understandably nervous, since Steven said it was a matter of faith that he wanted her help with. That put her in a position of great responsibility. She wished now that she hadn't told him she was too tired last night. If they'd talked then, the whole matter would be behind her, one more problem dealt with. It was this terrible waiting, waiting and not knowing, that was so nerve-racking.

"You're very quiet today," he commented.

"I'm still tired," she said. "And there's another performance tomorrow night." That, at least, was the truth. "These things take a lot out of me."

Steven nodded. "I should guess so. Are there many parents like our dear Mrs. Patterson?"

With a sense of shock, Rachel realized that she hadn't thought of Megan's mother once since they'd left the theater. She'd been so busy trying to figure out what Steven wanted that she'd completely forgotten the woman's snide remarks. She laughed. "Fortunately not. Most of the parents are appreciative. Several of the mothers are wonderful with costumes, too." She laughed again. "Like the mothers at church. No, there aren't many Mrs. Pattersons. Thank God."

This last was in the nature of a heartfelt prayer. Parents could cause a lot of trouble. Mrs. Patterson could have been a lot worse.

Steven pulled into Kitty's parking lot and shut off the motor. He glanced over his shoulder at the girls in the back. "Ready for lunch, you two?"

"Yes, Daddy."

Karen seemed unusually happy this morning, her cheeks rosy with something more than the cold.

"Good. Eat hearty. It'll be cold out there."

And it was, very cold. Though her stomach had been in rebellion, Rachel had managed to force down her food. The girls, who didn't seem to notice her quietness, were in high spirits. Laughing and chattering over some private secret, they managed to keep the lunch from becoming too serious and, incidentally, to keep her nervousness from being too apparent.

Standing beside the car while Steven unloaded the sled, she knotted a scarf over her stocking cap and pulled on her heavy mittens. She didn't want to be out here in the cold. She wanted to be at home in bed, safe and warm. Asleep, so she wouldn't have to think. Except that even in her sleep she wasn't free of Steven.

She was beginning to dread those dreams. Initially, not only did she find herself lying in Peter's arms, sometimes she was running to meet him, sometimes she was carrying him cake and coffee as he sat by the fire. But whatever it was they were doing, whenever she got close to Peter, his face inevitably turned into Steven's. And with that peculiarity of dreams, she couldn't stop herself, even though she knew he wasn't Peter, from going into his arms.

"Momma!" Abby tugged at her sleeve. "Come on. We're ready."

Pinning a smile on her face, Rachel followed them to the top of the slope. "Oh, boy! It looks great."

Steven put the sled on the crest of the hill. "You get settled first. Then I'll push you off."

Abby turned to Karen. "You steer. It's your sled."

Karen took her place in front. Then Abby clambered on behind.

"Watch out for those trees to the left," Steven said. "Keep to this side."

"Yes, Daddy."

"Here you go!"

Laughing and screaming, the girls flew down the hill. Rachel tried to smile. It wasn't fair to let her anxiety over the evening spoil Abby's day.

Steven came to stand beside her. "Being young is wonderful," he said. "Children enjoy the simplest pleasures."

"Yes." She watched the girls trudge back up the hill, dragging the sled behind them. "I suppose adults can do that, too."

"I suppose so," Steven said thoughtfully. "I've enjoyed our skating."

"Me, too." She kept watching the girls. It was easier to talk if she didn't look at him.

"The trouble with being an adult," he said soberly, "is that you have to be responsible for yourself, too. Being responsible for others, like your children, is hard enough. But being responsible for yourself is the hardest."

As he moved toward the girls, Rachel thought about that. She worried a lot about her responsibility for Abby. And certainly it was her sense of being responsible for Karen in her need that had led her into this relationship with Steven. But maybe he was right. It was her sense of responsibility for herself that was causing her present troubles. She tried to shut off her thoughts. They led nowhere, just round and round in never-ending circles. She'd simply have to wait till this evening. Steven had no intention of discussing the matter, whatever it was, while the girls were present.

She moved over by them. She'd forget about that for now and enjoy the afternoon. That was one advantage children had. They could live for the moment much more easily than adults. She pulled in a breath of crisp air, looked up at the blue sky, felt the warmth of the winter sun on her face. She'd think about those things, about what was happening now, and forget the rest.

She wasn't entirely successful in forgetting the coming evening, but she did join in the laughter and jokes. She did, at least, present a cheerful face.

%

It was after three when Steven looked at his watch. "Half an hour left," he told the girls.

"You and Momma haven't had a ride," Abby said, her face glowing.

"So we haven't," Steven said.

"I can't," Rachel said. "I've. . .I've gotten a terrible headache from the glare, and I can't see very well."

Steven was all concern. "Maybe we should go now."

"No, no. It'll be all right. You go ahead. Take a ride." She managed a smile. The lie was only half a lie. She did have a headache, but it wasn't from the glare. This was a worry induced headache if ever she'd had one.

"If you're sure. . ."

"I'm very sure," she said firmly. "I'm not leaving here for another half hour."

"Okay. You win." He turned to the waiting girls. "I'd love to do a belly-slammer like I used to as a boy." He grinned. "But it's been a long time. I'm not sure either the sled or my belly can handle it. I think maybe you'd better just push me."

They set the sled near the top of the hill. The girls watched, eyes wide, smiles on their lips, as Steven stretched stomach down on the sled and folded up his legs.

"Now," he cried. Giggling and laughing, the girls pushed the sled over the edge.

His laughter floated back up to them, making even Rachel smile as she watched the sled race along. Then it happened. Something hidden in the snow seemed to catch the runners, and the sled veered suddenly, sharply, to the left, directly into the line of trees that stood there.

"Steven!" The scream tore its way out of her throat as the sled slammed into a tree. Steven rolled off, only to lie silent in the snow.

She was already partway down the slope, slipping and sliding, before the sled came to a complete stop. "Steven!" She could hear childish screams behind her, but the girls would have to wait. "Dear God," she mumbled under her breath. "Dear God, don't take Steven, too. Please don't take him."

She reached him, after what seemed centuries of running, and fell to her knees in the snow beside him, her breath coming in great gasps. "Steven! Steven! Speak to me. Oh, God!" She prayed aloud now, scarcely aware of the words she used. "Please, God, please. I need him. I love him. Please!"

Sobbing with exertion and fear, she leaned over. He was so still. But there was no blood at least. She jerked off a mitten and felt for a pulse in his throat. Thank God, he was breathing. She was afraid to move him. So many internal injuries were made worse by wrong handling.

"Steven." She spoke his name gently, all her love and longing pouring into that one word. How foolish she'd been. She loved this man already. To lose him would be just as bad as losing Peter. She'd been afraid, afraid to admit she loved him. The dreams were clear now. Her unconscious mind knew what her conscious mind hadn't dared admit. If only it wasn't too late.

"Steven," she repeated, bending lower to feel for his breath on her cheek. "Steven, oh, please speak to me."

"Say it again, Rachel. Say you love me." His voice was low, but she heard the words distinctly.

She straightened, heat flooding her cheeks. "Are you all right? Do you hurt anywhere?"

His eyes full of love, he looked up at her. "I think I'm okay. I just got the breath knocked out of me."

She looked toward the tangled wreckage at the base of the tree. "But the sled. . ."

"I rolled off just before it hit. But say it again, Rachel. Say you love me."

She didn't think of denying it. She couldn't. "I love you," she said. "I. . .I didn't know."

"I hoped," he said, pushing himself slowly to a sitting position. "I hoped. And I prayed."

"Prayed?" She searched the face so close to her own.

"Prayed," he repeated. "You know that matter of faith that I mentioned to you?"

"Yes."

"Well, you're it. I asked God to make you realize your love for me. And He did. Though I didn't expect it to happen like this. Oh, Rachel." He reached out, pulling her over to the snow beside him. "I love you. I love you so much. These last weeks have been so bad. I've been so afraid of losing you, so afraid you'd never admit to loving me. Will you marry me?"

He stopped suddenly, his hands gripping her tighter. "Oh no," he groaned. "I didn't mean to rush you like that. You don't have to answer right away. It's just—I've been wanting to ask you for so long. I've been wanting, and I've been scared to death."

"Yes," she said simply.

"I think I began to love you that first night I got stuck in your driveway. You were so understanding, and when I looked into your eyes—that's when I decided that a special shade of brown was my favorite color. I don't want to marry you just because Karen loves you, you know."

"Steven," she interrupted, "you're not listening to me. I said yes. I love you. I want to be your wife. I want to be a mother to Karen."

He stared at her for a long moment and then he bent and kissed her tenderly. "We don't have to wait for a spring wedding, do we?" he asked anxiously when he released her lips. "I know spring is your favorite season. But our rebirth came in winter. How soon can we get married?"

She touched his face tenderly. "Very soon, dear. But first we'd better see if you're all right. And the girls. . . where are the girls?"

"I'm right here, Momma," Abby said from behind her.

"Karen, too. We're all right."

They moved up in her line of vision. "I told you so!" Karen cried, jumping up and down in the snow. "I knew he wasn't hurt. I knew it! Oh, Abby, isn't it wonderful! We're going to have both a momma and a daddy."

Steven got slowly to his feet and brushed off the snow. "I'm fine," he said, extending a hand to help Rachel up.

Then with an arm around her, he turned to the girls. "Abby," he said, "how would you like to have me for a father?"

Abby's smile was a joy to see. "I'd love it," she cried, throwing her arms around Karen. "We're going to be sisters, too!"

"That's right," Steven said. "We're going to be a family—the four of us."

His voice sobered. "God has been very good to us," he said, his arm tightening around Rachel. "Knowing how much we need each other, God brought us together. God brought us together, and He gave us the greatest gift of all—love."

Steven opened his free arm at the same moment that Rachel reached out to Karen. The four of them stood hugging in a circle in the snow, the ruined sled forgotten behind them.

"I think," Steven said gently, "that it would be a good thing to thank God right now for blessing us with such love."

"Yes, Daddy," the little girls said together, bowing their heads. Rachel, her heart full to overflowing, hugged them all tighter to her and sent up her own silent prayer of thanks for that most wondrous of His gifts—love.

Eagles for Anna

Catherine Runyon

CATHERINE RUNYON makes her home in Michigan with her family. She is a news editor and columnist at the *Advance* newspaper. Catherine writes inspirational romance because she wants "to make a positive contribution" to the romance genre and to let her readers know that "though all hope seems lost, He [God] remains faithful."

Chapter One

The rending screech, like fingernails on a blackboard, brought Anna fully awake. She sat straight up in the confining motor home bed, tired and aching after a restless first night in the Smokies. Hoping the noise she had just heard was only a part of her dreams, she shivered and wrapped the insulated blanket around her shoulders against the early June morning chill. She listened, half-afraid, the confusion of sleep just beyond her senses.

Perhaps the noise was only within her own skull. The trip from New York, driving the unfamiliar vehicle, had been exhausting. She had begun developing a headache long before she crossed the Tennessee state line. Then, instead of being able to drive to Granny's old homesite, as she had planned, she had driven for hours looking at one place after another, recognizing none and wracking her brain for memories of the trips she had made with her parents so many years ago. Finally, with the gas gauge fluttering on empty, she had given up, pulled the small motor home off the road, and fallen into bed disappointed, lost, and confused.

Above the pounding of blood in her temples, Anna heard a noise, something like soft knocking. *Of course,* Anna thought, *I've parked on someone's property and they've come to investigate.*

*

She called, "Who's there?" but no voice answered.

Whump! Whump! came the sound at the side door. Then Anna heard the awful screech again. Shivers moved in waves across her body.

"What are you doing?" she cried, then jerked back the curtains on the window near her bed, not caring if someone saw her smeared makeup and tousled hair.

A black bear grinned back at her through the window.

Anna gasped and whipped the curtains together. She jumped into the middle of the bed and pulled the covers close. What could she do? Could the bear get in? Quietly, she peered out the window again. The bear was walking around sniffing, pawing at the side of the vehicle, and occasionally raising up on hind feet to give it a good cuff.

Anna felt the vibrations from the blows. Climbing out of bed, she went from window to window, watching the bear. Apparently it was not angry, only curious. The bear walked around, nose to the ground, and finally found the apple core that Anna had tossed out the window last night just before dropping into bed.

Great! Now it thinks this is a traveling restaurant. It will probably be here all day! She sighed, a sudden image of Barry Carlson coming to her mind. *If he were here, he would be laughing at me,* she thought. Sometimes she wondered what kept her attached to this man who managed her career. He was seldom available when Anna wanted his companionship, but he expected her to be ready at a moment's notice to accompany him to a party or show. Though he was witty and fun, he sometimes seemed quite insensitive about things that Anna felt were important, such as this trip to Tennessee. He certainly was good-looking and was always fashionably dressed with his jet black hair elegantly styled. His dark mustache was so thin and perfect it could have been penciled on. He carried an aura of excitement about him, was always in a hurry, and always laughing.

Anna could still hear Barry making fun of her decision to come to Tennessee.

"Anna, dear, don't you know that after you get south of D.C., you drop off the edge? And in a camper at that!"

"It isn't a camper, Barry. I've rented a motor home. It has a bathroom and everything."

He had waved away her explanations and flashed the brilliant smile that was probably his greatest asset.

"Tell me the truth. You've been out digging for accounts behind my back, haven't you? You've been hired to do a spread for *National Geographic*—no, they don't use models. I know! It's *Farm Journal* or something like that, isn't it?"

Anna could not help but laugh with him, though she wished he could try to understand the feelings that had brought about her decision to come south. Anna knew she should have said yes immediately when Barry offered her a partnership in his modeling agency a few weeks ago. It was the chance of a lifetime in some ways, but Anna had doubts.

Anna had confidence in her own ability to manage a business and to work with other models as a manager, but she was unsure just what her relationship with Barry should be. He had said he wanted her to share his business and his life but had said nothing about marriage. He said "I love you" as casually as he said "Good morning," and Anna wondered if he understood how much she wanted the deep, passionate commitment for life that she had witnessed in her parents' marriage. If he understood, did he care?

As a child, Anna had visited the Smoky Mountains with her parents. She remembered a loving great-grandmother, standing in a farmhouse doorway waiting for Anna to come in, a woman out of tune with her times but completely at peace with herself. Anna had experienced a deep sense of wonder while standing on the high ridge near the house, gazing out at wave after wave of blue-green hills. The memory of that feeling had helped seal her decision to return to the mountains.

Anna peered out the window again. The bear was still nosing about. With a burst of determined energy, Anna pulled on the red plaid shirt and khaki pants she had worn the night before, rolled her sleeves up past the elbows, and headed for the door. As soon as she opened it, the bear trotted toward her.

"Scram!" Anna yelled as loudly as she could. "Get away from here! You don't scare me, understand?"

The bear continued toward her. It knew as well as Anna did that her threats were empty.

Anna scurried backward, closing the door just as the bear reached it. Again she heard the awful screeching of the claws on the metal.

"You're ruining the paint!" she screamed. "This thing is rented, you know! I have to take care of it." Anna rubbed her tired eyes with the back of her hand, taking off some of yesterday's makeup. With a deep sigh, she got into the driver's seat. If the bear wouldn't leave her, maybe she could leave it.

Anna had been hoping to get directions from a passing motorist before she started out on the road again, but it was full daylight now and there had been no sign of a car. Now she was going to get out of here as fast as she could and just hope she found a gas station before the tank went completely dry.

With one bare foot on the accelerator, Anna turned the key. The engine started, then died.

"Come on, come on," she begged. "If there's enough gas to start this thing, there must be a little bit left to get me out of here." She turned the key again. The engine came briefly to life, then died. Anna leaned her head against the steering wheel, drew a long, deep breath, and exhaled slowly, trying to relax. She forced down the rising panic that accompanied the knowledge that she was no longer in control.

Maybe this is a sign, she thought. The letter from her lawyer, urging her to revisit the property where Granny Huddlestone's home had been located in order to determine whether she wanted to sell it, had seemed like a message from the God she had so recently discovered.

"The Tennessee property that once belonged to your mother's grand-mother is included in your parents' estate," the letter had said, and the lawyer had mentioned a copy of a deed that had been in her parents' safe deposit box. She had not seen nor thought of the old place for years. "If you wish to sell the property, I will arrange for the sale through local real-tors. However, in your own best interest, I urge you to visit the site if at all possible to help determine its true value."

The timing was perfect, taking her away from her work to a serene place just when she needed to think over her relationship with Barry, but maybe she had been fooled by her own emotions. She had certainly been fooled by her memory and had behaved like a fool when she took off without first obtaining a copy of the deed with its indications of location and property boundaries.

On impulse, she decided to pray. "God, I think You brought me here, but things are not what I expected. Help me."

The motor home began to sway a bit. The bear had stopped clawing at the door and was pushing against it with its full weight. The small vehicle began to rock, and Anna's throat once again tightened in fear. Was the bear strong enough, heavy enough to overturn the motor home? Anna began to look for some sort of safety in case that happened. Just as she started to crouch beneath the dash in front of the passenger seat, she thought she heard a car approaching.

❧

Peter McCulley had plenty of time. He had been up since five o'clock and didn't have to be at work until eight. *The nice thing about tourists,* he thought, *is they usually like to sleep late.* That gave Peter time to enjoy the best part of the day before having to give himself to meeting their needs at the Sugarlands Visitors' Center. He had already been fishing and had taken a drive up on the ridge to catch the last reflections of the sunrise on the dew. He began whistling "Wildwood Flower," feeling good, knowing he could make it through one more exasperating day at the park information center now that he had some good memories to carry him along, and now that he decided that after fulfilling the one-week notice he was giving today, he would never have to go back to work there again.

Peter had no idea where he would go or what he would do. He only knew that the thought of leaving Gatlinburg was the most satisfying idea he had had in years. It did not matter where he went. Even if he moved only as far away as Sevierville, he would not have to make excuses for not coming to Sunday dinner with his mother. He would not have to pass the little strip mall where his photography studio had been four years ago. He would not have to feel guilty about hating his own brother if Darron did not honk and wave on his way home from work each day.

He knew he was leaving nothing in search of nothing, but he had made the decision and it seemed right. The only question he had now was why he had not made this decision sooner. There was nothing here for him. He should have left long ago.

The sight of a bear, scratching its back against the door of a motor home, caught Peter by surprise as he came around a bend in the road. He hit the brakes and his pickup slid around on the loose gravel, then came to a stop. Seeing the New York license plates, Peter shook his head and sighed. When would people learn that they could not use the entire state of Tennessee as their personal backyard?

He honked the horn to get the bear's attention, but nothing happened. For some reason, this bear was particularly taken with the motor home. Peter took his mess kit from behind the seat of the truck. He got out slowly and began to beat on the skillet with a wrench.

"Hey!" he shouted. "Git! Beat it!" Slowly he advanced toward the bear, pounding the pan, carefully judging the distance between himself and the bear, and between himself and the truck. The bear sat down on its haunches, scratched behind one ear, and gave a tremendous yawn. Peter scooped up some small rocks and threw them one by one at the bear's feet. "Go! Scat!" he shouted.

Finally the bear reared halfheartedly, shook its head, and got up. Lazily, it ambled off toward the woods. Peter watched until it was well out of sight, then walked toward the motor home. He wondered why anyone would be parked here so far from the main road.

Just as he was about to knock, the door flew open in his face and a woman stepped out, almost knocking him over.

"Thank you, thank you!" she cried. "I was trapped in there. I was so afraid the van was going to tip over. I. . .was just. . .afraid." Anna closed her eyes and breathed deeply, welcoming the flood of relief, though it threatened to make her knees buckle.

"You weren't in any real danger," Peter said. "That ol' mamma bear would have left soon to take care of her cubs, but she just came to see what you all were having for breakfast. You never know. Maybe it was better than what she was having herself."

Anna covered her eyes with one hand and Peter saw, with some alarm, what looked like a wide bruise across the back.

"I feel like a complete fool," she said, "and most of all, I can't believe I was so frightened. I should have known that bear wasn't a real threat." She felt her face growing hot. All the poise and sophistication that she had cultivated over the years vanished. "I'm a first-class dunce, and you put yourself in danger to help me. If you had been hurt, it would have been my fault."

The sarcastic speech that Peter had prepared moments ago faded from his mind as he watched the woman in front of him. She was nearly as tall as he was, very slim, but without the fragile look that he disliked in some women. Peter was forced to admit to himself that when he went to the door he had been expecting the kind of gushy gratitude he usually received when he helped people out of the stupid situations they got themselves into. Now he hardly knew what to say.

"What are you doing here anyway?" he said at last. "This road's hardly wide enough for your vehicle. Where are you headed?"

Anna, her strength returning, smiled ruefully. "I was asking those very questions of myself just as you came along. I was looking for a place. . .my great-grandmother's farm. . .that I thought was right around here, but I couldn't find it last night. Or maybe it's gone. That's a possibility. To be honest, I don't know where I am. . .or where I'm going."

"Got a map?" Peter asked.

Anna nodded and went inside the motor home, glad to be away from the eyes of the man who had rescued her. She could not remember a time when she had felt so awful. She picked up the map of Tennessee that lay spread out on the dash where she had left it last night. As she turned to go back outside, she caught a glimpse of Peter through the window. He had an air of patient suffering about him that made Anna feel more ashamed of her own thoughtlessness and lack of preparation for this trip. She had never run out of gas before in her life. To Anna, it symbolized a total lack of responsibility and organization.

Suddenly, it seemed important to her that this man should not think badly of her. She glanced into the rearview mirror, grabbed a tissue from the dispenser on the sun visor, and rubbed out the worst of the makeup smudges, then quickly combed her hair and fluffed it with her fingers. She went back outside to greet this welcome stranger with her best professional smile.

"Let me start over, please," she said, extending her hand. "I'm Anna Giles. I live in Manhattan."

"Peter McCulley, from over near Pittman Center," he said. Anna liked the way he spoke.

"Are you hurt?" Peter asked. Instead of releasing the hand she had offered, he turned it slightly, looking at the smear across the back.

The small gesture touched Anna and, for a moment, she wondered what to do. It was such a little thing, but so close, so personal and caring. It made her realize how alone she had been since she had left New York.

"It's just makeup," she said, laughing slightly. "It will wash off. I must really be a mess."

"No, ma'am, you're sure not," Peter said, glad that she seemed more at ease. "You look just fine." He made an effort to control his voice because she certainly did look fine to him. Her hair was expertly cut and hung in a plain, natural style. The color reminded him of good honey held up to the sun. She had very large eyes, blue-gray with dark-rimmed pupils, with a quality like deep, clear water, set above sculpted cheekbones. Peter allowed himself the pleasure of glancing down the length of her legs and was startled to see bare feet with pink polished toenails.

"Let's see that map now," he said, to keep himself from staring. He took the map and refolded it so the Gatlinburg area was clearly visible.

"I came in this way last night," Anna said, pointing to a red line on the map, "and turned off. . .here, I think. . .south of Sevierville somewhere, but I got turned around. There are so many little roads that aren't on the map, and they all seem to go in circles."

"Well, the place we're standing on isn't marked on this map. You'd need a pretty detailed county map to find this road. You sure did drift, though."

He drew a tiny circle on the map with a ballpoint pen. "Here's our approximate location. Now, where do you want to go?"

Anna chuckled ruefully. "If I only knew! I'm afraid I can't tell you. You see, I came down here to find my great-grandmother's place, but I can't give you an address. I just thought that once I got here, I'd be able to find it. Pretty stupid, right?"

Peter paused, his quick reply checked by a note of sadness in Anna's voice. "Maybe not, if it's important to you." He wondered at the odd expression that came over Anna's face. "Does your granny have a phone? Maybe she could give you directions."

"Oh, Granny isn't here anymore. She's been dead for years. My parents are gone, too." She didn't tell Peter that it had been only two months since her parents had died in a plane crash, and that their deaths were the reason the Huddlestone property now belonged to her. The memory was still painful.

"I haven't been to Granny's place in twenty years. When I was little, my parents would bring me to visit but, of course, I have only mental pictures of the trips, not road numbers, in mind. I'm not sure whether my mind has gone bad or whether the landscape has changed. The memories are so vivid that I was just sure I could drive right there."

Peter smiled. He knew the power of memory both for good and for ill. "Did you ever know of a name she called her place? Where did you send letters to her? Was it Gatlinburg or some other place, like Coon Creek or Pine Bluff?"

"Yes, it was something Hollow, someone's name. Marshall Hollow? Does that sound familiar?"

"How about Martin? Martin's Hollow?"

"Yes! Is that on the map?"

"Not on this one. A lot of those little places are just wide spots in the road. Only the people who live there know where they are."

"But you know where Martin's Hollow is, don't you? If I could just get in the general area, I know I could find Granny's place. It's so clear in my mind!" Anna put her hands together, her fingers touching her chin, and gazed at the tops of the pines. "There were trees that we don't have up north. Granny called them cucumber trees and I learned in school that they are a kind of magnolia that has a long, cylindrical seed. There were tall pines, but not the same color as these, and they were a deeper green and not as bushy looking. The road went practically to the door of the farmhouse, which was low and near a creek. The rest of the land rolled away behind the house, rising and rising." Her voice was soft now. "It was the happiest place I've ever known."

Peter listened quietly, amazed at the freedom Anna felt to express her feelings, her fears, her joy. She was looking for more than the land. She was looking for something, some part of her that had remained there since childhood, something that was lost to her as an adult. He felt a quiet stirring deep inside, an idea he had pushed away for a long time, but today, now, for just a fleeting moment, he remembered its presence, and it was because of Anna. It was the hint of a possibility that he might still share the beautiful things of life with someone who could appreciate them.

"Look here, Miss Anna. I've got to get on over to Sugarlands. I want to help you find your granny's place, though. Why don't you follow me over there and we'll do some asking in the right places?"

"But I can't let you do that!" she protested. "You must have work to do and—"

Peter cut her off with a gesture of his large hands. "You got my curiosity up now. Besides, how could I keep on telling folks about Tennessee hospitality if I let you wander around with no help?"

Anna shrugged and rolled her eyes. "What can I say? I'd be a liar if I said the help wouldn't be appreciated. Oh! I forgot! This thing is out of gas," she said. "That's why I couldn't pull out and get away from the bear. I can walk to a gas station and get some gas if you need to get to work."

"I guess you could, if you really like walking. It is fourteen miles, though, one way." Peter laughed at the look of despair that came over Anna's face. He remembered the humble gratitude when he had not berated her for having no travel plans, and the softening of her sophisticated smile when he had remarked on what he thought was a bruise on her hand. *She can't hide anything! Everything she feels is written all over her face.*

"Just hold on a minute," he said. He went to his truck and got a three-gallon can from the back. Anna unlocked her gas cap and Peter poured in the gas, then helped Anna get the vehicle started, pouring gas into the carburetor until the engine continued to run.

"Now, follow me," Peter said. "There's just barely enough gas in that thing to get you to the station, so don't get lost on me, hear?"

Anna nodded silently, got back into the motor home, and put the vehicle in gear. As she followed him along the winding road, she wondered if God ever sent angels in pickup trucks.

Chapter Two

When Anna came out of the ladies' room at the gas station, she saw Peter hanging up the receiver of the pay phone. She had changed into fresh clothing, brushed her hair, and properly cleansed her face, restoring the natural dewiness of her skin. A dash of eye shadow, mascara, and some light plum lipstick would be all the makeup she would use for the day. As she put her bag back into the refueled motor home, Anna knew that Peter was watching her.

She did not mind. She was used to the admiring glances of men and accepted the silent compliment that this one offered. In fact, his dark brown, slightly wavy hair, and his tan, angular face worked together to make Anna take a second look. He had none of the polish of the men in her life in New York, and certainly did not have the pretty good looks of the men with whom she modeled. His clothes were useful, purchased for durability instead of to emphasize the strengths of his build. Anna could not help but notice, though, that the simple uniform with its poor cut and careless fit could not hide the deep chest, the thick strong arms, and the solid figure of the man who wore it.

As Anna approached Peter, he waved a finger up and down, indicating the denim jacket, cotton turtleneck, and pleated duck pants, all in shades of blue and purple.

"L.L. Bean?" he asked.

Anna drew back slightly in surprise. "How did you know?"

"I just know," he said, a mischievous look on his face.

Anna was just a bit defensive. "Why not? I figured if I was going to rough it, I might as well rough it in style. Besides, I love nice clothes."

Peter lounged against the phone booth, his arms crossed. He winked broadly, pulling down one corner of his mouth. "We'll keep your tenderfoot status a secret, but if you want people to think you're a native, don't wear new boots. It's a dead giveaway."

Anna laughed at his teasing and good humor. "Mr. McCulley, I can't thank you enough for all you've done. Now I've made you late for work. Please let me at least pay you for your time lost on the job."

He shook his head. "No need for that, Miss Giles. I called and told my boss I won't be in. He can find somebody else to empty the trash cans today." He dropped his eyes, suddenly self-conscious. He would prefer that Anna thought of him as a hero than the glorified janitor he really was—or had been until five minutes ago. Angered by his manager's patronizing refusal when Peter had asked for the morning off, he decided to skip the week's notice.

"Find yourself another boy," Peter had said. "I quit."

"Well, you won't be hard to replace," he had heard as he replaced the receiver.

"Anyway," Peter continued, "you caught my interest. Your granny's place, I mean. Well, you, too, but. . .I was kind of hoping you'd let me tag along and see that old farm. There aren't too many of them left."

"Are you interested in old houses?" she asked.

"Yeah, and young women." Peter was rewarded with another laugh from Anna, and it seemed to him like a Christmas gift. Even if it had meant being fired, at this moment he felt it was worth it.

"Did you get any breakfast before that bear came to call?" Peter asked.

"No, and I'm starved. The last time I poked food into this mouth I was in Kentucky. It seems like a long time ago, and like forever since I left New York."

"Tell you what," Peter said, "let's park that monster here at Albert's place. You can ride with me. I'll find you a real Tennessee breakfast and we'll figure out which direction to take looking for your granny's place. I can get us a county map at the ranger station at Greenbrier; that is, if the rangers aren't all out feeding the bears."

"I can see it's going to be a while before I live this down," Anna giggled.

"I said I was sorry. Don't tell me you're the kind who carries a grudge."

Without time to wonder at what has happening, Anna found herself getting into Peter's truck while he expertly backed the motor home into a space between two buildings. The smell of sheepskin seat covers, wood smoke, old metal, earth, and general manliness assailed her senses, which were sharpened by hunger. The smells seemed odd to her at first, far removed from her experiences in a scrubbed city environment, but quickly they were accepted as right. The sight of Peter approaching the truck and holding her pink enameled key holder between his thumb and forefinger made her think, *There's a real man, a good man who doesn't depend on the company of a woman to make him feel adequate.*

As they drove toward the ranger station, Anna told Peter more of what she remembered of the surroundings in the area of Granny's house.

"The thing I remember most vividly is a log church," Anna said. "Granny didn't go there to worship. She said the church was from the old days and there were no services held there, but you could see it from the road coming to her place. There was just a faint track leading off to it, not even noticeable enough to be called a trail."

"Was there a Grandpa Huddlestone?"

"Not in my experience, I'm afraid. He died when my mother was just a girl, shortly after her own mother died. Granny never remarried. Her life was very simple. The house is just an unpainted old frame place, all gray boards inside and out. She didn't have electricity or inside plumbing. I remember when she finally had electric lights put in because she was afraid of fire with the kerosene lamps, but she kept her wood-burning stove and carried in water from the pump. Isn't that odd? That was in the early seventies. I guess she didn't live much differently than her own grandmother did."

"Was it because of her religion?"

Anna hesitated. "No, my granny was very religious, but not in the way that inhibits the enjoyment of living. My father used to encourage her to get some comforts, like a gas furnace or an electric range, but she was just. . ." Anna spread her hands wide, her mind searching for the proper word.

"Satisfied?" Peter suggested.

"Exactly! She never seemed to feel she was underprivileged in any way. She didn't feel she was missing or lacking anything. She said she was happy and as long as she could take care of herself, why change what worked well? She would say 'If it ain't broke, don't fix it.' I used to love going there, the strangeness of it all, the feelings, my granny. . ."

Her voice trailed off and Peter did not question her further, leaving her alone with her memories. He wished his own thoughts were as pleasant.

He was glad the break with his job had been made, glad it was clean and final, but wished he had been more in control. Control! That was the magic word, the quality Peter was seeking, the one that always seemed to elude him, even as it had this morning.

Peter and Anna were both silent when they finally pulled up to the ranger station, got out, and in a few minutes returned with a map.

"Now we'll get something to eat and have a look at this map and make some plans," Peter said. "I know a little place—"

That phrase grabbed Anna's attention. It was so typical of Barry's conversation. "I know a little place where we can have some privacy," he would say, or "He's got a little place up in the Catskills that has to be seen to be believed," or "There's a little place just on the edge of the district where they've got an old Italian woman who cuts without a pattern but faster than a stamper."

By now, midmorning, Barry would be in the thick of his business day. "If I don't make a thousand by noon, the day's a waste," he sometimes said. Always trying to find the inside track, the inside tip, was Barry's approach to life. He never actually cheated, of course, but he was not above using people in subtle ways. He was so good at it, they did not mind, if they ever actually knew. Anna knew Barry would certainly never lose a morning helping some poor lost tourist that he had discovered alone in the park while jogging.

As Peter and Anna waited for breakfast to arrive, they studied the map. No Martin's Hollow appeared amid the dozens of locations noted in tiny letters between the winding roads.

"How can that be?" Anna asked. "I know we used to write letters to her at Martin's Hollow."

"Probably there was a post office at the general store and gas station. In the last twenty years, a lot of those little places have closed up and consolidated with the bigger stations. When the store closes, there's no more indication on the map. You said your granny was religious. Did she go to church anywhere?"

"Yes, when we visited, we used to take her to church. There was a little town, just a few buildings, with a white church." Anna frowned at the map again, saying the names of the towns out loud.

"This one! This is it. McMahan."

"Now we're getting somewhere," Peter said with obvious satisfaction. After the waitress placed plates of sausage and eggs, biscuits and gravy, and potatoes in front of them, he said, "McMahan's not all that far. We'll truck on over there after we eat and find that church. Could be someone still remembers your great-grandma and can tell us how to get to the place. In fact, that might be the postal station now, too." He scooped gravy onto his eggs, buttered a biscuit, and began to eat, his five o'clock breakfast now only a dim memory.

Anna stared at the food. "How many people were you expecting? This would feed a basketball team."

Oh, no, not another dieter! "Try a biscuit," he coaxed. "They're not the same as homemade, but they're real good."

She shook her head and sighed. "I wish I could. They look terrific." She sipped her orange juice and cut a small piece of egg, which she chewed slowly.

"What's the matter? Scared you'll get fat?"

"Not scared, just disciplined. Fat models don't make much money."

Peter did little to conceal the sudden look of surprise and distress that came over his face. "A model! You don't look like a model."

"Oh? What do the other models you know look like? Two heads, or what?"

"Well. . .it's not that. . .I mean, I don't know any other models, but—"

"No one? Surely you base your opinion on wide research, Mr. McCulley. If I don't look like a model, what does a model look like?" She stared at him unmercifully, enjoying his embarrassment and wondering how he would get himself out of this.

"I mean. . .you said 'model' and I just thought. . . well, you know, those funny dresses and piled-up hairdos, and the women all bent into unhuman shapes and their hollow cheeks and all. You're not that kind of model, are you?"

"What if I am?" Anna replied coldly. "High-fashion modeling is a very demanding profession. There are very few women who have the talent to make it in that area."

"Well, you'll have to skip more than biscuits to get cheeks like a corpse," Peter grumbled.

"Oh, yeah? Well, how's this?" Anna sucked in her cheeks and moved her lips like a fish.

Peter looked at her and his face brightened. He snapped his fingers. "Now I know where I've seen your face. I thought it looked familiar! You're on the cover of some magazine I just saw."

Anna was immediately pleased. "Which one did you see?"

"Field and Stream," he said.

Laughter burst from Anna like summer rain. "Just wait until I get hold of Barry!" she said, shaking her head. "Just see if I ever let him handle another account for me! *Field and Stream.* He'll love that."

"Barry?" Peter asked, relieved that he had managed to get his foot out of his mouth.

Anna looked at her plate and took another bite of her egg. She shrugged. "He's my agent, sort of." For some reason she did not feel like saying more. She looked longingly at the basket of still-warm biscuits. "I think I will eat one of these," she said. "I've got plenty of time to get back in shape." She spread a tiny dab of butter and some honey on half of a roll and munched happily. "I really do like good food," she confessed.

"Well, if you don't eat biscuits, you'll starve to death here," Peter said. "Now, how about some gravy to go with it?" He held up the small bowl of milk gravy flavored with spicy browned sausage and smiled appealingly.

Anna took a spoonful, tasted it, and sighed. "That is so good! It's been years since I've had gravy." The taste of the plain, delicious food, so far removed from her urban lifestyle, merged with the memories she had dredged up earlier. Nostalgia came in a wave. The smell of the sausage and biscuits put her back in her granny's kitchen, warming her feet at the wood-burning stove, hearing Granny hum, her small, thin body moving efficiently about the sparsely furnished room.

"Funny, isn't it," she said softly, "how you seldom appreciate the good things in your life until after they're gone. . .maybe forever."

"Don't be sad, Anna," Peter soothed. "It could be worse. You know they say, 'Better late than never.' It would really be a shame if you didn't understand how valuable your memories are or how important she was to you. Some people never do."

"Yes, that's true. I was only twelve when she died, and I hadn't seen her for a couple of years then. It's hard for a child that age to get a picture of things that last." She shook her head slowly. "I'm still wondering if I've done the right thing by coming here. Sometimes the reality is less than the hope."

"But you are here, and we'll find—"

"Mornin', Peter," came a soft male voice behind them. "Mornin', Miss—"

"Hey, Darron." Peter stiffened and did not look around. Anna sensed the tension immediately. Peter nodded in the other man's direction. "My brother, Darron McCulley. This is Anna Giles. She's visiting from New York City."

Darron's face showed childlike delight. "New York? No kiddin'? That's a good ways off. Come to see the park?"

Anna smiled. "No, not really, but I can see why so many people do. It's certainly beautiful here."

Darron pulled out a chair and sat down.

"Help yourself, Darron," Peter offered. "Anna won't eat her share, so you might as well finish it."

"Dorothy, bring me a plate, will you?" Darron called to the waitress. "I'm glad I stopped," he said to Peter. "I saw your truck outside. I'm just on my way up to Sevierville to pick up some parts for the shop, but I can count this for coffee break."

He proceeded to fill the plate the waitress brought him and, with obvious enjoyment, ate the cold biscuits and gravy. "Actually, this might be lunch, too. Alysia wasn't feelin' too hot this mornin' and didn't pack me a lunch. That's my wife," he said to Anna.

"Nothing serious, I hope."

Darron beamed. "She's pregnant, if you call that serious. I'm havin' lots of fun babyin' her. She cries a lot and runs me off, tells me I'm bein' silly and can't love a fat old woman like her, but I know she's teasin'." He dug a thick wallet out of his back pocket. "We got two kids already. Here. Here's Alysia with Wilford and Emily, taken a year back. This one's Alysia and me just after we got married. Peter took the pic—"

"Miss Giles is here looking for some family property," Peter interrupted. "You know anybody around McMahan who might know Martin's Hollow?"

Darron continued to eat in silence for a moment. "Can't think of a livin' soul, Pete. There was Hobe Gillman, but he's passed away."

"Well, we're going to drive over there and ask around town." Peter stood up and held Anna's chair, hurrying her a bit.

Anna handed the wallet back to Darron. "You have a lovely family, Darron. I can tell you're proud of them all." As Darron stood up and offered a firm handshake, she added, "I'm glad I got to meet you. I hope your wife doesn't feel ill for the whole pregnancy."

"Oh, she won't. Say, where are you staying?"

"I don't know yet," Anna shrugged. "I guess that depends on what I find in my travels today."

"Listen, you get set somewhere, you call me," he grabbed a paper napkin from the black metal dispenser and began to write on it. "Here's my number. We live up toward Cosby and you just have Peter bring you over and have supper with us. Tomorrow, next day, be fine." He pushed the paper in Anna's direction.

"Why. . .thank you." Anna glanced at Peter, who seemed irritated and anxious to leave. "I'll try to let you know what happens," she said. She waved as she left the restaurant, and Darron called, "Y'all come."

"That's what I call a proud papa," Anna said as she climbed into the truck. "Is Darron's wife as cheerful and pleasant as he is?"

Peter shrugged and concentrated on getting the door closed firmly.

"So! You're an uncle," Anna tried again as Peter got behind the wheel. Still he said nothing and Anna decided it was best not to pursue the issue. She could not understand how anyone could be at odds with someone as delightful as Darron McCulley, but strange things happened between brothers sometimes. Besides, Peter McCulley's personal life certainly was none of her business. She had totally forgotten that Peter was really a stranger. A day like this could never happen in New York, at least not to a New Yorker like Barry. She had heard of the magic of the South, the friendliness and easygoing attitude. Perhaps it was true. Still, she could not help but wonder at the sullenness that had overcome Peter since meeting Darron.

❧

When Anna and Peter finally reached the town of McMahan, the small white church where Granny had been a member was not hard to find. The maddening slowness of the mountain roads had begun to irritate Anna, who was still in tune with the pace of New York. It was nearly two o'clock and they were just on the verge of getting real information. First, they had gotten the name of the pastor from the sign on the church. They had driven to the pastor's home only to find that he was a young man who had been at the church for only two years and knew nothing about Granny Huddlestone. He sent Anna and Peter to find Deacon Parker. Deacon Parker had no telephone, so they drove to his farm, but he and his wife were both gone.

Peter was driving Anna crazy. He was silent in the truck, but when he got out to ask a question, he first had to chat about crops and weather before getting to the point. Didn't anyone in this part of the world hurry?

After leaving the Parker farm, they headed back toward McMahan to find the post office. Anna chafed as Peter made another of his leisurely inquiries as to the location.

"Well, what did you find out?" she demanded as he came back.

Peter turned the truck around in the middle of the street. "It's this way."

This time, when Peter pulled up in front of a small grocery store, Anna got out and went ahead of him. There was a desk in one corner with a red, white, and blue sign, and the familiar white eagle. Anna walked briskly to the desk, but no one was there. She rang the small bell. A girl who appeared to be about eighteen years old came from the office. "What can I do for ya?" she drawled.

"I'm trying to locate an old address," Anna began. "The name is Huddlestone and the previous address was Martin's Hollow."

The girl looked confused. "I don't know anybody by that name," she said. "You could try mailin' a letter and see if it gets forwarded, or you can have it returned with an address correction. That's what we do when we get bad checks here at the store."

"The woman is dead," Anna said.

"Then how come y'all want to write her a letter?"

Peter stepped in. "Howdy. This the post office?"

"Of course it's the post office; can't you see?" Anna snapped.

"No, sir," the girl said emphatically. "This here's just a contract station. We sell stamps and stuff. We don't handle any mail."

"Do you live here?" Peter said.

The girl nodded.

"Have you ever heard of Martin's Hollow?"

She shook her head.

"Peter, my granny lived in this county for sixty-three years! Why doesn't anyone know anything about her? How can someone just disappear without a trace?"

"She was your granny," Peter said quietly, the accusing tone all too obvious.

Anna had to look away. Part of her frustration was a sense of guilt at having lost such an important part of her life. Her pride injured and her energy sapped, Anna sighed, "What now? Should we look for a main post office somewhere?"

Peter shook his head. "I doubt we'll get any help that way. We could go on up to the county seat and check the tax rolls and so on."

Anna did not answer but wearily headed for the door. The day was ruined. She was looking forward to getting back to Albert's, pulling that motor home out onto hard, blacktop road, and finding the nearest stretch that would get her out of Tennessee. After a day of being shackled to a stubborn man in a bad mood, she felt that an evening of Barry's caustic humor would be great by comparison.

She glanced sideways at the man walking beside her through the parking lot, and suddeny she was ashamed. No doubt he was as tired and disappointed as she was, even if not for the same reasons.

"Peter, you've done so much for me. Why don't you take me back to Albert's? I'll look up the tax rolls by myself. If I don't find anything, it will be a waste of time for only one of us."

"Time is something I've got plenty of," Peter said flatly. "We are going to find this place, if it still exists. We will! I'm not going to quit. Even if you head for the city, I'm going to keep looking."

"But why? It doesn't mean anything to you."

"Do you want me to leave you alone? Is that it? Well, if you think I want to share in the work but not in the success, you're wrong."

"No, of course not, but it seems so hopeless—"

He gripped her shoulders with a fierceness that startled her. His face made her afraid, not for her own safety, but at the thought of what such intensity might accomplish if misdirected.

"Maybe you get only one chance, Anna," he said, his grip firm but not painful. "You came here looking for something. I don't know exactly why, but I'm mixed up in it now, too, and I'm not sorry. It isn't just the house and all your warm, fuzzy memories about your old granny, and it isn't just the challenge of finding something as big as an elephant that still can't be seen. It's you. . .something about you."

Anna stared at him, her lips parted, hardly breathing. What was he trying to say?

He let her go and stepped back, his face softening a bit. "If you really don't want me along, I understand. I know I'm not always great company. I apologize."

"Oh, Peter, why are we arguing?" said Anna, feeling weak with the tension of the moment added to the fatigue and frustration of the day. "I certainly didn't mean to imply that you weren't wanted."

He said no more and Anna tried to sort out the tangle of emotions that crowded the hot cab of the pickup. Unbidden, the thought came to her that perhaps Peter was seeking an intimacy that she had not offered. That almost brought a smile. Anna Giles had achieved notoriety in her social circle for her creative ways to say no.

Anna didn't ask for anyone's understanding or need anyone's approval. For her, it was all or nothing, and so far it had been nothing. She knew what she wanted and no one—not even Barry—had offered it to her. She wasn't about to settle for anything short of her own expectations when it came to commitment to a man. For Anna, that meant marriage to a full-time husband, a home, and children, in that order.

Anna's friends would have been amazed to know that Anna had never accepted anything more from Barry than a few living room kisses. Not that he hadn't offered more! In fact, lately it seemed that every date ended in an argument over what he and she wanted from their relationship. Perhaps that was why Barry had offered her the partnership with its implications of marriage. Maybe he was ready to settle down now, in business and in personal relationships. If so, was he the man she wanted?

Anna glanced toward Peter again. What exactly would he be expecting later this evening? Suddenly her thoughts were violently wrenched away as they came to the top of a ridge. She sat up straight and grabbed the dashboard.

"Stop!" she demanded. "Stop! There's the old log church."

Chapter Three

"This is the same church! It's exactly as I remember it, but it's in the wrong place," Anna said. She and Peter walked around the ancient building, peering through the tiny windows at the rough benches inside. A wooden lectern with a yellowed, ragged Bible on it stood at the front of the room. The door had been sealed and a thick bronze plate anchored to a boulder outside the church gave the history of the building. Anna sat on the boulder and read the information.

"It's been moved. The county historical society brought the building here to preserve it when the highway went through eight years ago. It used to be on County Road 406, south of McMahan." Anna stared at the plaque as though it had fallen from space. "What does that mean? Did they call that trail a county road? If they had to move this building, what's happened to Granny's place?" The doubts came rushing in and Anna no longer had the strength to hold them off. Tears began to come and she shoved both hands hard against her mouth to keep from sobbing aloud.

Peter approached tentatively. He had no encouragement to offer. He remembered hearing Darron remark on the extensive improvements in the area some years back, but it had meant nothing to Peter then. No doubt if they did find the Huddlestone home, the area would be drastically changed. Should he give in, tell Anna to forget it rather than be disappointed any further? He placed a gentle hand on her shoulder, not knowing what else to do.

"I'm just as out of place as this church," Anna managed to say. "I don't belong here. I'm just chasing some kind of foolish dream and I've wasted your time and mine, too. I'm going to find a telephone and call my lawyer and tell him to sell. What would I do with the place even if I found it? I don't know anything about property values."

Peter sat beside Anna on the rock, his arm falling naturally across her shoulders. "Do you really want to leave without knowing for sure?"

Anna breathed deeply. "Ever since last night when I couldn't find Granny's, I've had this fear that the house would be gone. I think that's why I didn't do more calling before I came all the way down here. I was afraid to find out the truth—that I am really all alone now, without anything left of my family."

"Your mamma and daddy didn't leave you anything to remember them by?"

"Last fall, they sold their house in Maryland, but it was just a house. We lived in so many places that no single house ever seemed like home. We were happy together and my parents had a beautiful marriage, but we didn't have. . .oh, you know, a place. I never thought about it much, but they were going to retire. Daddy was in the army; he was going to get out and they were going to build their dream house in the mountains. They had sold the Maryland house and they were on their way to look at a piece of property when they died."

Peter held her close beside him, knowing the sorrow was still so new to her. At last he said, "You know your granny's place will never make up for them being gone, don't you?"

Anna nodded, then leaned against him and sobbed openly, feeling the warmth of tears flood the fabric of his shirt. He said nothing, letting her cry until she was ready to stop.

He took a blue paisley bandanna from his pocket and offered it to her. "Come on," he said gently and led her to the truck. He helped her inside, hating to be separated from her even by inches, but knowing she would not want him near when she recovered her resolve, and he believed she would do that very soon. He got behind the wheel and waited until her breathing was once again regular and quiet.

"Anna, it's after five o'clock. It's a good hour to the area where this church came from. I think you ought to get some supper, then some sleep, and start again in the morning. There's probably still a lot of time on the road ahead of you. You'll feel more like it tomorrow."

Anna nodded wearily. "Take me back to Albert's."

They got hamburgers at a drive-through restaurant and talked about nothing on the way back to the garage. The stillness of evening had begun to set in when Anna found the owner, gave him ten dollars for using the space for the day, and chatted with him for a moment.

"Albert says he'd rather not have the motor home here tomorrow because of the liability," she told Peter. "I don't blame him. I know about insurance and all that. Besides, I wasn't looking forward to sleeping here with cars coming and going all evening. Maybe I should just look for a motel. I really hate motels, but it's probably for only one night, after all."

That was exactly what Peter was afraid of. He was ashamed to admit, even to himself, that he was just a bit satisfied that they had not found Anna's property today. A feeling that could only be called panic rose within him when he envisioned her in the motor home, heading north and out of his life forever. For a brief moment he thought of manipulating the situation, hiding evidence that might be discovered, in order to prolong her stay, but, of course, that was absurd.

The knowledge that Anna was once more in control made him realize she would not need him forever and, in fact, was already separating herself from him. He did not want to share her with other people at a campsite or at a motel, people who would have no idea of what she was going through and what the bond was that the two of them shared. His big question was whether Anna herself felt the unity that he was experiencing.

"If you want to stay in the motor home, and aren't afraid to stay by yourself, I can take you to a place I think you might like," he said, trying to keep his voice steady.

"It isn't in a park, is it?" she said. "I think I might like a motel better than a trailer park."

Peter laughed. "No, it's not a park. Why don't you just follow me? If you don't like it, you can leave the motor home behind and I'll take you to a motel. . .I mean, I'll show you where you can get a room." He spun around and jumped in his truck as Anna smiled, remembering her thoughts of the afternoon.

Once again, Anna was following Peter's truck. As the sun began to cast longer shadows, she barely recognized the scenery along the road they had traveled this morning. It seemed so long ago! The sight of the taillights ahead of her was both comforting and upsetting. She followed Peter off the good gravel road onto a narrow dusty one where she wondered if there would be room for a passing car. The motor home was difficult to handle. What if she had to slow down and she lost sight of Peter? No, of course he would be watching for her. As they wound upward into the hills and then down into the hollows, the darkness deepened abruptly, and she turned on her headlights.

It was the awkward time of day when headlights made no difference. Anna tried not to think about the steep drop-off on one side of the road and the sharp rock wall on the other side, which had a tendency to shed loose boulders from time to time. The way she was driving reminded her of the way she had played as a child, twisting the wheel back and forth, back and forth, working the brake feverishly in an exaggerated manner. But this was for real.

At last, Peter turned from the small road onto an even smaller one, and slowed his truck even more as he went along a steep decline. Now, thick clumps of laurel threatened to swallow the road that was little more than a path. Just as Anna wondered how much further they could go, Peter pulled ahead into an open area and stopped.

He got out of his truck, walked back to the motor home, and got into the passenger seat. "You all right?"

Anna nodded. She mustered a false good humor and said, too brightly, "Some drive! Well! Is this the place? I don't see anybody else camping."

"Come have a look," Peter said.

When they got out of the vehicle, Anna was immediately cheered by the effect of the sunset above the distant mountains, the soft light reflected on the late spring colors of the surrounding woods. The shadow of an early full moon hung in the east, waiting its turn. The chill of evening had settled the breeze. The air was perfectly still and crisp as she followed Peter along a footpath of bare rock toward a rushing creek that glistened in the fading light. As they came closer, she could hear the water muttering as it babbled along through the shallow bed, following its destined course toward the big river.

"Like it?"

"Peter, this is like something out of a coffee-table picture book! It's hard to believe that such a place actually exists." She looked around at the variety of trees, the shapes of chinquapin bushes and honeysuckle vines, and she breathed in the rich aroma of blossomed air. The steadfastness of the rocks and trees and the purposeful journey of the stream settled her senses and reminded her once again of her own mission. She was happy. Somehow, she knew, things would work out.

"Yes, Peter, this is exactly right. I remember now. It was this sense of peace that I was really hoping I'd find once I got away from the city and back into the mountains that my parents and Granny loved so much. It is here, after all."

Peter touched her shoulder. "Do you have enough water for the night?"

"Yes."

"Are you afraid to stay alone?"

The question that had nagged at Anna's mind earlier returned. Was it payoff time? What exactly did he want her to say? More disturbingly, Anna found herself wondering what she wanted to say. Today, she had seen a melancholy, brooding Peter and a teasing, fun-loving Peter, and an understanding, thoughtful Peter. All of them were good looking and evidenced a definite appreciation for women. What if he wanted to stay? Could she say no?

Peter, suddenly aware of her silence, slapped his forehead. "I did it again, didn't I? I meant that I would sleep in the truck if you didn't feel like camping out here in the wilderness all alone. If you want to be alone, I'll go home. What's your choice? I'm here if you need me."

Yes, as usual, it was her comfort, her well-being that he had in mind. *I should have known he isn't the type to use people in any way.* "I'll be fine, Peter," she said. "Please, get a good night's sleep and don't worry about me. If there aren't any people around, I guess I don't have anything to be afraid of, do I?"

She pulled his bandanna from her jacket pocket then turned and met him face-to-face. The light of the rising moon fell on one side of his face, and Anna felt for a moment that it was the face in a painting, one of the old Dutch masters where the faces were full of wonder and curiosity, shining through a dark world. She handed the still-damp fabric to him. "Sorry about all that crying."

He took the kerchief and held it. "I'll come back first thing in the morning and we'll know soon enough if what you're looking for still exists."

For a moment, they simply stood together under the trees, the darkness falling rapidly around them.

Anna murmured, "This land belongs to someone. You're sure it's all right if I stay here? I should make arrangements with the owner, shouldn't I?"

"It's mine," Peter said, and deliberately folded the bandanna so that she would not see in his face the feelings that came with those two small words. He began walking toward the truck and she walked with him.

As he reached for the door handle he stopped and turned to her. "Anna, I hope. . .hope. . ." What could he say? He had no right to tell her that whatever it was she was looking for, he wanted her to find it here and that he wanted to be the one who showed her the way. He looked at her trusting, open face, and for one horrible moment, he visualized himself coming back in the morning and finding her gone without a trace—back to

New York and out of his life as though she had never been stranded on that road this morning.

She's a stranger, a city girl who'll run back to Barry Whoever-He-Is as soon as she disposes of her inheritance, or finds out it's nothing but an improved public roadway, he told himself. But more than anything he could remember in a long time, Peter did not want that to happen.

"I hope you get a good rest," he said, despising his lack of skill in the language department.

"Thank you again, Peter. I never imagined anything like this."

"I'll be out early. I'll cook. You get some rest."

Anna wanted to ask another question, to hold him there for a few minutes, but he was gone, bumping over the rough trail. The sound of the engine faded and she knew she was more alone than she had ever been in her life, and yet not alone at all.

Chapter Four

The persistent knocking at the door of the motor home penetrated Anna's sleep, and, for a moment, she thought of the bear. Then she remembered. Peter had said he would be there.

"Peter?" she called. "Is that you?"

"Were you expecting somebody else? Come on out or I'll eat everything myself."

Anna snuggled deeper into the blankets, savoring their warmth in contrast to the cold, crisp air inside the motor home. She had left one window open and slept deeply. She felt rested. The problems of yesterday did not seem so insurmountable this morning. Peter had been right.

Still reluctant to leave the warmth that surrounded her, Anna dragged the blankets along as she crawled to the end of the bed. She reached into the small bureau built into the motor home and took out a pair of jeans and a heavy, cowl-necked sweater. She dressed quickly, brushed her hair, and fastened it at the back of her head, then stepped outside into the morning. The smell of ham and wood smoke went straight to her stomach and Anna was suddenly ravenous.

She saw Peter near the stream and jogged toward him. "I hope you have tons of food," she said. "I'm so hungry I could die."

"What about your diet?" He broke an egg into the skillet and put the shells back into the carton.

"What good is being thin if you're dead?" she asked, sitting down on an outcropping of rock beside him.

Without makeup, Peter noticed, Anna's face lost some of its definiteness. She looked softer, more vulnerable. Her hair was bundled into a granny knot and small tendrils escaped around her neck and ears. A little air of sleepiness remained about her as she huddled close to the fire and hummed to herself. She held her hands out to the warmth, and Peter saw that her nails were of a moderate length and bore no polish. His image of the big-city fashion plate was fading. He began to feel that Anna was something else entirely. Suddenly, he felt a need to concentrate on his cooking.

"Why are you doing that?" Anna nodded at the skillet as Peter moved it in and out of the small flames.

"Regulates the heat," he said, "so the eggs don't burn."

"You must cook this way a lot. You don't waste any movements."

"A fair bit. Not as much as I'd like to. Having a job tends to interfere with living sometimes." But now there was no job. Maybe he could live again.

Anna smiled. "I get the impression that you aren't exactly fond of your job."

Peter shrugged. He scooped the eggs onto tin plates, served thick slices of ham from a plate that had been resting on the rocks near the fire, and then poured coffee from a battered and blackened percolator. Anna took the plate, then watched as Peter scraped away hot coals and pulled out a small Dutch oven. He lifted the lid and Anna saw that it was filled with golden-brown biscuits. The heat and aroma rose to her face, and she knew that she would rather be here than in the most exclusive supper club in New York.

"Peter, I almost hate to eat this. You've worked so hard. You must have started breakfast hours ago!"

He sliced a chunk of butter from a stick, slipped it inside one of the biscuits and handed it to her. "Believe me, I can't think of a better way to spend a morning. Don't feel too sorry for me. I didn't butcher the hog and cure the ham and feed the chickens and gather the eggs the way our grannies did."

"I used to feed the chickens when I came to Granny Huddlestone's," Anna remembered. "I was so afraid of them! I used to stand just at the edge of the yard and throw handfuls of feed overhand like a baseball. Granny coaxed me and encouraged me until I got over the fear. She would say, 'People are like chickens. There's banty roosters, all noise and feathers and no meat. There's old hens that are always in a stew. There's little biddies that don't know enough to stay home in their nests.' She called me her little chick, said I belonged right next to her under her wing."

"I like the way you talk about her. You're a good talker."

Anna grimaced. "That's a very nice way of putting it. My friends tell me my mouth needs a new transmission because it won't stay in neutral."

"Nice friends you got. Want another biscuit?"

He handed her another without waiting for her to answer. "How did you get into the modeling business? Were you discovered, or what?"

"My high school home-and-family-living teacher encouraged me to try it," Anna said. "I went to a big consolidated high school in eastern Virginia."

"What? I thought you were a Yankee."

"Oh, no. I didn't go to New York until, oh, a little over six years ago. I went to one of those charm school places when I was a senior and learned how to walk straight and keep my nose in the air, you know. I started working in Richmond, then I went to Baltimore for a few years before trying the big time. Believe me, the girls that come to New York straight from Iowa or Tennessee. . .they seldom have a chance."

"Where were you born?"

"I was born in Tennessee and my family lived here for two years after I was born. My father was in the army. We moved around a lot, four years here, two years there. New York is as much my home as any other place I've ever been. What about you? Is Tennessee home to you?"

"Sure. Born and bred in the briar patch, you might say. I only left Seviere County to go to college in Memphis, and I stayed there for two years."

"Tell me about your work, Peter. You must like helping people all day. You certainly saved my life yesterday."

"Well, it was my gain," he said, beginning to stamp out the fire without answering her question. Anna watched him as he quickly disposed of the garbage and cleaned the utensils without leaving any sign of human presence. From the bank of the stream where he cleaned the skillets using only sand and the cold water, he called, "As soon as you're ready, we'll drive over to the county seat. They can look up the location of your granny's property. We might as well get scientific about this thing."

❧

As Anna and Peter drove toward the county offices, she once again broached the subject of work. "I'm really afraid you're giving me too much time, Peter. I'd hate to have you lose your job because of this."

"It's all right," he said. "I'm taking some time off. Stop worrying."

The tone of his voice told Anna the subject was off limits, but her curiosity burned on. He was so full of secrets and so full of surprises! She wondered if, when the time came to leave, she would still be trying to figure him out.

She also wondered if her questions would be answered. Would she know if the new faith she had adopted as her own just weeks ago would really change her life, as her friend Brianna had promised?

Brianna had taken Anna to a luncheon where a businesswoman had shared with the listeners how she had asked God to forgive her sins and make her life His own. Anna had heard such stories before, but had assumed such experiences came to one in a supernatural, mystical way, not through logical decisions like the ones the speaker asked the audience to make. Still, when Brianna explained to Anna that without the forgiveness of God through the death of Jesus, there could be no communion with the Creator, Anna decided to pursue the idea. After reading the Bible and talking more with Brianna, she decided to make the personal connection to the God she had always assumed was rather disinterested in individuals.

The opportunity to get away from her work and her surroundings had so far given her little insight into the effects of that decision, but Brianna was right about one thing: Anna knew there was a Divine Presence in her life now, guiding her, helping her, though she could not guess in advance where it might lead.

As she listened to Peter talk about fishing, she knew he had come to her for some reason known at this time only to God. Maybe it was simply to help her find the property or to solve some problem connected with it. Maybe it was to be a friend at a time when she especially needed one. She didn't know.

The county clerk sent them to the assessor's office, who first did a flurry of computer work, then rummaged in a large file drawer, and pulled out a yellowed document.

"There's good news and bad news," said the man. "I'd say from the records I've got here, the Huddlestone house is still standing, though the road right of way has been changed considerably. The bad news is, the taxes haven't been paid in nearly two years. Actually, that property's due for sale in about. . ." he glanced at a large calendar on the wall, "let's see, the auction is in four days."

"But my attorney didn't say anything about taxes," Anna protested. "He has the deed. The property belonged to my parents."

"I can look up the correspondence for you, if you like," the clerk said. "All I know right now is that this parcel is on the list for auction unless we get full cash payment."

"Well, I'm not going to pay it until I see the place," Anna said, trying to control her emotions. "Can you tell us how to get there?"

The assessor showed Peter the location of the property, and he and Anna quicky got back into the truck.

"Two years," Anna said. "How could that have happened? Tax notices must have been mailed to the wrong address after my parents moved the last time. Two years' worth of taxes!"

"If you need money, Anna, I've got some put away. I can help."

She stared at him. "Peter, you are a wonder. I've known you for only a day and a half and you're behaving like family. That's the most generous offer I've ever heard."

He reddened a bit. "Oh, well, you didn't hear the terms of the contract yet: I demand you name your firstborn child after my grandfather."

"Is it worse than Rumpelstiltskin?"

"Jonadab Subulocious McCulley," he said.

"What if it's a girl?"

"She'll really hate her name," he said.

As Peter slowed the truck, Anna at first thought they were in the wrong place, but then she saw the house, standing as always near the ancient pines. The house had not moved, but the road had changed so much that she was at first disoriented. She had thought she would jump from the truck and run to the old place the minute she saw it, but now she hesitated.

"Come with me, Peter."

He walked quietly beside her as they walked down the hill and stepped up onto the porch. On the kitchen door was the tax notice. Anna took it down and tried the door. It was open, as always. Granny had no locks.

Anna pushed open the door and smelled the rush of air with its odor of vacant rooms, spiderwebs, earth, and insects. Carefully, she stepped inside and surveyed the room she had not seen for so many years.

"I would give anything to see my granny one more time," she whispered.

Peter said nothing for a time, then asked, "Did your mamma and daddy ever come back here after she died?"

"They came for the funeral, of course. They took some of the things that were left in the house. But I have a feeling they never quite got around to making any decisions about the place. See? So many things have just been left here. How can it be that vandals haven't destroyed the whole place?" She crossed the kitchen threshold. "There are some dishes still in the cupboard. Here's a can of corn still in the pantry."

"It doesn't make sense," Peter said. "Seems like a perfect place for a high school beer bust or worse. For some reason, the place escaped damage. It must be well built. The weather doesn't seem to have done much damage."

Roused from her reverie, Anna began looking through the rooms, one by one. As she did, the memories of her early years came to life. The house was no longer a sad place, but the piece of her own history she had hoped it would be.

"Peter, I'm going to keep this place. I might even fix it up and keep it for a vacation home or something like that. Do you think it needs much work?"

"I'm not much of a builder," he said, "but Darron's pretty good at it. He could tell you what would have to be done to put it in shape. Of course, you'll want plumbing, maybe a bigger electrical service, but it doesn't appear there's much structural work."

"I never thought to ask how much the taxes were. Let's go back and find out. Then I'm going to rent a car for a couple days—that is, if you don't mind if I leave the motor home on your land."

"Wouldn't have it any other way," he said, delighting in her enthusiasm and purposefulness. This was the Anna he had seen yesterday morning, set on a purpose, knowing her mind, yet not afraid to admit she needed help.

≈

Anna and Peter reached the assessor's office about fifteen minutes before closing, then were sent to the treasurer, who obviously didn't appreciate their visit.

"You owe three hundred twenty-two dollars and sixty-eight cents," she said abruptly, staring at Anna.

"No, I want to know the total amount," Anna said firmly.

"That is the total amount," said the treasurer. "That's the taxes for two years, plus interest and penalites."

Anna paused, not wanting to be rude, but said once more, "That's all? Are you sure?"

The treasurer wearily laid the tax bill before Anna for her approval and suddenly Anna laughed out loud. "Three hundred and twenty-two dollars? For two years?"

The treasurer was surly. "Well, I'm sorry, but we built a new school a few months back. The money mostly goes to the schools, you know, and there is a house on the place. If you have a problem with the charges, you could ask for a hearing."

"Can you take an out-of-state check?" Anna asked.

"I'd rather not," said the treasurer.

"I'll be in tomorrow with the cash," she said. "Thank you."

Once outside, Anna wrapped her arms around Peter and hugged him tightly. "I thought it would be thousands!" she gasped between peals of laughter. "It's a gift! An outright gift!"

"Real estate values are different here, I guess," Peter said, laughing with her.

"I guess I don't need the loan," Anna said. "Thanks anyway."

"Too bad," said Peter. "Jonadab would have been proud."

"Peter, come and celebrate with me, please. I need to go to Gatlinburg and arrange for a transfer of some money from New York. I can also rent a car there. Then I'd like you to come out and have supper with me later. Would you? I haven't been able to do anything for you and you've been wonderful. Say you will."

"I wouldn't miss it," he said. "Are you cooking?"

"Well, I'll serve something," she said. "I don't promise to cook, but it will be something edible, trust me."

੨ൠ

When Peter opened the door for Anna at the bank in Gatlinburg, he said, "I'll see you about seven. Are you sure you can find your way back now?"

Anna patted her handbag. "I've got my map, and as long as I don't wait until after dark, I'll be fine." She waved as he drove off, then she went into the bank.

After getting a rental car, Anna visited a grocery store and then did some shopping. She found a dark mauve jumpsuit in a quasi-military style that she decided she would wear for the evening. She rationalized her own motives for the purchase, telling herself she was not really dressing to please Peter, just making a wardrobe investment.

When paying for her clothing, Anna noticed in her handbag the napkin on which Darron had written his phone number. She remembered what Peter had said about Darron's talents in the building trades, and she decided to call him before she left town.

"Is this Darron?" she ased the person on the phone. "This is Anna Giles. Do you remember me? We met at the restaurant."

"I wouldn't forget you, Anna," Darron answered. "Are you all ready to come and have supper with us? I'm fixin' spaghetti."

"I'm afraid I can't tonight, Darron. You're awfully free with your hospitality, aren't you?"

"You know what they say. Love isn't love till you give it away. Just remember you're always welcome. Is there something else you need?"

"Well, I found my granny's house, the one Peter and I were looking for in Martin's Hollow."

"You did? For sure?" He lowered the receiver and Anna heard him call, "Alysia, Peter and that gal I told you about found that old house." To Anna he said, "Is there anything left of it?"

"It seems to be pretty sturdy, but Peter said he wasn't qualified to give any kind of estimate on repairs. He said you were good at building. Would you be willing to look at the place and tell me if you think it's worth fixing up? I don't want it to completely go to ruin. It's already been vacant for several years."

"I'll be glad to look at the place. Can you tell me where it is?"

Anna hesitated. "You know, I'm afraid I can't. I have the map we got at the clerk's office, but I couldn't tell you how to get there. For one thing, I don't know where you are. I could bring the map to you, though. I've rented a car and I'm doing some shopping in Gatlinburg."

She told Darron where she was and he gave her directions to his home in a neighboring small town. Anna was surprised to find the home was in a crowded and not-too-pleasant area. The duplex where Darron stood waiting on the porch was in need of paint, and the small patch of grass was rimmed with bare dirt. Anna would have thought she was being welcomed into a palace, however, by Darron's warm, enthusiastic reception.

"I'm sure glad I was home a little early today, otherwise I would have missed your call. Come on in and meet my wife."

Alysia was short with dark eyes and hair and a cupid's bow mouth. Her hair was windblown and curly and she wore a huge tee shirt over walking shorts. Though more shy than Darron, she welcomed Anna with a handshake and a smile.

"You'll know the place when you see it," Anna said after showing Darron the map. "For one thing, there are those huge pine trees below the house." She took a hundred dollars out of her bag and handed it to Darron. "This is just for your gas and time," she said. "If you need more to pay for estimates from contractors or anything like that, let me know."

Darron stared at the money. "I didn't think about getting paid."

"But. . .I couldn't ask you. . .this kind of work is expensive, Darron," Anna stammered. "I wouldn't feel right asking you to use your time and your own vehicle and not pay you."

"Well, if it makes you feel better; I won't say I don't need the money," he said, but he was obviously uncomfortable. He excused himself and left Anna with Alysia.

"Oh, I hope I haven't offended him," Anna said.

"You can't offend Darron," said Alysia. "It just never would have occurred to him to ask for payment, and he wishes he could afford to give it back, that's all. He won't think badly of you for it."

"Alysia, I've never met people like you and Darron. I don't know anyone who would invite me to their home on a moment's notice like this. They might meet me somewhere, but this is wonderful."

"Don't give us too much credit," said Alysia, laughing. "It's the way we were raised. We don't know any other way. Anna, I hope you stay a bit. I really like talking to you. I'm going to tag along with Darron to the house, too, if you don't mind."

"I don't mind at all. I think I'd better go now, though. I know you'll want to be feeding your family soon, and I've invited Peter to the motor home for supper. He's been such a big help."

A shadow of sadness passed across Alysia's face, and a small smile that was not a happy one lingered. "Peter has so much to give," she said. "I hope you and he can be friends." Suddenly she thought of something. "Anna, would you like to come to church with Darron and me? It's a little place, but we're happy there. We'd love to have you come."

Her invitation prompted Anna to share her own recent spiritual decision. She was pleased to see that Alysia understood perfectly what had happened.

"Darron and I both love and follow the Lord Jesus," she said. "Now I just know you and I are going to be friends even if you don't get to stay in Tennessee."

"Oh, I couldn't stay," Anna said. "I have my work, you know, but I am beginning to think I might be staying longer than the week I had originally planned. We'll see what happens."

Chapter Five

After she got things ready for a light meal, Anna still had time for a relaxing beauty treatment and the production of a more sophisticated hairdo. Her feeble attempts to convince herself that Peter would not be expecting her to dress up were lost in her natural love of elegance. When she opened the door to Peter's knock, she was surprised to see that she was not the only one who had dressed for the occasion.

"Peter! You look very nice," she said. He was freshly shaved, and Anna caught a hint of spicy cologne as he brushed past her. He wore cotton slacks that broke precisely over casual but well-polished loafers. His plaid sport shirt, though it bore no designer label, was crisp and bright and, Anna noted approvingly, tailored nicely.

Briefly, Anna wondered if she had misled Peter. Had he dressed out of courtesy, or was he trying to please her? Then she mentally slapped herself. Of course he would shower and shave for dinner. He was not a slob. And what if he were trying to make an impression? He had already done that, but the new image he presented to her this evening made him seem less like a wise uncle and more like an available man.

Serving the fondue supper that she had prepared, Anna said, "Sorry, no biscuits."

"I don't mind a bit," he said. "I can go without biscuits when the cook wears such a nice uniform."

"Oh, thank you," she smiled. "I saw this in Gatlinburg and it called my name. It's my favorite color. Let me guess yours. I'll bet it's blue."

He nodded. "What was your clue?"

She shrugged. "Most people like red or blue, and you don't seem to be the red type. Anyway, I think you're a bit romantic. I'll bet you even keep souvenirs."

He reddened at the thought of the small cedar box in his bedroom that held treasures from past years. Why could he not read her the way she read him? The only thing he had learned to predict about this woman was her definitely female effect upon him. He thought of the vulnerability she had shown last night. She had made no move to conceal it nor had she used it as a ploy to gain his sympathy and attention. She simply had a need, and he had been present to assist her.

Anna was saying, "Peter, are we friends?"

He smiled. "If I have anything to say about it, we are."

"I want to ask you something...tell you something, I guess. A few weeks ago, something happened to me. I went to a luncheon with a friend of mine and heard a woman talk about how she had given her life completely to God. She said she realized she was separated from Him because of her sins. She asked God to forgive her and make her acceptable to Him. Have you ever heard anything like that?"

Peter nodded. "Sure, lots of times. It's what they call the Gospel message."

"Yes, she used that word, Gospel. She said it meant 'good news' and the news was we could have peace with God and a personal relationship with Him. I prayed that God would take away my sin, too, Peter. I believe, though it's all new and strange to me, that I'm changed somehow. It isn't that I was some kind of lowlife before and now I'm an angel. I just know God is at work in my life. I can say now that I know Him. Does that make any sense?"

Peter nodded. "Around here people would say you got converted or maybe saved or just got religion. It depends on if you're Baptist or Methodist."

"This is important to me, Peter. It's one of the main reasons I came here, maybe the whole reason. Do you think it's weird?"

Peter could hardly believe she could lay before him perhaps the most personal decision any person could make. Didn't she fear his laughter and rejection? Could she be so sure of herself that his opinion would not change her mind? He understood that she was not seeking his approval, but only asking whether her experience paralleled anything in his own life.

"It isn't weird, Anna. If it's real to you, that's all that matters."

"I want to know if it is real or just an emotional reaction," she said. "That's why I decided to get away from work and the city and my friends and just think about this for a while. It's easy to get separated from the really important things when you are so busy and the lights are so bright." A picture of Barry flitted through her mind. He would be telling her that her ears were deaf from hearing things like horns and sirens and that there was something basically unwholesome in silence. He would not even try to understand the quiet stirrings in her soul.

Peter searched Anna's face. "It doesn't much matter where you are,

Anna. You can still lose touch with what's real."

"What's real, Peter?" Anna asked softly. "What's important to you?"

He shrugged slightly. "A few things. . .land, family. Maybe only those two things."

"Speaking of family, I met Darron's wife today. She's the most friendly, relaxed person. They invited me right in."

"You went to Darron's place?"

"Yes, he's going to look at Granny's house and help me get some idea of whether it's worth investing money in repairs. Alysia seems to think highly of you."

"I don't appreciate people talking about me behind my back," Peter snapped.

Anna stiffened. "No one was talking about you behind your back. What a thing to say!"

"Neither one of them will be happy until they—just leave them alone, all right? They can't do anything for you."

"Maybe they can. They can be my friends, which, by the way, I choose without your permission." Anna felt her own temper rising and was unhappy with herself for sniping at Peter.

"Well, I won't stand for you all taking me apart. Darron knows better. I've told him to let the past rest, but he won't."

"Peter, I have no idea what you're talking about. Darron wasn't even in the room when Alysia said—"

"So now it's Alysia," he shouted. "I should have known she couldn't live with it forever. She just had to tell somebody. Did she tell you the whole story or just her side? Did she tell you everything?" He was standing now, leaning over Anna in an almost threatening manner. "Did she tell you we had been engaged?"

"You? You and Alysia?"

Peter sat down again, obviously struggling for control. "What's the use? Everybody in this town who knows me knows what happened. Eventually, you would have known, too. You might as well hear it from the source."

"Peter, Alysia didn't say anything about it." Suddenly, the animosity she had seen between Darron and Peter made sense. Certainly Peter would resent the younger brother who had stolen his sweetheart, but that had happened years ago! Anna looked at the man before her, knowing at once that he was capable of such intense feeling and that he was also paying a price for his emotions.

"It doesn't matter," he said, calmer now. "It was a long time ago. Anyway, they won't have to be reminded of me much longer. I'm going to be leaving Tennessee."

Anna was stunned. "Peter, you love this place. It's as much a part of you as your own nose. You couldn't leave Tennessee."

He shook his head slowly. "You don't know anything about me, Anna. You think I've got some exotic, glamorous job. Did you know I am actually unemployed? The job I left was sweeping out bathrooms and cleaning windows. I assume I've already been replaced."

Anna did not know what to say. It must have happened recently, because Darron didn't seem to know his brother was no longer working. She remembered the phone call at Albert's garage. Could it have happened then?

"Oh, Peter, I knew you were going to get in trouble for taking time off to help me!"

"Anna, I was on my way to work yesterday with one thought on my mind. I was going to get free. I had my plan all figured out. I was going to give my notice yesterday then serve my time and get away from here. Quitting over the phone just moved the timetable up a bit, I guess. I should have left years ago. There's nothing for me here."

"But you might find someone else, Peter. Don't throw away everything you love because one relationship didn't work out. It's true I don't know you very well, but the sound of your voice when you talk about Tennessee is like love. And your land! I know it's important to you. Give yourself time."

"My mind's made up, Anna, but thanks for listening. Don't worry; I know this is the best way. I need to make a new start, and Darron and Alysia sure don't need me hanging around town, bumping into them on every corner. It's best for everybody."

"What will you do?" she asked.

Peter smiled. "I'll find something. Meanwhile, though, I would like to help you with your granny's house. You'll need someone to run you around the county, and Darron's a working man with three and a half mouths to feed."

"I'd love to have your company, Peter, and your help."

He stood up to leave, and Anna found herself feeling unsettled, wishing he would stay and somehow talk through the hurt she knew he must be enduring. But she had no control over him. Maybe, as Alysia had said, they could learn to be friends.

ஃ

The next day, Saturday, Anna decided that she would not see Peter for a few days. She wanted to settle her own feelings, and she knew he would be uncomfortable with her after having shared such a rare confidence. She met Darron at the Huddlestone home for an initial review of the property, and she was pleased to see that he had brought not only his wife but both of their children.

"Well, what do you think of the old place?" she asked Darron after a brief tour through the house.

"They sure don't build them like this anymore," he said. "I suppose by today's standards this wasn't a luxurious home. But look at the wood. Look at the way the doors and windows are set. It's as strong as iron."

Anna was as proud as if he had directed the compliment to her personally, for in an odd way, since she had found the place and decided to keep it, it was her home.

"Would you like to help me fix it up?" she asked.

Darron squinted up at the tin roof. "What are you going to do with the place once it's fit to live in?" he asked.

Anna shrugged. "I don't know. I might rent it or just keep it as a vacation home. Who knows? I might come back here someday when I'm too old to be a model anymore."

The words had a hollow ring in Anna's own ears. Even if she decided to stop modeling, there was the agency and Barry's offer waiting for her. Anyway, she was not exactly at the end of her career, though she had noticed many of the new models seemed like children to her. The truth was that she simply couldn't bear to see the old place empty and bare, remembering the home that it had once been. She wanted to give it life again.

Darron kicked at a loose board on the front porch. "How far do you want to go with this? Do you want to make it into a new house or just put it back the way it was?"

Anna hesitated, trying to focus the picture in her mind. "I just want it to be a home again," she said. "No one today would want to live here without plumbing and electricity, of course, but I wouldn't want to change everything. The place is sturdy, as you said. If the roof is sound, don't change it. If the windows keep out the cold, don't change them."

Darron nodded. "I always did want to do this kind of work, but I never figured I'd get the chance. I'm handy enough with a hammer, and I can find good people to do the plumbing and wiring, if you trust me. I can only give you Saturdays and evenings, though. I have to keep my job."

"Of course you do," Anna said. "Would you try to get some cost estimates for me pretty soon? If I could get some idea of how big the project is, in say a week or ten days, before I go back to New York, then I could make some plans. Pay yourself whatever is fair, Darron. I'm not rich, but I can just about do what I want right now, since there's only myself to think about, and this is important to me."

Over Alysia's picnic lunch, while the children climbed trees and raced in and out of the laurel thickets, Anna, Darron, and his wife worked out details. Anna would open a bank account for the project, and Darron was to draw a weekly salary from the account, pay all contractors, and get the necessary permits.

"Anna, why don't you and I come out this evening and clean the place up?" Alysia said. "It can be just us women, and we'll tie our hair up in rags and do some good old spring cleaning."

"Whoa now!" Darron cautioned. "The place is just going to get dirty again once the electricians get started."

"Oh, I know," Alysia said, "but we could do the windows and get rid of the cobwebs."

"I'd like that," Anna said. "I don't mind doing some of the work twice if I can see good results right away. There's nothing like a little success to keep hope alive."

Darron took the children home with him and Anna and Alysia headed toward the library to see if there were any historical records about the house or family.

"I can't get over how different Peter is from Darron," Anna commented. "Darron seems to be the more. . . well, I hardly know what to say without making it sound derogatory."

"Average? Normal?" Alysia prompted. "That's what he is, Anna, just the kindest, most self-sacrificing man in the world, and I love him to death. They aren't so different, though, really. See, they're like two Confederate soldiers who believed in the cause and were willing to die for it. One went off to the battle, that's Peter, and one stayed on the farm to grow food for the troops, that's Darron. Trouble with Peter is he keeps thinking that because he can't win the war and plant the corn, too, there's something wrong with him."

Alysia, who had gone to the same high school with Peter and Darron, told Anna that their father had died when the boys were in junior high school. The man had charged his sons to be faithful, to take care of their mother and sister, and to honor the family name.

"Peter thought that meant becoming rich and famous," said Alysia. "He had so much talent and potential, but he practically killed himself trying to be absolutely the best at everything. He was class valedictorian and football captain, held down an almost full-time job, and hated it all. Darron practically worships the ground Peter walks on, but his heart's just about broken because Peter won't ever forgive him for marrying me."

"Peter told me you two had been engaged," Anna said.

"He did? He never talks about it anymore. I thought his head would fly off the night I broke our engagement, but the day Darron told Peter he was going to marry me was worse. Peter never said a word. He packed up and headed for the woods and didn't come back for a week. Peter's special, all right, and real fine, but he's just not the man for me. I knew that years ago. I wanted a man like Darron who would just love me to pieces and be as dependable as the sunrise and not think about everything so much."

While Anna turned the car into the library parking lot, she was thinking of Alysia's words. She had had glimpses of the fiery Peter and, unlike Alysia, the image was exciting to her. If only she could find a man whose strength and determination would be directed toward the same goals as her own, she knew she would snatch him up in a minute.

❧

Later that evening, the two tore into the upstairs bedroom where Granny Huddlestone had given birth to Anna's grandmother, who had died before Anna was born, and where Granny had quietly died in her sleep at the age of ninety-seven. In the room was a bed so large and heavy, her parents must have decided to leave it when going through her things after her death.

Anna dusted and polished the bed while Alysia washed the inside of the windows and swept down cobwebs. They cleaned the floor and the smell of wet wood rose to Anna's nostrils.

"Oh, wouldn't this be pretty with some good hard wax rubbed into it?" Alysia said, touching the boards. "You weren't thinking about a carpet, were you?" she asked.

Anna shrugged. "To be honest, I haven't thought about much of anything. Sometimes I feel like I'm just riding a wave where this house is concerned. It seems to be pulling me along toward something; I don't know what."

"God is in charge of your life now," Alysia reminded her, "because you gave Him permission to take over. You might find a lot of your ideas will change." She picked up an oversized trash bag she had brought with her, and which Anna had assumed contained cleaning rags, though she wondered why Alysia would bring so many. Alysia removed the twist tie and withdrew a quilt made of blue and white cotton in a double wedding ring pattern. She spread it on the bare bed springs and the room came alive.

"Alysia! It's beautiful. Where did you get it?"

"Made it. I make about one a year, and I've had lots of time to work since I got pregnant and haven't felt so good. Anyway, that's as good an excuse as any to waste time on foolishness." Though Anna's obvious pleasure embarrassed her slightly, she could not hide the pride in her work. "Anyway, you keep that," Alysia said, patting Anna's arm. "The place isn't a home without a quilt."

Impulsively, Anna hugged her new friend. "Thank you, Alysia. I feel that all of you—Darron, Peter, and you—have given me so much, and I don't have anything to give back."

"No matter. We don't keep accounts on friends, and you musn't either. Come on; let's go home. I need to get things ready for church tomorrow. Would you like to come with us?"

"I would love to. I haven't been to church very much. I just started going with my friend in New York before I came here."

"Well, our church is little and plain, but we like the people. Darron likes it because it's country people and he doesn't have to wear a tie."

Anna pulled into the driveway at Alysia's home. "I'll come and meet you in the morning," she said, "and we can ride together if you like."

Alysia waved from the porch and Anna backed out, somewhat reluctant to return to the motor home but knowing it was only because of the closeness she had enjoyed today with Alysia.

❧

As Anna lay in the dark, the moon shining through the window, she wondered what God had planned for her. Alysia had said that her plans—her very life—might change. Did that mean she and Barry would become partners? Had God directed her to this new friend to help her make that decision? As she thought of Barry, however, she remembered the analogy Alysia had used to describe Peter and Darron. Barry, she knew, was neither the soldier nor the farmer. He was more like a Rhett Butler, turning every situation to his advantage, regardless of the cost in terms of relationships. Oh, he would never be cruel or even dishonest, but he would manage to avoid any association with the cause itself.

When she finally drifted off to sleep, it was Peter who stalked her dreams.

≥∙

It was also Peter who, on Sunday morning, walked into the church and sat down in front of Anna, his hair freshly cut and his white shirt emphasizing his deepening tan. As Anna listened to him sing, she was more confused than ever. It had never occurred to her that Peter attended church anywhere. Darron and Alysia, did not seem surprised, so it apparently was a normal occurrence.

When the fiery message, followed by a long altar call, was over, Peter turned and met Anna eye to eye, but did not smile. He nodded curtly at her, then Darron and Alysia, and left the church.

"Did you know he's going to move away?" Anna asked Darron.

Darron's lips tightened and he seemed to droop like a flower in the sun. "I suppose he will someday. I just don't know what else to do."

"Darron, does Peter have convictions about following Christ the way you and Alysia do?"

"You'd have to ask Peter. It's been so long since we said more than hello and good-bye, I hardly know him anymore. In fact, he's told you things I thought he'd never tell anyone. You just might be good medicine for him."

Chapter Six

While Anna was trying to cut the tallest weeds in the yard with a grass whip that she had bought, Peter drove up. Anna saw him take ladders and a toolbox from the back of his truck and come toward the house.

"Am I too late?" he called.

"I think we can still find something for you to do," she said, glad to see him but embarrassed to admit it, even to herself.

"I was surprised to see you in church yesterday," she said.

"I was surprised to see you, too, so I guess we're even," he answered. He set up a ladder to reach the top windows and began pulling away the old sealer and replacing it with soft, pliable glazing. "Are you going to try to make the old place energy efficient?"

"I told Darron I didn't want to change things too much. As long as the doors and windows keep out the weather, I would be happy to keep them."

Just then Peter glanced through the window and caught sight of the quilt on the bed. "Alysia gave you that, didn't she?"

"Yes. It's perfect for the room, and she does lovely work."

"I can't argue with that. She's a good wife to Darron, always has been."

Anna waited, saying nothing, but Peter did not continue, so she returned to cutting weeds. After half an hour, she slumped on the porch, her nails broken and small blisters forming between her thumbs and forefingers.

Peter came down the ladder and sat beside her. "I suppose you don't do a lot of physical labor."

Anna smiled. "Well, whirling and twirling in front of a camera can be tiring, but I admit it's nothing like whacking weeds."

"Got to be done, though. Fact is, the copperheads have probably already nested around here somewhere. They love old deserted places where there's an old porch to get under and weeds to hide in."

Anna glared at him. "I don't scare easily, Mister, and I'm not afraid of snakes." A sudden movement at her feet, however, caused her to gasp and jump up on the porch. When she saw the small twig in Peter's hand, she pummeled him soundly on the shoulders while he laughed and covered his head with his arms.

"You're just plain mean," she said, knowing that if she had not boasted, he would not have been tempted.

"True, true. I ought to be staked out on an anthill and have honey dripped on my nose. I'm serious about the snakes, though. Be careful working around here. They love any old quiet spot like this away from the road."

"I've been thinking I might bring the motor home over here," Anna said. "It would save miles on the rental car, but I hate to leave the hollow. It's so beautiful and peaceful there." Suddenly she remembered her discovery. "Peter, come and see what I found! I had forgotten all about this." She hurried to the back of the house and further down the hill to a place where a rock ledge protruded from the ground. A thin trickle of water came from below it and traveled downward on a path devoid of soil.

"I'll bet this was your granny's water supply," he said.

Anna nodded. "I used to bring the dipper from the house and come here to get drinks because the water was so cold. There was a pool then. I think there's a creek down there where the springwater runs." She stooped down and let the cold water run on her hands, relieving the burning of the irritated flesh. When she stood up, she said, "I hate to say it, but I think I'm done for the day."

"Would you like to go exploring?" Peter said. "I'd like to show you some more of the mountains before you head for the flatland. Let's go on a hike over on my land."

"That sounds great. I usually do a lot of walking and running, but since I left New York, my life is all turned around. I could use some good exercise."

Peter followed her car to the motor home where she put on jogging shoes and together they started out along the road, which was little more than a two-lane track. Gradually, the track became a path and, within twenty minutes, they were hiking up a steep grade on which a thin layer of soil hosted mosses, short spring vegetation, and an occasional white pine.

Anna was exhilarated by the exercise, especially when combined with the beauty of the landscape. She and Peter spoke only occasionally when he pointed out a tiny flower or spectacular view. All the while, she sensed they were moving up and up.

She took great deep breaths of the morning air, glad that she had resisted the temptation to begin smoking in order to stay thin. At this moment, however, her modeling career seemed faraway and almost unimportant. For the first time, she realized with wonder and amazement that everything before her was the product of the creative mind of God, the God whom she could now say was her friend.

"You should be here in the fall," Peter said. "The hardwoods turn and it looks like the mountains are on fire. The air is different and the earth gives off an aroma. You can hardly walk by here without stepping on a squirrel." A few minutes later he said, "You really ought to be here in the winter when the tree cover is gone and you can see the way the land swells and rolls. Even when there's only light snow, the bareness and wildness of it all is like a sweet sadness. There's nothing like the mountains in winter."

For a change, Anna just listened. The unfamiliar terrain was demanding, and she needed to concentrate on her footing, but hearing him talk in such a relaxed way was refreshing. When he started to say, "You should be here in the middle of the summer. . ." she couldn't help but laugh.

"Why don't you just say it's always beautiful here?"

Peter offered the crinkling grin that Anna had not seen since their first morning together. "I do love this place," he admitted.

"How can you think of leaving, Peter? You'd be so unhappy. You know you'd be longing for this sight with every change of the seasons."

"Well, we don't always get to have what we want. Anyway, this will be here if I want to come back."

They were approaching a summit where a tall pine pointed straight to the sun. When they got there, Peter leaned against it and said, "This is the middle of my property. I bought my first two acres when I was still in high school and I've kept on adding to it every time something came available. It's one of the few things I've done right in my life."

Anna surveyed the timbered hills before her, over two hundred acres according to Peter. "Do you plan to build anything on it?"

"Under the right conditions, I would put in a few homes, but it won't happen soon. There aren't any roads and there aren't any plans for them, either. Besides, I don't have any investment capital. For now, I just like the idea that it's here."

Anna sat down, feeling the effects of the exercise and the thinning air.

"Have we come too far?" Peter asked. "I can carry you piggyback if you're too tired." He sat down beside her, his back against the tree.

"I just need a few minutes to catch my breath. I get a lot of exercise, but it's all on cement."

"You're strong. You weren't even winded when we got here, and it's a pretty rough climb."

"I have to stay in good shape. These last few days have been a lazy time for me."

"I figured all you had to do was stand around and look pretty. Tell me about your job."

Hearing her life's work referred to as a job rankled Anna, but she did not comment on it. "Modeling is very diversified. Most people are familiar with the real stars who get the big, name-brand television commercial accounts, but there's a lot more to the industry than that. Usually, those girls start working at fourteen or fifteen, some as young as twelve, and in five years they disappear. When their faces aren't new anymore, they're out of the business. I didn't begin that way. I went to a modeling school and started out small and worked into a good, steady career."

"But what do you do all day long?"

Anna hesitated, then burst out laughing. "I stand around and look pretty! I have my picture taken all day long. Sometimes I do department store fashion shows or some other kind of live product demonstration. I work through an agency and Barry Carlson is my agent. He's responsible for making sure that I have enough work to keep bread on the table. He screens the offers, and I make the final selection, now that I don't have to take just any job I can get."

"Do you just model clothes?"

"I've done makeup ads and posed with dishes and pots and pans. Like I said, anytime you see a picture of someone in a magazine or on a billboard or a package, it's a paid model like me. I get lots of work because I'm versatile and I'm not temperamental."

"And you left it all to wander in the woods and think philosophical thoughts."

"Barry has asked me to go into partnership with him," she said. "I don't know if that's what I want. Then, on top of that, I'm seeing a whole new facet of life—a spiritual dimension—that I still don't understand. When my lawyer wrote to me about Granny's property, it seemed like a good time to take a vacation and sort out the pieces of my life."

"You didn't mention any man being one of those pieces."

"Well, there's Barry."

"But do you love him?"

"I don't know. Maybe I could."

Peter offered a small, derisive laugh. "If you have to get away from some-body to decide if you love him or not, it can't be too great. You're too smart and too determined to settle for less than exactly what you want, Anna. I don't know another woman in the world who would do what you've done. Don't sell yourself short. I don't know Barry, but if it were me—" He stopped talking abruptly and pulled a candy bar from his pocket and began to eat.

Anna stared at him. "What?"

He shrugged. "I guess I'm not the one to give advice about love." He stood up and pointed to the east. "We'd better head back. Looks like a shower's coming up on us."

As Anna stood up, she noticed something in the sky. "What is that bird, Peter? It looks like it's coming right toward us."

He moved behind her, looking over her shoulder.

"It is. Watch a minute."

Larger and larger the bird loomed in their vision, the filtered sun glint-ing on waxy feathers and giving the creature the stark contrasts of renais-sance art. Anna's heart beat faster and she stood absolutely still as the bird, a golden eagle, pounded the air in its steady course. When she thought it would surely smash into them, it veered upward, spiraling into the sky until it was lost from her view.

"There's a nest just on that next ridge," Peter said. "I've been watching him for years. He doesn't like us on his turf. He knows we're too big to fight, but maybe not too big to scare."

"So beautiful," Anna murmured, "such color and grace. I will never for-get this moment, and I promise I will never again go to a zoo as long as I live."

Peter laughed. "Just seeing one makes you feel like you can fly, too, doesn't it?"

"Yes, yes!" Anna exclaimed, turning to him. "I just felt I could reach up and follow him along to the sky."

"They have more character than bald eagles, in my opinion. It's a real gift, to be able to see one. I've seen the adults maybe only ten times over the years I've had this property. I'm glad you got to see it. . .with me."

Anna was subdued. "I can't explain the feeling of watching that bird, Peter. It has a special meaning for me. Just one more thing to think about, I guess."

Going down was nearly as difficult as going up, and Anna could feel the breeze stiffen and cool from minute to minute. Within fifteen minutes, the sky had darkened and in ten more, the first drops of rain fell.

"We'll take a little detour here and find some shelter," Peter said. "Sometimes these little cloudbursts bring lightning, too."

Anna's heart quickened. At the first peal of thunder, she felt a rising panic. She did not like storms. Peter seemed to think she was some sort of superwoman, but she knew her own secrets. In small things, like snakes and thunder, she was often afraid. Perhaps it was one reason she had chosen city living.

Soon Anna could hear the thunder rolling peal upon peal in the distance. On the horizon, the lightning flashed. She wanted to ask Peter to hurry, but he seemed rather unconcerned. *Maybe he's used to being out in the woods in the rain,* Anna thought, *but I'm not.*

"Peter, I think. . .I'd like. . ."

"This way," he said and they left the game trail they had been following, crept through some laurel, and entered a small cave. Immediately, the thunder was outside instead of all around, and Anna felt safe.

The serious rain began then, smacking the laurel leaves and running together down the slopes. The storm came hard and fast and the wind blew, but the cave opening was protected. Peter and Anna sat side by side, their knees drawn up to their chins, backs to the cave's interior wall, and catching glimpses of the lightning through the laurel bushes.

Peter did not ask Anna if she was afraid. He could feel that she was now relaxed, and if she was not enjoying being here, at least she was content to wait. He was disturbed by an overwhelming desire to draw her close, to tell her she was safe and that he would always protect her and help her through this kind of unsettling time in her life. But how could he, knowing himself as he did? He had nothing to offer her, despite his obvious boastful show of property. She did not need land or money. She needed a man, as he had said to her, who would be there for her when she needed him.

He thought back over the past few days and wondered when he had first begun to sense that he cared deeply for her. Was it seeing her in need or seeing her in control? Was it the fragrance of her hair in the heat of the sun as she cried against his chest? Was it the sincerity in her voice as she spoke of her relationship with God? Was it simply that she loved everyone she met? Or was it only this moment, sharing the wonder of the earth with her as the wind brought the aroma of rain and leaves to them? All he knew for sure was that he dared not look at her.

"You're very quiet," Anna said.

"When I don't have anything to say, I don't talk."

"I think that may not be entirely true. I think you have a lot to say that you've never said. Maybe nobody listens?" she asked, turning toward him.

"Maybe," he mumbled, resisting the urge to meet her eyes. He willed her to keep talking, to somehow say for him what he could not say himself, to discover his secrets without having to form the words in his own mouth. But she was quiet; the storm was over.

They left the cave and were greeted with showers from the laurel leaves as they passed through them. By the time they reached the hollow, they were thoroughly drenched.

"We might as well have walked in the rain," Anna said, wringing water from her sweatshirt. "Would you mind building a fire for me before you go? I don't have any heat in this vehicle." She was beginning to shiver. The sun had not returned and she dreaded the prospect of a gray, cold afternoon.

"You grab some dry clothes," Peter said, "and come with me. We'll dry off at my place and get something to eat."

Anna was too uncomfortable to argue. She shoved a change of clothes into a plastic bag and climbed into Peter's truck. In minutes, they were pulling up to a log home, set in a small clearing. There was no lawn, only young trees planted around the house, apparently to replace those lost during construction.

"Peter is this your house? It's lovely!"

"And I've got hot water."

"Hot water? I never realized how much I could miss it! I've got a shower in the motor home, but not enough fuel for the water heater."

Anna stayed in the shower until Peter noticed steam coming from under the bathroom door. He built a fire in the fireplace, and after Anna was dressed, she sat cross-legged on the floor in front of the fire, engulfed by the big, cowl-necked sweater he had seen on her the other day.

Anna was pleasantly surprised by the interior of the cabin. She had half-expected to see traps and flintlock rifles hanging on the walls, but the place was outfitted with strong, masculine furniture in good fabrics that were not too heavy for the room. There were no curtains, but the windows were made of double insulated glass and there were louvered shutters that could be closed against the sun. A collection of portraits was grouped on the wall above the sofa, and a few knickknacks, mostly small wooden carvings, softened the stark log walls.

Peter, now in a sweat suit and wool socks, put one more log on the fire, then sat down beside Anna.

"Is that your family?" she asked, pointing to the portraits.

"Uh-huh. That's Mamma, her name's Audrey; that's my sister Rose, and Darron and Alysia, you know. Some other odds and ends of relatives."

She smiled. "I like your house."

"That makes two of us."

"Will you rent it out when you leave?"

Peter almost said, "Leave where?" then remembered that he had made the commitment. He shrugged.

"I don't know. I guess I haven't thought that far ahead. I don't think I'd like to have anybody else living here."

Anna spied a rocker, obviously of some age, with a quilt draped over the back. She got up and went toward it, then paused. "Is it all right if I sit in this chair or is it just for looks?"

Peter smiled. "One thing I don't have is stuff that's just for looks. That's one of Alysia's quilts, by the way. The rocker was my granny's. Mamma gave it to me when I built the place."

Anna settled into the chair, pulling it closer to the fire and wrapping the quilt around her shoulders. She thought of Barry's expensive apartment, its white wool carpet immaculate, the windows offering a view of the city, the kitchen that was never used, the custom-made sofa. It was gorgeous and tasteful, but Anna knew she could never go there in wet boots. Of course, in her other life, wet boots were not a problem.

Gazing at the fire, she thought of a conversation she had had with Barry when she had been looking for a new apartment and suggested she might like a fireplace.

"A fireplace?" he had said, looking at her as though she were from outer space. "I'd have to redo the whole place if it had a fireplace in it. Besides, they're dirty. There's one at the club and somebody's always running through with an ash can. You're such an impossible romantic sometimes. Be practical."

It was good advice, Anna knew, but sometimes hard to take. She had to make a conscious effort to remain independent. It was easy for her to give herself to others, even to Barry. She only hoped that when the right time came, she would be able to put aside her deliberate separateness and form the kind of working relationship she imagined love could build.

❧

"Anna? Anna?" Peter was gently shaking her shoulder. Her head was at an odd angle, her neck stiff. "You'd better wake up. You'll break your neck sleeping in that chair."

Anna willed herself awake. "It must have been the fire." Her voice sounded faraway. "How long have I been asleep?"

"About an hour. I hated to wake you, but I was afraid you'd suffer if you stayed in that position too long."

She rubbed her neck. "I think I already have, but it was worth it." She walked to the window and looked outside to see a steady drizzle blanketing the late afternoon sun. "What a day!" she said.

"I like a day like this once in a while," Peter said. "It puts things in perspective. And it's a good day to bake cookies." In the kitchen, separated from the living area only by a breakfast bar, he was pulling a sheet of chocolate chip cookies from the oven.

"I thought I smelled them," Anna said, joining him at the kitchen table for hot coffee and warm cookies, "but I thought it must have been part of a dream."

"Ah, wait until you see what we're having for supper."

"What's it called?"

"Bologna cordon bleu."

After sandwiches and what Anna felt were far too many cookies, Peter made popcorn in a wire basket over the fire. Together they looked through a photo album filled with snapshots of mountain scenes, his friends, and his family. When Anna glanced at the window again, she saw stars shining in a clear sky.

"I'd better go, Peter," she said reluctantly.

"Why?"

"I. . .I don't know. Just because that's what one is supposed to say, I guess. Shouldn't I go?"

"Back to your old, dark, cold place?" His closeness to her as they shared the photo album was even more intense than in the cave. Could she possibly not know how much he wanted her?

Abruptly, Anna closed the album and stood up.

"Peter, take me back, please. I. . .I wouldn't want to do anything tonight that I might be sorry for tomorrow. I have so many decisions to make these next few days." She felt she was beginning to babble, but couldn't stop herself. "I can't let the circumstances of the day keep me from thinking clearly. And there's work to do and we hardly know each other. It's nothing you've done, but I have this idea about marriage, and I can't stay here, Peter, please."

On all the nights and afternoons and mornings when Barry had suggested she go to bed with him, she had never behaved so immaturely. She had always been ready with a witty remark and a clever dodge. Was it because those times had held no temptations for her?

Peter only said, "Well, have you got plenty of blankets? It will be cold tonight."

Anna nodded while she picked up her bag of wet clothing.

Peter took it from her hand. "I'll hang these out on the line for you. You can get them the next time you come over."

"Thank you," she whispered, for the kindness, and for the understanding shown by his open-ended invitation.

Peter drove her to the hollow. He opened the motor home's door and looked inside before standing away, allowing her to enter. "I'll see you in the morning," he said, not waiting for an invitation this time.

Anna nodded. "I have an idea, Peter," she said. "I'm so pleased with the change that came over Granny's room when Alysia's quilt was laid out. I want to find some nice things to go in the house—a few pieces of furniture and some wall hangings—just so that, when I get ready to leave, it won't seem like I'm leaving behind an empty shell."

"Anna, is that sensible? If you leave the place unoccupied, it would be an invitation to vandals and thieves."

"No, it's ridiculous. It's the most foolish thing I've ever done in my life, but I want to do it anyway. While Alysia and I were at the library I saw pictures of old houses like Granny's. . .like mine. Alysia said there are lots of antiques around here and that we might be able to find some things that would look right in the house without making too large of an investment."

"If that's what you want. Has Darron said anything to you yet about the contract work?"

"I'll see him tomorrow before he goes to work. I'm going to take Alysia shopping with me after the children leave for school."

"I'll find you there," Peter said.

"Don't tell me you like shopping?" Anna said skeptically.

Peter wondered if he dared say he would do anything in order to spend time with her. No, she was not ready for it, and he knew in spite of his longing, he could not make a commitment to her. He said good night and drove away, scolding himself for asking her to give more to him than he had a right to have, and in despair because he knew he could never rightfully claim her as his own. Yet, like a drugged man, he could not say no to spending time with her, talking to her, or just looking at her.

ॐ

Alone in his own house, he wondered if Anna were as lonely as he was. The moonlight through the window in his bedroom fell like a beacon on the closet door, and, in an impulsive moment, Peter threw the door wide open, dragged out a dusty leather case, and opened it. There might yet be a way to keep a part of her for himself.

Chapter Seven

"Peter is coming here?" Darron asked as Anna joined him at his tiny kitchen table for coffee.

"That's what he said," replied Anna.

"Miracles still happen," he said as he got up and pulled on his cap. He picked up a large lunch box and Anna tried not to invade their privacy as he and Alysia said good-bye at the door.

"This thing between you and Darron and Peter, just how bad is it?" Anna asked Alysia. "Or maybe it's none of my business."

Alysia looked uncomfortable. "I don't think it matters much, but I can't really explain it all, either. Darron and I knew that Peter would be mad when we started dating and then got married, but we thought he'd get over it, especially after we had little Wilford and then Emily. But it's like he avoids us more and more as the years go by. Darron has quit trying to mend the fence because it just seems to drive Peter further away. Darron loves him to pieces. It just breaks his heart that Peter won't visit."

"Well, all I know is he said he'd be here. Oh, there's his truck. Do you suppose he was just waiting for Darron to leave?"

"I wouldn't be surprised, though he barely speaks to me." She smiled broadly, a twinkle in her eye. "I just think he's crazy about you, Anna Giles, and he's going to do whatever he has to do to be with you. What about you? Do you like him?"

"Oh, Alysia, don't be silly. He's been wonderful to me, but I certainly didn't come here looking for romance."

"Nobody has to look for romance. It's everywhere. You've just got to reach out and grab it when it flits by." She went to the door to greet Peter and offer him breakfast.

❧

The three took Anna's car; Alysia insisted on sitting in the back. On the front seat between Anna and Peter lay a list of yard sales, flea markets, and antique gallery addresses.

"This is going to be a shopping spree to be remembered for years to come," Anna said, laughing. "The boost in Tennessee's economy this week will make headlines."

Alysia tapped Peter's shoulder. "What did you put in the trunk?" she asked.

"Camera equipment," he said curtly.

In the rearview mirror, Anna saw Alysia's startled expression. "Alysia? Are you all right?"

Alysia nodded, glanced quickly at Peter, then at Anna, but said nothing.

As the two women darted in and out of shops, turned over needlework pieces, and examined pottery and carved wood, Peter followed along like a puppy. Around his neck hung a camera that Anna knew was expensive and versatile. From time to time, she watched him change lenses and filters and knew that he was at least a very good amateur, and probably more. Alysia was too caught up in the shopping to be aware of Peter's constant photographing of them and the scenes about them, but Anna knew. She also knew Peter did not want her to pose and so she ignored him.

Anna found some furniture she liked and made arrangements to pick it up later with Peter's truck.

"I told you I'd come in handy," he said as they ate hot dogs at a roadside park.

"My mother used to say if you can't be decorative, be useful," Anna said.

"Oh, Anna, you're beautiful," Alysia said. "Isn't she, Peter?"

Peter smiled and took a big bite of his hot dog.

"Darron says the electrical contractor is going to start on the house early next week. Somebody's coming to dig a well the day after tomorrow and then the plumbers will start. Darron thinks the old pantry off the kitchen will make a good bathroom, and that will save tearing up too much of the house."

The easy camaraderie of the group made Anna wonder what all the fuss had been about. This was a normal way for friends and family to behave. *Alysia must be overreacting to Peter's moods,* she reasoned. However, when they were alone in the ladies' room at a rest stop, Alysia said, "I've been dying to tell you! This is the first time Peter has had his camera out in the open for at least five years! I'm telling you, Anna, there's something going on here. You've changed him."

"Why would he not take pictures? He seems to be quite good at it."

"You will have to ask him that," Alysia said firmly. "I've probably blabbed too much already."

When Anna had finally made all the purchases for the house that she could possibly justify, plus a few things to take to friends in New York, they called it a day and drove back to Alysia's house. Anna received the biggest hug Alysia's expanding abdomen would allow, and Peter took his equipment and headed for his truck.

"When do we get to see the prints?" Anna asked.

"Maybe never," Peter said. "Mostly I shoot for my own enjoyment."

"A true artist," Anna said.

"You think photography is an art?"

"Of course!" she answered. "A good photographer is just as creative as a painter or sculptor. I've had photos done that, when I saw the finished product, I could hardly believe it was me. A photographer can alter a whole situation by changing the angle of the shot a few degrees or by using a different light. I don't know how they do it, but I do appreciate it."

Anna saw the dust still clinging to the camera bag. "Alysia said you haven't done any photography for a long time. Why not?"

"Maybe there was nothing worth photographing. . .until today. Listen, it's early. Come to my place and have supper with me, or at least let me take you out."

"I need to go back to the motor home and deposit some of my treasure. Follow me, and we'll decide when we get there."

When Anna approached the hollow, she was startled to see another car there, one she recognized. It was Barry's white Ferrari. A hilarious image of the low-riding sports car, bumping along over the rough track, filled her mind. Barry would be fuming.

"I can't imagine how. . ." She got out of the car and went toward the motor home. Suddenly the door burst open and Barry bounded to the ground in front of her.

"Darling, where have you been? I've been waiting here for hours, bored to death. How can you stand it?" He grabbed her and kissed her.

Peter watched from his truck, knowing at once that the man embracing Anna was Barry Carlson. He did, then, love her enough to follow her and he would ask her to return to a life Peter could never be part of. Instead of shutting off the engine, Peter hit the accelerator and drove back the way he had come.

"Who's that?" Barry demanded.

"Peter McCulley. This is his land. He helped me when I first arrived and—"

"Great spot for a chalet, if the road were improved," Barry said, looking around. "Some trees would have to go, of course."

"Barry, how did you find me?"

"An odd set of coincidences, Anna. I stopped at that Sugarlands place to ask for directions to Memphis, and when they learned I was from New York, they said another New Yorker was staying in the neighborhood in a motor home. I knew it had to be you, especially when the guy said she had great legs."

"But how did you find your way here?" Anna tried to hide her disappointment at the fact that Barry had not actually been looking for her, but had only been passing through town and bumped into her accidentally.

"Well, this guy said the New Yorker had been seen with a former employee and thought that you might be camped here on his property, so I gave it a shot. Just my luck! One chance in a thousand, and I come through. I tell you, I am truly amazing."

They went into the motor home, sat down, and Anna showed Barry some things she had bought during the day. "They're for the house, Barry. I found it. I found my granny's house. Would you like to see it?"

Barry waved the idea away with a slim hand. "Not especially. Are you going to sell?"

"I don't plan to. I just want to keep the place. It holds so many memories."

"Well, that's ridiculous. You know it isn't practical. It will degenerate in no time at all, sitting empty. . .or will you turn it into income property?"

Anna thought of Peter and remembered him saying he couldn't imagine anyone else living in his house. Who could live in Granny Huddlestone's home and do it justice?

"I don't have all the details worked out yet, but it will happen. How long can you stay? I've missed you!"

"I was hoping to hear you say that," he said, "but I was also hoping to hear you say you'd be coming back to the big town. The question is, how long do you plan to stay here? I've got people clamoring for you, Anna. You're very popular in the district, you know."

"They'll be there when I get back. I need a little more time, Barry."

He sighed. "Time, Anna, time is what we have so little of. We don't get younger, now do we, any of us? Have you decided on the partnership offer?"

Anna hesitated. "Barry, tell me exactly what you have in mind."

"A full partnership, dear, fifty-fifty, and you don't have to invest a cent."

"Why not?"

"Just think of it as a gift."

Anna watched his face, looking for some show of emotion. She had hoped for some indication that he had been considering marriage, that he would share the business with her as his wife.

"Do you love me, Barry?"

"Anna, of course I do!" he said, holding his arms wide. "I've always loved you. I've told you that hundreds of times."

"I mean, do you really love me? What if I couldn't work any more, or if I weren't a model at all? What if I were a little shop girl with fat ankles? Would you love me?"

"Oh, don't be stupid. You are what you are and I am what I am. This offer won't wait forever, Anna. I've tried to be gracious and understanding, but Phil Curtis is after me to get in, too. He's offered me a million five for what I'm offering you for free, Anna—free! I don't often give things away, you know. Give me an answer and then I can get on with the paperwork."

"I. . .I just don't know." How could she make him understand she wanted more than a business partnership?

Barry babbled on. "Well, you've got to stop prowling around in the woods like some demented scout leader, ruining your skin with insect bites and too much sun. I saw Larry Tulloch the other day and he said to get you back into town immediately, even begged me to tell him where you'd gone so he could come and see you personally. He has a marvelous contract waiting for you that involves the Bahamas in January. And Albert Haines was hanging over the bar at Sherry's party last night. He thinks he can get you into daytime television."

"I don't want to do television," Anna said flatly.

"You don't say no to Albert, dear. You can have the job on a plate, or you could have had it if you had been there last night. Opportunity is a temporary thing, love."

She nodded. "I agree." She felt cheated. Seeing Barry's car had given her so much hope. The experience was turning out to be something like buying a box of cereal to get the prize and finding it to be much smaller than the one pictured on the box.

"I'm exhausted, Anna. Why don't we go into town, have dinner, and find a room at one of those lovely hotels we tourists like so much?"

"I thought you were on your way to Memphis?"

"Oh, Memphis, that can wait," he said, moving closer to her. "I have to get this buying trip out of the way as soon as possible. Can you believe I left Sherry's party half-drunk and drove to Charlotte to make an appointment at a mill this morning?" He laughed uproariously. "Life is outrageous sometimes. Then I decided as long as I was on the road, I'd go over to Memphis and see Arlen, you know, the guy who does those shirts with the painted designs? We handled that spread for some magazine; I forget which. And here I am. Are we going out?"

"You didn't really come to see me, did you?"

"I'm here, aren't I? Don't pout; it's so teenage. Anna, isn't there anything to drink in this place? I've got to have something."

"Orange juice, bottled."

A look of disgust covered his face. "Here you are in the place where they make some of the finest whiskey in the world, and all you have is orange juice. Come on, come on," he begged. "Let's get out of here. I'm becoming claustrophobic."

"I think you'd better go ahead without me," Anna said. "If you have other offers on the partnership, then I think you should accept them. You accused me of being impractical, Barry, but you can't refuse a cash offer for half of the agency. I'll be happy to continue working for you, though."

Barry was growing impatient, something that didn't take long to happen. "I won't take no for an answer, Anna. You must come in with me." He pulled an envelope from his pocket and unfolded the paper inside. "Here's the contract. I had my attorney draw it up, but you had already left town by the time he delivered it to me. Just sign, and stop playing hard to get."

"What's the hurry?" Anna asked, irritated. "There's something you aren't telling me, Barry." She took the contract from his hand and began reading.

He rolled his eyes and sighed, "It's you, Anna. The reason I want you in the partnership is that with you comes a host of people who like you. Let's face it. Phil Curtis has cash, but nothing else. Everyone in New York— well, maybe not everyone—loves you. You'd bring a hundred times as much business my way as Curtis would. I could expand. We could expand, I mean. We could run the biggest agency in New York. No one could touch us."

"That is a monstrous exaggeration," Anna said. "I know I'm popular, but certainly not that popular." As she scanned the paper, she caught sight of the phrase "credible individual." She read a bit further, then let the paper fall into her lap.

"Well, as usual, you've told half the truth. Why didn't you just tell me you needed someone with good credit to underwrite your debts, Barry? You've mortgaged the agency practically out of existence, haven't you? What's the matter? Wouldn't Phil Curtis settle for anything less than buying you out? Where are all your rich friends?" she asked, her voice rising. "Are you so near the edge that you have to come to me, nothing more than a working model, to bail you out?"

Barry jumped up. "You're missing out on something big, Anna. And remember, if you don't sign, it will be very tough for you once you get back to town. You think you can get by on your personality? Well, personality doesn't print. You're at the worst possible age for a model, dear, too old to do the glamour features and too young to pose for false teeth cleaners and vitamin supplements. The years ahead are going to be lean, and I can make them leaner than you imagine. Or you can go into business with me and we'll both get along just fine."

"This is all I've ever been to you, isn't it, Barry? I'm your safety net. You knew it the day you signed me up. I am New York's biggest fool, next to you."

Barry reached out to slap her and she lunged against him, afraid, furious, and humiliated.

"I'm sick of your games, Anna," Barry said, grabbing her shoulders. "I haven't made this awful trip for nothing. I'll get some satisfaction, one way or another." He pushed her down and she was amazed at how strong he was. She could not push him away, and the touch of his mustache against her cheek as he pulled her to him felt like wire.

❧

Peter drove furiously along the dirt road, unsure whether to go home or just keep driving, out of Gatlinburg, out of Tennessee. This would be as good a time as any to leave. He had his camera with him, and, trapped inside, the most beautiful day he could remember in many years.

If only I could tell her everything. He knew she would understand him and be conciliatory, but he also knew that it would change nothing. It was not her acceptance he wanted. That would only make the leaving harder.

The sight of her in Barry's arms had been like a bullet to his brain. Was he destined to spend all his life loving people who were beyond his reach? He braked to a halt, laid his head on the steering wheel, and fought the despair that rose in him like a sickness. *I have to try. I have to try just once more.* In a rush, he wheeled the truck around and drove like a madman toward the hollow.

≈

"Barry, don't do this," Anna begged. "We've been friends for so long."

"You know you've led me on for years," he growled. "I won't take it anymore. You and your cleverness, always just out of reach. It could have been different between us, but you had to have your own way." He slapped her, and her scream pierced the thin walls of the motor home as Peter came walking up.

The movement of the vehicle told Peter she was struggling and he bolted for the door. In a lightning-fast movement, he jumped inside, tore Barry away from Anna, and tossed him headlong out the door, then jumped outside himself.

"Stay there!" he ordered Anna, who now cowered on the sofa.

"Keep her!" Barry shouted, as he pulled at his shirt and walked toward his car. "Where I come from, there's one like her on every corner."

The words were like a bomb in Peter's brain. He shot forward and wrenched Barry away from the car door, taking grim pleasure in the look of terror that crossed the perfectly shaven and moisturized face. Grabbing Barry by his designer tie, Peter punched him soundly in the nose and felt the satisfying gush of blood on his knuckles. Still holding the tie as Barry howled, he pulled out his bandanna-style handkerchief and shoved it in Barry's collar.

"Wipe your nose," he said, and opened the car door and pushed Barry inside.

Barry spewed profanity as he pulled away, but Peter wasn't listening. He went inside where Anna was wiping her eyes and holding the contract in her lap.

"Are you all right?"

She nodded. "I thought we were at least friends. He never wanted anything from me except what was of personal benefit to him." The sadness in her voice was so profound that Peter found tears in his own eyes. "I don't know what to do," she said, looking at Peter. "If you hadn't come. . .why did you come back?"

"I don't know, exactly. Something in me just said, 'Go back and try to take her away from him.' I love you, Anna. I love you with all of me that there is, which isn't much, but I would do anything for you." Quietly, Peter encircled her with his arms and let her rest there as she tried to make peace with the fact that the most significant relationship in her life was over, and that a man she had known for only a few days was declaring his love for her.

"Take me somewhere," Anna said at last, "anywhere, just away from the motor home. I want to open the doors and windows and let the place air out. I don't even know if I can sleep here tonight. Barry has just ruined everything."

"He's definitely a spoiler," Peter said, "but I did a little damage myself. He's not quite as pretty as he was when he came here."

Anna smiled in spite of her heavy heart. "You're better than a dose of medicine," she said.

"And easier to take. Come on out when you get changed and we'll go out to eat."

In fresh clothing and with a hot meal inside her, Anna once again felt that she could carry on with her life, though the terror of Barry's attack continued to haunt her. The physical threat was less offensive to her than the betrayal, yet she chided herself for believing for so long that he could treat her differently than he treated everyone else. What was it her granny used to say? "The fruit doesn't fall far from the tree."

As they left the restaurant, Peter said, "Do you feel like going to a place I like, here in town? It's kind of quiet and different."

Anna nodded, wanting only to be cared for.

"It's sort of a tourist trap," Peter said as they parked in the lot of a place called Christus Gardens, "but there's a part of it I like." They bypassed the tour of wax figurines illustrating scenes from Scripture and went into a courtyard where pools and vegetation softened the patio area. Peter took Anna's hand and guided her to a small bench. The place was empty except for the two of them.

"I know you were surprised to see me in church, Anna, and I'm not sure exactly why I haven't been able to share with you my true feelings about my faith. I suppose it's pride. That is a problem for me sometimes."

"Only sometimes?"

He smiled at her, knowing she understood his hesitancy. He pointed across the courtyard toward a statue representing Jesus, placed against the far wall. "Look at that for a minute," he said. Then he got up and, taking Anna with him, they walked to another corner of the courtyard. When she looked at the statue, she saw that the gaze of the figure seemed to have followed them.

"It doesn't matter where you go," said Peter, "the statue is always looking at you. When I was little, we lived in a neighborhood just about like the one Darron and Alysia live in now. I used to run to the woods whenever I could, though. We went to church every Sunday and I liked going. One day I got down on my knees beside the creek, and I promised God He could do whatever He wanted with me and that I would always try to live by His rules. I said I believed what the preacher had said about Jesus dying for my sins. I was glad for that, I told God, and said thanks a lot. I was looking forward to seeing Him in heaven someday. I think I was eight or nine then. First thing you know, my daddy died. Mamma said it wasn't God punishing us, that everybody dies and we weren't being singled out, but it was hard for me."

Anna listened, sensing how hard it was for Peter to speak. All the while, his eyes met the eyes of the statue.

"I lived clean and right, Anna, all through high school and college, but I never felt like it was a two-way street. God didn't seem to be doing anything in return. I didn't understand. I knew I was forgiven and accepted, but where was He? After a few years, it just seemed like what had been so important when I was a kid wasn't that important anymore.

"Then one day I came here and found this place. I saw that statue and I thought, He's watching, there's no doubt about that. He always has been. The question is, is that a good thing or a bad thing? Is He pleased or not? He sees it all, but does it make Him happy? I don't know.

"When I heard you talk about your decision, I just wanted to feel that close and personal to God again. I think sometimes one reason I keep close to the creek banks is because I want to find that feeling that's gotten lost over the years."

"How lonely you must be," Anna whispered. "You don't think of that gaze as being a look of love and concern and approval?"

"It could be," Peter said. "I hope it is. I keep trying. But I keep thinking that maybe behind the look, He's saying, 'Yes, Peter McCulley, don't think you've got Me fooled. I'm watching you. I know what you really are.'"

"And what is that, Peter? What are you?"

He shrugged. "I'm a not-so-young-anymore man with no visible means of support."

"That's not what I see." Anna waited until he was looking directly into her eyes, then said, "I see a man with character and principles. . .and pride, who is loved by many people as well as by God."

"Do you love me, Anna?"

Now it was Anna who looked away, wanting to say yes and perhaps heal his pain, but knowing that she could not say it with certainty.

Peter said simply, "Let's go," and in silence they walked back to the truck.

As they drove, Anna's mind raced over the events of the past few days, retracing her emotions as she thought of Peter's sudden involvement in her life. *Do I love him?* she asked herself. *Do I even know what love is?* She knew she needed time to put Barry completely out of her mind before she could begin to think of Peter as anything except a good friend.

Peter interrupted her thoughts. "If you don't want to go back to the motor home tonight, you could go to Darron and Alysia's or come to my place."

"Darron and Alysia hardly have room for their own family. I don't want to inconvenience them. Where are they ever going to put a baby?"

Peter shook his head. "Hang it on a hook, I guess. Darron just doesn't have the cash to get into a bigger place right now, though I know they've been saving. Don't worry. One thing you have to say for Darron and Alysia is that they make do with what they have."

"There's a lot that can be said for those two," Anna said. "Peter, there's more between you and Darron than his marriage to Alysia, isn't there? Alysia told me she realized shortly after her engagement to you that you were not right for each other. Surely you would have known it, too. You wouldn't have wanted her to be unhappy. What is it? What keeps you from enjoying the companionship of your own brother when he obviously worships you?"

"Worships me?" Peter questioned. "Maybe when we were kids, but that was a long time ago."

"Has he done something to you or taken something away from you? Why can't you be the brother to him he wants you to be?"

"I'll tell you why, Anna," Peter said. "It's because I am so jealous of him, I can hardly stand it, and it has nothing to do with Alysia. What I want is not her, but what they have together. Have you watched them? Have you heard the way they talk to each other? There's no place they would rather be than together. That little apartment's a sanctuary to them. They're so happy, and I would give anything, anything I have or ever will have, to find that kind of happiness."

Quietly Anna said, "And do you think I'm the one who will make you that happy? Is it a matter of finding the right person, or is there some other ingredient in their magic formula? I want to know, Peter, because I want the same thing."

"I know how I feel," Peter replied, "and right now, that's all I know."

"My parents had enough money to live as they wished, and they loved each other, but I think there was a restlessness about them. For years I've said I wouldn't settle for anything less than the kind of marriage that Granny Huddlestone used to talk about, and I was waiting for something—fate, I suppose—to make it happen. But now I wonder."

By the time they had reached the hollow, Anna had made up her mind to stay alone, despite Peter's protests.

"Don't worry," she said. "Barry is much more interested in making money than in hassling me. He's halfway to Memphis by now. Come over to the house in the morning if you can, and we'll move all this stuff into it."

"I'll be there," he said.

"You always are," she answered.

Chapter Eight

Anna was up early and, after a breakfast beverage and a swim in the freezing creek water, she drove to the house. The trunk of the car was already loaded with cleaning supplies, and Anna felt a sense of anticipation as she thought of the items she would place in the various rooms of the house.

She arrived at the house, and when Peter got there she was beating the dust out of the cushions of a sofa and chair that were older than she was, but dry and still in good condition.

Anna waved as he came down the hill from the road. Her hair was tied back with a cheap scarf, but she wore a rose-pink linen peasant blouse with an ankle-length batik print skirt. On her feet were sandals. Somehow, the image of housemaid did not imprint on Peter's mind.

"Are you ready for your furniture?" he asked, pointing to the back of his truck.

"Oh, you have it already! I think I'm just about through with the cleaning. Frankly, I'm not much good at it. Come to think of it, I've never kept house. I've lived in apartments and usually hired people to do the little that needed to be done. As a matter of fact, I guess I've never really lived in a home much. I suppose they get pretty dirty when you actually do all your cooking and eating and laundry and everything right there."

Peter laughed. "They do, and if you throw in a couple of kids, the dirt piles up like everything else."

"Come and see what I've done," Anna said, pulling Peter along with her into the house. She showed Peter the dishes she had found, now clean and displayed artfully on a sideboard in the kitchen. The shelves were simple oak slabs, smoothed with years of use and cleaning. In another room was a chest, and inside it were half a dozen tablecloths and some crocheted doilies and lace curtains. Here and there were other remnants of her great-grandmother's life—a cotton dress hung on a hook in the bedroom where there were no closets; a metal washbasin on the porch used for rinsing bare feet covered with garden dust; an ax embedded in a stump overgrown with weeds.

"I wonder what my parents did with her personal things?" Anna said as she and Peter walked through the house. "There must have been papers, photographs, things like that."

"Maybe that lawyer fella knows," Peter said. "If he's got the deed to this place, chances are he knows about the rest of the stuff."

"It hurts to know that my family is gone, Peter. We should have spent more time together. My parents should have saved Granny's things for me, or at least let me see them after she died. It's my fault, too. I was busy with my career and didn't stay as close to my parents as I should have."

"Anna, there's no good in blaming yourself. You did what you could. You did the right thing by coming back here and finding this place. You'll have another family someday and you can share this with them." He took her hands in his and pulled her outside. "Look; I want to show you the pictures I took yesterday."

They scrambled up the hill and Peter spread out about two dozen color snapshots of Anna and Alysia on their shopping spree. Anna laughed at the expressions of delight that Peter had captured, at the weary shoppers with bedraggled hair eating hot dogs in the park, and at the trunk of the car filled to overflowing with household items.

"Let's start taking things inside," Anna said. "I don't want to clean anymore. As long as the spiders are chased away and we aren't leaving footprints in the dirt on the floor, I'm ready to start playing house."

They lugged in wooden footstools, table lamps, kitchen chairs, and a table from Peter's truck, then started on the boxes of decorative things in the trunk of Anna's car. She scurried about the rooms, placing wooden carvings on an old corner shelf, a brass vase on a window ledge, an antique oval picture frame with bubble glass on a living room wall where a nail had been waiting, empty, for more than a dozen years.

"Maybe you'll find a photo of your granny and you can put it in that frame," Peter said.

"Maybe. I wonder if there is a photo of her somewhere."

As they made one more trip to the road, Peter said, "Maybe you could use this other one, if you like it."

He opened the door of the pickup and took out an envelope. Inside was a black-and-white print of Anna sitting in a rocker, her hands together at her chin. She remembered sitting in the chair the day before, pleased with the feel of it, but not noticing that Peter had been busy with his camera.

The photo had a soft quality that emphasized the serene expression on

Anna's face. The light in the shop where the rocker had been purchased had come through several four-paned rustic windows, one of which was captured in the photo. If Anna did not know where the picture had been taken, she would have assumed the setting was a real home.

Silently, she looked at Peter, not knowing what to say. His expression showed his anxiety, and she remembered that Alysia had mentioned that Peter had stopped taking photographs years ago.

She was drawn back to the photograph again, pulled into the emotional aura it presented, even though she herself was the subject. *This is truly art,* Anna thought, *a factual photo that creates a timeless moment so much greater than the actual event.*

Again she looked at Peter. "You printed this, didn't you?"

He nodded. "I've got a darkroom at the house."

Slowly, she shook her head. "I. . .what can I say? I've been photographed by hundreds of people, but never anything like this. Can I really keep it?"

"Yes," he said. He had made the photo for himself, knowing the instant he had seen her relax in the rocker and raise her hands to her face in an unconscious gesture of pleasure, that it was a perfect setting for a perfect subject. He remembered the feeling of excitement as he had focused and shot at least a dozen frames before she became aware of his activities and laughed and waved him away.

"Why did you stop?" Anna asked quietly. "Alysia said you had given up photography, but she wouldn't say why. This is the best work of its kind I've ever seen, Peter, and I work with some very talented people."

"Talent doesn't count for much at the grocery checkout. I haven't had a lot of time for hobbies lately. It just seemed like a good day to get the stuff out."

"Oh, all right, don't tell me if you don't want to," Anna said, frustrated at his tendency to quickly cut off communication. She put the photo back into the envelope.

Peter walked over to her and, as she turned, he said, "I want to, Anna. I wish I could just tell you everything, but I can't."

She nodded. "I'm sorry. It's wrong for me to expect confidences from you. After all, we hardly know each other."

"I know you, Anna," Peter said. "I can't stop thinking about you. I thought for a long time that I was in love with Alysia, and in a way I do love her. She's a wonderful woman, but almost from the minute I met you, I have felt for you what I've never felt for anyone else. Anna, how can

I make you love me, too?"

"Make me love you? I don't think that can happen, Peter. You and Alysia were very close once, but you simply did not love each other. Love is either there or it isn't." She searched his face, wanting to be as honest as she could be without raising false hopes. "I know we're together for a reason. I believe God directed me here, and it's no accident that you've become a part of my life. You're everything a woman could ask for. There's just something that keeps me from saying the words you'd like to hear."

"Just don't say, 'Can we be friends?' That's one thing I don't want to hear."

Anna smiled. "We certainly are more than friends, Peter, much more. You've changed my life forever."

They were interrupted by the arrival of a utility truck. "This the place where we're supposed to bring power?" said the driver, checking a paper on a clipboard.

"Darron must have called them," Anna said. "He seems to be enjoying this project almost as much as I am."

"Darron is good at a lot of things," Peter said.

"Are you proud of him or are you being sarcastic?"

"Both, I guess."

"Take my advice," Anna said. "Don't lose the ones who love you most. A memory—even a good photograph—is never as good as the real thing."

Peter took the last box from the trunk of Anna's car and carried it into the house and set it on the kitchen table. Then they stood on the porch and watched as the line workers established the connection to the house.

Suddenly the man on the ground yelled and jumped sideways. "There are snakes everywhere!" he declared. "You two gonna live in this dump, you better get yourself a pig."

"A pig?" Anna asked. "What's he talking about?"

"Pigs kill the snakes," Peter said, "but if you'd rather, we could get a goose. They kill snakes, too."

"Maybe I should try to get some more of the grass cut. I'd hate to have any of the workers who are going to be around here get bitten."

"Once people start working here, the snakes will catch on to what's happening and leave. If it makes you feel better, though, I'll get a gasoline-powered trimmer and mow the tall stuff."

"Would you? I'd feel much better about it. Promise me you'll be careful."

"I promise. Are you going to be here for the rest of the day?"

"I expect Darron will be by after work, so I'll stay at least until he gets here."

After Peter left, Anna went back into the house, trying to imagine how it would look when lighted. She remembered the kerosene lamps that had been there when she was very young and recalled the pungent odor of the fuel. Sometimes, as Granny lighted a lamp, she would sing a song like "This Little Light of Mine" or "Thy Word Is a Lamp Unto My Feet," which had no meaning whatsoever to Anna but were fun to listen to. Granny had once told her the story from the Bible of the foolish women who had no lamp oil when it was time to go to a wedding; she had admonished Anna to, "Be ready, honey. When God gets ready to move, you be ready."

Anna looked out at the linemen and wished once more for her granny's companionship and wisdom. She also made a mental note to find that Bible story and read it again. Perhaps it would make sense now.

Anxious to see how the work was progressing, she pulled the chain on the single electric light that hung in the kitchen. Though she had replaced the bulb this morning, there was no light. She sighed and went outside to fill a flower box by the window with petunias, where Darron found her when he and Wilford arrived.

"Linemen still here?" he said, squinting into the sky. "Must be they had some problems. I'll go see what's taking so long."

"Have you got any jobs for me, Miss Anna?" Wilford asked. "Daddy said I could come along if I promised to help and not be a pest."

"If you could get some water from that old spring and bring it for these flowers, that would help me a lot." She handed him a small plastic pail and he trotted off.

"Well, they're just about done," Darron reported when he came back. "Now you and I talked about not having a whole lot of wiring done. There's no problem with codes in a remodeling project like this, so you can pretty much get what you ask for. You want a light and an outlet in each room, right?"

Anna looked up from the flowers. "A light? I'm sorry, Darron; I guess I wasn't paying much attention."

"You got your mind on something more interesting than power lines," he said with a smile. "I passed Peter on the way over here. Alysia's determined to get you two together somehow."

Anna smiled. "Darron, your brother is a most unusual man. Come here. I want to show you something."

Together they went to the road where Anna's car was parked. She gingerly picked up the envelope containing the portrait Peter had made and handed it to Darron.

Darron slipped the photo out and gazed at it, offering a long, low whistle. "Well, he sure hasn't lost the touch, even after all these years."

"What happened, Darron? Why did he quit photography? He has so much talent, and he obviously loves the work."

Darron shook his head sadly. "Peter isn't an easy guy to get close to, Anna."

"I've found that out."

"Well, you've gotten closer than anybody else has in a long time. If he's going to tell anybody his secrets, it will be you. When he's ready, and I think he's almost ready, he'll tell you. Don't worry; it isn't anything so deep and dark as all that. In fact, when he does tell you, you'll probably wonder what all the fuss was about, but Peter. . .well, he feels things more than other people do. It's part of the reason he can do things like this," he said, handing the photo back to Anna.

As they went toward the house, Darron said, "Anna, I just have to say I'm awful pleased to see Peter working again. I don't know exactly what's between you two, but I'm hoping, praying, that he'll find himself soon. If you're one of the pieces of the puzzle in his life, and God brought you here to fill up a certain spot, then I hope Peter doesn't do anything stupid to mess it all up. And maybe we can all be something special for you, too."

"You have been, Darron," Anna said. "I came looking for support and I found it in you and Alysia and, in a way, in Peter, too. This old, worn-out house is sort of the glue holding us all together, I suppose. Isn't it funny how—"

A scream, followed by another that was higher and longer, stopped them on the porch, and Darron immediately bolted toward the spring.

"Wilford! Wilford! Where are you?" he shouted.

The linemen looked toward Darron and the one on the pole began pointing and shouting. Darron saw the tall grass waving and barged through to where Wilford lay, rolling on the ground, clutching his ankle.

"A snake bit me, Daddy!" he howled. "My leg hurts!"

Darron lifted the boy in his arms and hurried toward the house, hearing as he went the lineman's words, "I kicked up some copperheads a while back. Be careful."

"Anna, he's been bit," Darron said, his voice trembling. "I'm going to take him to the hospital. Is Peter coming back here?"

Anna nodded. "He just went to rent a grass trimmer."

"Wait here for him. Tell him what happened. Ask him to get Alysia and bring her to the hospital. He'll know where to go." He was on his way up to the road before Anna could answer.

Anna paced the front porch until Peter returned. "How serious could the bite be?" Anna asked as they drove toward Alysia's home.

Peter's shoulders hunched briefly. "Depends on the size of the snake and what it was. Darron doesn't even know for sure if it was a copperhead, does he?" Peter didn't want to mention rattlesnakes.

෴

Anna stayed at the apartment with Emily while Alysia and Peter drove to the hospital. Darron was waiting for them and enfolded Alysia in his arms as soon as he saw her.

"He's hurt, it's a bad bite," he said. "They're doing what they can. The doctor says it isn't life-threatening, but they have to try to prevent tissue damage right away or his leg might not be right again."

The three sat together in the waiting room, and soon Peter and Darron's mother, Audrey, and their sister, Rose, arrived.

"Poor little Wilford," said Rose. "What was he doing running around that old place, anyway?"

"Helping," Darron said defensively.

"I never should have let her start working there until the grass was cleared," Peter said. "I even teased her about the snakes. How could I have been so stupid?"

His mother, Audrey, sighed. "Oh, Peter, there you go again, thinking the whole world is on your shoulders. Darron told us exactly what happened and it could have happened to anyone. It's nobody's fault. People get bit by snakes every year. I'll tell you something. I know in my heart Wilford is going to be all right. I've prayed and prayed that this family would be healed and although my heart breaks for Wilford, and I'm sorry he's the one to pay the price, I'm happy as I can be to see you two boys together again, talking face-to-face like two human beings. Now there, that's just how I feel."

"Never mind, Mamma," Darron said in his typically soft, conciliatory voice. "Peter and I never did have a quarrel, did we, Pete?"

Peter glanced briefly at Alysia and in her pleading look caught the full effect of her faithful acceptance of him and her absolute, unyielding love for Darron. As he looked at Darron and understood that the door to his return always had been and was even at this moment wide open, he knew that he no longer had the strength to be angry with them for their success.

"I never did have a quarrel with Darron, Mamma, except maybe when he wore my new jeans to the football game without asking."

"If I'd have asked, you would've said no," Darron said.

"Guess we'll never know," said Peter.

They returned to their silent waiting, each one knowing that at least one wound had already been healed. When a doctor finally came to give an update, the whole family crowded around him like a group of schoolchildren.

"I asked him what color the snake was," said the doctor, "and he said it was orange, which leads me to believe it was a copperhead, especially with the appearance of the wound. The swelling's stopped. He's in less pain now." He nodded at Darron and Alysia. "You two can go in for a few minutes, then you might as well all go home because he's going to be sleeping a lot."

Audrey said, "I'll go stay with Emily. Peter, you take me over there. We'll give your friend the news. She might want to come and visit tomorrow herself."

❧

Anna was amazed that the moment she was introduced to Peter's mother, the woman hugged her warmly and treated her like a long-lost friend.

"Thank you so much for helping," Audrey said, but Anna had no idea of just what she meant.

"Peter, I'm so surprised by your family. They are wonderful people!"

"Kind of makes you wonder how I got in, doesn't it?"

Anna laughed. "You know what I mean."

"Mamma is a wise woman," Peter said. "I told you the other day that I was jealous of Darron. I think I've finally been able to admit it to them, too, while we were all together. Mamma understands what's happening, and she knows you're a part of it. She's grateful. So am I."

"It could have happened without me."

"But it didn't," Peter said.

❧

When they arrived back at the motor home, Anna invited Peter in to eat. Anna made tuna sandwiches and warmed up some soup on the stove. Just as it reached serving temperature, the flames of the tiny gas burner flickered and went out.

"Well, I guess this is my last hot meal," she said. "I'm out of fuel."

"You can always get another tank of propane," Peter said.

Anna turned and asked, "Why, Peter? I won't be here that long."

Peter continued to eat. There was nothing he could say.

"And what about you? You've been reunited with your family. Can't you make a life for yourself here now? Do you still think you have to leave the only place that's ever going to be home to you?"

"Do you like Chinese food?" Peter asked.

Anna raised her hands in frustration. "What does that have to do with anything?"

"Sweet and sour, Anna," Peter said, leaning back in his chair. "You take a bite, and you can't decide. Is it sweet, or is it sour? The sour turns the sweet, and vice versa. That's how this place is to me."

"I know about the sweet. But what about the sour? What is it that's keeping you from your life and your work?"

He crossed his arms on his chest, partly to keep from reaching across the miniature motor-home table to stroke Anna's hair or caress her hand. His crossed arms also shielded his heart and symbolically pressed away the ache that came from knowing that the same thing that kept him from his work also kept him from Anna.

Certainly she had a right to know about his past, but telling her, he knew, would only drive her further away. Things were going well now. They were friends. If she knew more, that would end. *Not only would she not like me*, he reasoned, *she would certainly never love me*. Yet, how could he say he loved her when parts of his life were marked off limits?

"Let's take a walk down by the creek," he said. "Maybe we can talk."

Chapter Nine

"It's a pretty place, isn't it?" Peter asked as he and Anna stood at the edge of the water and looked up and down the stream. Ragged pines hung over the bank where the stream widened and deepened; further down, a series of short falls took the water around a curve and out of sight. Mosses were greening up for summer, and the leaves on the hardwoods were beginning to lose their brightness as their unfolding became complete. The mountainsides were shady with sunlight penetrating only in the clearings where rocky outcroppings soaked up the heat.

"Yes, Peter, it's lovely," Anna said, wondering what Peter was trying to say and why it was so hard for him.

"This is where I started doing serious photography," he said. "I got interested in cameras when I was in high school and took some pictures for the yearbook. Then when I went to college, I studied a bit more, but this is the place that made me want to do nothing except take pictures. This was the first land I bought. I was nineteen, and I used the money my daddy left me for college. That's one reason I went for only two years."

"Photography is expensive. How did you keep yourself in supplies?"

"I went to work, like everybody does. I sold a few pictures, but I had this idea that somehow I could take all of this," he waved his hand toward the scene before them, "to the rest of the world through my work." He laughed briefly. "Pretty grand idea, wasn't it?"

"And worthwhile. After all, that was Ansel Adam's desire long before environmentalism was a buzzword. He did it, too."

"Well, I didn't do it. I opened a studio in order to make a living doing something I was reasonably good at—or thought I was good at." The image of the empty storefront in the strip mall came to Peter's mind. He could even see the old cars parked on the blacktop, the empty soft drink cups and hamburger wrappers lying around, and the sun beating on the treeless lot.

"A studio? You did portrait photography?" Anna thought of the photo he had given her.

"Portraits, weddings, graduations, little kids." He nodded. "In the first year, I worked fifteen or eighteen hours a day sometimes, trying to get up and running. It just never did fly. People quit coming, but the bills didn't. Finally, it came down to a choice. I could sell the studio or I could sell this land. I decided to sell the studio."

"I don't understand. Your work is so good. Why did the business fail?"

Peter shrugged then tossed a pebble into the creek. He shook his head and said, "I don't really know for sure. People were polite, but they just never came back, and they sure didn't bring their friends."

Anna waited for more, but Peter seemed to be finished with his revelation. She remembered Darron's statement that she might wonder what all the fuss was about.

"Peter," she began cautiously, "are you saying that because your business failed, you gave up on your life, your art, and your family? I don't understand. Businesses fail every day."

"Something just ended for me there, Anna. I walked out one day and locked the door. I wouldn't even go back for my equipment. Darron went over one day and collected everything before the new tenants moved in. If he hadn't dumped it on my doorstep, I wouldn't have it today."

"But surely you understand now that your engagement to Alysia didn't end because the photography studio went under."

"It was a good excuse at the time. I told Alysia I couldn't support a family and we couldn't get married, but she had already told me it was over between us. It sort of helped me keep my pride to think the breakup was my idea. Then she started dating Darron, so the studio was another reason to keep him at arm's length."

"What does the studio have to do with him?"

"He told me not to start it in the first place," Peter said.

"And you didn't want to hear him say, 'I told you so.' "

"No, especially not while he was walking down the aisle with my ex."

"And the look, Peter? What about the eyes of God? Did you think He was watching then?"

Peter turned toward Anna, not missing the earnestness in her voice. He did not want to damage her faith, but he knew he could not hold up his own as an example.

"I knew," he said. "But like I said, it didn't seem to make any difference."

"Did you ask for help?" Anna could almost feel the pain Peter must have experienced in his failure, and she suddenly understood that what seemed like just another step in life to Darron and Alysia was devastating to proud, sensitive, artistic Peter.

"Did you call to God for direction? I did, Peter. When I didn't know what else to do, I just put myself in His care, and He led me here, to you."

"Did He?" Peter smiled. "You don't love me, Anna. If He led you here, it was for your benefit, not mine. For me, knowing you and loving you is one more failure in my life."

Anna could hardly keep the tears from flowing and she turned her pain to anger. "You and your stubborn pride!" she cried. "You have all these wonderful things in your life and all you can see is an empty photo studio where you were probably wasting your talents trying to get spoiled brats to smile for the camera. You just thought you couldn't be the best, so you refused to try. How can you throw away your life like this?" She wanted to make him try again, to demand that he stop resisting God and making petty excuses for his own choices.

As she stood trembling with emotion before him, Peter forced himself not to take her into his arms. He would not take advantage of her sense of right in order to satisfy his own longings.

"Don't be angry," he whispered. "You're the only one who knows how much it hurts. . .and it still hurts. You're right; I'm proud. When Daddy died, I decided I would take over. I was the good student, the athlete, the leader in the family until I got old enough when it would really count for something. Then I lost my livelihood, my fiancée, my brother's respect. It's been downhill ever since."

"You never lost Darron's respect," Anna said. "He's always loved you and admired you. It happened in your own head and your own heart. You learned that today, didn't you? When a crisis brought you all together, you saw that the love is still there."

"Well, blood is thicker than water, you know. Family really can't disown you."

"I don't believe God has disowned you, either," Anna said. "I think He's just waiting for you, just like Darron and Alysia and your mother have been waiting all these years. Don't quit, Peter. Don't stop trying, please. You have so much to give."

Peter was quiet for a moment. He remembered the first day he had spent with Anna, and he realized that something about her made him want to go on, to reconstruct the dreams that for so long had been associated in his mind with pain. He had to acknowledge that, except for Anna, he would have packed his truck a week ago and gone in search of something to fill the hollowness in his own soul. He just didn't believe he could do what she was asking of him.

"Will *you* wait for me?" he asked.

In a moment, Anna knew that if she could not love Peter, she could never love anyone. She realized that in feeling his pain and loss, she had been joined to him in a way she never could have been even through all the good times they might share.

"I'll wait," she said, "if you'll work."

Silently, they followed their shadows to the motor home. Anna said, "I'm going to go in to the hospital for a while. What should I take for Wilford?"

"He likes puzzles. He's a math whiz." At the door, he asked, "What about getting that propane?"

She searched his face, knowing he wanted her to stay.

"I'll see about it tomorrow." At least they both knew she wasn't going anywhere that night.

₰

At the hospital, Anna found Alysia in the waiting room. "I'm so glad you came!" Alysia said. "Darron had to get to bed; the poor man was exhausted with all that's happened. I wanted to stay a while yet. They said Wilford would be awake before too long and I could see him before I go home for the night."

"I didn't really expect to see him," Anna said, sitting next to Alysia on the hard sofa. "You can give him this when he wakes up." She handed Alysia a pocket calculator and a book of games that were played using calculations.

"Oh, it's just perfect!" Alysia declared. "He'll be so excited. How did you know he likes this kind of thing?"

"Peter told me," Anna said and then smiled at Alysia's knowing grin. "Alysia, you're just like a schoolgirl. You have to get over the idea that Peter and I are going steady."

"I won't get over it. I'm hoping to get you as a sister yet."

"Well, you've got me as a sister one way or another," Anna said. "You know, Peter did finally tell me just this evening why he quit photography. You and Darron don't understand why he was so devastated by his failure, do you?"

Alysia shook her head. "No, he just gets so worked up over every little thing, bless his heart. At the beginning, Darron told him it was a bad idea because Darron had seen Peter's work. He didn't think Peter was going to be happy cooped up inside all day with runny-nosed kids in bow ties who didn't want their pictures taken, but Peter insisted he could make it work. The trouble was, Peter was too good. People wanted nice posed pictures that flattered them. Peter takes the kind of pictures that show people as they really are, if you know what I mean."

Her own portrait flashed in her mind. "Yes, I do know," she said slowly, trying to imagine the response of a self-promoting debutante to such a work. No, people would have responded badly to Peter's style of portraiture, and he would never have compromised his work to curry favor with customers.

"Another problem Peter had was that he's no accountant," Alysia said. "I offered to keep the books for him, but he didn't want that, especially after we broke up. By then it was too late, anyway. He didn't want to advertise, either. Said it made him feel like a prostitute. Can you imagine? The whole thing was a bad idea. But being Peter, he just used that old studio as proof that it was he, not the business, that was a failure."

Alysia turned on the calculator and pushed a few buttons. "Peter's not much good at taking help and Darron's almost as bad. You saw how he was about the job offer. Why are men like that?"

"I don't know, Alysia. The men I've known in the fashion industry are always asking for help." Once again, Anna's stomach churned at the thought of Barry's deceit. "For all the problems it causes, I think it's better for men to be like Peter and your husband."

Alysia put her arm around Anna and giggled. "They are awful nice to marry."

Chapter Ten

Anna lay in the too-short motor-home bed, watching the moon drift past the tops of the pines. The day had been exhausting. After her visit to the hospital, she had returned to the hollow and immediately gone to bed, but had been unable to fall asleep.

Listening to the night sounds, she realized how comfortable she had become in this environment in only a few days. New York seemed so far-away, especially now that Barry was not there waiting for her. The trouble was, she had no plans for tomorrow. None of the reasons that drew her to Tennessee still remained.

Granny's house had been found and would be available to her if she ever wanted to go there. Anna now knew that the important thing was not living there, or even having the house, but having made peace with her own past by accepting the changes that had come with the death of her parents. The house was a monument to the love she had known in her life.

There was no more question about going into business with Barry; there was certainly no possibility of a continuing relationship with him. *He will probably never even speak to me again,* she thought, *and I don't mind that at all.* It was not the answer she had hoped and prayed for, but it was an answer just the same.

Watching the shadows in the sky, she knew that the faith in God that she had developed in New York would carry her anyplace in the world. Day by day, she had become more comfortable with God's dealing in her life, more aware of it, and more trusting. Meeting Darron and Alysia had been a joyful part.

Once more, she looked at the photographic portrait of herself that Peter had made. With some sadness, she admitted that learning about his life also had helped her to cling more tightly to her own faith. Seeing his suffering and believing that it was largely a result of spiritual turmoil made her determined not to make the same mistakes.

She dared not think about the effect he had on her personally. There could be no future with Peter because he refused to return to the point of simple faith where he and Anna could begin a life together. Seeing Darron and Alysia and remembering her granny had shown Anna that a

good marriage had to begin with that kind of mutual belief. She con-
sciously erased the vision of Peter's face, knowing that their separation
was coming soon.

Though it left her with a hollow feeling, Anna knew that there was no
reason for her to stay in Tennessee. Tomorrow she would begin preparations to return to New York. A sense of urgency was gradually building in
her. There was business that needed her attention. At the same time, she
knew there were serious decisions ahead of her, because Peter's photo, as
Alysia had said, had shown her the truth about herself. Barry was right—
she was not getting any younger.

Once more, she looked at the picture before slipping it back into the
brown envelope. Though Peter had captured perfectly her feelings and
even a part of her life, the facts were also there. She was getting too old for
the work she was now doing. She thought about Barry's angry words.

"You're at the worst possible age for a model," he had said.

The truth of those words was all the more bitter because it was Barry who
had said them first. She would have to begin thinking about other work.

&

The next day Anna got up early and went to see Darron before he left for
work. On the way, she had an idea.

She sat with Darron and Alysia at their kitchen table with a cup of coffee, carefully planning her words.

"Anna, I just wish you'd stay a while," Alysia was saying. "We're just getting to know you. At least promise me you'll visit when the baby comes."

"I wouldn't miss that for anything," said Anna. "You know, you two have
done so much for me, I hesitate to even ask this, but I need the help.
Granny Huddlestone's house is just sitting there. I did the few things necessary to satisfy myself, and now I have to leave. Would you two consider
living out there as caretakers of the house? I'd pay you, of course. It would
certainly ease my mind."

Darron blinked as Alysia squealed and tugged at his arm. "Darron,
Darron, we could get out of town! The kids would just love it. Let's do it."

Anna interrupted, "Remember, it doesn't have the kind of conveniences
you've been used to. There will only be the one small bathroom."

"That's all we've got now," Alysia said.

"There's no modern kitchen," Anna added, "although I wouldn't mind if
you put in a range and sink."

"Say yes, Darron," Alysia pleaded. "I just love that old house. I have since the day Anna and I went out there to clean. I've been so jealous, I'm ashamed of myself."

Darron finally spoke. "I won't take any money, but I'll just tell you I've been worried about that old house since you two started filling the place up with stuff. I'd hate to see anything happen to it now that you know it's what you want. We could live there. We'd have some more room and I'd be closer to work."

Alysia bounced on her chair like a child. "Thank you, Anna! Thank you, thank you." She made a final bounce up, took two steps to Anna's chair, and hugged her.

Anna laughed. "Don't thank me yet. You may be sorry once you get into the old place. It isn't exactly a palace, you know."

"It is to me," Alysia said. "Besides, knowing how special the place is to you makes it a home for me. And, remember, the house is yours. You can have it back or come visit whenever you want."

Anna looked at her two friends, unlike any friends she had ever had before. *How long until I see them again?* she wondered. "I'll be leaving in a day or two," she said. "I may not see you before I leave."

Alysia looked away. "I won't let go of you, Anna. I believe God brought you to us —to all of us —and somehow it's going to work out."

"You'll always have me," Anna said, "just as I'll have you. Now don't fret. What do you think Wilford will say when you tell him about the move?"

"I think he'll say he wants a pair of high-top boots," Alysia said.

❧

High-top boots were what Peter was wearing when Anna found him, cutting grass in a wide swath around the house. He had already mowed beyond the spring and was working at the back side of the house when Anna cautiously approached. The noise of the gasoline-powered trimmer was deafening, and Anna had to wait for Peter to turn in her direction in order to get his attention.

"I had breakfast with Darron and Alysia," she said. "Wilford had a restful night. He'll be coming home later today."

Beads of perspiration clung to Peter's skin just above his eyebrows, and he wiped them away on the back of a gloved hand. "Well, I don't think anybody will see any snakes close by here, as long as the grass is kept short through the summer. If it gets long, though, they'll come back."

"Darron will keep it cut, I'm sure," said Alysia. "They've decided to come here and live."

"No foolin'!" Peter's face brightened in a way that surprised Anna. She had half expected an argument from him. "That's real fine. Darron's kind of a mother hen. He isn't happy unless he's got a certain amount of things to take care of. He'll like the old place."

It occurred to Anna that she should tell Peter she was planning to leave, but the words would not come. There was still time, of course.

"Come over here and see if you think this might have been your granny's garden," Peter said, leading Anna along the edge of the cleared area. The ground was level and had a softer feel under Anna's feet than the rocky yard. Peter pointed out the points of iris foliage.

"I think this is sage," he said, pointing to another plant, "and here's mint."

Anna turned and looked at the house. The place where they stood was directly in line with the kitchen window. "It's the garden all right," she said. She turned ninety degrees and pointed. "The henhouse was over there." Through the bushes they could see a few remains of the old building.

"This was a wonderful spot. I didn't like the chickens, but I loved the garden. Every morning while I was visiting, Granny and I would walk out here and see what had changed since the day before. It was like visiting friends for her. 'Oh, look how the radishes have grown,' she'd say, or, 'Why, would you look at that? While we were asleep, the mustard sprouted. It puts me to shame. It worked all night long while I rested.' "

"Have you ever had a garden of your own?" Peter asked.

"No, I don't even keep house plants."

Suddenly Peter said, "Anna, let's go back to the mountain where we saw the eagle. Come with me, please. I want to take some pictures up there later this afternoon. Let's go about three o'clock."

Anna hesitated only a moment. "All right. Come over to the hollow when you get ready to go. I'll be there." She did not say she would be packing.

When Peter arrived at the motor home, Anna was sitting on the ground outside, in the shade, reading a book. "What have you got there?" he asked, taking her hand to help her up.

"T. S. Eliot," she said. "Do you like poetry?"

"Some, if it's the kind that doesn't paint everything as a disaster. After all, 'Humankind cannot bear very much reality.' "

"So you do like Eliot," Anna said. It was a good starting point for conversation and launched them on their hike on a wave of camaraderie that reminded Anna of other days during her stay. She was going to miss Peter. For all his prickliness and black despair, she liked spending time with him. For a moment, as they walked along, she wondered whether any of her old friends in New York were really friends at all. Was she returning to a void? The urge to simply accept Peter's love and stay with him was very tempting just then, but she made herself put the thoughts aside.

"Will you try to photograph the eagle?" Anna asked as they neared the place where they had seen the bird before.

"If we see it, and if the light is right, and if, if, if, yes," Peter said. "I spent almost a whole year tramping around here, taking pictures of the birds and their young. I don't have any pictures from this point, though. I'd like to have some for the collection."

They walked around examining the tiny wildflowers that grew in the sunlight of the summit. The blankets of green, which Anna had never taken time to look at before, now offered an almost infinite variety of shapes and hues, from tiny mosses on the rocks to tall trees of half a dozen varieties.

"There's so much to see," said Anna. "In New York, there are maple trees planted in rows and surrounded by cement. It's pleasant enough, but there isn't much variety."

"I knew a photographer in college who published a whole book on lichens that grew in the county where he lived," said Peter.

"What about you? Have you published any work?"

"Oh, half a dozen photos some years back. Nothing you can point to with much pride. Strictly illustrative stuff."

"Have you decided what you'll do now, where you'll go?"

"No."

Anna sat with her back against a tree and watched the blue haze above the mountains deepen and intensify as the sun inched along the horizon. Peter brought his camera and sat beside her. Silently they scanned the sky, waiting.

"Does the eagle come every day?" asked Anna.

"No. It hunts other places, too, but I was here yesterday and the day before and I didn't see him. It's about time for him to make a pass through here." He raised his hands, forming blinders at his temples. "I think. . . looks like that could be him."

Anna could see just the smallest speck in the sky. Beside her, Peter raised his camera and focused the telephoto lens, changing it moment by moment as the speck came closer.

Suddenly Anna cried, "Look! There are two of them!"

Sailing through the air, slightly behind and to one side, came a second eagle.

"Well, he's brought his wife," said Peter softly. He stood up and moved quickly to a different position.

Anna heard the familiar click and whirr of the motorized camera, but knew this time she was not the focal point. She watched the birds in their path, realizing that they would not come directly toward the place where she and Peter stood watching as they had the other day. At first she sat very still, but as they came closer, she could not help but be drawn into their quest. Slowly she stood up, and it was as if they called to her, and even made eye contact, inviting her to rise above the common life she now knew, and fly.

The moment was poignant, but brief. In only seconds, the sky was again empty as the pair vanished into the distant haze.

"Don't you just wish you could go with them?" Anna said quietly as Peter returned to her side.

"Every time I see them," Peter said. "In my collection, I've got some pictures of one that was wounded. It made a dive for a young raccoon and smacked its wing against a rock. It stayed on the ground for a couple of days. Every time I tried to get near it, though, it would fly off, so I knew it could fly. You know what I think? I think it was afraid to fly. After about two weeks, I found it dead."

" 'Because these wings are no longer wings to fly, but merely fans to beat the air,' " Anna quoted T. S. Eliot. "We could all fly, I suppose, except that we're so afraid to fall." She looked directly at Peter. "And once wounded, it's very hard to trust, isn't it?"

When he did not reply, she said, "The eagle died, Peter. For an eagle, there are only two choices: fly or die. God has given you wings. He's the very air that holds us up. You have to believe."

Peter watched her face intently, revealing nothing of his own emotions. At last he said, "You're leaving, aren't you?"

Anna nodded ever so slightly. "It's time. I have to go."

"I thought you said you'd wait."

"I will, but not here, not being next to you while not really being with you."

Behind them, the sky, completely free of clouds, deepened to form a magenta curtain. In the shadow of the great pine, Peter slowly enfolded Anna in his arms, and she answered his embrace. Her eyes closed, she pressed her face against his sunburned neck and felt the heat of his skin against her cheek and the soft brush of his hair against her temple.

He held her for a long moment, sensing her heartbeat even as his own quickened. When he felt her gradual movement away from him, he held her just for one more moment and kissed her softly.

"Knowing you're right doesn't mean I can just do what you want," Peter whispered. "I am what I am."

Anna nodded, forcing herself to step away from him. "And I do what I have to do."

Chapter Eleven

Except for brief snatches of conversation about returning the rental car, finding the best route to the interstate, and preparing the motor home for the trip, the walk home for Peter and Anna was silent. Peter's terse good-bye left Anna sad and lonely.

For her last evening in the hollow, Anna went into the motor home but found the space too confining. Dressed warmly for the night, she took blankets and a pillow, a flashlight, and a book and found a place near the creek to spend the night. Although she was not afraid to sleep alone in the woods, the habits she had acquired in New York were strong; she took her handbag containing her money and identification and locked the door behind her.

She read by flashlight until the light began to dim, then settled down for the night, but the strangeness of the sounds and shadows made it hard to sleep. She lay awake thinking of Peter, wondering if he, too, had slept here and whether she would ever see him again.

She did not know she slept until she was awakened by some unknown sound. She lay still in the darkness, watching the woods, wondering if the slight movements she heard could be those of an animal. After a few minutes, she heard what she knew was the closing of a car door and she realized that someone else was in the hollow.

Peter must have returned for some reason, she thought. He would be worried if she did not answer his knock at the door. *Why would he be here now?* she wondered. She estimated the time to be somewhere around three A.M.

She got up and walked along the creek and, as she peered through the trees, she caught a glimpse of a white car. It was Barry's car! She dropped down behind the bushes, waiting to see if he would go away when he realized she was not in the motor home. Barry was not in sight, but soon he came around from the other side of the motor home. He did not knock or call for Anna. Instead Anna saw, to her horror, that he had in his hand a gasoline can and was splashing the liquid onto the sides of the vehicle. Calmly and silently he produced a flame on his cigarette lighter and ignited the fuel.

Quickly he stepped back and, in the light of the flames, Anna could see his smug expression. She pressed her hand hard against her mouth to keep from crying out as the flames leaped around the door. Had she been inside, it would have been impossible for her to get out.

Barry then walked to the rental car parked nearby, poured the rest of the fuel inside on the upholstery, and set it afire. He stood, watching the blaze.

"See if your Boy Scout can help you now," Anna heard him call. Then he got into his car and drove away.

Anna huddled at the edge of the woods until she was sure he would not see her. The flames danced higher and higher, roaring as they consumed everything in the motor home. The car exploded, sending a ball of flames into the sky, and Anna was suddenly afraid that the woods might also begin to burn.

She stood helplessly as the heat shriveled the ferns and melted the pine needles of the trees closest to the clearing. She could not decide whether to sit and wait or try to get help. Certainly there was nothing she could do about the fire. At last she began walking, knowing that many miles separated her from any other person.

Before she had rounded the first curve on the track that led out of the hollow, she heard a car engine. She stumbled off into the trees, afraid that Barry was returning to check on his work, but ran out again when she saw that it was Peter in his truck.

She ran behind the truck as Peter drove to the clearing; he jumped from his truck and started toward the remains of the motor home. She heard him screaming her name, peering into the blaze.

"Peter! Peter! I'm all right!" she shrieked. Gasping for breath, she came within hearing range just as he was about to rush into the flames. "Don't! I'm here, Peter!"

He turned and saw her then, and ran to her and held her once again. "What happened? You could have been killed!"

"Barry came back. He set everything on fire. He actually tried to kill me, Peter. How did you know? How did you get here so quickly?"

"I guess I have to tell you I haven't been completely honest with you," Peter said. "Each time I drove up here with you, I took the old county road off the highway. The fact is, if you go on that old logging trail that runs off into the woods just beyond that bend, you come out at my house in about fifteen minutes. This is my backyard."

Anna stared, her mouth wide open. "You mean, all this time. . . ?"

"You haven't actually been alone. Did you think I'd let you stay here with no one else around? I was only about half asleep when I heard the explosion. I could see the flames from my place. Oh, Anna, I was so afraid. . . ." He clung to her as the flames poured their wrath into the night.

"Well, there's no sense calling the fire department. By the time they get here, it will all be over," he said. "Come and stay at my place, and in the morning we'll take care of the details."

≈

Anna slept late and awakened in Peter's spare bedroom to the smell of bacon and coffee. She showered and put on the same clothing, the only clothing she now had. After breakfast, she and Peter started toward Gatlinburg.

"This is going to be hard to explain to the insurance people," Anna said. "I suppose I should get a police report."

"They can confirm that the fires were set deliberately, but it might be hard to prove it was Barry who did it. You can't go back to New York," he said firmly. "You can't even think about it as long as that loony person is there."

Anna remembered the steely look on Barry's face as he watched the fire. *What could have happened to him?* she wondered. *He was callous, but what would bring him to the point of murder?*

As Peter and Anna came to a point where the road took a particularly sharp turn and the mountain dropped steeply into the river below, they came upon a police car. There was a break in the guardrail.

"Looks like somebody went over the side," Peter said. "I'll go speak to one of the officers about stopping up at the hollow to look at the fire damage."

He pulled the truck over to the side of the road and walked back to the place where the guardrail had been broken. One officer was helping another up from the bank.

Anna watched in the rearview mirror, then saw Peter coming back toward the truck.

"Anna, can you come over here? I think maybe it's Barry's car down there."

Anna felt a wave of nausea and found it hard to catch her breath. She got out of the pickup and walked to the side of the road, afraid of what she might see hundreds of feet below. There, half-submerged in the river and looking like a discarded toy, was the white Ferrari.

"Is he in there?" she whispered.

"The driver's body is in the car, ma'am," the officer said. "It's a white male, maybe about six feet tall, dark hair, thin mustache."

"That's Barry," she said, and her voice broke into sobs.

"There aren't any skid marks here at all," he continued. "After hearing what Mr. McCulley had to say, I believe the driver must have deliberately accelerated and slammed into the rail. He must have been doing close to sixty. The car practically flew more than halfway down. I'd say he did what he came to do and killed himself."

Anna sobbed quietly, thinking of the waste that characterized Barry's life and death. She would not see him flitting in and out of the modeling sets. She would not see him in his apartment or her own. His carefree, haughty smile was gone forever.

"He was on the verge of financial collapse," Anna said when she could speak. "He had been on his way to Memphis to see business acquaintances there. He. . .had asked me for money, but I refused. If they also refused in Memphis, it may have been too much for him."

And so, by the end of the day, Anna was on her way to Louisville to catch a plane to New York.

❧

For days, Peter remained secluded. After the motor home and car rental companies had investigated, he worked at the hollow, clearing the debris caused by the fires. Photography was his only pleasure. He shot rolls and rolls of film at the creek and around his home, and stayed in his darkroom for hours at a time.

Three weeks after Anna left, Peter was sitting in a straight-backed chair on his porch when Darron drove up. Darron marched toward him, obviously resolved to accomplish a mission. Peter sighed, knowing he would have to deal with the man.

Darron tossed a magazine into Peter's lap. "Pete, I'm mighty tired of seeing stuff like this and knowing you could do better," he said. The open pages of the magazine showed photo illustrations of a deep-South family reunion—the food, the people, and the home.

"We've been all though this, Darron. Photography will never be a business for me. I can't make it work."

Darron's lips were set in a firm line and he seemed like a schoolmaster about to berate an errant child.

"How much are you going to have to lose before you look up and pay attention to what God's trying to show you?" Darron demanded. "You were good to me all my life. When Daddy died, you were a father to me. I loved you like a daddy, but when I got old enough not to need one anymore, you felt like you'd failed somehow. You didn't. I just grew up, that's all. I wanted you for a brother then. But no, you wouldn't have it any way but yours. I wanted to help you in your business, and so did Alysia, but you were too stinkin' proud. You were willing to let all of us just disappear out of your life rather than admit you needed anybody else.

"Well, now look at you. You haven't even shaved in a week, holed up here like a hermit. You let the best thing that's come into your life slip away from you rather than get down on your knees and tell God you need His help. You know He's waitin', Pete. You know He's been knockin' the chucks out from under you for years in the hopes you'd give up and let Him do the work Himself. Instead, you just keep trying to find new props. You called the shots when we were growing up. Now I'm telling you something. You get yourself right with God and get to work using the talents He gave you, and if you got one single brain cell in that thick head of yours, you do anything you can to win Anna. So help me, if you throw your life away, I'll beat you myself."

"Anna doesn't love me, Darron. It takes two, you know."

Darron grabbed the magazine and slapped his brother on the side of the head with it. "Make her love you, Pete! All she's waitin' for is for you to give in and surrender to the Lord. I know you've been wrestlin' with Him, just like Jacob, for years now! You can't win unless you surrender. You've got to do it!" He smacked Peter again, then threw the magazine to the floor of the porch. "Anna can't commit her life to a man who's too proud and stubborn to take orders from God. Be the man you used to be when you were a kid."

"That doesn't make any sense," Peter said defensively, rubbing his ear.

"It's the only thing that makes sense. I'm through tryin', but Anna, God bless her, I think she'll pine for you 'til the day she dies. Not because she needs you, but because she wants you to enjoy the kind of spiritual life she knows you could have. It's what I want, too, you big fool." He spun around, strode off to his car, and drove away.

Peter sat on the porch, watching the dust clouds form behind Darron's car. He wondered how long Darron had been working on that speech and how he had worked up to its delivery. Something in the act had touched Peter deeply. Maybe it was that Darron would risk losing their newly discovered relationship in order to do what Darron thought was the best thing for his brother. Darron was wrong, of course. Anna's lack of love for him was just one of a series of failures in his life. He wanted to think of it in terms of fate, but somehow he could not.

He also could not dismiss Darron's accusations and challenges as easily as he wanted to. Though he busied himself as best he could, Darron's stern face kept coming back to him. Finally, he walked across the porch and picked up the magazine and glanced at the photos. They were good photos and illustrated the story, but they gave no hint of the relationship of the people to the event. The people might all have been hired models, models like Anna. No, even a poor photographer could not make Anna look as stiff as these people, as removed from their experiences as these laughing faces seemed to be.

All his efforts to clear his mind of her face and presence had been useless. With each passing day he missed her more. When he drove past the Huddlestone property, he imagined her face at the window. Had she really come into his life, and then, taking part of him with her, gone away?

Peter left the porch and went into his house. He pulled from a drawer the color snapshots of Anna and Alysia on their shopping expedition and looked at each one. Would he ever have anything except her likeness on paper? If Darron were right—a possibility difficult for Peter to concede—there might be one chance left for him. It involved tremendous risk, however, and Peter once again felt the familiar sensation of fear. What would happen if he actually trusted God with his life?

≈

Later that evening, people walking through the courtyard at Christus Gardens noticed an unshaven young man sitting on a bench and staring at the carved figure of Christ.

Chapter Twelve

Anna ignored the conversations around her in the restaurant, stared at her plate, and lined up the julienned carrots as she thought about Phil Curtis's offer.

"It's what you would have done for Barry," Phil was saying, "but with no strings. I know you'd make a good partner and a good manager. The younger models look up to you and respect you."

Phil's reference to younger models had nearly as much emotional impact on Anna as his reference to Barry. She had known for some time about Phil's changes in the management of the agency, which he had purchased when it had gone into receivership after Barry's death. Now he was offering Anna the job of manager.

While many people had been sympathetic to Anna after her return to New York, she found few jobs once her existing contracts were fulfilled. With fewer jobs came fewer friends, fewer nights away from the apartment, and more and more memories of Peter. Knowing she had made the right choice was little consolation. She had never been so lonely.

Phil Curtis had begun asking her out a few weeks previous to his offer to let her manage the agency. He was an old friend and a good businessman. Anna was glad to spend time with him and she knew that his offer was sincere. If only it didn't seem so hollow! She could not help but remember that only about four months ago, a similar offer had helped take her away from New York to what now seemed like another world.

"I just don't know exactly what I want to do right now," Anna told Phil. "Can I take a week or two to decide? I'm not sure I want to give up modeling yet."

His attempt to conceal surprise was not missed by Anna. "Oh, well, sure, if you want to be in front of the camera a while longer, that makes sense. You have a history of good work, after all. I'm sure the work's there for you. If you decide to handle the business, though, I'd love to have you."

He took Anna to her apartment, offered a friendly kiss on the cheek, and was gone. Anna went inside to finish a letter to Alysia that she had begun earlier.

I can hardly believe it is halfway through October, she wrote. *I suppose the* mountains there are beautiful. I haven't even been out of the city since I returned in June.

In addition to feeling torn in half when she had left Peter at the bus station in Gatlinburg, Anna returned to New York to find that funeral arrangements for Barry had fallen to her. He had left her plenty of responsibilities, but no resources. His assets were all gone. She paid for the funeral herself and acted as hostess to the few who bothered to pay their respects. Then she got on with trying to put away the memories of both men.

The summer and early autumn had passed slowly for Anna. She had struggled with Barry's death, even though a call from his contact in Memphis helped her to understand that she had nothing to do with his suicide.

"He was as angry as I've ever seen anyone," the designer had said. "I told him I couldn't give him the money because I didn't have it, and he nearly went crazy. He said if he couldn't live well, he wouldn't live at all. He said you were the only person who had ever really loved him, and since you probably hated him now, he might as well go out in style."

"If he thought I loved him, why did he try to kill me?" Anna had asked.

"I'd say it was an illogical and crazy way to get back at your boyfriend. You know Barry. He had to blame somebody," the designer had replied.

Anna wrote, *I'm so glad you're all moved into Granny's house. I hope you'll be happy there. What am I saying? You and Darron will be happy anywhere. You'll never know what your friendship means to me. Be sure to tell me when you get the phone installed.*

What she could not write were questions about Peter, whether he had moved away from Gatlinburg, whether he had found a job, whether he ever spoke of her. He had not written or called. How real could his love have been? Anna could not answer that question, but since her separation from Peter, she had come to understand the reality of her love for him. Had she not physically torn herself away from him, she knew she would eventually have surrendered to him.

The letter continued, *Remember, you're supposed to be eating well now that you're in the last part of your pregnancy. You want to have a smart kid, don't you? Get lots of protein. I'll be there to see you as soon as you're ready for company after the baby is born. Have you picked out a name yet?*

Jonadab. Anna laughed to herself, thinking of Peter's joke about naming

454 Contemporary Collection No. 4

a baby after his grandfather. She wondered if that were really his grandfather's name. There was so much about Peter she didn't know, and now, probably would never know. She sealed the letter and dropped it in the mail slot in the hallway, then went to bed.

⤖

In a week, Phil called again and asked her to attend a show of new products with him. They looked over the booths one by one, comparing the techniques of the live models demonstrating various products and speculating on the possibilities for income from such events for the agency.

As they sat in the hotel lobby and sipped coffee from styrofoam cups, Phil said, "Anna, I want you to know I care about you a great deal. I'd like to be more than a friend to you." He slipped his arm lightly around her shoulders and moved a bit closer on the sofa.

Anna stared at him, knowing from the change in his expression that he could read the doubt and surprise registering in her look.

"Don't think I'm trying to pull a Barry Carlson maneuver here," Phil said quickly. "My affection for you remains whether you want a job with the agency or not. I would have made serious efforts to win you long ago, but Barry seemed to be first in line." Anna started to protest, but Phil silenced her with a wave of his hand. "I understand, Anna. You need time to get over Barry. That's fine with me. I just want you to know where I stand. You and I are adults; we don't have to tiptoe around. I find you very attractive. I want to have a special relationship with you."

Anna's mind was whirling. If she could not have Peter and the kind of complete love she had dreamed of, perhaps it was best to settle for friendship and security, the kind of relationship she knew she could develop with Phil.

"Phil, do you have faith in God?" she asked.

Phil's expression softened. "Yes, I do, Anna. I heard the rumors about your decision, and it made me do some serious thinking. I've been reading and studying the Bible for months. I've come to believe in Jesus Christ as my Savior. I'm learning a lot about the Christian life."

⤖

That night Anna lay awake, wondering if a whole new part of her life was opening before her. Phil had always impressed her with his reliability and common sense, existing as he did in the midst of a crowd of frenzied socialites. He had always been a gentleman and, even before his conversion, she had never known him to be dishonest or even unkind to the models with whom he worked. As for love, she had heard that people were often surprised by it. Sometimes it just grew if the seeds were planted and nurtured.

She thought once again of her granny's wisdom. "There's no flavor like that of a wild strawberry," she had said as they bent over the hillsides, picking the stems laden with fruit. "A berry patch in the garden is handy, though, and makes life a lot simpler. You just have to decide what you're willing to give up."

Could she give up the dream of perfect love she had come so close to with Peter and accept the kind of life she would have with Phil? She did not know, and it seemed unfair to have to make the choice.

Tears rolled from the corners of her eyes onto the pillow as she tried to understand why the God she had honored had brought such heartbreak into her life.

It did not seem to her that He was managing things well. It was very confusing. Remembering the summer, however, reminded her that she really had no choice except to trust Him.

&

The next morning, when Anna collected her mail, there was a plain envelope, rather wrinkled, with no return address. Inside was a piece of lined paper, ripped from a small spiral-bound pad. On the paper was written, "What we call the beginning is often the end, and to make an end is to make a beginning. The end is where we start from."

"T. S. Eliot," she breathed. She knew it was from Peter, but what could it mean? Where was he? Did he just want her to know he was safe? Or was he ending it all?

She paced about the apartment, nervous energy driving her into mindless activity. At least twice she reached for the phone, then remembered that Darron and Alysia would not answer at their old number.

When the doorbell rang just before noon, she practically ran to answer, glad for any interruption of her wild imaginings.

Peter stood before her, smiling, a small portfolio at his side. His crisp, white shirt made his tan face seem even darker, and the suit he wore was obviously new.

Anna stared at him for a moment, then pointed to the suit. "J.C. Penney?" she asked in a voice barely audible.

"How did you know?"

"It's my business to know," she said and then backed away to let him into the room.

He looked about, saying nothing for a few minutes. "So, this is where you live," he offered.

She nodded, gazing at his back until he turned and faced her.

"Anna, can we sit down? There's something I want to show you."

For a moment, Anna considered asking him to leave. She was tired of being hurt, tired of saying good-bye, tired of hoping and despairing. Simple courtesy, however, caused her to go and sit down at one end of the long sofa. She kept staring at him as though he were an apparition.

Peter saw the envelope and notebook paper lying on the coffee table. "You got my note. I didn't know what to say, so I thought I'd let a master speak for me." He laid the portfolio between them on the sofa cushion and unzipped it.

"I've been working," he said simply, and spread out before Anna both the original prints and the published counterparts that chronicled the progress on Granny Huddlestone's house. The accompanying article was titled "When Love Comes First," and it detailed Anna's decision to fill the house with beautiful things before starting the improvements.

"This is a magazine published by a historical society in Tennessee," said Peter. "They liked my work. They want me to do three more features this year."

Anna's gaze was drawn back to the photos, which included shots of herself smoothing out Alysia's quilt on the bed and pouring water from an old, chipped porcelain bucket onto the flower boxes.

"Did you write the article?" asked Anna.

"One of the society members wrote it. She had plenty of material after she got through interviewing Alysia."

Anna could not help but smile as she imagined Alysia's enthusiasm. Peter's work, however, crowned the story.

"I'm very happy for you," Anna said. "You've crossed a long bridge. Don't ever go back, Peter. The world would be a poorer place without your work. Just look! You've done what you always wanted to do. You've brought some of what's best from your home and shared it with. . .well, maybe not the world, but a lot of other appreciative people."

"Alysia's been doing my bookkeeping. You'd think she has enough to do with two kids, but she says she needs brain work once in a while. She does letters for me, too. I work from my house. No more storefronts."

Anna searched his face, hoping for a clue to the mystery, but finally had to ask. "What happened?"

Peter stretched against the back of the sofa, his hands behind his head. "You remember when you came to Tennessee last spring, you had a question. You knew there was a God, and you knew your life was influenced by Him. Your question was, so what? Does it make any difference? And maybe a bigger question was, could you trust Him to do the right thing? Anna, I had the same questions, exactly the same. Finally one day I had to start over, like the poem said and like I did that day down by the creek when I was little. I just promised God I'd quit looking for results and just do what He wanted me to do."

"I know it was hard for you. What made you do it?"

His hands still behind his head, Peter turned a few inches to catch sight of Anna. "Because Darron threatened to beat me if I didn't," he answered.

Their laughter was followed by a noticeable silence until Peter said simply, "I love you, Anna."

He replaced the items in the portfolio and carefully zipped it shut. He moved forward on the sofa, sitting with his elbows on his knees, his fingers loosely intertwined. "I couldn't come to you until I knew I could succeed in the work I wanted to do, and you wouldn't have me until I was ready to surrender to God. If you'll say you love me, there's nothing else in this world I would ever want."

"Nothing?"

"Well, one little thing, I guess. Marry me."

In an instant Anna was in his arms, wrapped in the strength of his healed life and cradled in the comfort of the knowledge that while more questions might come in the days ahead, there would always be answers.

"I thought I might never see you again," she said. "I just about went crazy when your note came. I was afraid you had gone off somewhere all alone and were just brooding."

"Well, I did that for a while, I admit," Peter said, holding her close. "But I'm back. I'm not afraid anymore. I want you to come with me just as soon as you can and promise me you'll never rent a motor home or even go near a bus station again."

"You know what my granny used to say?" Anna asked. "I can still see her, sitting on the porch, soaking her feet and saying, 'No matter where you are, if it isn't home, it's too far away.' "

"What was your granny's first name?" Peter asked.

"Evangeline. Why?"

"Just in case we have a girl. Otherwise—"

"I know, I know," Anna said. "It's Jonadab." She kissed him and thought she could taste wild strawberries.

A Letter to Our Readers

Dear Readers:

In order that we might better contribute to your reading enjoyment, we would appreciate your taking a few minutes to respond to the following questions. When completed, please return to the following: Fiction Editor, Barbour Publishing, Inc., P.O. Box 719, Uhrichsville, OH 44683.

1. Did you enjoy reading *Inspirational Romance Reader, Contemporary Collection, No. 4?*
   ☐ Very much—I would like to see more books like this.
   ☐ Moderately—I would have enjoyed it more if

   _____

   _____

2. What influenced your decision to purchase this book? (Check those that apply.)
   ☐ Cover   ☐ Back-cover copy   ☐ Title   ☐ Price
   ☐ Friends   ☐ Publicity   ☐ Other

3. Which story was your favorite?
   ☐ *A Whole New World*   ☐ *A Matter of Faith*
   ☐ *The Fruit of Her Hands*   ☐ *Eagles for Anna*

4. Please check your age range:
   ☐ Under 18   ☐ 18–24   ☐ 25–34
   ☐ 35–45   ☐ 46–55   ☐ Over 55

5. How many hours per week do you read?_____

Name _____

Occupation _____

Address _____

City _____ State _____ Zip _____

If you enjoyed *Inspirational Romance Reader*
Contemporary Collection #4 then read:

Inspirational Romance Reader

Historical Collection #4

A romantic collection of four
inspirational novellas including:

The Promise of Rain
Sally Krueger

Escape on the Wind
Jane LaMunyon

Hope that Sings
JoAnn A. Grote

Lost Creek Mission
Cheryl Tenbrook

Classic Fiction

Readers of quality Christian fiction will love these new novel collections from Grace Livingston Hill, the leading lady of inspirational romance. Each collection features three titles from Grace Livingston Hill, and a bonus novel from Isabella Alden, Grace Livingston Hill's aunt and a widely respected author herself.

Collection #4 includes the complete Grace Livingston Hill books *The Finding of Jasper Holt, Miranda,* and *The Witness,* plus *Diverse Women* by Isabella Alden.

paperback, 352 pages, 5 ³⁄₁₆" x 8"

❤ ❤ ❤ ❤ ❤ ❤ ❤ 🖤 ❤ ❤ ❤ ❤ ❤ ❤

❤ ❤ ❤ ❤ ❤ ❤ ❤ 🖤 ❤ ❤ ❤ ❤ ❤ ❤